Masters in This Hall

* * * *

Marty Smith

* * * *

© 2018
published by

Blotter Books
a division of
The Blotter Magazine, Inc.
www.blotterrag.com
ISBN: 978-1-7323938-0-6

Masters in This Hall

(This is a work of fiction. All the characters, except for some Famous Persons glimpsed at a distance, are figments of the author's imagination; and all the events depicted take place in an extremely alternate reality.)

(Cover design by author.)

*(A portion of the chapter SIXTEEN COACHES LONG appeared in the February 2018 issue of **The Blotter Magazine**.)*

Now Arriving

The day before his missing brother came back, Rick left Haw Court for his dad's house in Raleigh. He thought the Wizard's barrier on as he approached the gates, an action by now as automatic as clicking his seatbelt. No pleaders, protesters, Aidan groupies or general crazies were lying in wait for him. They seemed to have learned, even the most stubborn, that the barrier would always keep them at bay. He honked as he drove through, in case Leslie was watching from the gatehouse.

*

"Richard Grace Shew-Kingsley," say his files at the FBI, CIA, NSA, and other, darker agencies. Height, five-eight; weight 170. Hair, dark "copper" red; eyes blue. Clean-shaven, except after vacation when he lets the stubble grow, even though his girlfriend complains it scratches. Born November 10, 1987, to Linwood George Kingsley of Grantsville, N.C., and Beverly Zellman Shew of Upper Darby, PA. Graduate of Jordan High School in Durham, N.C. and North Carolina State University in Raleigh. Bachelor of English with minor in Education; Master's in English from University of North Carolina at Chapel Hill, N.C. Last job, "Customer Service Representative," Duke Energy, Durham office. They've got his work history, political affiliation (average Democrat), master's thesis ("The Butler Didn't Do It: Master / Servant Dynamics in Golden-Age British Mysteries"), e-mails and texts and porn sites visited (hetero, infrequently); even down to the name, origin and breed of his dog ("Baxter," Independent Animal Rescue, mutt). Yes, they have files on him: because of his dad's position and his mom's politics; because he's the Master of Haw Court; because he has seen a Ghost Train with his own eyes; and because in frustration, they're obsessed with learning anything they can about anyone who might hold any clue to the mystery of Aidan Stephenson Kingsley.

*

Women sometimes told him he was handsome. He'd accept the compliment gladly and follow up on it, hoping to steer the conversation bedward, with an average man's average success. When he looked in the mirror of a morning, though, he couldn't see the "handsome." He saw the hair, the freckles, pale skin that always burned when he wanted it to tan (along with the lighter-red bush and quite average set of man parts). He looked like the annoying kid sidekick in an old movie, the one who gets gunned down if it's a gangster picture or blown up in a war epic, so the star can have a big emotional scene over his death. "Oh my god, they killed Kenny! You bastards!!"

*

His parents met during law school, he at UNC, she at Duke. Mom was, by her own admission, less self-confident, far from home, stretched almost to snapping by the pressures of school, and coming to terms with the growing certainty that she was lesbian. Dad was charismatic, sexually magnetic, persuasive, handsome enough that Mom's classmates were envious on seeing him with her. He was completely self-confident in his views on law, politics, society and religion; and on the way his girlfriends were supposed to behave. These views, nine times out of ten, were absolute matter-antimatter opposites of hers. Attempts to combine them did not go well. "When we weren't fucking, we were fighting," she once told Rick, when he was teenaged enough to be neither shocked nor grossed out by the information. On Graduation Eve, after one fight too many, she went to a party, drank a whole lot of wine, and took home a member of the Duke womens' lacrosse team. Dad caught them *in flagrante*, a possibility she had noted but decided to not give a fuck about. That ended the relationship. She graduated; returned to Philadelphia; and a month later, discovered herself pregnant.

Her family heritage included Quakers, Unitarians, refugees from Hitler, liberal-arts academics, and authentic Sixties hippies. Her sense of fair play, instilled by this heritage, made her call Linwood with the news that he'd be a father. Her self-confidence, strengthening in her family's loving support, made her state "I'm going to raise the kid myself. I know what you think about gay parents, but tough shit. And if you think about starting trouble, remember two things: what possession is nine-tenths of; and which one of us aced the Family Law exam." He conceded her the parenting; she conceded him visitations, and that the child would carry both surnames. The following November, Richard Grace Shew-Kingsley arrived.

He had plenty of cousins to play with, aunts and uncles and grandparents to help look after him. The uncles and Mom's man friends, straight and gay, provided plenty of male role models. "Daddy" was a strange man, from a distant realm called "North Carolina," whose visits were only slightly more frequent than the Tooth Fairy's. Neither of them knew quite what to make of the other. A snapshot in a family album shows "Daddy" holding up baby Rick like a football he's just caught, and grinning with the gleaming charisma he was already making good use of in Republican politics back home. Rick, aged eight months, is regarding him with perplexed concern – *Who is this person, and what is he planning to do with me?*

Mom, meanwhile, passed the Bar, worked in the Public Defender's Office, and dated. By the time Rick was nine, she and Annie were a settled couple. Anne Rodriguez had left the Navy in disgust over "Don't Ask, Don't Tell," and returned to college for a biochem degree. Rick quoted her to fourth-grade classmates: "They can put that 'Don't Ask Don't Tell' where the sun don't shine." They were delighted, but a fifth-grader called him a Fag and had to be punched out. Mom gave him an earnest, muddled talk about nonviolence and words versus fists. Annie listened with a smile of quiet amusement. She took him aside later and said "Your mom's right. But sticking up for people is right too."

The year Rick turned fifteen, the Public Defender's Office got reorganized. Many of the colleagues Beverly Shew respected and worked well with were put down, while ones she didn't approve of – and who didn't seem to approve of her – were raised to power. Annie, now Ph.D'ed, was offered a job with a pharmaceutical firm near Durham, North Carolina. A law office in the same city, with good progressive credentials, agreed it could use an experienced former public defender. They moved down in early February.

The transplanting turned out to not be that bad. The bus system sucked compared to SEPTA, whose trains and trolleys he'd been navigating on his own since age eleven. On the other hand, spring came earlier, things cost less, the schoolwork wasn't as hard; and that fall, he lost his cherry to a classmate who thought his Philly "accent" was sexy. A rival for her favors, a boy who smoked unfiltered Marlboros and wore a Confederate-flag trucker cap, called him a Yankee Faggot and had to be punched out. (The grownups didn't learn of this incident, so Rick escaped more earnest lectures.) Duly punched, the boy turned out to be of a forgiving and even friendly disposition. He admitted that his Uncle Bobby, who'd fought in Afghanistan, was gay; he invited Rick and the girl to a party at his house, where he served authentic North Carolina mountain moonshine. At one a.m., Mom and Annie came out seeking the source of certain strange noises, and found a very unsteady Rick projectile-vomiting into the camellia bush. They both shook with laughter when he managed to explain, and sent him to bed with Annie's custom-mixed hangover remedy.

*

Dad had vetoed any publicity of Aidan's return, with Mr. Boulware and the State Bureau of Investigation in full agreement. It could be another false alarm, another cruel hoax, though the Bureau's experts were certain the handwriting – a short note on the back of another Polaroid – was Aidan's. (The photo itself, like all the others, showed nothing from which a location could be deduced. Aidan was seated on a wooden deck, sipping from a steaming mug held in both hands; bare trees in the background, their fallen leaves lightly dusted with snow.) If he did appear, they'd whisk him back to Raleigh, where SBI agents, and therapists who specialized in handling missing / exploited / abused children, awaited Dad's call. His return would be headline news, as much as, if not more, than his vanishing. Scores of kids might go missing every day…but not all of them left behind a controversial and damning video explaining why. And, not all of them had as their father a controversial Tea Party Republican, and possibly the next Lieutenant Governor; one of many races in the

guidelines to accommodate transgender students: "The end of public

most fiercely argued election the country had ever seen; whose contests were all, from Dad all the way up to President, shadowed by the question of "The Wizard."

The Wizard, whoever, or whatever, he was. He? – he, she, them, it; nobody knew. Frantic conspiracy theories throbbed like inflamed nerves through the Net's synapses. Cyber-attacks by terrorists; a cyber-intelligence grown self-aware and rogue like in dystopian sci-fi. Evangelicals were sure he was the Antichrist, come to bring on the End Times, especially after what he'd done (or had he?) to Arlene Hooker. Progressives praised him; but even the most extreme leftists were wary of his powers. Was it him psychologically wrecking "bad guys" – terrorists, mass murderers, refugee traffickers, religious fanatics – all over the world? (Like Arlene Hooker; or TeShaun Williams, Mom's death-row client, who was now a wretch so devastated by Wizard-struck remorse that the prison had put him on suicide watch…) If it was him, what were his criteria for who he would or wouldn't take out? Anybody could be next.

All the weird shit of the past four years seemed to have begun when Aidan disappeared. The way he'd vanished so completely, and stayed vanished without a trace, except for the anonymous Polaroids. The extreme weather: round the time his first photo arrived, there'd been a vast tornado outbreak, from Oklahoma as far east as upstate New York (!), some of the biggest ever, two miles wide in places. Records were being broken everywhere. Hottest years in history, killing thousands in India and forcing Australia to add new colors to their weather maps. "Thousand-year" storms. Floods in Colorado, floods in West Virginia; California in critical drought. Wildfires in Yosemite, in

education!"…Communication Workers of America union says it faced "SWAT

Alberta, right now in North Carolina, burning the mountains between Boone and Asheville. (Even here, several hundred miles east and under a clear sky, Rick could smell smoke.) The Rainbow Gathering and Burning Man disasters, with their huge death tolls...and the Ghost Trains, which might, just might, have made those tolls inaccurate, if rumors were to be believed. Rumors of long-gone trains on long-gone railroad lines reappearing, passing by; even pausing sometimes at long-gone stations to rescue people in distress, then vanishing again. Heard, seen; even filmed, as at Ithaca. The rumors still hadn't emerged from the Internet's thickets to become a full-blooming news item, and even on the Net were often as not chaperoned by experts with doubtful looks and plausible explainings-away. *Yeah right,* Rick could've told them. *That wasn't a "rumor" outside my sleeper window. I know what I saw.*

Weird, crazy, scary shit. Human disasters, like the chemical spill in West Virginia that took out Charleston's water supply, and lead pipes poisoning everybody in Flint. Attack dogs loosed on Standing Rock resisters. White racists claiming they were "victimized" by Diversity. Refugees drowning by the hundreds off the coast of Italy. Brexit. (What the fuck – had some James Bond villain spiked all their tea?) The turbo weirdness of Donald Trump, that monstrous buffoon, running for President – and with armed supporters threatening civil war if he didn't win. (The election was three weeks off. All the polls and pundits predicted for Hillary, but the constantly growing number of TRUMP signs along Chatham County's back roads gave Rick a feeling of queasy dread.)

And, of course, there was Rick's own bizarre situation.

team with automatic weapons" after uncovering "massive" Verizon offshoring

None of the other runaways had an elder half-brother who, through no fault or doing of his own, and for reasons known only to a mysterious, reclusive and now dead guy, had been made "Master of Haw Court" and all that it entailed. He had no more wish than Dad to publicize this trip. He'd told Mom and Annie; his estate manager David; and Leslie. He'd gotten in the habit of telling her things. He'd often talk to her before he talked to his "official" advisors, about ideas or ethical questions involving his inheritance; use her as a sounding board to help him think things out. (One thing they still didn't talk about, though, was last summer's swimming pool incident...)

*

He'd left early enough to beat rush hour, but the drive was still stressful. To keep his temper down, he took care to not look at the big billboard by the 540 / Capitol Boulevard interchange: text in varying sizes, all seeming to tremble with indignation as they offered "**$1,000,000 REWARD** FOR INFORMATION LEADING TO THE ARREST, TRIAL AND **EXECUTION** OF THE PERSON OR ENTITY KNOWN AS THE WIZARD, FOR **HIGH TREASON** AND" (redundantly) "**CRIMES AGAINST AMERICA**;" with a picture of a wizard looking like Ian McKellen as Gandalf – a good-guy wizard, ironically; if the Wizard was that evil shouldn't it be Christopher Lee as Saruman? The sign had been put up by a rich, vicious arch-conservative, who'd caused a hellacious uproar some years earlier by mounting the exact same billboard except with Obama as the target. The furor had made national news.

Letters, phone calls, e-mails and tweets had deluged everyone: the Governor, Dad, the billboard company, and the vicious arch-conservative, who'd refused to back down by so much as a font size. The sign had been regularly defaced, and just as regularly repaired. Two people were currently in jail, and three more facing steep fines and stringent probation, for trying to burn it down. Dad, pressed for comment, had finally pointed out that (a) it was the man's own money, to spend as he chose (like for instance, on arch-conservative Republicans running for North Carolina office); and (b) while the sentiments of the sign were clearly offensive to many of the "liberal persuasion," they were not illegal. Now if it had called for Mr. Hussein's – beg pardon, Mr. *Obama's*, assassination; well then, the man would've had some explaining to do to the Secret Service; but as it stood, it was merely his Opinion, and therefore sheltered beneath the First Amendment. The sign guy had gloated at all the "liberal tears" he'd caused. Even Dad had smirked a little for the cameras.

Legal or not, it was still *wrong*. It was deliberate, bullying hatefulness, the kind which assholes like that guy, and the whole right-wing FOX-News Tea-Party horse he'd rode in on, had been brutalizing "liberals" with for as long as Rick could remember – if by "liberals" you meant people who held that compassion, honesty, fairness, restraint and the scientific method were good and right. These ideals were like visceral imperatives for him; he couldn't not want them any more than he could stop breathing. Bullying, deliberate cruelty, deliberate unreasonableness, made his temperature rise and his hands ball up into punching fists. Especially when it was done with arrogance, a sick delight in hurting people. Like, for instance, Lin Junior and the way he'd

him what Jesus "really" thinks about immigrants...Right wing outraged over

treated Aidan, to take it from the abstract to the specific. How could Dad and Eunice have watched Aidan's video and not *seen*? Yeah, he was melodramatic and self-dramatizing; because he was thirteen years old. To a thirteen-year-old everything's intense, because it's happening for the first time; plus their hormones are firing them up like nature's version of crystal meth. But Aidan had had some damn good reasons to be melodramatic. Scores of people all over the country agreed; Aidan was a hero to bullied kids coast to coast. Eunice seemed to put a lot of energy into denial, sweeping unpleasantness under the rug and pretending she had the Traditional Christian American Family she thought she was supposed to have. But Dad – what did he feel? Was he too busy (as Aidan had accused in the video), or did he not care? Or, did he find Aidan contemptible and weak, and want him to "man up" i.e. become as hard and mean as Lin?

(Was forgiveness easier if you knew the person you were giving it to had had seared into the very core of his soul all the shock, terror, pain, heartbreak, despair and helpless rage he had caused, and was being forgiven for?)

Where are you, Aidan?...I wish I'd said more than I did, stood up for you more than I did...The reasons I didn't are just lame excuses...Have you been riding the Ghost Trains?...

*

He was checked in by one set of security guards at the community entrance and another at the house. Eunice hugged him. She looked haggard. She'd always seemed painfully high-strung; and the years of worrying over Aidan had not been kind to her. Dad and Cal Boulware, his campaign manager and all-around factotum (stout, sleepy-eyed, sonorous-voiced, and that rarest of species, a black Republican), came in from a fundraiser dinner an hour later; and as soon as they'd changed, they all headed down I-40 to Grantsville. The dark-clouded sky grew even darker with the approach of autumn night. Every few miles, highway crews worked beneath bright lights, clearing away downed trees and debris left ten days earlier by Hurricane Matthew. Though officially downgraded to a "tropical storm" by the time it made landfall, everyone was still calling it a hurricane. It had flooded Lumberton and most of Robeson County, even closing Interstate 95; drowning several dozen people, and leaving hundreds more homeless. (Rick had sent a truckload of Haw Court produce down to the shelters.)

(Here too was the exit where Rick, years later, had turned off, gotten lost, and met the odd New-Age-y family, on their little farm that he never could find again. More strangeness...)

*

How many times had he made this trip in the past fifteen years? Once they'd moved to North Carolina, every few months he'd spend a weekend with Dad in Grantsville, a rural county seat near Wilmington. Mom would hand him off on the neutral ground of fancy restaurants in shopping-sprawl wildernesses, where Dad was usually meeting either constituents, lobbyists or Republican lever-pullers. They were always men. They'd eat steak, hit on the waitress with a "good ol' boy" vibe, drink bourbon (though when they offered Dad some he'd decline, saying with a clumsy hand on Rick's shoulder, "I got me some important cargo today.") Rick would keep his profile low and say little. He'd think about secretly recording their conversations on his phone and slipping them to whoever Dad was running against that year, but never worked up

Mexican descent means he can't be trusted to handle Trump University

the courage. Instead he'd take a picture of the sprawl, with maybe a left-behind huddle of sorry-looking anemic pine trees, and text it to friends back in Philly. "Welcm 2 fukin South."

Once on the freeway, Dad would pull out his own phone and start working it, talking a mile a minute about political or business stuff in a don't-piss-me-off tone. "You tell him from me, he's not the only one who can [yadda-yadda-something-or-other] for us. He knows that. I swear, his hogs've got more sense than him." He'd speak to Rick only briefly, referencing someplace they were passing: Spivey's Corner and its "Hollerin' Contest," or Bentonville Battlefield, where some Kingsley ancestor had gotten a field promotion for doing some warlike thing or other.

The two-lane road into town didn't change much through the years. Pines and hardwoods; 1930s cottages, shabby trailers and ramshackle barns; and metal buildings housing either repair shops or, with only the addition of an aluminum steeple perched on top, Fundamentalist churches. The few people they would see were black, walking slowly along the road with heads bowed by summer heat or slouched, elderly and immobile, in chairs on deep porches. Dad would wave at the porch sitters and stop to say hello to the walkers. The houses grew closer together, smaller, more ramshackle, then gave way to farm-supply lots and a closed peanut mill. A broad space of grass, weeds, gravel and a few randomly parked cars, with a dusty brick train station facing a single rusted track. A neo-colonial courthouse with a clock-tower cupola on a square of old storefronts, mostly empty. The First Methodist Church on Caswell Street, looking all superior in brick and stone and stained glass. Dad's house was a sprawling brick ranch fronted by an immaculate emerald-green lawn and framed by huge magnolia trees. Their leaves and blossoms looked shiny, as if made of plastic. The house was always dim and cool inside, with a faint scent of cleaning products. In the living room, the first time he saw it, every sittable piece of furniture wore a clear plastic slipcover.

Eunice had been an archetype he'd never encountered before: a small-town Southern Lady. Pigeon-toed walk on small feet, delicate fussy gestures, bouffant-ish hairdos. (Hair salon day was the highlight of her week: "my Girl Time," she'd titter.) Conservatively dressed: frilly blouses, knee-length skirts with matching jackets. She wore reading glasses on a gold chain. She'd patted his hand. "So you're *Rick*. I've *so* wanted to meet you." Her lamblike voice was more Southern than Dad's. She looked vaguely over her shoulder and called. "Addelie? When you have a moment can you get their things?"

An elderly African-American woman, short and hunched over, wearing a plain gray dress with white collar and cuffs, emerged from further down the hall. "This is Addelie, our housekeeper. She'll take good care of you."

The slipcovered living room had merely been freaky, but this was astounding. OMFG, a *black maid*?! – like Hattie McDaniel? In 2001! He'd tried to be friendly to her, asking if she liked her job. She'd given him side-eye and croaked "I just blessed to be workin'." Many years later after she'd passed away, he'd learned from her grandson that she hadn't "approved" of him, because he was born Out Of Wedlock.

His bedroom had been equally pristine, though not slipcovered. He texted more pictures to his Philadelphia friends: *if i wantd 2 beat off theyd mak me use condom rubber gloves &*

biohaz bin. There was never anything worth reading in the house. Dad's den had books on law, history and political strategy, and works by conservative celebrities, many personally autographed. There were childrens' books in Lin Junior's and Aidan's bedrooms; in the family room a selection of Christian self-help manuals and a movie almanac, and in the living room a large ornate Bible in pride of place.

There'd be Saturday lunch with Dad in the café across from the courthouse, where Rick encountered Southern foods like Brunswick stew (thick and rich), turnip greens (painfully bitter), and grits (tasteless unless slathered in butter). Dad would be getting up every ten minutes to greet some new local who'd walked in the glass front door with its tingling bell. He was a different person in public: jovial, joking, self-deprecating, "country;" talking about "them folks up in Raleigh" who "hadn't got the sense the Lord gave a squirrel." Summer Saturdays could include a trip to the beach, an hour away on rural roads, and nothing compared to Atlantic City or Wildwood: no boardwalk, stores or amusement parks, just huge houses on stilts, perilously close to the sea. Sunday was First Methodist, all in their very best clothes. Dad continued to be Mister Gladhand in public, frowning and don't-waste-my-time impatient in private. Eunice chattered Grantsville gossip concerning who was sick with what, or nervous-Nellied over immigrants or Muslims or whatever new nastiness Obama might be up to; and nowadays, over the Wizard's horrid sins. They both introduced Rick to more people than he could ever possibly keep track of, and told him random stories about family history, mentioning relatives he had met, could meet, might meet, or would never meet due to their being long-deceased. He was

inspired Tennessee Congressional candidate erects "Make America White

glad when his bus brought the Durham skyline back in view, the SunTrust Tower and the ballpark and cranes building the new courthouse: Reality, once again. As they pulled into the terminal he might see Muslim cabdrivers bowing towards Mecca on prayer rugs behind their vans, Mecca seeming to lie in the same general direction as the Teasers' Palace Gentlemens' Club across the tracks. "It's another planet," he'd say, when Mom and Annie asked about his visit.

*

Eunice woke them all at six. She was wearing the same clothes, and looked as if she'd slept in them, if in fact she'd slept at all. Rick hadn't gotten much sleep himself, for a horrendous, deafening, blinding thunderstorm had hovered over the house for what seemed like hours, and he'd lain awake wondering when, not if, the tornado sirens would start howling. The Grantsville house, like many in east Carolina, had no basement, only a crawl space, so they all would've had to pile into the little powder room off the hall and hope for the best. The morning light's slow and grudging increase revealed a thick mist, of penetrating clamminess and a faint briny aroma from the ocean twenty-some miles away. Dew soaked every surface, and sounds had a muffled sub-aqueous quality, as if Grant County was already submerged beneath global warming's risen seas.

Cousin Mason soon joined them. He was compact but solid and square as a concrete pillar, with silver hair swept back from his forehead and the profile of a cigar store Indian. (Like many East Carolinians, he suspected some Lumbee in his bloodline.) He was usually in jeans and an old U.S. MARINES t-shirt, usually pitted out from working on some outdoor repair. His father and Eunice's were half-brothers. His family had taken her in at age five after her parents' death in a car wreck, which had happened as they were on their way to see a lawyer about the divorce everybody in the family had been saying they should get almost from the day they were married. (Eunice had been the main, if not only, reason the marriage had been necessary in the first place.) Cousin Mason had done eight years in the Marines followed by ten on the Wilmington police force, and now ran a home-security company. He and his husband Danny, a corrections officer at the New Hanover County jail, lived on the Bates family farm southwest of Grantsville. Eunice revered him; but even though they lived openly, albeit quietly, as husbands, she, not unlike the proverbial trio of monkeys, could not seem to see, hear or speak the word "homosexual." (It was a very Southern situation, Rick told friends.)

Aidan's note had read "I'll be at the Grantsville train station after 7 am, October 18." They were there by 6:45, gathered on the weedy gravel where the tracks once had been. Sheriff Laney was there at Dad's request, with a patrol car and a couple of deputies. The mist was still thick. The only sound was the distant grumble of trucks on Route 117 downshifting as they reached the town limits. Lin Junior (Dad and Eunice's elder son, a pre-law student at East Carolina) had brought a thermos of coffee. "Little fuck better not keep us waiting," he muttered. "Don't tell Mama I said that."

They heard the courthouse clock strike the hour, a mournful damp *clong, clong, clong, clong,* trailing off into thick silence. Nobody spoke, listening, waiting. Then suddenly, as if it had appeared in a split second while they were looking elsewhere, a figure was standing on the loading dock at the depot's far end.

The day before Aidan left, Rick almost got in an argument during lunch. His whole morning had been a string of "hell" calls: irrational, clueless, mule-headed, hateful people, all wanting to rip him a new one personally over Duke Energy bill-paying rules which he was powerless to change but compelled by employment to enforce. At McDonald's, a businesswoman in a beige tailored suit decided to have a fit and hold up the whole line: himself; three Hispanic guys in paint-spattered coveralls, two black men with the hard hats and orange vests of highway workers, and a slatternly-looking girl with purple hair, pushing a large baby in a small stroller. (The baby was glassy-eyed and drooling, as if she'd given it one of those laudanum tonics popular in Victorian times.)

Ms. Tailored Suit had an expensive-looking haircut and expensive-smelling cologne. Her nose seemed sculpted for looking down on people. She wanted to use a child's Happy Meal coupon, which said "Child must be present for discount." Her daughter, though, was at home "not feeling well." When the counter girl demurred, Ms. Tailored wanted the assistant manager. When he wouldn't play along, she demanded the general manager. He had the bad luck to be there, helping with the lunch rush; and when he said No, she pulled out her tablet and demanded the number of the regional supervisor, "so we can discuss this further." Their usual McDonald's did it all the time, she insisted. "I don't think I'm being unreasonable, do you?" she said, not to Rick but in his general direction, as if his being Caucasian, clean and conservatively dressed made him the only human worthy of her notice. As if.

"She got your Philly up," Leslie said.

"She got my Philly up, yeah." He put his Upper Darby childhood's inflections into his voice. Even after twelve years away, he could still do the accent at the drop of a cheesesteak. "'You want my opinion, ma'am? Yes. If it says your kid's gotta be present, then she's gotta be present. You can obviously afford it: nice clothes, nice bling, and you're driving an Escalade. And you're holding up a bunch of people on their lunch break, who don't have the time to wait while you try to screw Ronald McDonald out of a buck-fifty.'"

"And then?"

Leslie Deramus worked in the opposite cubicle. She was good with "hell" calls, showing patience which she said came from working at a day-care center during college. When he got customers who were distraught instead of hateful he'd pass them to her. That morning, for instance, there'd been a woman with two minimum-wage jobs and three kids, one of whom had some kind of medical issue; so she was having to choose between meds, food and keeping her power on. Leslie always had a current list of charities and social services at her fingertips. She dressed dumpy because she liked to be comfortable. She often wore orange, which didn't look good on her, but she didn't care because she liked orange.

"She glared at everybody. Then one of the Mexican guys whispered something to his friends and they all started laughing. So she stomped out. I hoped the baby would hurl on her expensive shoes, but it didn't."

"One can't have everything," Leslie sighed, leaning on the top of the partition.

A call came up. "Billing; this is Rick. – Good afternoon, Ms. Colter, what can we do for you? – Yes, ma'am, it still says here six weeks past due. – You gave your son the money and told him to come pay it. – And that was? – Last month. He told you he'd paid it. – Was it a check, or cash? – Cash; right." Rick grinned ruefully up at Leslie. "Just out of curiosity, ma'am; but how old is he?" ("Thirty-one," he mouthed to Leslie.) "Yes, I – yes, ma'am, we – Ma'am, I honestly don't know. All I can think is, somewhere between your house and our office, he found something else to spend it on…"

*

His contretemps with Princess Country Club was on Friday. Saturday dawned to beautiful spring weather, with clear sunny skies and temperatures at the perfect balance between cool and warm. He and Claire had just come back from brunch when the phone rang. "Hi, Dad."

"Is Aidan with you?" Dad sounded like he was seething. Eunice was weeping in the background.

"No –"

"Have you heard from him?"

"Not since the last time I talked to you. Has something happened?"

"Do me a favor: check online and see if he's contacted you."

"Hang on…" Rick pulled out his phone. Claire gestured and mouthed *what's the matter?* and he put up a hand to ward her off. "Is he missing or something?"

Dad gave a short, angry huff of breath before replying. "He has gone and run off. And he's left this video saying we're to blame."

"Shit…when?"

"This morning sometime. Eunice didn't find the note until Bobby Laney brought Randy Hewitt over asking for him. I didn't know about it until I get a call from some goddamn reporter, because he's also put that damn video all over the goddamn Web."

"(Aidan's run away,)" Rick mouthed back to Claire, who made dismayed sounds. "Okay – no; no e-mails from him; let me try Facebook…Weird – his page is gone."

"He says he's gone offline. Try e-mailing him and see if it bounces."

Aidan, whats up, u OK? Youre causing a ruckus. "Who were the other two? – Bobby Something, and –"

"Bobby's Chief of Police. Randy's some kid that's been talking shit to Aidan. Baiting him. I tell him, just sock him a couple times and he'll leave you alone; but he goes into his whole weeping and wailing – 'Ohh, he's bigger than me, he knows how to fight, he's gonna kill me and you don't care' bullshit. You know. Instead, he gets himself a *hidden camera* and goes round *filming* every damn body these past three weeks. Every kid who says two cross words to him, and then Bobby and Gil the principal and Eunice all telling him to man up and fight back; and he puts it all up on YouTube, saying we're a bunch of *criminals* for not defending him."

Aidan's e-mail address was also gone. "Do you want me to come help look for him?" Rick offered, while wondering how much time off Duke Energy might allow him for this sort of crisis.

"No, you stay put, in case he turns up there or at your mama's. And if anybody from the press calls you, send them to

made"…Stockman: "If babes had guns they wouldn't be aborted"…Jeff me or Cal."

"You think it's going to be that big a story?" Dumb question, Rick thought even as he spoke, considering Dad's prominence. His father would be, if he wasn't already, looking at the story through a political lens, thinking of ways to show the concern he surely felt for Aidan that would do him credit. When you're a career politician, anything and everything that happens to you is liable to have a political plug-in somewhere; and if you don't find it first and plug it in the right way, you're likely to get zapped. Dad knew how to play the power games. It was everybody else's shit luck that he played them for the wrong team.

"He's done every damn thing he could to make it big," Dad growled. "Says he's posted it to all the child-abuse prevention sites too, goddammit. And says he's not gonna come back for three years, after he's learned self-defense. Left a note too. Saying, you're negligent, you're criminal, this video proves it so don't try to destroy the evidence. Eunice found it."

"Shit. This is a mess. But he can't have gone far, unless someone gave him a ride. Did he take his bike?...Then it'd take him an hour, maybe, just to walk out to I-40. Or he could be hiding at a friend's. Maybe he went to Mason and Danny's...Well, like I said, he can't have gone far. If he's hitchhiking he may not even have been picked up yet...Okay, I'll call if I hear anything."

He filled Claire in while pulling up Aidan's video. "He's your younger brother, isn't he? How old is he?"

"Thirteen. Crappy age to be."

"He's the one who loves trains so much, right? Maybe he took a train."

"No, they pulled up the tracks through Grantsville a long time ago. The nearest working tracks are something like twenty miles away, and they're only for freight."

"This is terrible. I feel so sorry for his mom"

Aidan's video was titled "Why I left." There was no description. White subtitles at the lower left corner indicated date and time. The first image was a close-up of a note on his desk.

I am going away.

You have made it brutally clear that not one single one of you is willing to do your job *as adults and defend me. Therefore you leave me no option but to learn how to defend myself.*

You will find proof on the DVD. I have also posted it to YouTube, and to anti-bullying and child-abuse prevention groups worldwide. The DVD is a copy. I have the original with me. Other copies are hidden in various safe places. If you try to take it down – in other words, if you try to destroy the evidence *of your* deliberate, criminal *negligence – it will be immediately reposted. I have meanwhile closed all my online accounts, and am leaving my phone behind. You will not be able to track me.*

I will not return – if, indeed, I return at all – until I have learned every kind of self-defense there is to learn. This process will take up to three years. I will send photos at irregular intervals, to prove that I am still alive.

That was Aidan, all right. Poor guy; everything for him

became a melodrama. The thought felt like an obscure betrayal. After all, it wasn't Aidan's fault that he was the way he was.

The next scene was from three weeks earlier. It must have been from his hidden camera, worn somewhere on or in his shirt, judging by its point of view. He walks into Linwood Junior's bedroom and confronts his older brother. The family has returned from church and Lin is shedding his Sunday best as quickly as he can, tossing his jacket on the bed, then his loosened tie. It slips off the edge and hangs briefly, like a noose, before falling to the floor. Lin Junior, seventeen; inheritor of his father's handsome features (broad forehead, strong V-jaw, slight dimple in the chin; gleaming thick chestnut hair sleekly brushed back) and some aspects of his father's personality: the impression of easygoing friendliness, and the direct blue-eyed gaze, when he talks to you, that makes you feel like the only person in the world to hold his interest; or for some, the single prey on whom this predator has focused; looks and persona together forming the kind of glamour wary people suspect is too good to be true. The hint of a smirk pulls up one corner of his smile.

"Give me back that DVD," Aidan's voice demands, creaking with puberty and fear.

"What DVD?"

"The one you *told* me you *stole* from my room, the one with my station project."

"That I told you? Maybe I was just messin' with you. Maybe I got it and don't know. I can't find half my own shit." Lin indicates the messy room, rarely cleaned.

"I kept it on the same shelf as my other projects. I spent *three months* working on it. You *know* because you *asked* me what I was working on. When I couldn't find it, you *said* you had taken it. And you wouldn't give it back unless I did something."

Lin's smile shows how he's enjoying his power to torment. "'Less you did what?"

"You know."

"Did what?"

"You *know*."

"Maybe you oughta show me." Lin's hand goes to his waist, thumb and finger taking the little gold tab of his zipper.

"No. You have to *say* it."

"Say what?"

"What you said I have to do to get my project back." Aidan's hand appears, pointing towards Lin's crotch. *"That!"*

The zipper is slowly descending. Lin looks down. "That? What, my junk? What about it?...You want some of it?"

"No I don't."

"No?"

"No."

"That's a shame…Bet you'd like it…I'll tell you: you don't know nothin' about this yet, but when you grow up to be a man you'll know what it's like to be horny. All the time. So much you can't even concentrate, like when somebody asks you to find something…So, *maybe*, if you help me out there, just a little bit, I can help you find your train-station shit."

A long pause, while Lin says nothing and grins. "You know what a blow job is, right?"

Aidan's voice is hard. "So unless I give you a blow job, you won't give me back my project."

Lin raises both hands, disclaiming responsibility. "I ain't sayin' nothin' –" but Aidan has already turned and is walking out. There's a brief glimpse of him reflected in the dresser mirror: portly like his mother; plump round face with nerdy glasses; and the ridiculous clownlike orange curly hair which he so wants to cut short but his mother won't let him, because she loves to run her fingers through it while cosseting and petting him. His face is burning in a misery of fury and helplessness and humiliation.

(Claire was appalled. "That's *horrible!*" "No shit," Rick answered. "Fucking asshole...Lin always was kind of a shit, but...Man, I hope Dad beats the crap out of him." Baxter trotted back and forth between them, looking up at their faces with faint half-whinings. He hadn't a clue what was going on; but if his Pack Leaders were upset he was going to be upset too.)

Next scene, a few days later, ten in the evening. Dad's home, a rare occurrence when the House was in session. The family had a place in Raleigh, a McMansion in a gated development in the northeast suburbs, discreetly bought by a consortium of Dad's wealthy supporters and discreetly rented to him, but Eunice and the boys joined him there only on special occasions or when school was out. Dad's in his study, on the phone, surrounded by thick copies of proposed legislation. "What is it?" he demands, once he notices Aidan.

"I need to show you something," Aidan's voice asserts, or tries to, in a quavery tone.

He places his opened laptop on Dad's desk, plays him the video of the confrontation with Lin. Before it even reaches the zipper part, Dad has marched to the door and demanded of the hallway that Lin "get in here." Lin presently appears, a bit wary but bluffing indifference. "You been messin' round in his room

held" religious beliefs...TX Baptist church: "Biblical precedent for strict racial

again?" Dad growls at him without waiting for an answer. "Give him back his damn CD, or whatever it was."

Lin claims he has no idea. Aidan charges him with his crime. "And he won't give it back unless I give him a blow job! Watch the video!"

"What??! – No *way*! That's sick. He's makin' it up!"

"You did something to him. Give him his thing back and quit messin' with him."

"I'm *not*! He's messing with *me*!"

"He's *lying*!" Aidan's voice rises to a scream. "WATCH THE VIDEO!"

"Goddammit – Aidan, I have *told* you, –" Dad's pointing finger jabs – "do not *ever* yell at me like that. Lin – give him back whatever it is. Aidan, just stay out of his way and leave him alone."

"Make him leave *me* alone!" The scream has turned to tears.

"He's making it up –"

"He's *lying*! It's –"

Dad isn't having any of it. Every phrase Aidan tries to start, he cuts off with a harsh clipped noise, palm flat against his son's words. " 'At – 'At – 'Ut – No; Aidan –" while Aidan pleads "It's – You won't – You always – You never LISTEN to me –"

"I am going to count to ten; and if both of you aren't out of here by…I do not have time for this bullshit."

"You ALWAYS believe him and not me –"

"Ten; nine; eight; seven…"

Aidan's hands seize the laptop. The picture blurs as he runs out. Then it jolts, and there's a brief flash of Lin's grasping fist, his furious face above snarling in a whisper "Why'd you tell on me, boy?" Shakes him. "Why'd you do that?...I find that damn project of yours I'm gonna *erase* it. Wipe it out. All your damn work: *bzzzt!* Gone. Un-*less* you...No – I'm goin' tell everybody you already did. Tell 'em you slurped it right up and asked for more. So you want your thing not erased, you have to make me not be a liar. They all think you're a faggot anyway." He lets go, and strolls down the hall making disgusting slurping noises. Pauses at his bedroom door, looking back with a hateful grin; and pulls a finger out of his cheek with a popping sound.

("I may have to punch that fucker out myself," Rick growled.)

Short takes. Lin making more of the slurpy sounds, or the finger-in-cheek pop, then pretending to hitch up and zip his jeans. Pointing at an imaginary CD in his hand and going "*bzzzt!*" He repeats these motions: walking past Aidan's open door, in public places where their parents won't see; even in church, attracting his attention with a serious look as if he has something important to say, then grinning cruelly as Aidan falls for his ruse. Distracting Aidan so he could snatch away a report for school due the next morning. "You want it back? You know what it'll cost you." Thrusting his finger obscenely in and out of his mouth. Aidan yelling for his mom, who comes trotting in and fusses at Lin until he drops the paper on the floor and walks away smirking. He is taller than her by a head, just like his father, and she seems fearful of him. "I don't know why you have to be so hateful all the time; why you can't be sweet to him just once in a while, like you used to when you were babies; you just don't care that it breaks my heart. Poor baby; with everybody at school giving him so much trouble, why you have to add to it I just do not understand..." Lin doesn't even trouble to answer her. She hugs Aidan to her (a close-up of her blouse approaching at alarming speed), murmuring "Poor baby, poor baby, why is he so mean? Come, I'll get you some cake, to make you happy." An enormous wedge of cocoanut cake appears, accompanied by a scoop of ice cream, and a knife and fork arranged daintily at one side. "Just a small slice, without ice cream," Aidan's voice begs, but to no avail. He takes the knife and cuts a thin third off the wedge, placing it on another plate. "*This* is what a small slice without ice cream looks like," he sighs. Her mouth turns down like a meek little child harshly reprimanded. "I made it special for you, darling, because you love it so. If you don't eat every bite you'll hurt my feelings."

"I need to show you something." He plays the video. For a moment, she does appear concerned. Her mouth puckers, her long lashes flutter. One hand, with its well-trimmed, painted nails, its pearl and amethyst ring, lifts itself to touch the frilly blouse beneath the satin jacket and the cross on her necklace, then rises in a vague lost motion towards the elegant hairdo. Her large dark eyes are uncomprehending. She half-staggers to her feet. Says nothing. Hurries away. The master bedroom door shuts, cutting off daylight to the dark hall; and there is a long pause of motionless silence.

("That's your stepmom?" Claire ventured. "She's...")

(Rick shrugged. "Yeah...She does make good desserts; but – yeah.")

Some sort of parental reckoning must have taken place, for the next scene opens in a blurred hurry at dinner, where Lin is open-mouthed and indignant at a command Dad's just given him.

fertilizer plant explodes; 15 dead, 200 injured...Gun activists plan massive

"What??"

"You heard me. Go get Aidan's project and give it back to him. I am not going to tell you again."

Lin rises, disrespect in every move, and saunters out. He's gone for a while, long enough for Dad to yell his name. He returns with a jewel case, which he flips onto the table next to Aidan's plate. The DVD inside has "Grant Park Station" handwritten in black Sharpie. "There's your damn train shit. It was right where you left it, on your shelf."

"You mean where you put it back after you *stole* it."

"Aidan Stephenson, look at me," Dad orders. "We are *done* with this issue. You got your project back. We are *not* gonna talk about it any more. Linwood Ervin: you are *not* going to go in his room. Is that clear – both of you?" Their replies of "Yes sir" come as reluctantly as though dragged in chains. Afterwards, Lin corners him in the hall, not grabbing him but blocking his path. "You know I was just messin' with you, right?" he grins. "Havin' some fun. You gotta let me have a little fun once in a while." As Aidan walks away, there's another "schlurp!" sound from behind him.

The damage is already done. A hallway at school, girls clustering in a cloud of giggles and hand-hidden whisperings as Aidan passes. He goes on, perhaps ten paces, when a female voice calls "Slur - pee!" followed by even fiercer giggling.

("Oh no," Claire said in sorrow. "Mean Girls.")

The filthy nickname spreads like wildfire, following him down every hall. "Slurpy!" someone calls, then calls again, getting closer. "Hey Slurpy!...*Slurpy!*" The caller grabs him and yanks him round: another boy, tall and hulking, with dark black hair and

march on Washington, with rifles slung illegally over their shoulders...

Vanishing Act / 30

darkness in his eyes. He looks like the kind who'd be a poster child for Bad Attitude; who gets his height and strength and tormenting hormones before anyone else his age, and doesn't know what to do with them except lash out at others. "You ain't gonna answer me when I call you?"

"You were calling somebody else. That's not my name. And you know it."

"It is if I say so. Slurpy."

Aidan says nothing and walks on, but the boy darts round in front of him and blocks his path. "Don't you turn your back on me, fucker. Answer me when I talk to you."

"Then use my right name."

(Back in Philly, Rick would've simply punched out an asshole like this and been done with him, saying "Fuck off, dickwad!" Aidan, poor meek Aidan, a bully magnet if ever there was one, can't. His stubborn but helpless voice is heartrending.)

"I *did*." The boy dances before him like a boxer, jabbing, feinting, taunting. "You wanna fight about it? Huh? Wanna fight?" Other kids have quickly formed a circle of spectators, laughing, mocking. Several of the Mean Girls watch with open glee. "Wanna fight? Or you just gonna stand there and cry? Come on, lemme see you cry. Cry for me, boy. Whatcha gonna do, tell your momma and daddy?" He's grinning now; he knows he can inflict limitless hurt and suffer none. Aidan stands mute.

("*God*, I hated middle school," Claire moaned)

A teacher appears round a distant corner, strolling oblivious up the hallway. At his approach the spectators turn, in the quicksilver instant way of a shoal of fish, each back to their own business as if nothing is happening. The bully, though, leans in to whisper as he passes from view. "I'm gonna *kill* you."

Later that day the chief Mean Girl approaches him, with a couple of her acolytes. "We're doing a survey about teenage sex lives. It's an *official* survey from the Health Department, so you *have* to answer all the questions. It's the law: if you don't you'll go to *jail*." She has her tablet in hand. "'What does a dick taste like?'"

("'Suck mine and find out, bitch,'" Rick exclaimed, wishing Aidan could've thought to say it.)

"*I – don't – know*," Aidan's voice answers in tight fury.

"'Delicious,'" she types in. Her voice drips sadistic sweet venom. "'How many times a day do you suck dick?'"

"I *don't*. Stop putting down what I didn't say!"

"'A dozen.' Remember," she says archly, "you have to tell the *truth* or go to jail!"

"I AM!"

She prims up her face in a smirk and makes kissy noises at him, then runs away laughing with the others.

Between her and the hulking bully, his last week is a misery. The bully jumps out at him, feinting and taunting. "Wanna fight? Wanna fight? I'm gonna beat your ass. I'm gonna *kill* you." The Mean Girl appears at his side as he puts things in his locker, saying in a voice of mock concern "Aren't you worried that being so *fat* is bad for you?" against a backdrop of her posse's vicious snickering. Thursday the bully corners him as he walks home, backing him up against something – a telephone pole, a mailbox. Across Caswell Street the old Robbins place is visible, boarded up and derelict and half-hidden beneath its mound of kudzu. "You little piece of shit, you ain't gonna disrespect me *any more*. You are *gonna* fight me. Next Saturday at the mill. You are gonna *be* there, and fight me, and I'm gonna *kick your ass*. If you don't show I'm gonna come to your *house* and fuckin' *kill* you, and ain't nothin' your mama or daddy or *nobody* can do nothin' about it." He stalks off, high-fiving friends who've followed to watch. Friday morning the Mean Girl announces to him, "We've talked it over; and everybody's decided you should just kill yourself. Randy's going to hurt you so bad you'll want to die anyway…I'm sad you're going to be dead; but you're such a complete loser you'll never be anything anyway. You're just wasting space and air that *normal* people need…'Bye!" She gives a coy little wave over her shoulder as she walks away, her smile as sharp as a serial killer's dismembering knife.

("And God, think what they must've been doing online," Claire said. Even as she spoke, screenshot of Twitter and Instagram threads appear. *#FuckingDieAidan*. The posts are merciless. "Loser faggot turd Slurpy.")

Friday afternoon. The principal's office. A clock shows "3:07." Gil Johnson is a black man of late middle age, with an shiny bald egg head. He looks put-upon and exasperated, and sounds like the kind of old-school administrator who'd regard demands for anti-bullying programs as just another case of liberal whining.

Aidan shows him the video of Randy's threats. "How did you get these?" he demands.

"A hidden camera."

"Did he know you were recording him?"

"No, sir."

"Are you recording *me*?"

"Yes, sir."

"You turn that thing off right now."

"No, sir. Not until you tell me what you're going to do about this." Aidan motions at the laptop.

"I'm not doing nothing unless you turn that camera off."

The picture goes dark, but the voices continue. "All right, then...Does your Daddy know you're doing this?"

"He's in Raleigh. I sent him a copy."

"What'd he say?"

"Nothing. He probably hasn't even watched it. He doesn't care."

Johnson sounds taken aback by the bitterness in Aidan's voice. "Well...so Randy Hewitt's made a lot of noise about calling you out. Suppose you don't go? No law says you have to."

"He swore if I didn't, he'd find me and kill me anyway. I *showed* you."

"And you believe him."

"Yes."

"You really believe he's truly going to kill you."

"*Yes.*"

"Let me tell you something: guys like him *talk* a whole lot more than they *do*. I bet you he won't be half-surprised if you do show up. Maybe *he* won't. Maybe he'll forget all about it by Saturday. Or, maybe you should go, and stand up to him."

"Even though he's a year older, twice as big, has been fighting all his life and is way better at it, and hates me so much he wants to destroy me?"

"I'll tell you a trick: kick him in the knee. He'll go down, I guarantee you. Then jump in and start whalin' on him. Even if you do have to take a few punches everybody'll respect you for not backing down. I bet you he will too. You'll make your daddy proud, for once."

Aidan's voice saying, "So even though I've *shown* you him swearing to kill me, and I've *told* you that I am *in fear for my life*, you *refuse* to do anything about it." Accusation rather than question.

"Aidan, we've had this talk before. You take this stuff way too seriously. It doesn't *mean* anything. It's how kids let off steam. Now if he does I'll send a big damn wreath saying 'I'm sorry' to the funeral. But I can't go pulling people out of class, and go through all the processes I'm required to go to for a complaint, plus get all kinds of grief from the parents often as not, every time somebody makes a face at you."

Bobby Laney, Grantsville's chief of police, has a round face with a flattened nose and double chins, and his uniform is a little too tight. He seems more upset by the secret recordings than by Aidan's being in mortal fear. "Damn. I'd have to ask everybody from the City Council up to the damn Attorney General to get permission...Did they know? That you were recording them?"

"No sir."

"Because that may not be legal."

"It is, sir. I looked it up. We're a 'one-party consent' state. Statute 15A-287."

The chief frowns, probably not liking some thirteen-year-old kid to best him in law knowledge. He too demands the camera be turned off. "I don't know what you think you're trying to do...if everybody finds out you've been taping them I wouldn't be surprised if they wanted to kick your ass. You shown this to your daddy?"

"I sent him a copy, but he'll never watch it."

"Your mama, then. Because if you're bound and determined to, I don't know what, press charges against him, she'll have to file them for you since you're a minor. So's he. And the most he'll get, if he gets anything, would be community service. A couple Saturdays picking up trash out by the freeway. You'd be better off having your folks talk to his."

Aidan's voice comes from the dark screen, repeating his accusation: "…you refuse to do anything."

Chief Laney sighs. "If that's the way you want to look at it. Ask your folks; and if they want to come talk to me they can."

The kitchen at home. Aidan sits at the table, his computer open and the video playing, loudly. Eunice is again trying to serve him an enormous wedge of cake, red velvet with chocolate-chip ice cream. She adamantly refuses to watch, or even listen, shutting the laptop and placing the cake plate on it. "It's nothing but hatefulness and I'm not going to pay it any attention, and you shouldn't either. Getting your brother to say all those horrible things…"

Aidan's hands move the plate and reopen the computer. "This is different, and worse. Randy Hewitt is going to *murder* me."

"Oh, pooh." She waves a hand in dismissal. "Why you even talk to him I don't know. That whole family's no good and never has been. Never wanted to do anything but live off the government…I bet you he's jealous because Daddy's successful and can buy us nice things. Was it about your clothes? I cannot get over that; mocking you for having nice clothes. Do they want everybody to look like trash, like them?...Now eat your cake all up, and you'll feel better."

"So you're not going to watch."

"Not a second. I don't ever want to see it again. It breaks my heart that you'd even do something like that; you used to be so sweet..."

"He *swears* he's going to kill me, even if he has to break into our own *house* to do it. That doesn't break your heart?"

"Aidan honey, it *never happens*. All the time you've come home saying somebody's going to do something to you, they never have, have they?"

"Plenty," Aidan insists; but she keeps talking over him. "It's nothing but *talk*, and you don't have to pay it any mind. What they think doesn't matter one little bit. When they tease you and call you fat and all – Honey, I'm your *mother*, and I think you're just right? Now who are you going to care about, them or me?" she simpers.

Nothing from Aidan but a long sigh, weary and sad. His hands close the laptop; the view turns and walks away. Her voice cries plaintively, "Don't you want your cake?"

The screen goes black.

(Transcripts – 1)

(*to:*) Lesliramus@google.com
(*from:*) woodstranscrip@rmwoods.com
(*subject:*) transcriptions

Dear Ms. Deramus: please find attached Word documents of the tape transcriptions. I am sending the tapes back via FedEx. My invoice is also attached.

The recordings are all of one person speaking. There is nothing in the content to indicate in what order they were made. He appears to have been recording himself at random, turning the recorder on and off. I have marked these instances as [*break*]. There are also long pauses when he seems to have left the recorder running. These I have marked as [*pause*]. His volume ranges from soft to extremely loud, sometimes in the course of a single sentence. I have used *italics* and CAPITALS to attempt to convey the differing levels.

Thank you again for your business and have a blessed day.
(Respectfully) Rose M. Woods
Woods Transcription Services

*

[*Tape #1 (?)*]

[*singing*] "*...got a job to do, you got to do it well; you gotta give the other fellow HELL!...* "

Give 'em hell. Give 'em back the hell they gave, with interest.

[*pause*]

To confront you and corner you with nowhere to run, no spin-doctoring; *force* you to see and *feel* all the pain you've ever caused, and *grind your faces in it* like a dog that's shit on the carpet.

I want it seared into the very core of your mortal souls.

I want you to realize – and I want it to destroy you – that you destroyed and hurt *absolutely innocent* people, who never did you any harm or even wanted to or even *thought* about it. And I want that realization to *break your hearts beyond repair* for every waking moment of the rest of your lives; and make you *scream* in the agonies of *Hell* for every millisecond of the rest OF ETERNITY!

I want it to hurt you so badly – I want you driven fuckin' *insane* by remorse. Where you'd *sell your soul* to undo the pain you've caused. But I want you to be absolutely *helpless* to do even the tiniest thing about it – like *you* made *us* helpless to stop you from hurting us.

[*break*]

Consequences. Real-world consequences. That guy who got gay-bashed, because you're all about Family Values and homophobia? Guess what? – he was the only doctor who could've cured your grandma's terminal illness, that keeps her in constant pain. That woman who got shot fifty times because she stood up to some open-carry fascist who tried to bring his Uzi into her day-care center? She was the only teacher who could've brought your special-needs kid out of himself.

Where every wrong, evil thing you do destroys everything you need to live. And leaves you helpless, watching, as *your* kids are drowned in global-warming hurricanes, screaming for you to save them. Crushed by tornadoes. Poisoned by pollution. Blown up by fracking explosions. Blasted into hamburger by some gun nut. I want *you* to be laid off, evicted, foreclosed, bankrupted, denied health care, *your* kids murdered before your eyes by police, who get off scot-free. To go begging into church food pantries and find them stripped bare, because *your* policies and *your* laws have made so many *Americans* so desperately poor that they – Oh, we don't need welfare, you say; the churches can take care of that – that they can't feed even a tiny fraction of all the desperately starving people out there. And all the while, every talk-radio show and FOX host and newspaper is mercilessly vilifying you as lazy and worthless and a disgrace because you're poor; because you're unemployed, even though there's no jobs anywhere to be had. Relentlessly, *mercilessly* shaming you.

To go to Social Services, *pleading*, My children are *starving*. And for them to not give you food, shelter, help, anything – but to *take your kids away* – big military-weaponed cops literally *tearing your babies from your arms* as they SCREAM in helpless terror and despair, saying You're a Bad Parent because you're Poor. And you never see them again as long as you live, no matter how hard you look for them. I want your babies' helpless screams to *rip your hearts in half*, every day of the rest of your life.

All your policies, all your laws, everything you do, seeks to destroy everything good and fair and right and compassionate in the world. You think compassion's a *weakness*, to be mocked and humiliated, and crushed whenever possible. You *hate* compassion, because it'd force you to share your power and wealth. And if there's anything history's taught, it's that your kind will stop at nothing, *nothing* – cheating, stealing, lying, mass murder even – to keep your wealth and power from being diminished.

[*break*]

A film in science class, when I was little. The slides for old-fashioned microscopes: they had a thick piece of glass on the bottom and a really thin light piece they put on top. They put a cell between two of the heavy bottom pieces. This was all in close-up. The weight was too much. The cell struggled and struggled but couldn't escape. Its cell wall broke and the, the plasma came oozing out, and it died. The narrator described it like it was nothing.

That's what they do.

They put on weight they know will crush us; and *don't care*.

[*pause*]

That's the kind of world you want; and by God that's the kind of world you deserve.

I want to see that. I want to see you totally successful in destroying everything: the ecology, the economy, the poor, human rights, civil liberties, tolerance, democracy – and I don't want you to realize you've destroyed all Creation until it's totally too late to undo the tiniest bit of it. Not even God can save you; because you've crucified Him so many trillion times over, in among the trillions of people you've driven to death, that even He has no more power. Or even consciousness. That's what I want you to realize, too late: that your deliberate evil has destroyed Him, and all Creation, for all eternity.

I want each and every last one of you to suffer the full –

[*break*]

There's a kind of insect that shoots a blast of corrosive acid at its enemies, leaving them nothing but a smoking husk. That's what I want my psychic power to be like.

I want to sear into the very core of their mortal souls, every single solitary measure of every last bit of pain they have inflicted on innocent people. Willfully, knowingly, sadistically, *gloatingly* inflicted. On *absolutely* innocent people. People who *wanted* to do goodness and love mercy, *wanted* compassion and fairness and reason and honesty. Who were *vilified*, shouted at, spat on, called traitors, *terrorized* mercilessly, tortured, *murdered, because* they wanted those things.

I want you trapped for the rest of your lives in a world where every last consequence of all the evils you've done backlashes onto you like corrosive acid. Where evil is invincible and good utterly helpless. Where there's nothing *but* injustice and cruelty; where even the tiniest little *attempt, thought* even, to do kindness is massively, brutally, psychotically crushed and crushed and crushed again. I want your hearts to be broken and broken and broken and broken and broken, relentlessly, with no hope of it ever ending. I want your world to be nothing *but* mass shootings and gunfire, and poisoned air and poisoned water, and starvation, and homelessness. I want you forced to watch in total helplessness as the food is literally *torn from the mouths* of your starving children, and then them be butchered into carnage before your eyes, for the "crime" of being hungry, being poor.

I want you ground down by relentless work for no money, and utterly helpless to resist even the slightest bit against whatever oppression your bosses take against you. Work eighteen hours! Work in mortal danger, work in poisoned environments! Work for nothing but pennies! What? – you have a *family?!* *You disgusting, filthy, pathetic, TREASONOUS piece of SHIT, how DARE you put*

your humanity before our profits! DESTROY HIM! DESTROY HIM! DESTROY–
[*End of tape*]

Poor Wand'ring One

"That is the damnedest thing I've ever seen," said Annie.

"God. I am so glad I didn't let them raise you," Mom told Rick. "Poor little guy."

They were at Mom and Annie's, gathered round Mom's computer. Baxter was asleep by a heating vent. "I still think we should go help them," Claire said. "Be there for them, at least."

"Dad wants me to stay in case he comes here. And I've told him a few times, if he needed to get away for a while he could stay with me. I feel bad about it, because if what if that's what he's trying to do? He doesn't need to be out there hitchhiking, not at his age."

Claire agreed. "Some crazy person could pick him up and never be seen again."

"And the way he is, too meek to say No to anybody."

"Maybe they need people for search parties," Claire suggested.

"There's professionals. Dad can turn out the whole SBI if he needs to."

"You shouldn't feel bad," Mom told him. "He needs all the support he can get."

"I didn't tell Dad and Eunice I'd offered him refuge. If it turns out he was trying to get to me and something did – does – happen to him, I'd be a steaming pile of dogshit."

"No offense, Baxter," said Annie. "Now what was his 'station project?'" She was stout, but strong from regular exercise, her steel-gray hair streaked with white. Her sharp nose and rimless glasses gave her the look of a humorless turtle, although it was mere appearance: she had a thriving sense of humor, dry humor on the lines of Jane Austen and Miss Manners, and absurdist humor as in Monty Python and Firesign Theatre. Rick was glad she and his mother fit so well together, each seeming grounded in areas the other wasn't. Cooking, for instance: Mom couldn't, and Annie was a natural-born chef.

"He read something about Amtrak needing a new Chicago station because the one they've got now is too small, so he designed one. He showed me last time I was there. He had it all worked out: the trains would come down this ramp to the lower level and let off their passengers, then go round this big loop to a train yard south of the station where they'd be cleaned and serviced. Then they'd back into dead-end tracks on the upper level, to board passengers before departing again. It'd be downtown on the lakefront, at Grant Park, so it was 'Grant Park Station.' He had moving walkways, baggage carousels, stores and a food court – He kept explaining all the details, on and on, totally geeking out; and I wanted to say 'Okay, I get it' but I couldn't, because I could see how much it meant to him."

"Did he not have a backup?" Annie showed a scientist's alarm at such a perilous oversight.

"You'd think. I would've, if I lived there. Knowing Lin; that's exactly the kind of asshole thing he likes to do."

"Why is he so mean?" Claire exclaimed. "Is he jealous?"

"Maybe. He was four when Aidan was born."

"Is your dad mean to them?"

"Not mean; but – He's not demonstrative. And he's always busy: he's either at the Legislature or committee meetings or campaigning. When he's home he's usually on the phone. He doesn't have a lot of time for family stuff."

"He should've made time."

"It's kind of like, Lin is like Dad, and Aidan's like Eunice," Rick speculated. "Only since they're teenagers there's no filters."

"Not to speak ill; but the term 'mama's boy' comes to mind," Annie remarked.

"Yeah...kind of. She tries to treat him that way. It drives him crazy; like if they run into some of her friends and she's fawning and gushing all over him, he'll stand there totally tense like this –" he assumed a stiff, trembling posture, eyes downcast – "not saying anything but looking like he's about to explode."

"Does he ever?" Mom wondered. "Explode."

"He has hysterics. A couple years ago he was going down to see his grandparents at Hilton Head, and we were taking him to the train station in Fayetteville. Coming into town Eunice sees this new thrift store that's opened, so she pulls in saying 'I'll just have a quick look inside, I won't be a moment.' He freaks. 'No you won't! You never are! You'll talk and talk and talk and be there for hours!' And it's true; she does have no sense of time. But she's like, 'Don't worry, they'll wait for you, they know you're coming.' I went with her, to kind of make sure she didn't get caught up. I gave her about five minutes, so she could say hi to the owner and talk a little, then steered her out. The car's empty, and Aidan's walking down the road half a block away, trying to drag his big heavy suitcase with both hands and bawling his eyes out. *'You don't care! You don't care if I miss the train and don't get to see them! You don't WANT me to go! You WANT me to miss the train and force me to stay home!*...We got him to the station and we're on time; but then she has to make it worse, trying to prove to him he didn't have to worry. She asks the ticket clerk – and she gets her Southern Belle condescending-to-the-help attitude – she says, 'The train waits until everyone's gotten on, doesn't it?' Yes. 'And everyone's ticket has their name on it, so you know who's supposed to be on board, don't you?' Yeah, sorta. 'So if someone wasn't on yet, you'd wait for them, wouldn't you?' The ticket guy starts trying to explain the concept of 'on schedule' to her, but she gets this superior look and says 'Well, if I paid whatever-amount dollars for a ticket with my name on it, and that train wasn't waiting for me when I got there, I'd have something to say to my lawyer.'"

Mom stared. "Seriously? How often does this woman travel?"

"Aidan completely loses his shit. Screams at the top of his lungs. 'IT DOESN'T WORK THAT WAY! TRAINS RUN *ON A SCHEDULE*! THEY *DON'T* WAIT FOR YOU! YOU WANT THE WHOLE RAILROAD *SYSTEM* TO STOP DEAD SO YOU CAN BE *SELFISH*!'" Rick tried to keep his own voice at a conversational level, while still conveying the shrieking steam-whistle force of Aidan's fury. "If he'd been able to lift his suitcase he would've killed her with it. I got them both out the door and way down the platform, away from everybody."

"It's a good thing she and I never met," Mom remarked. "I'd have some things to say to her, by God."

"It'd be a salutary experience," Annie agreed.

"I don't think she could handle me. Everything FOX News has ever told her to be scared shitless of –"

"Sometimes I can't handle you," Rick grinned.

"Lesbian, feminist, lawyer, Democrat, Planned Parenthood

Poor Wand'ring One / 47

defender –"

"Edumacated," Annie added.

Mom made an explosive noise, hands flying outward. "*Her* head would explode. That conservative mindset…And passive-aggressive, which makes it worse. I *hate* dealing with it. A meek servile 'Christian' wife – arrgh! When you argue with your dad at least he meets you head-on." She bumped her fists together. She gestured a lot when she talked, and got passionate about things. Dance was a hobby of hers; she'd taken numerous courses over the years, to where the suppleness and good posture control of a dancer was embodied in her everyday moves, even as her gesturing hands and unruly mass of dark brown curls flew in all directions. "But she would drive me up the wall. It's impossible to reason with someone like that."

"Aidan found that out pretty quick. And he tried so hard, at first. Even when he was little, he always seemed to know what he was doing. And if they asked him, what are you doing, he'd look like 'What? – why don't you get it?' Especially if they didn't ask but demanded; like Dad. You know how he is; with constituents he's Mister I'm-Your-Best-Friend, but with family he's like 'What the hell d'you think you're doing?'…Like the time he had the hematoma…"

*

Aidan was a year old, and Lin Junior five, when Rick first met them. Lin was a fast-moving monkey-clever packet of energy, already showing signs of athletic skill, which pleased Dad greatly. Aidan waddled after Lin with eyes full of wonder. His hair was already curly and orange, which everyone found hilarious except Eunice, who called it Adorable. Lin mostly ignored him, except in

Commenters threaten writer with rape after she argues against rape jokes...

Poor Wand'ring One / 48

situations where he could use him as a kind of interactive toy; sometimes against his wishes. When alone, Aidan could entertain himself at length by working out elaborate dramas among his population of toys (Thomas the Tank Engine and colleagues, G.I. Joes, Lego people, the occupants of a deluxe Noah's Ark playset drydocked by his bed), speaking all their dialogues in his edge-of-language sounds. Eunice sometimes tried to join him, assuming he was acting out, for instance, Bible stories, and making the figures speak and move accordingly. Aidan would stare at her with, successively, bewilderment, dismay, anger; and finally, loud tears. "Oh now, baby, don't do that; I'm just trying to help you!" Lin would rewrite the script as War, bringing his tanks and Star Wars fighters to mow down Aidan's cast. This brought on the howls and tears much faster. Dad had no patience for any of it; grabbing Aidan, putting him on the bed and slapping his pajamas down beside him. "Look at me. *Look at me.* I do NOT have time for this crap. When your mama tells you to do something, you *do* it. GO – TO – BED." Eunice would stand in the bedroom doorway dabbing a tissue at her eyes. Later she might sneak Aidan a plate of leftover dessert.

Not long after Rick's first visit, Aidan suffered a bad fall from a seesaw – an accident Rick suspected Lin had something to do with, noticing guilty looks on his face when Eunice talked about it. Aidan had landed with legs akimbo on a jagged rock, leaving a deep gash between his thighs, extremely sensitive and painful. Diaper-changing times became a torment of agonized screaming. The first time Rick heard it, his first impulse was to turn right around and head back to Durham. Sometimes it was too much for Eunice to bear on her own, and she'd get Dad to hold Aidan down.

(Rick flat-out refused to do so.) Aidan was just beginning to form coherent sentences, and trying to explain himself in them.

The tub of the Grantsville house's master bath had a detachable shower head on a hose. One day Aidan had climbed in, managed to dislodge the head from its cradle by reaching up with one of Dad's shoes, shed his loaded diaper, and tried to wash himself. Dad had caught him, and there'd been hell to pay. Rick, peering in the doorway with Cousin Mason to see what the uproar was, remembered the sodden shit-filled diaper by the drain, the head and hose swaying like some ominous slow pendulum; and most of all Aidan's look (big dark sorrowing eyes like a Keane painting) of dismay and anguish. *How can you not understand?*

*

"...Mason figured out what he'd been trying to do and explained to Dad; and after about a month the hematoma went away. But that's only the worst one I remember. Every time I was there – every time they yelled at him – Dad would yell but Eunice'd do her passive-aggressive 'Oh, how can you do this to me, you're breaking your mama's heart;' he'd get that look. 'Why are you hating me, I'm not being bad on purpose!' It hurt to watch."

They'd gone to Francesca's for ice cream. There they chanced to meet Leslie, who'd been round the corner at Cosmic Cantina getting a burrito. She escaped by a hair's breadth a great melodramatic spring storm, with thunder and lightning and sheets of rain pouring down. They sat in the front patio, recessed in the building and well-sheltered by its side walls and overhung second floor, cozy and dry in their little separate world, while just a few feet from them the deluge flooded gutters and slowed cars to a

KKK"...Klansman, accomplice charged for building "Hiroshima on a light

crawl, headlights on and wakes of water arching from their wheels.

"Poor guy was born in the wrong family," Mom said, shaking her head.

"Or the wrong era," Annie suggested.

"The wrong something," Leslie concluded.

There was a crack of thunder, and the rain came down even harder. "Yeah...If I ever found a wardrobe that went to Narnia, he'd be the first one through it," Rick said.

"Maybe he did," Claire murmured.

*

Saturday passed, with no news. Saturday night, Sunday morning; nothing. Sunday afternoon, Sunday evening, Sunday night. Monday morning; back to work. Colleagues had seen Aidan's story on the news, but most didn't know or hadn't realized that Rick was related to him, or to Dad. "He's your father?"

"That's a situation," Leslie remarked. "Has he ever tried to trot you out during his campaigns, like he does with the rest of the family?"

"No. For one thing, I wasn't born in Holy Matrimony," Rick smiled. "His 'Family Values' types might get pissed off. Anyway, I never wanted to be part of his political life. I totally disagree with him about everything political. Naturally."

"I was thinking, you two must have had some intense dinner-table conversations."

"And I grew up with Mom and her family and Annie. He only came to visit once in a while. And by the time we moved here I already knew from reading about him that I wasn't going to agree with him on stuff, so we've never talked about it. It's a Southern way; like his wife having an out gay-married cousin but never saying the word 'gay.'"

"I'm Southern too, remember. I grew up in Columbia."

"He asked me a few times if I'd like to go to an event with him. I said 'No, thank you;' and he seemed okay with it."

*

"He's your daddy?" Jimmy exclaimed. "Damn! You never said nothin'."

They'd just finished playing, he and Marcus against Jimmy and Scott, and he was still winded. Darnell dozed in his car seat, despite the gym's bright lights and loud echoes. Scott walked to and fro, blowing out gusts of breath and flapping his soaked-through shirt. Marcus was lying back against the bleachers, arms outstretched and eyes closed. "(whoosh!) – You two ran me ragged!" Scott panted. Marcus smiled.

Jimmy and his family lived up the street from Rick. They'd met when Baxter and Darnell escaped from their respective back yards, and were found happily frolicking together on a neighbor's lawn. Rick and Jimmy talked college basketball (Jimmy was a Carolina man; Rick pulled for State). Rick played pickup ball one night a week at the Walltown Park rec center. Jimmy asked if he could join. Rick figured they found each other equally exotic: Rick with his lesbian two mommies and big-city childhood; Jimmy, a sixteen-year-old redneck ("damn right, and proud of it") with a year-old, mixed-race son.

Darnell had happened in an all-too-usual way. Jimmy and Darnell's mother were schoolmates. They'd been making out at a friend's party, at which there was cherry vodka but no adult supervision. Neither had ever been taught any strategies for pulling back before things went too far; both feared that doing so would bring scorn and mockery from their friends. Things went; and in a couple of months, Pam learned she'd be joining the Teen Moms club.

There was grudging agreement, in both families, that Jimmy and Pam were far too young to marry. There was agreement that abortion was out of the question. There was partial agreement – Pam's family but not Jimmy's – that adoption wouldn't do either. Mr. Cotterill wanted Pam to learn about Responsibility, and Mrs. Cotterill feared a mixed-race child might languish for years in foster care before being adopted. Pam was sullen about everything, never having agreed to become pregnant. For Jimmy, though, the idea of fatherhood came upon him with all the might of Saul's vision on the Damascus road. He'd tell the story of how, on hearing that Pam was in labor, he'd deserted his friends, leapt on his bike, and raced at death-seeking speeds to the Duke Hospital birthing center. (He had his learner's permit, but no time to track down Daddy, Momma, brother Sam, from work to come fetch him.) He fought his way into scrubs and into the delivery room. And when they placed the warm, wriggling, tiny little figure in his arms, he sat there stunned, tears of joy and amazement streaming down his face; and all he could say, over and over, was "He's *beautiful*....He's *beautiful*..." Rick had seen him when he returned: though completely sober, he was still higher than a dozen kites. He stayed in school, but now worked as many part-time hours as he could get at his dad's towing company. He hoped to buy his own truck someday.

Scott, stocky and sandy-blond, was a nurse at a private rehab center. He'd sometimes come from late work and play in his scrubs, not bothering to change. Marcus, tall, lithe and black, was a loan officer at Wachovia. He wore impeccable suits and cufflinked shirts. His hair was a great sheaf of dreadlocks, harvested in bandannas. They might go out for a beer later, someplace where they could sit outside and downwind of other patrons. (Jimmy was too young, of course; not that that stopped him, he'd brag, from finding his own sources of drink.) "Guy time," Marcus would say. "*Beer* time," Scott would echo. Marcus was married; Scott had a girlfriend and a year-old daughter.

"Shoot. I bet he's got every cop in the state out looking for your brother," Jimmy said.

"He's doing all he can, I'm sure."

"He's got the resources," said Marcus.

"SBI, FBI, trackers, bounty hunters –" Scott listed. "Oh, tell you what – he should get what's his name that's on TV! Blond guy with the mullet; you know who I'm talkin' about? Has his whole family in the business?"

"Dog," Marcus said, eyes still closed. "Dog the Bounty Hunter."

"Yeah, him!"

"They'll find him," Jimmy assured. "He can't drive yet, right? So he can't go far. They got security cams everywhere now. Somebody's bound to see him."

"Your dad being who he is, they'll put everything on it," Marcus agreed, slowly levering himself upright. "Not like if he left from McDougald Terrace," (Durham's version of "the projects").

"Sad but true," Rick sighed.

"They'll find him," Jimmy repeated.

*

Everyone was kind and sympathetic and made what they thought were helpful suggestions about finding Aidan. He listened and thanked and said that Dad would surely try the ideas if he hadn't already, telling the more level-headed (such as Leslie) that in his own outlying position all he could really do was hope, and hold a watching brief. He too held a thin tension of worry; a waiting apprehension, like being in a plane and expecting at any moment the sudden drop of turbulence.

The Internet, meanwhile, was whirling up a perfect storm, as only the Internet can, round Aidan's story. His video struck a nerve for a whole lot of people, and by God they were going to say something about it, from the safe anonymity of their keyboards. There were demands, and offers, to pound both Lin and Randy Hewitt to a bloody pulp; and to do far worse to Kayleigh Werthan, the chief "mean girl." The thread of #LYNCHLIN was thriving. There were offers of safe refuge to Aidan, wherever he might be, and even adoption. Eunice was excoriated, not just for her mothering skills or lack thereof, but for her clothes, makeup, hair, rural Southern speech; there was even an entire sub-thread on how she'd "abused" Aidan by forcing unhealthy desserts on him. As for Dad, the comment was made, and widely circulated, that what Linwood Junior had tried to do to his little brother, Linwood Senior and his Republican cronies were doing to North Carolina as a whole. A small but vocal movement wanted pressure put on him to resign, or be removed, because of the "revelations" of his harsh, uncaring treatment of his youngest child.

There was a TV interview with Randy Hewitt, on a sofa flanked by his uncle and mother, and his grandmother in an adjacent chair. The imitation-wood-paneled wall behind them held

DREAMers "drug smugglers with calves the size of cantaloupes"...PA. police

a window with a precariously mounted air conditioner, and a portrait of a surfer-dude Jesus, with long flowing blond hair and basset-hound eyes and a nebulous golden glow round His head. A cockatoo twittered and screeched off camera. "I don't know what to say except that is not how he was brought up," Uncle insisted. Grandma made a derisive noise. That set Mother Hewitt off. "If his father was here, but he's *not*, because Laney keeps putting him in jail for stuff he *did not do*, because every [bleeping] time anything happens everybody says 'He's been in jail before, it must be his fault!' and bam! they put him back again!" More derision from Grandma, and a screech from the bird. "Hush up!" Grandma shouted at it.

"I have not got the *time* to deal with this [bleep]! I got two jobs and have to drive fifty miles a day in a car that's about to die any minute, and I *still* can't hardly keep my kids fed!"

"If their baby daddies would man up..." Grandma muttered.

"Now Mama, you know Elton's doing what he can," said Uncle. "He just now got him that Port of Wilmington job..."

"And neither one of them'll give me more hours no matter how much I ask; and now that goddamn Obama's going to force me to buy insurance with money I don't *have*..."

Randy looked like he wished he could vanish too. When the reporter, with valiant effort, managed to persuade the grownups that she'd rather hear from Randy himself, he hung his head and mumbled. She had to repeat her questions before he'd look up and speak audibly. There was no trace of the arrogant bully from Aidan's video. "I wasn't gonna *do* nothin' to him...Just wanted to mess with him a little..." (Why?) "I don't know...we just did."

(We?) "Me and my friends…we mess around like that…It don't *mean* nothin'…"

"And I can assure you it is not going to happen again."

"If he's so [bleeping] sensitive he can't take it, why don't they take *him* out? Send him to some fancy-pantsy school in Raleigh where they got counselors and shrinks and all and don't let nobody hurt anybody's feelings?!"

("SQUAARK!") *"I said hush up!"*

Chief Laney and Principal Johnson, faced with cameras, repeated how astonished they'd been by the existence of Aidan's video. They neither defended, nor apologized for, their responses to Aidan's pleas. Laney promised full cooperation with the SBI, and Johnson went on "administrative leave" pending a "full investigation." Kayleigh Werthan was incommunicado. Her father, owner of Grantsville's Chevy dealership, refused to even say where she was, let alone permit an interview. Friends (and reporters) trying to reach her found all her social media accounts shut down. "My daughter's life has been destroyed," Mr. Werthan said, holding back righteous tears. "My thirteen-year-old daughter is receiving death threats. Death threats. For what? For saying things. Saying the kinds of things little girls have always said to each other. They say things, and fight; and the next day it's forgotten and they're friends again. Whatever she may have said – and I don't deny she may have – it cannot, can never justify what he's brought down on her. A deluge of vicious hatred, from all over the world. I am talking to my lawyers about possible courses of action."

Rick did not go unnoticed. That Monday, his phone, e-mail and Facebook began to fill with queries from reporters. This was

"faggots;" wanted to start paramilitary "Constitution Security Force"…NRA

the first time he'd really had to deal with the public side of being Linwood Kingsley Sr.'s son; he wasn't sure how to deal with it, and didn't like it. So instead of replying, he took Baxter and went for a run round East Campus, to clear his head. He showered; ate; fed Baxter; then sat down and worked up a Statement, which he sent off to Cal Boulware along with all the messagers' contact info. *"I don't have anything to add, except I hope Aidan is safe and comes home safe. I'll do what I can to help. I support my Dad and his wife in trying to find him, and ask that others do the same."* Sometimes it was useful to have been an English major, after all.

The phone rang as he was going to bed, with Dad's private number. "Yeah, Dad, what's up? – any news?"

"Nothing. Not a trace. I got your statement. I appreciate your sending it. I was going to ask you, but…"

"I understand. I figured – you probably know, I don't agree with you on a lot of stuff, but this isn't the time for that."

"Thanks. I appreciate it."

"How's Eunice holding up?"

"She's a wreck. She picks up the phone Sunday and some sonofabitch starts screaming abuse at her."

"Shit. I'm sorry. You should've told her not to answer."

"You know how she is; you tell her things and half the time she's not listening…She and Lin are here in Raleigh. Lin – at school nobody'll talk to him now. He's had death threats. Somebody slashed his tires last night, brand new ones I just got him. Randy Hewitt and Kayleigh Werthan, they had to pull them out too, for their safety. Have you seen the goddamned shit they've been saying about her?"

Rick had glimpsed an entire "Suicide Girl" webpage, where

ideas for horrific vengeances against Kayleigh were constantly being added: for instance, that she be gang-raped and given to ISIS as a sex slave; this idea accompanied by crudely-made .gifs of her in a burqa, being sodomized by Osama bin Laden and a camel. "The Internet's a total jungle. It's feral."

"Twenty years and he's supported every one of my campaigns, and now…And you know that same day, Bobby Laney went and found Randy and gave him a talking-to, and even brought him to the house so's he could promise Aidan not to pick on him no more?…I tell you, I'm gonna have a few things to say to him when he comes back."

"Yeah, well…I watched his video; did you?"

"That goddamned thing…"

"Do you think he knew all this would happen? He had to have. At least guessed. He's not dumb. And I have to think, how desperate he must've been, to do that."

"If he could've *waited* half a day. If he'd just sat down and et his cake like his momma asked him to…" His father's voice lowered, cautious about Eunice overhearing. "Now every day that goes by, you know this, the chances of finding him alive go downhill quicker."

"We're all keeping our eyes out here: me, Mom, Annie, even people I work with."

"The SBI's got all their experts on it. They've got tracking dogs coming in tomorrow. If that doesn't work – and I'm not telling Eunice – they'll start with the cadaver dogs."

*

Aidan's trail, according to the dogs, went east on Third Street to Caswell, past the open bay doors of Wardell's Auto

Repair, although Mr. Wardell did not recall seeing him. Mrs. Haywood and Mrs. Pinyan, tending the rose garden at First Methodist, thought they might have; but weren't sure if it was that Saturday or some other, or for that matter if it was him. Adela Pinyan also had the impression, though she couldn't say why, that he'd gone into the old Robbins place across the street.

If a small town contains a long-vacant, derelict house, the children of that town are sure to decide that it is Haunted. Grantsville's version was The Old Robbins Place – though no one could remember any Robbinses having lived in town for ages – a nondescript two-story structure of vaguely 1850s vintage, porches sagging and chimneys crumbling. Its emptiness was for some mundane reason: no clear title; or the heirs responsible for its upkeep unwilling, unable, or unfindable. The story, relayed by Grantsville's older children to their juniors, was that on moonless nights, if you looked at it from just the right distance and just the right angle you could see lights and hear voices, sometimes even music and laughter. The entity in charge of these hauntings was known as That Arnett Boy; though again, there'd never been any Arnetts around that anybody could recall. (There was an extended clan of Arnetts in the county's northwest corner, up towards Fayetteville; but they were all Negroes, which for some reason disqualified them.) That Arnett Boy was a juvenile delinquent who was arrogant, abusive and cruel to his poor widowed mother. Every year his behavior had grown nastier; until, one moonless night, he had either slapped her, stabbed her, or bashed her head in, with an excess of gore. He was packed off to Central Prison in Raleigh, or its next-door neighbor Dix Hill, the state insane asylum. He escaped; and though many in Grantsville had fearfully

same time"...Nearly 1/5 of scientists considering leaving U.S. due to funding

locked their doors at night against his return, he was never seen or heard from again. But he *had* come back, of course, the children told their enthralled listeners, and now lurked in the depths of The Old Robbins Place like some great evil spider waiting for the touch of an unwary victim on its web. Lin had frightened Aidan with these tales; Randy Hewitt and others had dared him to climb inside through the haphazardly boarded windows. He'd always refused (yet another thing he was mercilessly teased about), would even cross to the opposite side of Caswell rather than pass the place; but that Saturday, the dogs indicated, he'd walked right in. They went through the weeds, underbrush and briars, past the half-fallen back porch, and on through the trees beyond, to the shallow gravelly depression where the railroad track used to run. Here they lost the scent, darting to and fro or turning in circles with a strange uneasy whimpering, behavior their handlers said they'd never seen before.

The SBI's cadaver dogs, searching lonely and secluded places in a wide radius, found two cadavers, but neither belonged to Aidan. When the first week had gone into the second, still without any leads, Eunice brought a psychic down from Raleigh. Nobody else in the family thought any use would come of this, but by then any opposition to any untried tactic got Eunice distraught almost to hysteria, which was just too exhausting to deal with. They went down very early on a Sunday, leaving Raleigh before dawn, and in secrecy: Eunice because she was terrified the people still vilifying her by Internet and anonymous phone might show up to attack in person, Dad concerned that his largely-Christian-conservative base would object to psychics, and that his liberal / centrist / everybody-else opponents might seize the opportunity to roar laughter at him. Rick was with them, visiting for the

cuts in climate-change research...Yosemite Rim forest fire burns 281 square

weekend. He felt he ought to show his support and sympathy in person; also, Claire kept urging him to "do something" – exactly what, she couldn't think to specify; but "something." Eunice was grateful for his presence, craving the support of every member of the family. He, Dad, Lin, Cousin Mason, Calvin Boulware, they all went.

Sister Betty was herself a Christian, middle-aged and quite ordinary. Rick would have easily taken her for one of Eunice's friends from First Methodist. Greying hair, grandmotherly smile, modest shirt and slacks and comfortable walking shoes; no great claims about her powers – "a small gift, and all from Our Lord and Savior," she said. "Even if I don't read anything, honey, you can be comforted knowing you've tried."

They took her along Aidan's trail. At the Robbins place Mason chopped away the thickest undergrowth with a machete. They walked in single file behind the house. Rick had heard the "haunted" stories from Lin, and of course didn't believe them; but still… The house was half-invisible beneath a mound of kudzu, slowly devouring it like some monster out of H. P. Lovecraft. There were random pieces of tin fallen from the roof, with rusty sharp edges; wrecked scraps of lumber with rusted nails sticking out. An old coil-topped icebox stood on the back porch, its door hanging open by one hinge. Storms had blown leaves and trash inside, to rot and drip nasty liquid over the bottom lip. An upstairs window had fallen away entirely, to show pitch-darkness within that could conceal things even nastier. Rick shivered as they passed.

They reached the old railbed. The air, even that early, was thick and muggy and soundless, and the morning light otherworldly through the trees. Sister Betty's pace slowed, and became a dazed wandering. She swayed. Her knees buckled. Rick and Mason caught her just before she hit the ground. She had turned pale and was trembling. Her eyelids fluttered, and she breathed shallowly, mouth open. Lin ran to bring the car in. They lay her lengthwise on the back seat and propped up her head.

After a moment she blinked, and slowly tried to sit upright. Mason offered a water bottle. "Oh my," she said, "oh my." Eunice, peering in, one hand on the car roof and the other at her breast, kept asking "What did she see? What did she see?"

Sister Betty seemed to be looking at another dimension. "He walked through a doorway," she said in a colorless voice. "Then he closed it – *and took it with him.*"

She could not explain her vision. She asked that they return to Raleigh right away. "I need some prayer time with this. I've never felt anything that strong. It was – frightening." Eunice pressed her for details. "He isn't dead. I do feel that. But anything else…it's all slipped away." Back in Raleigh, she would not take any money, and left as soon as was politely possible.

*

The following week, Rick got interviewed – or was it interrogated? – by the SBI, a pair of Special Agents who appeared at his door one evening. They didn't look the part. One was tall and thin, with a youthful bearded face behind retro horn-rim glasses. His superior, Agent Leinster, was more towards the cop stereotype, with a blond buzz cut and no visible neck, though the tip of a tattoo occasionally peeked from beneath his shirt cuff. Rick let them in, one hand holding Baxter's collar so Baxter wouldn't slobber doggy welcome all over them. They made friendly with him anyway, petting him and saying *"Good* boy!" and making him wriggle in delight. Leinster took Rick's armchair without being asked, and indicated for Rick to have a seat on the scruffy old sofa. The other agent brought in a stool from the kitchen table.

What kind of secret psy-ops techniques might they use on me? Rick wondered. These days everybody knew about "good cop / bad cop," so had they developed new ones? Like that European method of detecting guilt from eye-movement patterns, which the French police had offered to teach American security people after 9/11 (but which the Americans, apparently still stuck in the same mindset that produced "Freedom Fries," blew off). He didn't have anything to feel guilty about, though. (Well; aside from some occasional porn-watching…)

Leinster made small talk, asking about basketball: Duke, UNC or State? What did Rick think of State's lineup this year; and had he ever gotten to see them play under Jim Valvanno? By the way, had Rick ever brought Aidan up to see a game? Oh, so Aidan wasn't a sports guy. Maybe a movie or a play, then, or that model train show they had at the Fairgrounds every year. "A model train show?" Rick said. "I didn't know. If I had, then sure, I would've asked him. I did tell him a couple times, he was welcome to visit if he wanted. But I never knew things were that bad until I saw his video."

It was shocking, wasn't it? So Rick had sympathy for Aidan, what he was going through. "Well, who wouldn't? I hope I was never that shitty to anyone as those kids were to him. But you don't always know how what you say is going to affect someone. If they're an introvert, and keep it all inside."

Had Rick's schoolmates given him that kind of shit? "Not more than once," Rick grinned. Leinster grinned back. So; suppose Aidan had called him and said "Rick, help me, I need to get the hell outa Dodge." How would he have done it?

I see where you're going. "How would I" can translate to "How did I?" "First of all, he'd have to convince me – and my mom – that he did need to escape. I'd get her to talk to Dad and Eunice and negotiate it. No way would I leave them out of the loop – that's too much like kidnapping. Then I guess I would've either sent him a bus ticket, or gone down to get him if I could." Would he have stayed here? No, at Mom and Annie's, since they had a guest room. The second agent, Dougherty, agreed that this was a pretty small place; speaking of which, could he use the bathroom? Behind its closed door, Rick thought he heard him checking in the medicine cabinet and behind the shower curtain. *I should've warned him about the cave crickets.* (They came up through a hole in the floor beneath the old claw-foot bathtub, in which he'd sometimes find them reposing when he went for his morning shower. Claire pitched a fit whenever she saw one, spraying it with layers of Raid as thick as Pompeii's ash.) Leinster continued to speculate how and where Rick might have met Aidan on the hypothetical rescue mission, and forwarded him to this or that secret refuge. Rick held his ground: yes, these were possibilities, but only once Dad, Eunice and Mom had agreed. Mainly Dad and Mom, of course; the whole idea would've made Eunice hysterical. Yes, Mom was quite outspoken in her dislike of Dad's politics (you should've heard her last year when he supported Amendment One), but she was far too sensible to risk her law career by helping spirit away an underage child.

change denialists press Congress to kill bill establishing honorary Science

Baxter, exiled to the back yard, whined, barked and pawed the kitchen door. "You can let him in; we won't mind," Leinster said. "I got a couple dogs myself." He followed Rick back through the bedroom and kitchen. "You don't mind if we take a look around?"

"Mom would probably say 'Ask for a search warrant!' But the only reason I would is because I've never seen one and wonder what they look like. So sure, go ahead."

They looked through every closet, cabinet and drawer. They peered behind and beneath the furniture. They shone flashlights into the crawl space. Leinster left his card – "if you remember anything, don't hesitate to call." They departed in the same friendly manner as they had arrived. Rick called Mom, with a heads-up that she and Annie might be next.

*

The weeks accrued into a month. Another month began; and was well underway when suddenly one mid-morning, Angela urgently motioned Rick to her office. Dad was on the phone. Aidan had sent them a photograph.

It had been addressed to the Grantsville house but forwarded to Raleigh with the rest of the family's mail, which Cal Boulware and his interns screened every day. Anything related to Aidan went to the SBI. Eunice, Dad said, had pitched a fit on learning she had not been shown the picture immediately. "But I would've had to pry it from her cold dead fingers to get it to the lab."

The envelope was hand-addressed, in Aidan's handwriting; postmarked at Waycross, Georgia. There was no return address. No one in the Waycross post office could recall its passing through, nor could they be sure from where it had been collected: home, business, public box or even the receiving slots at the main office itself. The stamp was one of the generic "Forever" kind. The envelope held no fingerprints save Aidan's, and those of various postal workers.

The photo was a Polaroid. It showed Aidan leaning against a fence, behind him a vista down spring-green fields to a distant pasture where ordinary brown cows grazed, with gentle rolling hills beyond hazy in the sunshine. There were no buildings or signs or indications of any sort, however, as to where in Georgia the vista might exist, or to say that it even was in Georgia (and investigators who went down to Waycross, a county seat some sixty miles northwest of Jacksonville, said it didn't resemble the countryside there). Aidan, in the foreground, leans with both arms outspread on the rails, one bent leg resting its foot against a post. His hair is cut short and expertly trimmed, with sunglasses perched on top. He wears sneakers, jeans and an unmarked t-shirt; not the clothes he left in, nor any he'd ever owned. He is grinning openly. A stalk of grass or straw is at the side of his mouth, insouciant as Franklin Roosevelt's cigarette holder.

The only fingerprints on the photo itself were Aidan's. No note was enclosed.

His picture and description were widely circulated through Waycross and its environs: to staff at the Okefenokee National Wildlife Refuge south of town; to crews on CSX freight trains passing through (it was a busy railroad junction); to the Amtrak stations in Savannah, Jesup and Jacksonville. Realtors and land agents were questioned about the vista, and even cattle brokers, concerning the ordinary brown cows. Not so much as a straw of new information was discovered. If Aidan had indeed wandered through Waycross, he'd done so without a single soul noticing. One local officer, tired, frustrated and aggravated after a hot day of driving all over saying "Have you seen this boy" to people who invariably hadn't, was being commiserated with by a dairy-farmer friend he'd stopped to visit. A Holstein leaned her head over the fence between them. "You seen this boy?" the officer asked her, showing Aidan's photo; which she promptly ate.

There was nothing else to be done. The SBI confided to Dad, and Dad to Rick, that the case was going cold. Every lead, every tip, had been followed to its dead end. The Robbins house and property had been thoroughly searched, twice. They'd checked every corner of the Kingsleys' attic, of Mason and Danny's farm. Aidan's picture was posted in rest stops and truck stops along the Interstates; appearing in newspaper inserts and flyers and pop-up ads. All the possible powers – forensic, analytical, informational – had been brought to bear, and come up empty. They could only watch, and wait, and hope. Eunice, when setting the table, always lay a place for Aidan, and insisted that the light in his bedroom be left on all night: a bedroom he'd left immaculate; bed made, trash emptied, shelves dusted; not so much as a stray sock out of place.

"The gist of it," Rick said, "was that since the ur-text of Golden Age mysteries was the restoring of a disrupted order...'Ur-text?' Crap, I'm spouting academic bullshit already!...The people of the Twenties and Thirties, they'd lived through World War One, which totally blew up everything they'd taken for granted about civilization. It killed off something like half the young men in England. So when they looked back on pre-war life and it seemed so – I don't know, simpler, part of that was a world where being a servant, being 'in service,' they called it, was considered a worthwhile job. After the war girls, women could work, as secretaries or in factories or telephone operators, instead of as maids, where you had to curtsey to Lady Cheddar every time she went past." Leslie smiled. "So you'd have this stable, closed community, standing in for the stable prewar world they nostalgized about; someplace like Miss Marple's village or Downton Abbey; then somebody gets murdered and it's 'Oh no, our order's been disrupted; call Hercule Poirot, call Lord Peter Wimsey!' And my point was, servants were part of that order; they could never be the disruption. They couldn't murder anybody; the most they'd do is scream and drop the tea tray when they found the body..."

He was trying, after a few beers, to explain his master's thesis to Leslie and Claire. Leslie still looked interested, but he could tell he'd lost Claire halfway through the monologue. They were cozy in a booth at Bull McCabe's on a Friday evening, as another thunderstorm lashed rain across the windows. Aidan had been gone three months. Rick would be busy at work, or out with friends like tonight, and suddenly realize he'd forgotten to worry about Aidan. He'd feel shitty for doing so, then wonder if he needed to feel shitty. Grieving process? But Aidan wasn't dead...

*

He sometimes dreamed about Aidan. Aidan, dealing with his bullies, the way Rick would've liked to see. Grabbing Randy Hewitt by the neck and throttling him, until his eyes bug out and his face cyanoses blue. Then *bam!* – punch him in the chest, smashing the wind out of him. Cornering Kayleigh Werthan and slapping the shit out of her, with each blow, a word: "YOU. WILL. NOT. TELL. *LIES.* ABOUT . ME."

Wouldn't the grownups intervene? Oh, he's *so* prepared for that. To Principal Johnson he says, "You *refused* to stop them when I *asked* you to. You will not stop *me* now. You will tell the *truth*: that you are too weak and cowardly to *do your job*, of protecting *innocent*, honest, *moral*, people like me from *criminal* bullies and liars like them. You will tell them that if they attack me, *they are on their own*. I *will* defend myself, by *any means necessary*. If I have to permanently cripple them, I will do so. If I have to *kill* them, I will do so, without one single second of hesitation or remorse."

And if Mr. Johnson objected to the "coward" label?" "You are a coward, and you know why. You're the only black official in a white, conservative school, and you're scared shitless for your job." Aidan's voice drops into a tearful Uncle Tom accent. "'Oh, Lawdy Lawdy: if Ah disciplines de white kids, Massa might sell me down de rivah!'" He's touched a nerve; Johnson rises from his chair, face frozen in offense. "Coward, and *stupid* too. You know my dad won't let them fire you. He needs you to point at when he's trying to get black votes. So you've got two choices: put them in juvenile prison, *where they belong*, until I'm safely out of this school and out of their reach; or tell them they persecute me at their own risk. And the blood be on your hands."

To Chief Laney he is just as merciless. "I came to you in *mortal terror* for my *life*, and asked you to *do your duty* and protect me. You *refused*. You refused to believe me. You refused to listen to me. I could have *proved* it, *but you wouldn't let me*. You *laughed* at my terror. *You are not fit to wear that uniform.*" His rage grows with every blow, as he thinks of still more hurts to avenge. Kayleigh Werthan and Randy Hewitt, all the mean girls and bullyboys, and Lin too especially: beat them and beat them and beat them and *beat* them, no matter how much they argue, threaten, beg, bleed, piss and shit themselves, beat them with all the monstrous strength of his righteous rage until their souls were broken and they could do nothing but scream their abject and absolute wrongness for ever after. *Whoa, dude, pull back! This is too far!* – Rick tries to warn, but he's immobilized like a fly in amber.

*

"Oh look, it's supposed to be nice tomorrow," Claire said, pointing at the TV, where clear skies and just-right temperatures were being promised. "Let's go to Pittsboro" – the seat of Chatham County, southwest of Chapel Hill; still mostly rural, though its northern and eastern edges were slowly being infiltrated by the Triangle's suburban creep. She'd heard there were fun thrift shops and an old-fashioned ice cream parlor.

"And speaking of Downton Abbey," Leslie added, "on the way we could go by Haw Court. You know about Haw Court, right?" she asked Rick.

"Vaguely…a big mansion out there, and the owner's a recluse?"

"It's a really sad story…" Claire sighed. (She had a fondness for sad, romantic stories.)

*

Hugo Jules Baum was sometimes described, on the rare occasions when people thought of him at all, as "the Howard Hughes of North Carolina." He was rumored to be of immense wealth, and lived in an enormous mansion known as Haw Court, on a several-thousand acre estate along the Haw River.

He had first appeared in California, surfacing in the Palo Alto area around the time the two Steves, Jobs and Wozniak, were building their first circuit boards. He went to many of the same Homebrew Computer Club meetings attended by Wozniak, with whom he had a nodding acquaintance. He'd seemed to be in his early twenties. He had prodigy-level skills at math and programming, and none at all for social interaction. A nodding acquaintance was the closest relationship he was ever known to have. No one knew his origins. All that his few acquaintances could recall him saying was that his family was "back East," and all dead. Some people said he'd had a faint Southern accent.

He applied to and was accepted at Stamford. He'd had to take the GRE's first because he had no transcripts, explaining that he'd been "home-schooled," a practice quite unheard-of in those days. His studies took an erratic course amongst mathematics, finance, and politics. He tried to have the University tailor him a degree in Strategy, but was unsuccessful, as was his run for Student Government and his attempt to start a Risk club (the board game, not the behavior). He worked part-time at banks, then at stockbrokers' offices. He took every scholarship he could get, while living with a frugality that bordered on obsessive: one of his proudest accomplishments, for instance, still remembered by his housemates with unnerved awe, was an intensely detailed chart of every place along the Peninsula where free food could be cadged, cross-referenced to bus, trolley and commuter-rail schedules.

He left Stamford, degree-less, after seven years, and signed on as junior partner / dogsbody / numbers geek at a venture capital firm. ("He was weird, but thorough," its founder said years later. "He knew his stuff and got things done.") All through the rise of personal computers and the Internet, Baum was there in the background: a face in the last row of group photos, a footnote in books or articles; an unknown unpredictable at the rare parties he attended, to be handled with discreet caution, like a firework of uncertain properties and dubious fuse. He never gave interviews. The only quote a journalist ever got close to extracting from him was second-hand via Wozniak, who vaguely recalled him saying "In a gold rush, be the guy who sells picks and shovels." When the bubbles burst, he always escaped ruin, some mixture of skill and intuition telling him to withdraw at the right moments. His wealth grew; and while other men might collect mansions and yachts and beautiful women, he collected profitable investments.

Shortly before the new century turned, Baum got engaged. There was considerable surprise. His socializing skills had not improved, and he had shown so little indication of any sexuality at all that his acquaintances had given up speculation on the "gay or straight" question. His fiancée was also a Stamford student, delivered to Palo Alto via scholarship from the Willa Cather prairies of south-central Nebraska, orphaned in infancy and raised in a Catholic childrens' home. She had a degree in counseling and an interest in the psychology of geniuses. They met as neighbors in an apartment complex. She found him fascinating; set her sights upon him, and won him. She brought him to parties with quiet pride, mothering his tiny steps towards sociability. People who saw him in those times recalled him standing beside her with a dazed smile, as if he couldn't quite believe what was happening to him.

They'd have picnics down at San Simeon, where she shared with him her daydreams about luxurious life in such a palace. He had come to own – no one knew when, how, or why – a dormant farm in North Carolina, along the Haw River in Chatham County; and added more acreage to it year after year. He designed and set to being built there what everyone guessed would be his secret wedding surprise: a great mansion.

2001 began. Bush the Younger smugly assumed his stolen Presidency. (Baum hated politics, his fiancée whispered to friends. He hated corruption; hated dishonesty; hated violence, arrogance and cruelty. He despised Republicans for all they did, and Democrats for all they were powerless to do.) On a morning two weeks after 9/11, at the height of that madness of paranoia and revenge-lust disguised as sacred Patriotism, his fiancée was driving up the Nimitz Freeway to a job interview in Fremont. A drunk in a minivan cartwheeled over the divider and struck her head-on. Death was instantaneous.

Baum was not seen anywhere until her funeral, where he spoke the barest few words possible to anyone who approached, and left as soon as was politely possible. Phone calls and e-mails from her family, and from his handful of nodding acquaintances, went unanswered. He sold his shares of the venture-capital firm to his partners. He gave notice to his landlord, threw his furniture in the dumpster (from where much of it had come), and returned to North Carolina, to the now-complete but empty mansion. He rarely set foot outside the estate again.

There were rumors, of course. He was said to hitchhike into Chapel Hill and sit drinking in dark corners of small hidden bars; to be writing brilliant mathematics articles for academic journals under assumed names; to be stockpiling food and weapons against whatever Apocalypse it was currently fashionable to fear; to be in conclave with ultra-secret government agencies, or space aliens, or both. The few people who dealt with him kept their confidence: his local accountant and lawyers, and the maintenance crews from a property management company. These last saw him only when direct explanation was needed to convey his wishes. The crews were mostly Hispanic, and on their first visit their supervisor had to translate. By their second visit, four months hence, Baum spoke self-taught fluent Spanish.

In general, though, the area gave him little thought. The only slightly newsworthy thing he'd ever done was to retreat into hermitage. No one was quite sure what he looked like, as the only extant photos were from California long ago. Of "Haw Court" (the name he had scribbled on one of the mansion's floor plans), there were only aerial views on Google Earth, and the permit blueprints tucked away in the Chatham County Planning Department. The estate was fenced and walled and well-guarded, with hidden cameras at all the gates. People did sometimes climb those gates and try to explore, but soon found themselves facing sheriff's deputies and arrest for trespassing. Among the region's population, now growing past the millions, many didn't even know of Baum's or the Court's existence.

*

They took "Sherbie," Leslie's lemon-yellow Mini Cooper, because it was a convertible (although it took them several minutes to figure out how the top was lowered), and because Leslie had a better sense of direction. Five or six miles south of Chapel Hill, they left 15-501 for a side road. They turned a second time, and a third; on old two-lane roads with the asphalt crumbling at their edges, winding down hills to cross narrow bridges and climb up round ninety-degree turns; through endless woods, save for the occasional clearing with a house or cabin, or overgrown cemetery, or pasture with an ancient silver-grey tobacco barn screened by distant trees. A brief flash of sunlight on water was glimpsed as they rounded a curve. "That's the Haw," Leslie said; "we're getting close."

"I'm glad you know where you're going," Rick said. "I'm lost."

"I'm good with maps," she shrugged, with a little smile.

"You know what would be weird?" Claire said. "If you were driving on this road you'd been over like a hundred times before, but it suddenly turned and went somewhere different."

A bright sunlit clearing appeared ahead, and a small green sign: LEWIS FERRY. They rolled into a tiny crossroads by the river. There was a derelict general store, a few old houses, some mobile homes, and the roofless brick walls of a nineteenth-century mill, half-covered in kudzu. A guardrail blocked one side of the intersection, and beyond it a row of crumbling bridge piers marched across towards the far shore. A quarter mile further, a high wall of plaster-covered masonry emerged from the left-hand woods to parallel them. Another mile, and it turned inward, and rose into a portal framing black metal gates. A gatehouse sat beside them, fanciful retro-Gothic, almost as if before leaving California, Baum had purloined some little corner off Disneyland Castle. The windows were curtained with what looked like faded tablecloths. An old pickup was parked behind it, dusted with pollen. Beyond the gates, the drive vanished upward into a mysterious tunnel of green shade.

They parked by the roadside. They stretched, breathed, looked about; saying nothing after the noise of travel, listening to the faint quiet woodland sounds of a still afternoon. Leslie walked over to peer through the gates. Rick and Claire joined her.

"Good afternoon," said a voice behind them.

All three nearly jumped out of their skins. Claire seized Rick in a breath-crushing grip. A door of the gatehouse was partly open, and an elderly man was standing there. They couldn't guess his age, as he was the well-preserved kind of elderly that could be anywhere from sixty to near ninety. He was perhaps six feet tall, though slightly stooped. He had fluffy white hair beneath an old brown fedora, and rough gray beard stubble. His face, though unsmiling, had a look as though a smile had just passed across it, like the fleeting touch of a ghost. He wore a dark green sweater, khaki pants, and deck shoes over mismatched socks. The cuffs were frayed, and the sweater unraveling in several places.

"I'm the caretaker. May I help you?" His diction was formal, his voice soft and unaccented.

"We weren't trying to break in or anything, honestly –"

Claire started to say. Rick managed to get her un-gripped.

"That's quite all right. Many are curious to see the estate."

"We know it's not open to the public," Leslie said. "We were just showing our friend where it is."

"Because the weather was going to be so nice today we wanted to drive around Chatham County," Claire babbled, "because Rick's never seen it – we're from Durham – and get ice cream at S & T's in Pittsboro, you know; and then we were talking about Haw Court –"

The ghost-smile returned to the man's face, and he gently lifted a hand, honoring and forgiving her flusteration. "No need to worry. As I said, you are one of many." He cocked his head slightly. "I beg your pardon – but are you Rick Kingsley?"

Rick did a double-take. "Well – yeah…?"

"Your brother disappeared recently, under unusual circumstances. You and your family have my sympathies." His voice had a slight tremble of age, but his speech was calmly assured. Rick thought later that he'd had the aura of some senior academician, from some Oxford college of long and ancient lineage, who carried a lifetime of authority within him and knew he didn't have to raise his voice to assert it. "Have you any word of him?"

"He sent us a picture of himself last month. But it didn't have anything to tell us where he is."

"I see. A painful situation." He paused, as if considering a course of action. "I'm not supposed to do this; but…The owner's away, and not expected back for some time. Would you like to go in and look at the grounds?"

A long sigh of – astonishment? delight? – from Claire.

Leslie was staring as if he'd told them some strange joke she didn't get. "The house is locked, of course, and there are cameras, but you may look in the windows. Now I would ask that you keep this a secret between us. No photographs either, please."

He took out a tablet and touched some buttons. The gates unlatched themselves with a complicated metal clanking, and swung slowly open. "When you come back," he said, "sound your horn and I'll let you out." They piled into Sherbie with a speed that would have impressed the Dukes of Hazzard, and zipped off upward through the green tunnel. The clang of the gates closing echoed behind them.

"I didn't know *this* was on the menu," Leslie said with a nervous laugh.

"Oh my god," Claire exclaimed. "This is totally…It's so *kind* of him to do this. I mean, he could get fired."

"Nobody'll hear about this from me," Leslie asserted. "They might not believe me."

"To let you in even though he doesn't even know you? He shouldn't get fired for that. For being kind. When we go back, we should tell him, if he gets in trouble we'll stand up for him."

"And I wonder where Baum's gone?" Leslie said. "I thought he never left. Hope he doesn't come back unexpectedly. We'd all be in trouble."

"It's weird," Rick said, though he couldn't pin down in his mind the exact reasons it was so. "It's nice that people are sympathetic for me, yeah. That they care…But when they go over the top with it. Sometimes they get way emotional. And it's not for me, it's about Aidan; the pain he went through really affected them. Because similar stuff happened to them."

"They're projecting on you," Leslie suggested.

"Yeah. And I don't know what to do for them."

"He didn't get emotional," Claire pointed out.

"No. But...I don't know. I get uncomfortable if I think they're giving me something I wouldn't get otherwise. I don't want to take advantage of them when they're that vulnerable, you know?...They've carried all this pain all their lives, and they meet me and think I understand, and they pour it all out. They let down their defenses. And shithead sociopath types can totally manipulate them, when they're in that state. Like, you know, these fucking scammers who keep telling Dad and Eunice they can find Aidan, *if* they'll give them a million dollars, or if Dad'll resign and repeal all his legislation. I mean, sure, I wish he *would*; but that's *not* the way you do it. You don't fucking blackmail the parents of a missing child."

"You *do* understand," Claire smiled, touching his arm. "That's why you feel like this."

"It's a power thing," Rick concluded. "...If Dad wasn't there, Eunice would've spent every penny the family ever had on those fuckheads."

The drive was lined with flowering trees: magnolia, Bradford pear, dogwood, mimosa and crepe myrtle, so that there'd always be something in bloom from early spring to midsummer. Low stone bridges spanned creek beds. They seemed to be climbing and curving gently lengthwise up the side of a hill. At the crest there was another view of the Haw and the distant countryside; and the briefest tantalizing glimpse, off to the right, of a broad chimneyed roofline below and perhaps a mile away.

The road turned and began winding down the far slope, still

surrounded by woods, but with the tingling excitement from that brief glimpse heightening their anticipation. A graceful curve across another stone bridge brought them to a fork, with a side lane going off to the left. There were no signs; but the arc of the main road continued forward, implying that they follow. Then at last, the woods narrowed away and revealed the Court, on the far crest of a broad lawn: a long classical front of pale grey stone, balustraded and pedimented, reminiscent of Versailles or St. Petersburg's Winter Palace. The drive brought them round the lawn and up to the central porte-cochere. They parked Sherbie and got out. "This place is bigger than Biltmore," was all Rick could think to say.

Broad stone steps flanked by empty ornamental planters led to the entry, white French doors with sidelights, leading to a vestibule whose inner doors were glass above and dark wood below. They took the caretaker's word about everything being locked. They spotted the security cameras: discreet, reflective black half-cylinders, tucked up in corners of the eaves. Through the doors they were able to make out an oval entry hall, rising the house's full height and softly lit by clerestories somewhere above, with twin curved stairs rising along the back walls to meet in the center, where archways on both floors led deeper within. There were oval windows to right and left of the porte-cochere, which Rick was able to look in at by leaping to grab the stone sills and pulling himself up. The left-hand one revealed a little coatroom, whose inner wall matched the entry hall's curve. The symmetrical right-hand space was a powder room.

They went left, or south-ish, as Leslie guessed from the sun's angle. Six windows showed them a long dining hall with an elaborate plaster ceiling, paneled wainscoting, and wall murals where figures in Jane Austen-era outfits posed decorously amidst pastoral classical ruins. Open doorways in the far wall gave onto a corridor, with what seemed to be an interior courtyard beyond. Next to it, three windows lit a corner room, which led into another decorated like a mock-Bavarian tavern, complete with bar and keg taps. Round the corner were two more windows, and a two-story screen porch wing with first-floor steps and outside door (also locked). Their way further was blocked by a high fence entwined with wisteria and morning glory, but through the leaves they could make out basement-level garage doors opening on a paved area of white concrete, and across it a wing with the proportions and window placement of a motel. "Servants' quarters," Rick thought, and said. They retraced their steps.

The windows all had half-drawn venetian blinds, but no curtains, and no furniture was visible within, so they weren't able to tell the purpose of the three equal-sized rooms along the north front – formal parlors or reception rooms of some kind, Rick guessed. These too opened onto a corridor and another interior courtyard. At the north end they found matching two-floor screen porch wings at east and west; and between them a balustraded terrace edging an ornamental lake, which seemed to have partly been cut from a hill, as the opposite side was a cliff of exposed grey stone topped with turf and trees. Opening onto this terrace was a ballroom, whose appearance set Claire to gasping and sighing again. Two stories high; another ornate ceiling, with chandeliers; doorways with white railinged, dark curtained balconies above; carpet round a long rectangle of polished wood dance floor. At the west end was a gently curved platform for musicians; and behind it, the wall was indented in the scalloped shape of a giant seashell, like the one from which Botticelli's Venus emerges.

Beyond the further porch wing, a level lawn stretched from the back of the house to a large, long swimming pool, with a trellised seating area backed by changing rooms and what looked like a small bar. The windows on this side showed bedrooms, presumably, with spacious adjoining bathrooms; save for the center, where a tall Gothic-arched window revealed a two-story English Tudor "baronial hall," with a large stone fireplace, raftered ceiling, and another curtained balcony up in the far wall. One last porch wing stood at the far end. Beside it, a hedge separated the lawn from surrounding woods. A gate led to a concrete walk, which in turn led to a patio and rear doors of the "servants' quarters." The servants apparently had their own kitchen, dining area and lounge all opening onto the patio. The walk, meanwhile, led on to a stairway down to the garage level.

Here they paused to rest. The service drive emerged onto the garage area from thick, tall woods, the walls of the house towering above it to form a secluded courtyard. Rows of blank windows blazed brightly in the sun, while the shaded air was cool and still. The sky was cloudless, without even the faintest contrail. Claire walked out onto the drive and spun slowly round, arms spread wide. "Wow. What would it be like to *live* here?"

There was a long, pensive pause. "I can't imagine," Rick finally said. "I don't know how Baum does it without going crazy. Or crazier."

"Careful – the cameras might record sound too," Leslie pretended to warn.

enforcement ignores right-wing extremism...*NY Post* editorial: City "too

"Rattling around in there all by himself, all the time."

"That's mean. You don't know that he's crazy," Claire objected. "Maybe he's still grieving."

"That's not how I'd do it. I wouldn't want to – like, bottle myself up, with nothing else to think about. I'd want to get out and be around people."

"I'd bring the people here. I'd have parties and balls, and fashion shows; and pool parties; and weekend guests all the time…what?"

Leslie was looking skeptical. "What would you do if they didn't want to leave when the weekend was over?"

"Oh, pooh. You're such a party-pooper."

As they drove away, the sun had shifted to where the front of the Court was in just the slightest hint of shade. Claire, sighing romantically, wondered why nobody lived in Great Houses any more, like on *Downton Abbey*. Why had they given up something so glamorous and wonderful? Rick repeated some of the talking points from his thesis, how the power structures of British country houses had been changed by economic shifts, a fading class system, and "domestic service" careers losing popularity to better-paying, more personally empowering jobs. Leslie had the opinion that the modern-day equivalents of Downton Abbey were the big corporate headquarters parks, like the one Annie worked in. They had the same kind of huge staff, of groundskeepers and canteen workers, cleaners, maintenance crews, drivers, security guards; they received a similar flow of income from multiple "fiefs," only instead of feudal tenant farms it was franchises or patents or contracts; they were the current centers of power, economic and political, that the "lords of the manor" had held back in Downton's heyday. Rick agreed. "You *could* still live like that," he said, "but you'd have to have money like Baum's to sustain it...I wonder what he's like as a boss? – does he pay well, does he offer benefits?"

"I wondered the same thing about James Bond villains," Leslie remarked. "Those huge secret lairs, with hundreds of minions running around: how did they hire them?...'Job opening: tech support for attempted hostile takeover of the world. Some risk of being blown up by Sean Connery.'"

Claire pouted. "I don't care. I'm going to stay in my fantasy world. So there."

They reached the gates, and Leslie honked Sherbie's horn. The gates unlatched themselves and swung open. The caretaker was nowhere to be seen.

They went on to Pittsboro, where the thrift shops and S & T's Ice Cream lived up to their promise. But Rick kept thinking of the caretaker: there'd been something about him; something in his look, in his eyes. That sense of authority, so deep and assured it didn't need to assert itself. Rick kept remembering that look; and felt somehow that the man knew much more than he had said, or would ever say.

As I was saying before I was so rudely interrupted…

Nobody'll get that, will they? Who even remembers Jack Paar anymore?

As I was saying, I left home because I overheard my parents plotting to lobotomize me.

They'd deny it, of course. They'd lie themselves black in the face, like always. "Why, *no*, honey, we'd *never* do nothin' like that!" Bull. I HEARD you. I *heard* you say the word "lobotomy" and talking about Dix Hill. Daddy saying "We could tell him we're takin' him up for the State Fair," and Mama saying "If it ever got out I couldn't never show my face in this town again."

Tough titty. It's your face; you can show it or not as you please.

Why? Because I exercised my powers of *thought*. Because I started *thinking* about things, and if they didn't add up I said so. No, Ma, Jesus did *not* mean for the coloreds to be segregated because they're not like us. No, Dad, rock music *isn't* a Communist conspiracy. Yes we *did* land on the moon. It wasn't faked; it's a scientific *fact*. So are fossils, and pollution, and…and Nixon's guilt, and My Lai, and Kent State; and everything else you get so smug and condescending about. "Oh, honey, now don't you worry none. You're just a baby; you'll understand once you're all grown up. All you need to do is read the Bible. Everything that's truly true is in there. What they say on the TV news, it ain't nothin' but lies of the Devil." LIKE HELL. It's scientific FACT and I can PROVE it, but you won't LET me because you refuse to *listen.*

[*pause*]

It always escalated. She'd start bawling because I was yelling. Of course I was yelling, because I was mad as hell and not going to take it any more. You're going to face the facts, the *real* facts, if I have to crack open your skull and brand them into your brain. Dad'd say "Now look what you done" and leave the room and go around muttering for days how he'd "done raised him a Commie traitor." Or then she'd go down on her knees and start praying for me, wailing, like I wasn't even *there* standing right in front of her. Until one night I doused her with a pitcher of ice tea. She about near choked to death. On her own prayers.

[*pause*]

The squeaky wheel gets the grease. The kid who speaks – squeaks – up, about fact versus pathological delusion, gets the lobotomy. Behind door number three, the rest of your life as a vegetable retard!

So I hit the road.

I was sixteen. It was the start of the hippie era, and hitchhiking was easy.

If they had lobotomized me, I would have killed myself. Taken Daddy's hunting knife and ripped my own guts out right in front of them, saying "I refuse to live with anything less than the full brain I was meant to have."

[*break*]

One guy I met, another refugee, he'd been in shock therapy. They were trying to cure him of being queer. It made me sick. We were both refugees from people, *family*, who should've *known* better, trying to boil our brains out and make us into good little all-American Disney audio animatronics. Which would have been a – a monstrosity in his case because he was *brilliant*. Brilliant. It would've been like burning the library at Alexandria. The first person I ever met who *got it*, why computers are so amazing. We talked for *hours*. He could've been Steve Wozniak if Woz hadn't beaten him to it. And if he hadn't become an acid head.

He said during his acid trips he went to parallel universes, ones he'd had glimpses of during the shock treatments. It was easy once you learned how, he said; but what if you could use, say, mild electric currents and magnetic fields to get the same results? Because LSD contains strychnine. It made him grind his teeth all the time. Plus it was hard to get; you couldn't trust the dosage or if it even was LSD. Besides the fact that it's illegal.

I wonder what became of him. If he ever discovered what I have. He'd be ecstatic.

I thought I saw him once in a picture from the Burning Man Festival.

We talked about that too: parallel universes. Did they exist, could we get to them, could we live in them. The thought, the wish, burned in me. We looked at the world like it was in '72, '73 and said "We gotta get out of this place –"

[*singing*] *"If it's the last thing we ever do..."*

We thought it couldn't get any worse. Ha! Boy, were we wrong!

He even told me about people who'd found portals to other universes, stumbled on them. Not fantasies like *Wrinkle In Time*, but people that friends of his knew! It *burned* in me. I wanted so much to go. A place where Nixon's Gestapo thugs would never find us, that Big Oil couldn't pollute, that the Pentagon couldn't

napalm flat – and by God you know that if they knew about it they'd try, in a skinny minute. Where they wouldn't *lobotomize* high school students for being *right.* And all the promise of computers, of electronics – computers; again, boy, how little we knew what was coming! – brain research, they were already starting to map; how could we harness that power, for good, to escape all the evil that was running berserk all around us. I asked him every detail he could remember, trying to determine what were the variables and what were constants. He said –
[*break*]

I've had a warning. This morning, a pain in my chest like a knife stabbed with a giant's force. My movements became slow and my face lopsided, my speech like Popeye's mutterings.

Thanks, family history of heart disease!

No doctors. I don't want the publicity. Don't want a cure, even if one exists, which I doubt. My work is done, my legacy secured. I have seen the Promised Land – and it has trolleys.
[*break*]

Our national tragedy, he said. It's hardwired into our nation's character, the delusion that we've got this whole continent to plunder to our hearts' content. Of course technically it *wasn't* ours; but between smallpox, guns and whiskey, oh my, the natives didn't stand a chance.

That's why these psychopaths believe they don't have to be responsible and clean up after themselves. Why bother? We can ride off into the sunset and find new resources in the next valley. The next gold mine, coal seam, virgin timber, Amway scam. And leave that fag Indian behind, to cry his faggy little tear on the garbage, in that commie environmental commercial.

To quote Daddy.

It's going to take a massive Darwin Awards die-off to make them see. See their own children and families and friends dying by the thousands daily, from the direct results of their own willful stupidity. Getting worse and worse and worse; and by the time enough survivors realize it needs to get better, it'll be too late.

But whose behind is going to get left now, eh?

[*pause*]

Laura would talk about Bodhisattvas. Comes from reading *Dharma Bums* too many times. Enlightened souls that don't go to Nirvana so they can bear the sufferings of others. Well now. Could it be that Christianity poached from other metaphysical concepts?

Uplifting others is all well and good. But choosing to suffer? Sounds more like masochism than metaphysics. After all, this is the, Buddha help us, 21st century.

If they can do it in *Avatar*, so can we. [*laughs*]

[*break*]

It's astonishing how much they've accomplished in the short time since finding the way through. If it was short, that is. I can't get clear data. Most say it was during, because, the Tea Party's rampage. No; it was when Bush the So-Much-Lesser was re-elected in '04, by Rove's foul tricks. Or 2000, when they stole the election for him. It was when the Gingrichites took over Congress. When Reagan was re-elected. When Nixon was re-elected. Rumors all the way back to the Spanish-American War, when we drowned our founding principles in Havana harbor and made an empire of ourselves.

No matter to me. They're looking to the future. A future

worth looking forward to, at last. Even if I don't see it.
[*pause*]
    I'm not worried about death.

    I yearned for it after Laura died. But not always. Some days I felt relief, that we both were spared the catastrophe of marriage. The little voice of conventional wisdom on my shoulder – devil, or angel? Ha! – what if it was Ann Landers? Saying "For shame; you should be mourning!"

    Ha!

    I gave up on conventional wisdom long ago.

    Trust your instincts. Says Young Friend. Your instincts, your hunches. Things that go bump in the night in your mind. That's how they found this new world.

    And how they've managed to accomplish so much. Trains and trolleys don't appear out of nowhere, rails and crossties and overhead wire...

    Or drive-ins. Durham has a Starlite Drive-In, run as part of the city parks. They were showing a Burt Reynolds retrospective this week. Burt Reynolds!

    Deliverance. What banjo song did the sirens sing? Laura had a crush on him when she was little, she said.

    Laura darling, my Aurelia, we've *found* deliverance.
[*break*]
    The traversing grows easier and easier. Here the forces are strong enough that a mere thought sequence puts me through as soon as I'm past the gates. I have to make sure the converter's on, of course, or the truck won't run. They're phasing internal combustion out completely. And coal-burning power plants, hurray hurray! All solar, wind, geothermal, hydro. But the

converters are cheap, biodegradable, made of recycled hemp – nearly all the paper products here are hemp-based – and found in any general store. Pre-assembled or build from a kit. If I knew the exact science I –

Hmm.

But then again; no. When things do collapse, Marzipan Cottage will be on the front lines; and if these tapes fell into the wrong hands...

So, no details on the science, of converters or traversing or any of the above. Science? How much of it is science? How much is mental discipline, geology, gemology, electromagnetism; ley lines and all that New Age-ish magic? Magic is unexplained science, it's been said. But God forbid scum like Karl Rove, or Governor – ha! – McCrory get their hands on it.

[*pause*]

There's still much to do, of course. But everyone has a voice, a measure of strength. Link your mind to the – hmm, wait; no trade secrets, remember? Tune your RCA to the right channel, and join in building the program, the coding. Evolving it.

Mind over matter. Says Y.F.

Do adjust your set; we *all* are in control.

Y.F. has had some input in station design. At Union Depot the tobacco-leaf capitals on the columns were his idea. He says it was easy to...let's say, "manifest" the commuter rail system because so many people in this area have been saying for so long we need one. Many already had one half-planned in their minds. Three, four decades of thinking it through. Blend the plans, the ideas, the desire, the energy, into one accord; and with the right...

No trade secrets!

[*break*]

That aunt who left my client the land – I wonder how much she knew? I remember he told me once she'd been a Wiccan, long before it was –

[*End of tape*]

Sixteen Coaches Long

The *California Zephyr*, over three hours late, persevered across Illinois at its standard 79-miles-per, lumbering along like a dinosaur trying to hurry. The coaches had the faint stale atmosphere of their three days' journey from Oakland. Passengers had colonized the seats with the usual detritus of pillows and overcoats, GameBoys and IPads, cardboard trays from the café car, dismembered newspapers from Sacramento, Reno, Salt Lake City, Denver. The fields blurring past were muddy, the roads glistening wet; the eastern horizon was one long wall of cloud, shading from dark grey down to indigo, and with split-second flicks of lightning. Whispered rumors of tornado alerts could be overheard while passing through the cars. Rick tried to not keep looking at his phone. Every minute they lost tightened his 6:40 connection to the *Capitol Limited* out of Chicago, and the *Zephyr*'s steward still had no word on whether it would be held for them.

He dreamed about Aidan that afternoon, as the train racketed eastward. Aidan, leaning over him, saying "Wake up; we're almost there." They'd left Aurora and were racing through the outer suburbs, at "one-hundred-ten per," Aidan proudly said. They were no longer on the Amtrak *Zephyr*, with its lurching double-deck Superliners, but on the original *California Zephyr*, the gleaming Art Deco streamliner built in 1948 by Budd of Philadelphia, where each car's name was prefixed with "Silver." They wandered through a few: *Silver Vision, Silver Future, Silver Society, Silver Sustainability*. Aidan was in heaven, talking about everything: heavy welded rails and advanced suspension keeping their motion smooth, dome cars now with wheelchair lifts, ADA-compliant sleeper rooms…Aidan the ultimate train-history nerd, who wasn't even born until decades after the old *Zephyr* had been retired, but knew every detail down to the choices on the dining-car menus…The suburbs speeding past looked surprisingly rural; there were open fields, groves almost big enough to be part of a forest; the houses on larger lots, with chicken runs, extensive vegetable gardens; – wait, was that a cow? Solar panels glinted on countless roofs. Even as the neighborhoods grew shabbier near downtown, with housing projects and burnt-out or boarded-up buildings, he saw community gardens and homemade playgrounds in vacant lots, old factories repurposed as solar farms, and many of the derelict structures aswarm with workers rebuilding. Past the freight yards and Western Avenue station; sailing over the Chicago River, slowing past State Street control tower with its Escher-like steel maze of switches; round the graceful descending ramp into Grant Park Station's lower level. Redcaps and free luggage carts waited on the broad platform, where at the north end a choice of pedestrian ramp or moving sidewalk led up into the high-clerestoried Arrivals concourse and its baggage-claim carousels. One o'clock: right on schedule. He could get a late lunch at the Berghoff and still have plenty of time to make the 4 pm *Carolina Special*…

He woke. They were at Chicago but not in the station yet; they were sitting just west of the yards, probably waiting for a signal. The other passengers were already gathering coats, laptops, leftovers and children, or getting in each others' way as they tried to maneuver suitcases down off the racks. Rain was coursing down the windows, blurring streetlights into fractal stars and the skyline to an Impressionist painting. His phone said 6:02. The

delayed workers' back pay, the Right saw shutdown effects as "left-wing plot"

steward's voice on the intercom was announcing that "all passengers traveling on connecting trains would please meet with an Amtrak Passenger Services Representative inside the station."

An outbound suburban train rumbled past. The commuters crowded inside, beneath bright fluorescent light behind tinted rain-wet windows, seemed like travelers in space capsules. Once it had gone the *Zephyr* jolted forwards, to creep round the northward curve and into the subterranean tracks of Union Station. Then more confusion and delay, as everyone sought to make their way down the narrow corkscrew center stair to the lower-level door, there to join the river of travelers already flowing up the platform, narrow and puddled and randomly asphalt-patched, with rent-a-cart machines and massive columns impeding; past the deafening roar of the locomotives and into the concourse: a scene chaotic and disheartening, like evacuees fleeing Godzilla. The station TVs, inaudible in the rush-hour uproar, were reporting something about tornadoes in the North Shore suburbs, along with another multi-twister outbreak in seven states from Texas to Georgia; the fifth one that year, with an aggregate death toll cresting three hundred. All the trains to and from Milwaukee were marked DELAYED. Rick talked to the Passenger Services rep, a drained-looking woman in Amtrak garb, who directed him through another gate to where the *Capitol* waited, hissing steam. It pulled out soon after he boarded.

The rain was still coming down. On a city street bridging the tracks there'd been an accident, a scene of arc-bright lights strobing blue, red and white, and cops moving hunch-shouldered in yellow slickers. Everybody up there must've been getting soaked, poor bastards...So there'd been a fifth mega-tornado attack. The weather kept getting more and more extreme, but politicians like Dad still didn't want to admit global warming. Just another one of those frustrating fucked-up things you couldn't do much about, except vote and sign occasional petitions and hope for the best. The kind of thing that would've had Aidan, poor tormented runaway Aidan, in a fit of passion. ("Why do you care about it so much?" you'd ask. And through his tears he'd scream back "BECAUSE NOBODY ELSE DOES!!!") Everybody saying, "the whole thing's gonna collapse, our civilization's gonna destroy itself" – while in the meantime, things like Amtrak kept struggling on, still running trains; maybe not on time, but still running…

Once the porter and conductor had come for his ticket, he called Mom. "Hey, kiddo! How's it going?"

"We just left Chicago. We're about twenty minutes late, but they say I shouldn't have any trouble making the Washington connection. Thanks for the upgrade." His tickets had been coach, but she'd paid the extra for a sleeper compartment.

"It's the least I could do. How was the interview?"

"It went OK. I don't think they were happy with me not having much teaching experience, but they were still friendly." The job, teaching English at a Catholic high school in Omaha, was a long shot; but these days any job application was a long shot. "Nothing to do now but wait."

"Wait and hope; it's all you can do. I don't suppose you saw any sign of Aidan."

"Nothing. Not from anybody I talked to either. I figured that was a long shot too."

"Yeah; long shots are usually just that. But, anything to help Eunice feel people are still trying."

tweets "this very expensive GLOBAL WARMING bullshit has got to stop"…

Aidan had now been gone for a year. The SBI had confessed, privately to Dad, that it would have considered the case stone-cold; except that every few months, another Polaroid would arrive in the mail. Each one showed him in a different locale: smiling against a backdrop of snow-capped mountains; running with arms joyfully spread across a prairie; pointing over a wide river; shirtless and up to his waist in ocean surf; in a wooded clearing, with a fire pit, log benches and a scatter of drums behind him. The pictures, implying Aidan's continued existence, had enabled Dad to pull some favors with the school board and get Gil Johnson back from his "administrative leave." Randy Hewitt, meanwhile, had returned to school. Lin didn't bother, as he'd been set to graduate, and start at East Carolina in the fall; Dad had also arranged for him to receive his diploma without having to be present. Kayleigh Werthan remained at the private academy in New Jersey where she'd been hidden, and was said to be delighting in its easy access to Manhattan. Her father had been persuaded by his lawyers to not sue anybody.

When Rick told Dad and Eunice about his upcoming trip, Eunice begged him to go by train. Aidan was traveling, out there somewhere; maybe, just maybe, he was riding the trains he so loved. Even though there weren't any trains in the pictures – or cars, or other people, or roads, buildings, landmarks, anything that might give away a clue. No letters accompanied them, no notes were written on the back, no return address on the envelopes; and as best as the Post Office could trace, they'd been dropped in random mailboxes on quiet suburban streets, far from any security cams. (And Polaroids?? Where the hell was he getting Polaroid film? The cameras themselves hadn't been made for years.)

Eunice was willing to clutch after the frailest of straws and longest of long shots. (She continued to leave Aidan's bedroom light on and table place set.)   Rick agreed to train travel, with Aidan's picture to show and ask, "have you seen him?"

"I feel sorry for her," he told Mom. The rain had stopped, and dusk was falling. The train raced past freight after westbound freight, as the steel mills of Hammond flared their unearthly fires. "He was always her 'baby.' And I think that's part of the problem. He didn't want to be 'my baby' any more. But she wouldn't listen."

"I know. Poor gal," Mom repeated. "She really needs some kind of support group."

"In Grantsville??"

"I'm sure they've got runaway kids even there…Even if they did it through their church. It'd give her something positive to do…"

"Yeah; but who's gonna try and persuade her: me or you?...Anyway, they just called my dinner seating. You know with a sleeper your meals are included?"

"No kidding. Wow! Living it up. Have a steak for me."

"Maybe I will. Bye; I'll call you tomorrow night. Love you."

"Love ya too, kiddo. Wait, wait – something I want to ask you."

"What?"

Her voice lowered. "(Gee, how should I put it?)…Have you had, like, any particularly weird dreams recently; like in the past couple nights? About wizards."

"Wizards?? No. That's a particularly weird question, Ma.

Like what; and why?"

"Never mind. Some story I saw online. It's too long to explain.'"

"Coming into Chicago today I dreamed Aidan and I were on one of his historical trains, and he was showing me all around, acting proud as if he'd designed it. But that's not particularly weird."

"I'll tell you about it when you get back."

"I will. Say hi to Annie."

The steward agreed to circulate Aidan's photo amongst the waiters and kitchen staff. None recalled seeing him, though a few remembered his disappearance. The porter had already made up the bed when he returned, and as he'd had to get up way early to catch the *Zephyr*, he decided to turn in early too.

That night he did dream of a Wizard, and of Aidan again. His consciousness rose from deep sleep into the dream. He knew it was a dream, for he could still feel the motion of the speeding train beneath him, and distantly hear the constant mournful call of its horn. He was in another historic train, in one of those single-person "roomettes" they used to have. The bed pulled down from the wall behind his seat. An Art Deco lamp was fixed by its head, lozenge-shaped with frosted lenses at top and bottom, and a toggle switch. Flipped up, the top lens was a reading light; flicked down, the bottom lens held a blue night light. Tiny slot-like closets were built into the side walls, and a stainless-steel sink could be folded down from the opposite end wall. A little circular fan perched at the top corner of the high ceiling, like a benign gargoyle set to keep watch. He felt comfortable, tucked away beneath warm blankets in the tiny space; cozy and safe and reassured, feeling he was in good hands: of the engineer, the conductor, the operators in control towers flashing past; and of the dispatchers in some faraway central hub, a large windowless room full of lighted track diagrams and banks of switches, humming with a sense of competent seriousness like NASA Mission Control.

The window shade was up, showing daylight outside. They were passing a broad lawn that sloped gently down to the tracks; and there, in the shade of a great oak, stood The Wizard. As in "Wizard of Oz," from the movie; and there was Dorothy, and / or Judy Garland, in a group of women sitting or laying on the grass listening to him. In her Garland aspect she'd cleaned up off all the drugs and hysteria and was now in a happy strong spiritual place. She waved to Rick. Beside her, Ava Gardner (one of Mom's favorite actresses) gave him a sultry wink. And wasn't that Lucy and Susan from the *Narnia* movies, and Hermione from *Harry Potter*? A figure in Biblical robes was Mary Magdalene, something kept telling him.

Aidan was standing beside the Wizard. He held a paperback the size of a phone book, whose title in Victorian letters read "THE OFFICIAL GUIDE OF THE RAILWAYS" round a display of six clock faces depicting Standard Time across the country. Rick's train was rolling past in slow motion. He looked at The Wizard. Their eyes met. The Wizard tipped his hat, in as gracious and friendly a manner as could be; and placed an approving hand on Aidan's shoulder. "He's doing an excellent job."

He was awakened by inertia dragging at him. The train was grinding to a sudden halt, brakes wailing and groaning underneath. He parted the curtains but could see nothing: an ink-black silhouette of treeline barely distinguishable against an equally black night sky. Footsteps hurried past in the corridor, with urgent staticky voices from a train-crew radio. "*...Negative, 29, he's waiting at Berea; this thing's right on top of you, Track Three westbound...*" A shaft of approaching light materialized, illumining rails, ties and trackside underbrush. The throbbing sound of diesel engines grew. Then the dazzling glare of the headlight blazed, and the other train was passing them.

It was another old streamliner, the front of the engine rounded in Art Deco curves. The cars were marked "BALTIMORE & OHIO." Coaches with drawn blinds and dim-lit vestibules; lounge with shaded lamps and a spotlit counter where bottles and glassware gleamed; bright diner with empty tables, already set for breakfast. Several cars had glassed-in observation rooms on top. The last car was another cozy, sleepy lounge, with windows at the rear and a lighted sign below them. Twisting round in his berth, he was almost able to read it: "(something) – OL LIMITED."

His train sat there for what seemed like ten minutes. Nothing happened. There were no more hurrying footsteps or radio voices. Finally he heard the engine blow two sharp notes on its horn, and they creaked into motion again.

Next morning in the diner, the steward told him they were running an hour late. "We had some traffic congestion around Elyria."

"Yeah, I woke up when we stopped for that other train."

"Other train?" The steward looked concerned. She was a perky grandmother-age lady, with greying blonde hair in bangs and big glasses on a silver chain.

"The old one, the streamliner. Was that the other 'Capitol Limited?' I thought I saw its sign on the back."

"No sir; we met Thirty just the other side of Cleveland. And we're all Superliners now. Have been since about '95."

He enjoyed an indulgent breakfast of French toast and bacon with plenty of coffee. At the other end of the car the steward seemed to be in worried conversation with the conductor. He thought they looked his way once or twice. What was up with that? – had he unwittingly spoken some top-secret railroad code word passengers weren't supposed to know? Like in thrillers such as *North by Northwest*, where some ordinary guy makes an offhand remark which is the password a nearby spy (a glamorous woman spy played by Eva Marie Saint; or maybe Ava Gardner) – the password a nearby spy is waiting for; and the ordinary guy finds himself all tangled in espionage and being chased by assassins on Mount Rushmore. Rick sometimes wondered what happened with the real spy the password was meant for. Was he still back in New York, kicking his heels and wondering where the fuck his contact was?

They lost fifteen more minutes between Cumberland and Martinsburg due to track repairs, backing into Washington Union Station at 2:30. As Rick reached the end of the platform, two people in suits approached him. "Mr. Kingsley?"

"Yes?"

"I'm Tricia Magonias, with Amtrak Security. This is Ed Dorsey, NTSB – National Transportation Safety Board. May we speak to you for a moment?"

"Yeah, I guess so; but, I have to catch another train at 3:05…"

"Number 91, the *Silver Star*, right? We can hold it for you, if necessary. If you'd come this way, please."

"Can I ask what this is about?" He'd always been a little wary of Suits – i.e. well-dressed but ominously official persons.

"There's no trouble, I assure you. There was an incident last night, which we understand you witnessed, and we'd like to get your story. It concerns rail safety."

They led him through NOT AN EXIT doors, with keypad locks that they operated with the familiarity of regular use, down corridors, and to an office where several other people from the train had been gathered: the conductors, a porter, possibly the engineer (a man in stained jeans with a yellow hard hat and battered metal lunchbox beside him), and two or three passengers. From there they took him to an inner office where more Suits waited, from the Federal Railroad Administration, CSX Railroad and the FBI (the latter saying he was "just there to observe.") Rick wondered if spooks from the CIA and NSA were hiding behind the curtains.

The NTSB rep led the questioning. He asked first about Rick's trip on the *Capitol*. Which room was he in, and which car; could he indicate on this diagram where his room was located; whether he'd been facing forward or backward relative to the train's direction. Had he slept through the night?

"No, I woke up when we stopped to let that old streamliner go past. But after we started moving again I went back to sleep."

As soon as he mentioned the streamliner he felt their attention focus, like a wire suddenly charged with current. They asked him to describe it in the minutest detail. Did he recall what time this had been? (No; it hadn't occurred to him to check his phone, but he would guess about 2 or 3 A.M.) What sort of sounds could he remember hearing? "Um…the other train's engines, and the – you know, the 'clickety-clack' as it went by – First it was our train's brakes. Then the conductor ran down the hall talking to somebody on his radio. And there was a kind of white noise, this faint blowing sound, maybe the heating system. And our train blew its horn twice before we started again."

How did he know it was the conductor? He didn't; he assumed it was, because of the radio. Could he remember what was said? Not exactly, of course; something about "no, that train's waiting somewhere else, this one's right on top of you." And was he sure he'd been awake, that this was not a very vivid dream? He had to think; but no, he was certain he'd been awake; he'd felt all his senses, including the inertia of his train stopping; that's what had woken him up.

Was he a frequent train traveler? No. When he was a kid in Philadelphia he'd ridden SEPTA; then in North Carolina he'd gone to Charlotte on the *Piedmont* a couple times. But this was his first long-distance trip. What had made him decide to go by train? He told them about Aidan, and saw that it made them stop and think. The FBI rep pulled up something on his phone and passed it round to the others.

Was there anything else about his trip that had seemed to him odd, or unusual? "Well yeah; I told the steward about the streamliner, and afterwards I see her and the conductor giving me funny looks. Then as soon as we arrive you grab me and bring me in here. That seems unusual."

The Suits exchanged glances. The Amtrak Security lady decided to field his comment. "I'm sure it does. We can understand your being puzzled. Did your brother tell you much about railroad operations? Railroad lines aren't public thoroughfares like a highway. A person can't own their own train and take it out on the tracks whenever they want. Trains have to be carefully scheduled, the way Air Traffic Control directs planes – and for the same reasons. All of you have reported seeing what looked like a train last night –"

"That wasn't supposed to be there," the CSX person said. He'd been tapping his fingers on his knee the whole time and looking like he wanted to put a word in. Now he flushed, as glances in his direction implied he'd put their collective feet in his mouth.

"No such train has been found anywhere along that line, so you may have seen something else; a row of truck trailers or mobile homes close to the tracks. However, it's still our responsibility to investigate."

The dispatcher saw it too, Rick thought, *if that was him on the radio. Meaning, he saw it on his indicators, meaning it was on the tracks. Anyway, lady, I'm from the South, I* know *mobile homes. That was a* train. He felt it safer not to argue, though.

She thanked him for his cooperation, and went to see about his connection. She returned with a very attractive Amtrak service rep, and the news that, while they hadn't been able to hold the *Silver Star* after all – doing so, it seemed, would've delayed or detoured every other train between D.C. and Richmond – he would be comped a Business Class seat on the next Northeast Regional to Petersburg, and a shuttle ride directly to Durham. "But in exchange, we'd like to ask you to keep this confidential. It remains an open investigation – like your brother's case. We'd rather not have rumors spreading. If anyone does ask you about it, especially anyone from the media, please have them get in touch with me, or Mr. Dorsey at NTSB. Here are our cards. Speaking of your brother, I wasn't aware that he was a railfan and might be riding trains. The investigators on his case didn't mention it to us. We can circulate his information and ask our people to watch for him." The service rep escorted him to the first-class "Metropolitan Lounge" (armchairs and sofas, free coffee and tea, WiFi, two TVs set to CNN and Bloomberg) and brought him his new ticket.

They were taking this mystery train a lot more seriously than they let on. Five Suits, including the FBI? Interrogation the minute he got off? The talk of "cooperation" and "confidential," with the faint implication of "we're the Government, we *can* fuck with you if necessary." (If he'd given them the smartass mouth he used to have in middle school, he might've been hitchhiking to Durham right now.) He didn't blame them, though. The idea of rogue trains running around was not good. "Rumors" could mean panic among existing passengers and paranoia in potential ones. Not to mention all the dangerous chemicals the freights often carried. He decided to do a little research, starting with the phrase "mystery train."

There was a Wikipedia page on the Elvis song of the same name. *Train I ride, sixteen coaches long*…(and it was actually written in 1953 by someone named Junior Parker. The entry didn't say, but he was probably black and more or less had it stolen from him, with Elvis getting all the fame and royalties). An Amazon link to buy several different movies called "Mystery Train," and a bunch of sites for "Dinner Mystery Trains" or "Mystery Dinner Trains." Down at the bottom, though, last above the ads, was a link to a website called *Anomalist*: "World News on Bigfoot, UFOs, the Paranormal, and Other Mysteries at the Edge of Science." *"Is this a* [Mystery Train](#) *high above Cayuga's waters? From station WTSM in Ithaca, NY comes this video showing what looks like a train in the background – on a railroad line gone since 1963....Also in New York State, a stretch of track that supposedly carries the ghost of* [Lincoln's Funeral Train](#) *each year on the anniversary of its 1865 trip. And in North Carolina, a ghost train not seen, but heard – and smelled – on the* [Old Saluda Grade](#).*"*

The TV station had featured the video on their local news two weeks earlier. Taken from a boat on Cayuga Lake, it showed children laughing and waving from another boat near the shore, where houses, docks and a road could be seen among thick trees; and up on the hillside behind them, a blur of motion, something long and swift darting past. It was barely visible at the top of the frame, but then the camera-holder seemed to have noticed the movement, for the view lifted up; to catch a quickly vanishing line of dark red coaches, their windows glinting in the sun. The video, taken during a family reunion the previous summer, had gone unremarked until March, when it was seen by a family friend who knew Ithaca's railroads and knew there was no way a train could have been there. The reporter spoke from a hillside road high above the shimmering lake, pointing out a tiny gap in the brush behind her that marked the former right of way, and a narrow strip of asphalt across the pavement where the tracks had been torn out. A team of paranormal-investigating Cornell students, studying the case, had found nothing save a historical detail which may or may not have been significant. The apparition had appeared in the exact same place, and time of day, that a train of that same appearance (the Lehigh Valley Railroad's *Black Diamond*) had passed there until its discontinuance in 1959.

He skipped the Lincoln Funeral Train in favor of the North Carolina story, a feature from last Sunday's Asheville *Citizen-Times*, dated "Tryon, N.C." Colton and Betty Vinlea had lived their whole lives in a little house beside the Norfolk Southern's Hendersonville - Spartanburg line, which harbored one of the steepest railroad grades in the East. "You could hear them coming from miles away," Mrs. Vinlea said, "wheels squealing all on the curves. And the brake shoes would get so hot you'd think they'd melt clean off. And smoking, too, and with a stink! I'd have to get my clothes off the line or that brakeshoe smell would get all up in them." The tracks had been out of use for decades, NS having easier routes down the mountains; but for some time now Mrs. Vinlea had been waking on random nights absolutely certain she'd heard the sounds, and smelled the aroma, of a descending train. Mr. Vinlea hadn't heard anything, but fancied he'd caught the brakeshoe scent on a couple of occasions. There was a photo of the elderly couple, next to rusted overgrown tracks and a signal nearly covered in a Grim-Reaper-like shroud of kudzu.

Rick next searched "Baltimore and Ohio," the name on his own mystery train. The B&O had been a railroad, fifty years and four or five mergers ago, linking Baltimore via Washington to Chicago, St. Louis, Cincinnati and other Midwestern cities. It had long since been absorbed into CSX. Its showcase train had also been named the *Capitol Limited.* He scrolled down to photos.

It was the exact same train.

There were the streamlined locomotives, the observation domes, everything; right down to the last car's lighted sign. He wondered if he should tell the Suits, and if they'd put him through another interrogation. *Aidan, you need to come home. You'd be totally creaming your jeans over this.* He bookmarked *Anomalist.* He wanted to keep an eye on this story.

Then he tried "Anomalist, Wizard." Lots of links to "The Wizard of Oz" and Harry Potter; occult sites both pro and con ("Demoniacal Real-Life Mysteries!"), indignantly Christian and trailing dire evangelical warnings. A 2008 story about a British general in Afghanistan, whose interpreter was a self-proclaimed "voodoo wizard," protecting them from the Taliban with spells involving seashells and stuff. Nothing, though, about strange dreams –

"Mr. Kingsley?" The attractive Amtrak rep was standing there. "Your train's ready for boarding."

homophobic...Paul Ryan: "People on food assistance have empty souls"...

Sixteen Coaches Long / 110

A Murmuring of Women

Dinner with Mom and Annie, telling of his interview adventures. The dean at Montana State in Bozeman couldn't seem to handle the news that he'd never ridden a horse. He'd been fifteen minutes late at Colorado State in Fort Collins, because of inept directions given over the phone. An assistant dean at the University of Wyoming, despite photos of a wife and children on his desk, kept sneaking glances at Rick's crotch and invited him to go swimming at the campus gym. An old nun at the Omaha school had the preconceived notion that he was an Atheist, because his CV and résumé made no mention of religious affiliations. "But the weirdest thing happened on the trip back: I saw a Ghost Train. And, I got Interrogated by the Government!"

He explained. "That is _amazing_, kiddo," Mom said. "My son the ghost hunter!"

Annie looked intrigued. "About a month ago I overheard a couple of Duke kids saying they'd caught a train from Carrboro back to Durham. They'd been out drinking, couldn't drive, didn't have money for a cab. So they figured they'd break into Carr Mill Mall, where it'd be warm, and sleep there. But when they woke up they were back in their dorm. They weren't too clear how they'd got there – they couldn't remember much about the night before - but they thought they remembered finding an elevator down to a train platform, and a train that brought them back and dropped them by 9th Street."

"Did they say what it looked like?" Rick asked.

"All they said was, 'a commuter train.'"

"That is weird," Mom agreed. "There's no commuter

trains within a hundred miles of here – and if your dad and his gang have their way, there never will be. I mean, if Triangle Transit found some money to buy a train and do test runs, we all would've heard about it. But they wouldn't do it in the middle of the night; and no way would they have let a bunch of drunk frat boys on board...Maybe they did get a cab and just don't remember...*Or*, or, the kid made it up. He told his girlfriend the story as a cover for something. Like he hooked up with some other girl and rode home with her."

"But listen, talking about weird stuff," Rick said. "Remember when you asked me if I'd had any dreams about a 'Wizard?' When I asked why you got all cagey and weird. Then that night I did dream about a Wizard. What's the deal?"

There was a silence. Mom and Annie exchanged looks. "Oh boy," Mom sighed. "You're gonna think I've really gone off the rails this time."

"Speaking of trains," Annie said. "Wait, Bev; first I want to hear his dream."

Rick described it. "He looked like the Wizard of Oz, from the movie. And Aidan was with him."

"What else happened?" Annie asked.

"That was all. Then I woke up because my train was slowing down, to let the 'ghost train' go by."

Annie nodded at Mom. "I see similarities."

Mom took a breath, preparing herself. "Here's what it is. Annie and I, and other women we know, have been having these really vivid dreams, with some guy calling himself 'the Wizard.'"

He would appear near to, but separate from, the dreamer's space: beside a river, for instance, on which the dreamer was floating. He'd greet the dreamer in a courteous and friendly manner. All the while, there was the growing knowledge, to absolute certainty, that he was in, or *was*, a separate consciousness, whose reality now abutted that of the dreamer's. At this point, some dreamers were so astonished that they shot wide awake, in dismay or even fear. A few nights would pass, and then the dream would come again, but with the Wizard at a greater distance, and apologizing for causing them distress. He emanated to them the knowledge – the way one knows in a dream world what its otherworldly laws and physics are – that, powerful though he was, he would never enter upon their consciousness without their express permission. He offered friendship, and help, which they could accept if they desired, at their own chosen speed and comfort level. "None of them know each other, never met –"

"That we know of," Annie added.

"Annie's niece Joan, in Mississippi. Desiree, who interned with me last summer. A client of mine."

"Our lab manager," Annie said.

"They all say their dreams have the same things: the Wizard figure, giving this feeling that he's powerful but totally benevolent; they're extremely vivid; and...this very *very* strong sense that he, or the dreams, are coming from *outside* their – our – own consciousness. He comes to them, and he offers them..." She paused, and blushed.

"He says he'll give them mind control over their reproductive system," Annie said.

Rick stared. "Seriously?...How??"

"That's not clear. The way Joan described it, they'd have the power to focus their mind on it, and control it. Their cycles

U.S. will never get its debt under control unless it denies food to the poor...

A Murmuring of Women / 113

would continue normally; but if they slept with somebody, the ovum wouldn't fertilize unless they directed it to."

"Then if they *were* pregnant," Mom added, "and something happened to make them change their mind, some serious life change where they couldn't afford to have the baby, or really strongly didn't want to –"

"If the dad turned out to be a total shit," Annie suggested.

"If they were truly certain. They couldn't be capricious; they couldn't say 'Screw this' and get rid of it if they just were having bad morning sickness or fighting with their boyfriend. But if they were sure, or it was seriously necessary, they'd be able to…re-absorb it somehow, like rabbits can if there's not enough food." Mom gave a small embarrassed laugh. "I didn't know rabbits *could* do that until I read *Watership Down*, and even then I hardly believed it."

"Wow," was all Rick could think to say. "Well…does it work?"

"We don't *know*! Besides the fact that it sounds completely impossible – even to *me*, who's always going on about the mind affecting the body – how could anyone tell?"

"You'd have to set up a hell of a lot of controls," Annie said. "There's so many variables involved in conception. Fertilized eggs sometimes abort spontaneously, without your even knowing you've conceived. You could try an MRI before and after and see if there were any changes in the brain…"

"Has anybody tried it?" Rick asked.

"Joan," Annie replied. "She's all for it. She told the Wizard, 'bring it on!' I asked her if she felt any difference and she said she could, but she couldn't put her finger on how. A sense of confidence, that she knew she could do it if she needed to. She did say she could visualize her uterus more vividly." Annie chuckled. "She wants to try it out, but doesn't want everyone to think she's turned into a slut."

Rick had a crude guy-thought, which he kept to himself: could that visualizing extend to the vaginal muscles, and make them massage a guy's dick in fun new ways? "Are other people dreaming it too?"

"We're asking around," Mom replied. "People we know. Very carefully, of course, because it *is* so weird. We don't want to sound like complete loons. Like you at fourteen when I'd try to tell you about body-mindfulness things, and you'd go 'Oh God, here's Mom with more of her New Age woo-woo.' Remember?"

"Yeah; and I stand by it," Rick smiled at her.

"And if we have any more Wizard dreams, we'll ask him. 'Is this a universal offer? It better be.'"

"'And why are you telling gals like us, who're way past menopause?'" said Annie.

"And why would he come to *me*?" Rick wondered. "If it was really him. Maybe it was just a regular dream, and you'd put the idea in my mind...If it was him, I should've asked him where Aidan is."

"He's telling us so we can reassure younger women," Mom replied to Annie. "At our age we're supposed to be Role Models, remember?...Wow. Wouldn't it be amazing, if it *was* real?...Total reproductive freedom, that no government could ever take away. We wouldn't have to depend on pills or devices or doctors or pharmacists, or worry about our employers trying to prevent it, or protesters – or *gunmen* – outside clinics; the people working at the clinics wouldn't have to struggle with any moral issues they might have with performing abortions, because they wouldn't be *needed* any more; if it was worldwide, we might even get the population under control…"

"There'd be fucking in the streets," Annie predicted.

"And God, it'd make Arlene Hooker and the rest so mad their heads'd explode. My God, it'd be beautiful."

Rick couldn't place the name. "Who?"

"God, do not get me started on her…"

"Don't start, Bev," Annie said. "Batshit-vicious 'pro-lifer' congressperson. From Joan's district. Another reason Joan's all for it."

As he left, Rick asked "Could you do something for me? Talk up that story about the Duke kids and the train. See if any more stories like that come up."

"Glad to, kiddo," Mom smiled. "And you ask Claire and other women you know about Wizard dreams, if you get a chance."

"If I can figure out how to get it in the conversation without freaking them out."

He phoned Claire on the way home. "Hey, it's Rick; how was your day?"

"Hi, Rick. Good, I guess; how was yours?" She didn't sound too tired, which was encouraging.

"It was OK. Just got done with dinner at Mom and Annie's…How about ice cream? Francesca's in half an hour?" Francesca's was a few blocks from his house, but Claire lived twenty minutes away. That longer drive back could be a bargaining chip in persuading her to stay over.

"Um – I don't know…"

"Please? I've got a bunch of stuff to tell you, from my trip. And Baxter'd love to see you." Baxter, hearing his name, stuck his head between the seats and whuffled. "Really, did you have an OK day? You don't sound sure."

"No, it was all right. It was dead, then it got way busy, then dead, then busy again; you know."

"Nobody was hateful to you?" A mean customer could put her in a funk for days. In that state she didn't want sex, no matter how gentle. She wanted cuddling and reassurance, in her own bed.

"No…not really…"

"Meaning?"

"I don't know…I just get tired of the kind of people who – Like they think they have the right to shop at Macy's. They *deserve* to be able to; that's it. 'I can afford this, so you should all bow to me.' Instead of 'Wow, I'm so lucky I can afford this,' which is what I would say."

"They think they're entitled."

"They think because they're rich they deserve to be rich."

"And sometimes it's not even their money, it's their husband's. Oops – was that sexist?"

Another slight laugh, giving him hope. "No, it's true. And they're usually the worst."

"Well, I think you need some ice cream therapy."

"All right…Is that the only kind of therapy?"

He felt his face, and other parts of him, brighten. "Any kind you want."

"Okay. Can I take 45 minutes instead?"

"Works for me. See you there."

climate-change denier pressure; retracts academically-sound study linking

At the house he let Baxter into the back yard; checked for messages (none); did a quick sniff test on himself, debated whether or not to change his shirt and decided against it, mouthwashed and rinsed, and brushed his hair. In spite of his better angels he felt prompted, looking at himself in the mirror, to murmur in a child's teasing tune, "I'm gonna get some *pus*-sy, I'm gonna get some *pus*-sy…" He grinned at his reflection, then frowned, reproaching himself. *Don't jinx it!* the better angels warned. He tidied up the bedroom and made the bed.

He and Claire had been a couple – or coupling, at least, as well as keeping company – for two years. They'd met at a party at Leslie's, whose cousin she was. She'd been chattering like a sorority girl, so he was further intrigued, as he got closer, to hear her chattering, with both knowledge and experience, about biochemistry. She was "way into Aromatherapy," she explained when he asked. Yes, he'd noticed her perfume, he said. He'd never worn cologne; nothing against it, he'd just never gotten the habit – Oh, that was because most mens' cologne designers were dumb; the best scents were customized, especially for redheads like him because they had different pheromones, especially if they'd been working out or were aroused. Yeah? Tell me more…

She was three years younger; beautiful and blonde and model-thin, but willowy, unlike most model-thin women who looked as fragile as a twig. His traditional-guy side enjoyed the pride of having a woman so blonde and beautiful attached to him. The downside – and it had been this way with all his girlfriends – was that sometimes she seemed to expect him to know how she was feeling without her having to tell him, and was hurt when he didn't. At least she'd never asked him – yet – if he loved her;

them to conspiracy theorists...Tenn. General Assembly passes "religious

A Murmuring of Women / 118

which was good, because he couldn't honestly say. He liked their being together; and if she left, for some reason (he'd run the scenario through his mind a few times), he'd be hurt and sad, but suspected he'd survive. They were in an undefined realm past friendship, but not all the way yet to love; or marriage proposals. (She didn't like the term "friends with benefits": it was passé, she said; "and besides, it mostly benefits the guy.")

He made sure to get to Francesca's before her, waiting outside so he could meet her with a strong hug and a kiss, and hold the door for her. "Where's Baxter?" she asked.

"Back at the house." (She'd tried several times to custom-aromatherapize flea-and-tick powder for Baxter. Now whenever her saw her he started sneezing.)

His story of the maybe-ghostly *Capitol Limited* unsettled her. She seriously believed in ghosts and was seriously scared of them, so she wasn't happy to hear that someone she knew might have seen one. He reassured her it must've real, because the dispatchers had seen it on their computers; real enough, in fact, for the NTSB to get all concerned. He told her about his questioning by the Suits. "They said, 'Maybe you saw some mobile homes; maybe there was a trailer park by the tracks.' I'm like, 'Man, I'm from the South, I *know* what a trailer looks like.' A lot of Daddy's supporters live in trailers, so I know what the people who live in them look like, too. *They* scare me." That got a laugh out of her, and a story of how she and her mom had almost had to move into a trailer after the divorce. She'd begged and pleaded against it, certain that everybody would call her "Trailer Trash" and her social life would be forever ruined.

"Do you work tomorrow?" he asked as they stood outside.

Meaning, as he knew she knew, "I'd like you to stay over." 9 to 5 every Wednesday, she answered; didn't he know that by now? But she wasn't annoyed. He walked her to her car, and saw that she'd brought a change of clothes and her makeup kit. He hugged her again and kissed her, longer and more serious; no tongue yet, but running his hands under her jacket, across her back and down her sides to suggestively just above her hips. She embraced back, pressing into him.

*

Rick had a childhood memory of 9th Street. He was toddler age, the legs of chairs and tables and grownups towering above him like California redwoods. He guessed they'd been in North Carolina to visit Dad, or for Mom to do some Duke reunion thing. They'd been in the little coffee shop near Francesca's. The counter was at the far end. Next to it and down one step was a long space lined on both sides with bar-height tables and stools. At the near end, by the entrance and down another step, a lounge with sofa, armchairs, and a low table. Mom set him down by the counter while she talked to the server, up there in the high altitudes where grownups spoke their mysterious dialogues.

He'd noticed an interesting picture on a magazine by the door and wanted to get a closer look. He clambered carefully down the first step and made his way along the aisle between the tables, a distance seemingly the length of a football field, then let himself down the second step. He looked around, to get his bearings.

He saw a man sitting in one of the armchairs, regarding him.

The man had light brown short hair and a grey goatee,

reading glasses and gentle blue eyes, and the hint of a smile. A book lay in his lap.

"Hello," he said, in a quiet friendly voice.

Rick stood astonished. Who was this person? Rick's limited toddler social skills weren't up to the situation. He pointed towards Mom, off in the distance, turning from the counter with cup in hand. He searched through the kaleidoscope of images and sounds tumbling in his mind, trying to guess what might convey his meaning.

"That's your mommy. She's getting coffee."

…and suddenly everything was all right. The man understood. He knew that Rick was there with Mom; that she was indeed buying coffee (a strange, hot, bitter-smelling substance grownups liked to laugh about); and that Rick, though appreciative of the friendly attention and benevolent intent, preferred to leave the social dealings to her, fluent as she was in Grownup. Now here she stood, smiling down at him – "Ready to go, bud?" – picking him up. The man rose, laying his book face down on the table, and held the door for them.

"That was good manners," Mom said as they went up the sidewalk. Rick agreed; and all was right with the world.

*

That night he dreamed the memory. He half knew he was dreaming. He was aware of the darkness of his bedroom, with the pale rectangle of curtained window and reflected glow of the bathroom nightlight; of Claire breathing in her sleep and the faint metal ticking of ductwork somewhere. Yet at the same time the bed was floating along 9th Street, which rippled gently like a broad river. Once in New York Mom had taken him on a Circle Line tour; the Hudson had flowed beneath and beside them in the same way, and the city skyline passed by in the same stately manner, as the storefronts of 9th were now doing. There was the coffee shop with its big striped awning. Through its glass wall he could see the man inside, reading in his armchair. The cover of his book had an animated image of a speeding train. The locomotive's guiding rods churned the wheels in a blur, with smoke billowing from the stack to stream backwards in the wind.

The man looked up over his glasses. His eyes met Rick's. He nodded, with a smile, acknowledging him. There came from him a warm glow, like hot cocoa on a chilly morning, of understanding and friendship and benevolence, full and absolute.

Flowing on water; passing scene; adjacent consciousness. "Good manners," and respectfulness. Remembering and understanding, without ever the need to explain. That was how the Wizard might be.

That man was what the Wizard might look like.

That was the Wizard.

*

He was awake. Morning light was brightening the window. He slipped out of bed and pulled on shorts, went to the kitchen to let Baxter in, and started the coffeemaker. (He was old enough now to understand the whole "coffee" thing, why Mom and her friends laughed about it.) While it brewed he took a shower, then brought mugs for himself and Claire. He wafted hers under her nose. She opened one eye just long enough to murmur "Hi."

IIc got back in bed, sitting up with the covers to his waist while he drank. Baxter trotted round giving the apartment his morning inspection, whuffling and snorting. After a few minutes

Claire sat up and reached for her mug.

"Mom told me a weird story last night. She says she and Annie and other women they know have been having dreams about a wizard. Now I've had one."

Claire snapped her head round, staring at him with eyes wider than he'd ever seen. His gut dove down and bobbed back up. In her expression he realized – realized for the second time, the first being when he found the old *Capitol Limited* photo and recognized his "ghost train" – that this, whatever "this" was, was *real*. Something was happening, something powerful and uncanny and outside the no-longer-impermeable bubble of Reality-as-he-knew-it. *That was the Wizard.* He had the irrelevant memory of feeling a similar thrill when the guy at Haw Court let them in.

"Oh my god. What did he tell you?" she gasped.

"Nothing. He was just there. He looked like this friendly old guy I met when I was real little. He saw me and remembered me, and then I thought, 'that's the Wizard!'"

"Oh my god. Last week I dreamed – He was just like you said, old and nice and all. I felt totally safe with him. He was like a mixture of all these people I've known who – Real people and fictional. Grandpa and my uncle, and Doctor Who; and, and…The guy at Haw Court too. He talked to me but he didn't *talk* talk, you know? He sent knowledge into my mind. And I knew, I *knew*, it wasn't my own mind making it up – I was having *actual telepathy* with another person!"

"What did he tell you?"

"He said he could give me the…mental power, to…control my, my…" She blushed, all the way down to the top curves of her breasts. "To only get pregnant if I wanted. To make my eggs fertilize, or not; or fertilize and slough out anyway. And I *knew* it was totally true!"

"That's what all the dreams have been," Rick said, hoping to reassure her. "The ones Mom's friends told her about. He offered them the same thing. And he was really respectful about it; he apologized if he scared them. And he didn't pressure them to take it. You're not the only one, either. I told you: Mom and Annie both had it, and a bunch of people they know. Maybe some of your friends have. You should ask."

She gaped at him. "*No*! They'll think I'm crazy!"

"Not if they'd had it too."

"I couldn't. I couldn't." She sipped her coffee, clutching the mug in both hands. He sidled next to her and put his arm round her shoulders. "This is actually the second time I've dreamed about him," he said, and told her about his vision on the train. "I don't know if it was *the* Wizard, or if I just thought so because Mom mentioned it. But the more I think about it the more I'm sure it was him."

"What is he? Is he a person, or a – a spirit, or –"

"He doesn't feel dangerous. Not to me. I'm freaked by the idea of, like you said, telepathy; but I'm not – He doesn't – I don't think he's going to hurt me or anything…Mom's really into it, because if it's real it'd solve the whole abortion issue. The right-wing shitheads couldn't do a thing…If it was real, and you felt safe: would you do it?"

"I don't know…I can't even process it right now."

Before leaving for work he asked her to listen for talk of the Wizard. "You don't have to say anything unless you want to. But if you hear anything, please tell me. Mom and I both want to know."

He told Leslie the story. She was fascinated. She hadn't had any such dreams herself, but readily agreed to keep an ear open for Wizard gossip. In fact, something odd she'd overheard a yoga classmate say last week now suggested that person had received the dream-offer. She doubted, though, that the Wizard's power would end the nasty melodrama over reproductive rights. "A lot of women wouldn't take it, on religious grounds. The church-lady types who believe God and Satan want to micromanage their lives. They'd freak over the telepathy like Claire did, and assume it was the Devil trying to tempt them. Then the Fundamentalist 'Quiverful' ones would say it's immoral, because it'd let women not be baby machines like the Bible says they should."

"Wouldn't some religious women think the complete opposite, that it was a gift from God?"

"Yes; but the anti's would make the biggest noise, like always," she sighed, with a heavenward glance of exasperation. "They'd still want to close Planned Parenthood, just for revenge."

*

(5/17/2014)
(*from*:) shewfly@nc.rr.com (*to*:) KingR008@yahoo.com
Hey kiddo – check this out! xoxoxo – Ma
(5/17/2014)
(*forwarded*:) (*from*:) AnnCRodrigu@nc.rr.com (*to*:) shewfly
Bev – just found this. Re what we & R talked about. Geneticist at U. of Adelaide located the phenotype in rabbit DNA which enables reabsorption of pregnancies. Here's a link to his paper. Hope they didn't stress the poor bunnies too much!

If Joan's DNA shows a similar pheno, that would be Very Interesting.

If a sample from Before DIDN'T show one, that would be Even More Interesting.

(5/17/2014)

(*from*:) KingR008   (*to*:) AnnCRodrigu

You gonna do the experiment?

(5/18/2014)

(*from*:) AnnCRodrigu   (*to*:) KingR008

If Joan's OK with it.

*

Joan was OK with it, and sent samples: hairs freshly plucked from her head, and from an old hairbrush. (She also sent word that her boyfriend was puzzled, but not complaining, at being taken to bed more often.) The experiment would have to wait, though, until the lab tech who owed Annie a favor could spare time.   Leslie, meanwhile, asked the yoga classmate, who confirmed dreaming of a Wizard politely offering birth-control abilities. (No, she hadn't accepted, because it was just a dream – wasn't it? No, she hadn't heard that other women were having the same dream. Was Leslie sure? Lord! – she'd have to do some praying over this. She and her husband wanted a baby, but had fertility problems...)   Leslie also posted a notice on several womens'-issues websites and bulletin boards. "Research study. Has anyone had dreams involving a 'wizard?'" She'd set up a separate e-mail to receive replies.

Rick was concerned. "You know you're going to get a lot of kooks and wingnuts."

"What if one of them tries to stalk you?" Claire added. At

Macy's she had overheard two women customers make a private joke about "simply Wizard," but hadn't had the courage to ask.

Leslie shrugged off the kooks and wingnuts as an occupational hazard. There were a few, mostly Fundamentalist types ranting religious invective. Over Friday beers at Fullsteam Brewery, she brought the most hilariously idiotic replies along and read them out loud. There were also increasing numbers of real responses. Each story had the same core: a gentle, courteous figure of powerful magic, offering them control of their wombs. The women replying were skeptical, or puzzled, or hopeful, fearful, thrilled, doubting their own sanity; sometimes all at once. Leslie set up a blog where they could share their experiences.

A few days later, she announced that the yoga classmate had come to her in excitement so intense it was almost a visible aura. She and her husband had prayed, and asked for a sign. The dream came again that night, and this time she accepted the offer. They had made love; and now she knew, she absolutely *knew*, that she was pregnant. She had almost been able to "see" the conception in her mind, steering the fertile ovum into the path of a vigorous healthy-looking sperm.

Rick made a grossed-out face. "Too much information."

"I think it's important. It means the ability isn't just for stopping pregnancy, but starting it too. I'm glad. It'll be a talking point against the antis."

Annie's lab tech found some time.

*

(5/29/2014)

(*from*:) AnnCRodrigu@nc.rr.com
(*to*:)shewfly@nc.rr.com,KingR008@yahoo.com,

Lesliramus@google.com, Clairefranch@google.com
JESUS ON A FUCKING DINOSAUR.
Here's the rabbit phenome. Here's Joan's before and after.
I'm gonna have to change my underwear.

*

The five of them met at Mom and Annie's. Mom had bought champagne. "What do we do now?" Claire asked.

"Do we go public?" Rick wondered. "Can you publish it?"

Annie shook her head. "An experiment with only one test subject? Won't fly. No matter how exciting the result. You'd need a whole study group of women to take the Wizard's power, get themselves pregnant, and then try to reverse it. And that gives me some serious ethical headache. Potential babies as just elements in a science project?" Claire looked horrified.

"But you can ask other people to replicate it," Mom suggested. "Put it on Leslie's blog."

Leslie had been on her phone, checking the latest responses. She made a surprised sound. "Damn. It's already public."

There was a clip from that morning's *The View*: Whoopi Goldberg remarking to her co-hosts, "Lemme ask you something. Have you heard this rumor about a guy who shows up in your dreams and says he's some kind of Wizard?"

Her co-hosts stared at her, not for the first time, like she was nuts. But a woman in the audience fainted, and another fled the studio in tears.

"What do we do now?" Claire repeated.

*

There didn't seem to be any followup, though. The news

governor signs bill allowing open carry in govt. buildings, churches, bars…

was too busy with David Brat's defeat of Eric Cantor for House Majority Leader, along with the shootings at Seattle Pacific University, Troutdale in Oregon, and Las Vegas (where a couple gunned down two policemen because they wanted to "start a revolution"). Leslie's blog, though, kept growing. Women from all over the world were coming forward to tell her they too had experienced the "Wizard" dream. (The dreams had begun, as far as anyone could later trace, at the end of April. The women who dreamed, had at first kept the dreams in their hearts and pondered them there, according to their conscience and character and their culture's views of womens' place; until some opportunity – a conversation on the subway, a chance meeting with a trusted village elder, a letter from home, a discovered link online – until some opportunity prompted them to share.) The blog got so busy that she didn't have time to manage it, so she passed it to old friends in Columbia who ran a womyns' center. She'd renamed the "Looney Bin" page, where she put troll-ravings, as the "Hate Mail Museum," with emoticons sticking their tongues out and a hand giving the middle finger.

Who is the Wizard? Why is he doing this? Some people tried asking him in their dreams. He was easily connected with; anyone who went to bed hoping with true intent to meet him, in sleep would presently sense him drifting towards their dreamworld. He appeared uniquely to each person, framed in the unique metaphors of each dreaming mind. He was the beloved teacher in the old village school. He was the patient, listening, witty uncle; beloved by, and refuge for, the quieter children at family gatherings. He was the gentle, eccentric librarian or used-bookstore owner who'd known just the right thing to read during a rough patch of life. He was the old family friend who'd brought flowers to a hamster's backyard "funeral," or hot chocolate to the aftermath of a grueling thesis defense. Thought-queries, though, elicited no details; just those same benevolent attributes of kindness, intelligence, humor, and compassion. These virtues, feeding a love of fairness and equity, were also the reasons expressed for his offer. "I am a fellow soul, who has found these powers," was all that dreamers could report back.

*

"Rick?"

"m?"

"Can I ask you something?"

What time was it? 12:35 AM. He'd been just a breath or two away from sleep. "I can't sleep because it's bothering me," Claire continued.

He rolled over. "Shoot."

"When do you think a fetus starts to feel things?"

When did a – who, what, huh? Oh brother. Jesus on a dinosaur, to quote Annie. "I have no idea."

"But what would you think?"

"If I *did* think…I'd guess, like…not until its brain has developed enough to have pain receptors and stuff. To have consciousness. You know, like a computer can't run a program if it doesn't have enough processing power. I bet Annie could give you a better answer; she's the scientist." He put his arm round her. "Is something scaring you?"

"No, but…And if it was big enough to be conscious; and its mother wanted to abort it with the Wizard's ability; do you think it could, like…somehow ask him to not let her?"

"Whoah. That is *way* beyond my competency. You might as well ask him."

"Because wouldn't it be terrible to be in there, and realize she wanted to get rid of you?"

Jesus on a dinosaur indeed. "I don't think fetuses have anywhere near enough consciousness for that. Babies don't even realize they're separate from their parents until something like a year after they're born. And the mothers don't abort them, they re-absorb them."

"But what does *that* mean?"

"I have no idea. Reversing the gestation process, or something. Besides; it only happens when they change their minds about being pregnant, and with the Wizard's patch they don't even have to get pregnant unless they want to."

He wondered if she was displacing grief over her father, whom she still missed and felt abandoned by. (Hey Wizard – think you could give her some father-comfort; or at least persuade her to find a support group?) All the same, the next time he and Claire went to dinner at Mom's, he put the question to Annie.

Annie made a wry face. "Not really my field. Your theory's good as any, though. I have read that the thalamus – the part of the brain that registers nerve signals – doesn't develop until five or six months into pregnancy."

*

Arlene Hooker, the Mississippi congresswoman, was and always had been intransigent on abortion, as well as related topics like birth control, sex ed, and welfare for "the undeserving." She'd joined the pro-life movement as a passionate Born-Again college student, protesting outside clinics. She had been one of the most

budget amendment forbids Pentagon from spending to study, prepare for

determined members of the group, using every tactic the laws allowed and trying to think up new tricks to push those laws' boundaries. She'd step right in front of approaching patients, dodging side to side to block them if they tried to pass her, not moving unless and until they or any companion they might have brought directly asked her to step aside. She would get up in their faces. If they looked aside she'd move to keep herself in front of them; if they looked down she'd crouch to glare up at them. She'd insult, threaten damnation, pray at the top of her lungs, weep, talk in a child's voice begging "Please, Mommy, please don't kill me!" She'd lay pictures of bloody fetuses before them anywhere they tried to walk. One day a woman tripped on the uneven sidewalk, dropping her purse as she fell. Her wallet tumbled out and open. Instead of helping her up (she'd scraped a knee and both palms and bruised an elbow), the future congresswoman read her name out loud, very loud. They all began shouting at her by name. "(A)'s killing her baby! (A)'s a child murderer! (A)'s a slut!" (Ms. A. said "Bitch, I'm just getting a mammogram," but they wouldn't listen. She later tried to sue them for assault, but the suit was dismissed by a Born-Again judge.) The times when some girl would be so battered by their vitriol that she'd break down in tears and run away, the future Congresswoman Hooker would literally dance with glee in exultant self-righteousness, gloating that she'd saved another innocent.

So on June 10, she, or her office, announced that she would put forth a bill requiring mandatory, monthly DNA testing and brain scans for every woman of childbearing age, with severe Federal-level prison sentences for any who showed evidence of Wizard-change. She made pointed remarks about "who did this

climate change...Hobby Lobby owners want "literal reading of Bible" in public

Wizard person think he was, allowing selfish promiscuous women to cannibalize their own unborn babies, and why didn't he have the courage to show himself?"

("Hooker?" Leslie remarked. "Oh my. Bill Maher's gonna have fun with that.")

*

"How is your girlfriend?" Eunice asked. "The one who does the perfumes. You've been seeing her now for, it seems like five years."

Sunday lunch in Grantsville, after the usual narcolepsy-inducing service at First Methodist. Baked ham, drop biscuits, cole slaw, deviled eggs; pitchers of sweet tea, a cocoanut cake in waiting. Aidan's place setting and empty chair, a Southern Gothic psychological negative space. "Your Daddy and I keep hoping you'll tell us you all are engaged. After all these years she must be wondering. And you realize, don't you, that it's more important than ever now, to get married and start a family?" When Rick didn't answer, she added "For people like us. You know what I mean."

"People like us," Cousin Mason repeated as an inquiry.

Eunice made little distressed gestures. "Respectable people. *Good* people. People who know…People who believe in right values, in living right and being good citizens…You must see that. Because of that Wizard, and what he's doing."

"The *Wizard*?" Rick almost exclaimed, restraining his voice at the last second.

Lin grimaced. Dad looked wearily resigned, as to a song he'd heard far too often coming up on someone else's radio. "It's so hateful! Letting women get rid of their babies any time they get the littlest fancy? Or not have children at all, because they want to live like those Kardashians and go out every night, or those 'Real Housewives.' 'Real' indeed! They've never done a lick of housework in their lives. In California there soon won't be any babies born at all! And you don't think all those immigrants and welfare types aren't going to have as many children as they can, so they can stay here and live off of us? If that Wizard isn't stopped we'll be outnumbered. We'll be foreigners in our own country."

"What Wizard? Where'd you hear about him?"

"Arlene Hooker's newsletter. Thank heavens *she's* standing up to him, even though everyone's laughing at her and saying that she's crazy as a bedbug and should be locked up. Just like they hate me because of Aidan. Horrible, horrible people all over the news. They hate babies and they hate this country and won't stop until they've wrecked it for good."

"I wouldn't worry about it, Neece," Mason said, helping himself to more ham. "Plenty of people out there still having kids. Danny's got so many nieces and nephews he can't keep track of them."

"So you need to start poppin' out Christian babies P.D.Q.," Lin told Rick. "Be a Christian stud."

"Christian Stud" sounds like a gay porn star. "You first," Rick replied.

*

A harried mother stood on the sidewalk outside Elmo's Diner. Her baby was wailing in its carrier and her two-year-old throwing a tantrum, refusing to be put into his coat despite the gusty winds and unseasonable cold. (Durham County was under yet another tornado watch.) "I didn't have to ask the Wizard after all," Claire mused, watching them.

The non sequitur stopped Rick with a forkful of pancakes halfway to his mouth. "Hm?"

"I dreamed about re-absorption and being in the womb and all. It felt really real – it felt true, you know? – and it reassured me."

"Well, that's good."

"I think you're right. They're not really *conscious* conscious. They sort of sense things like sound, or movement. In the dream it was like slowly, slowly waking up in tiny stages. Then in re-absorption it'd be like slowly going back to sleep. Then their souls would just go back to where they came from. That was the beautiful part of the dream. Don't you think souls are permanent?"

"I'm not a theologian; but if I did think about it: then yeah. I hope so."

She pretended to pout. "You. You're so skeptical."

The woman's husband came to the rescue, catching up the tearful little boy in his arms. "This is a change," Rick commented. "You used to be skeptical. When I talked about the Wizard or ghost trains you freaked out."

"I'm *still* scared of ghosts. This was just a dream."

"Could the Wizard have sent it to you?"

"No; he wasn't even in it."

"Sooo…" he ventured a smile, "going out on a limb here: is there a way I can ask if you've taken the Wizard's offer without seeming like a horny bastard?"

She giggled, but then got serious again. "No, I haven't. I still can't believe it would really work. I'm okay with the morning-after pills. I'm afraid with the other I'd think the wrong thing when..." She giggled again, blushed, and lowered her voice. "When it's happening; and get pregnant...I hope it's okay with you too."

He touched her hand in reassurance. "I'm good. Whatever you're most comfortable with."

She tickled it. "But yes, you are a horny bastard."

"And -?"

She gave him a sly smile and didn't reply.

*

On June 15, Arlene Hooker dropped out of sight.

Obamas for wanting daughters to empathize with minimum wage workers...

A Murmuring of Women / 136

How I wish it could've happened.

Mama and I are downtown, and run into…

I'm not going to say her name, not even here. Miss Princess, Miss Snob, Miss Hateful Bitch. With her dad Mister George Babbitt, Mister Hamilcar Q. Glure. Puffed up like the *Hindenburg* with self-satisfaction. "This your boy, Mrs. X? Looks like a fine young man. You gonna be at my daughter's party, son?" "No sir; I'm not invited." "Well, why not, boy?" "Well sir, I'll tell you why. The other day at lunch she and her friends come up to me. She gets this gloating look on her face and she tells me all about the party. All the cool stuff you've got laid on. Got the XYZ's to play" – whoever; some famous band the girls all scream over and wet their panties. He gets this look like, I did? – since when? "Then she asked me, 'Do *youuuu* want to come?' I say, 'If I'm invited, I'll think about it.' 'Well *sor* – ry, but you're *not*. I don't invite *retard creeps*.' And they run off all smirking and giggling. So I'm like, In that case, never mind."

Now he's all flustered. It's making him look bad. Asks me, is it true. "Yes sir. I'd swear to it on the Bible in court. And I can get you the names of a whole bunch of people who saw it – people who *aren't* in her girl gang, because you *know* they're all gonna lie for her and say it didn't happen, so *they* don't get dis-invited."

He can't believe it – my little girl'd never do anything like that. Says he'll talk to her; or he confronts her right there. It doesn't matter, sir; she's told everybody how she can get you to do anything she wants. All she has to do, she says, is make big sad puppy-dog eyes at you, and flutter her eyelashes and act – and fake like she's about to crumple up and cry, and she can wrap you around her little finger. Sit in your lap and bat her big blue eyes, and wriggle her ass against your crotch; and *bam!* Anything she wants. A Mercedes convertible with vanity plates, the day she turns sixteen.

She *boasts* about it, sir. And again, I can get you a whole cloud of witnesses.

She is caught, but *good*. Cut off every single way she could lie herself out of it and stripped her hateful true self naked to the world. *Corner* her where she can't do *anything* but tell the TRUTH, that she is a *lying hateful sadistic bitch*.

"Ohh, I can do anything I want to anybody, 'cause Daddy's the richest man in town and thinks I'm his little princess."

The kind who'll come up to you at your locker, out of nowhere, for no reason at *all*, and say, acting all fake-concerned, "How does it feel to know everybody *hates* you?"..."Even if it was true, which we *both* goddamn *know* it isn't: I don't hate me. And that's all that matters. How's it feel to know *you're* the kind of person goes around saying, How does it feel to know everybody hates you? How's *that* feel? Do you like it? It feel good to see the heartbreak on their faces? To see tears coming out of their eyes so you can gloat on them and mock them? Does it turn you on, make your pussy wet? To HURT people?"

Get up in her face and leave her broken and in tears, at what a hateful bitch she is.

Maybe she gets on me next day at school – "Why did you *say* those things, you *embarrassed* me in front of my Daddy." Back her into a corner, going "Bitch, I told the *truth*. You *know* that you said and did *every single goddamn one* of those things. You are not *ever, ever* going to lie your way out of it, because *I won't let you*. You are going to *face the truth* of what you did, and *deal with it*. And the consequences, that you goddamn well *know* you *deserve*."

Did I every do anything to you, before you began persecuting me?

Did I say anything, did I even look at you wrong? No.

Not one damn thing. Not a *thing* did I *ever* do, to give you *any* reason to attack me. You *chose* to hurt me for *no reason*. Because I was weird? No – because I was *me*. Because who I *am* makes you uncomfortable, embarrassed you. So you decided I didn't deserve to live.

You *deliberately, viciously, sadistically* CHOSE to *break the heart* of an *absolutely innocent* person, who never *once* did you wrong.

I want that knowledge to break *your* heart, for every waking moment of the rest of your God-damned life.

You're ruining my life, she says. Everywhere I go everybody laughs at me because of you. Well that's just too damn bad. Even if it was true, which you know goddamn well it's not, it's not my problem. Tough titty. You'll have to tell them I'm not your responsibility. You've got no power over me.

When they get smug – that makes me want to go lethal. They say all their hateful stuff in this voice of, We know so much more than you, we're so – exponentially better than you'll ever be, you shouldn't even *try* to argue with us when we tell you what a loser you are.

Pretending they care. Coming up to me and saying "We're

really *concerned* about you; if you don't change you'll be a retard all your life and never have anybody or anything. We're doing an intervention; you have to do *exactly* as we say, or…"

[*break*]

Modern version. Little Bitch Princess 2.0. She and her posse come to the house, saying "This is an intervention." They've get some guy, like somebody's older brother, to dress up as a cop. "This is an intervention, and you *have* to do *exactly* what we tell you or you'll go to *jail*." But I'm walking around this guy, looking him over and saying "Like hell. First of all, where's his cop car? You all drove up in that fancy – that, that Rich Brat-mobile your daddy bought you. He's no cop, he's too young. Look, he's got zits all over his face. And how come his uniform doesn't say what police force he's with? Are you city police, state, sheriff's deputy? It's a damn *costume* – I can smell the mothballs!"

Concerned, my ass. Bitch, you don't give a *fuck* about me, you just want to manipulate and control me, so you can force me to humiliate myself in front of the whole school, so much that they'll laugh at me for the rest of their lives and *never* take me as human. You *want* me to lose everything and never be anything. You think I *deserve* to be destroyed, just because I'm *me*!...IT. IS. NOT. GONNA. HAPPEN!

[*break*]

Or they create a fake e-mail address and start sending messages saying they're from this girl at school; she won't tell me who she is but says she likes me. Fine; next time you see me at school, introduce yourself. – No no no, I can't do that! – Why not? – I can't be seen with you, it'd…it'd ruin my reputation, or my parents would kill me; some bullshit excuse. Instead she tries to get me to come meet her in places that're in, like, a really dangerous part of town, or where gay people are known to hang out. That's so if I did go they could tell the whole school and smirk and gossip, Ohh, you were seen where all the *queers* go! But I keep saying No. I don't – I suspect from the start this whole thing's a setup, and I'm not falling for it. I tell her No, I can't, I don't have a car. You'll have to talk to me at school. They make her sound more and more distraught: I *have* to see you, I really *need* you. Then talk to me at school. *No I can't, I can't! You don't understand!* I can't be seen with you, if anybody knew I liked you everybody'd totally reject me like they do you and I'd be an outcast forever! You don't realize how weird everybody thinks you are; even the teachers talk about you…

Yeah, sweetie?...buncha goddamn shit. If they do, it's totally unprofessional of them, and I will *gladly* tell them so to their faces. And I'm not gonna be anybody's guilty secret. If you won't be seen with me in public, you can't see me in private. And I block her e-mail.

Next day Miss Princess comes up to me pretending to be all angry and tearful. "I hope you're satisfied; So-and-so *killed* herself last night because of you!" Bitch; *nobody* in this school's killed themselves; it'd be all over the news, and this place would be crawling with reporters and grief counselors. She tries to feed me this line about Oh, her parents covered it up because they didn't want anybody to know, but she told me all about it – Save your breath, you stupid fuckin' hag, I *knew* from the start the whole thing was a setup, you trying to trick me into doing something embarrassing so you could boast it all over the whole school. *It didn't work.*

[*break*]

The big reveal.

When they see me rise up, they see that fury blazing, they see the power I've learned; and they realize – that total shit-your-pants we're-screwed fear of *God* drops in the hollow of their stomachs...*Oh. Shit.* Everything we ever said to him, everything we ever did – there's no excuses on the face of this earth we can make – all those years we thought, Oh, he's helpless, we can knock him around all we want to and cream our jeans with gloating joy at making him cry sissy tears. He's too Good to even try to fight back. We can hurt you any way we want, and because you're a Good Christian you'll have to forgive us for every little bit of it. Right? Gonna cry for us? C'mon. C'mon. Cry for us...No excuse on the face of this earth is gonna stop him, nothing, *nothing*, we can ever do or say that'll ever make him not see us as the sadistic scum that we *are.* We pushed him too far, *beyond* too far, and now we've set off the Apocalypse. We've brought it on ourselves. We can *never* be sorry enough, for all the hurt we caused him, all he should have gotten that we tore from him. *We. Are. Fucked.*

God, how I want that. For justice to finally, *finally* come. To see the – to be the worm that finally turns, and it be as fuckin' big as the sandworms in *Dune*. Say, I want to hear you SCREAM, in helpless grief, despair and *agony*; like you *knowingly, willfully, deliberately, Christ-crucifyingly* CHOSE to make your victims scream, and REJOICED in their pain and death and *annihilation*. Like the little kids at Newtown screamed as they were gunned down. For everybody who was ever bullied by you. *You*; you gun nuts and polluters and gay-bashers and election-stealers: I want every last single solitary one of your hearts to be *broken beyond repair*; like you deliberately, *treasonously, Satanically* CHOSE to break ours.

　　　To confront you –

[*End of tape*]

Apocalypso

Rick hit stop-and-go traffic just past Benson. Cresting a hill, he saw the backup continuing all the way to the next horizon, a mile or more: a barely creeping ribbon of red brake lights and the square back ends of trucks, while in the distance curtains of rain fell from storm clouds as dark as righteous fury. 511 Info informed him that high winds had blown down trees and knocked over a semi just west of Newton Grove, ten miles ahead. Sampson, Wayne and Duplin Counties were all under tornado warnings for the next two hours. There was an exit coming up, though, so he veered off.

GPS twisted him further and further into a maze of back roads, until he'd lost any idea of whether he was heading south, north, east, west, or into some Mobius-strip dimension. The only name he recognized was "Spivey's Corner," on a sign pointing in the opposite direction. The GPS seemed to be losing certainty as well: it started to lock up, pixelate, fractalize more and more, until finally all it could do was helplessly repeat "Redirecting..." in its robot-lady voice, like a Stepford Wife with a short circuit. There were no gas stations, no country stores, no volunteer fire departments, where he might ask directions. Gusts of wind and showers of pelting rain washed across the road. Creeks were high and ditches near overflowing. The clouds grew even darker. Was he driving into the path of a tornado but couldn't see it? Thick trees pressed close on all sides. Where would he find shelter? He shivered.

The road suddenly turned to gravel. His car stalled, and died.

Supreme Court says Hobby Lobby can deny contraception coverage to its

He tried four times to restart it, getting only that frustrated, frustrating *rrr – rrr – rrr!...rrr – rrr – rrr!* He'd stopped at the top of a long, gentle hill, so he let the car roll forward in second with his foot ready to lift from the clutch, hoping sufficient speed might kick the motor awake. It didn't work. He juddered to a bone-shaking stop at the bottom of the slope, just across a little concrete bridge with the date "1933" cast in its balustrade.

The rain had stopped, and the wind subdued to a breeze. There were, miraculously, glimpses of blue sky and sunshine in the clouds racing overhead. There was a large clearing off to the left, at its center an old but well-kept cabin. Its red tin roof was lined with solar panels. A windmill tower also held a satellite dish. He saw an extensive vegetable garden, a tin-roofed stable from which a cow was sauntering, a chicken coop with a gaggle of hens cautiously poking their heads out. There was even what looked like a pig pen, complete with pig.

A gravel drive led up to the front porch. Rick approached it tentatively, half-wondering if the appearance of rustic content would prove only a front, and he'd be met with shotguns and / or banjo music to butt-fuck city slicker liberal Democrats by. Then, three small children scrambled into view from high grass by the roadside. They were wet and muddy and looked like they'd been having a grand time getting that way. "Hi, mister," said the eldest. "Are you lost?" She was perhaps seven years old and blonde, with dark gold skin.

"I am, yeah; and my car won't start."

"You must've come through the barrier. Is it storming out there?"

"There's a tornado warning until 5! The wind's blowing

down trees and knocking over trucks on I-40." Where were these kids' adults? Why were they letting them run around outdoors during a tornado warning?

"Then that's why. Bad storms sometimes make people come through. Fires and earthquakes and stuff do too. I bet you need a temporary converter. Mama's got a bunch of them." She pulled a bicycle from the weeds and pedaled off.

The youngest child, also a girl, was a tubby toddler. Her blue eyes seemed nearly as big as an anime character's, and her wispy hair was randomly gathered into tufts tied with little ribbons. She took a finger from her mouth and pointed it at the house. "Mama car fix," she affirmed.

Her brother had black hair, a broad face, and a thoughtful expression. He regarded Rick for a long moment. "Mister, do you think if a tree fell on your car otherside and killed your av, do you think you'd feel it?"

Rick had no idea what he was talking about. He looked back at the trees to see if any showed signs of toppling onto him. "What?"

"Mama and Daddy say you don't, but any time someone's does we have a special grieving coven for them."

The toddler pointed her finger again. "Daddy Mama was," she remarked. "Other Mama."

"She means Daddy transitioned," the boy explained. "He was a woman before. We had covens for that too. They're growing him a new penis up at the hospital. When they attach it we'll have another coven to help his body accept it. Daddy says otherside they don't know how to grow them yet. Is that true?"

Had this kid been eating special mushrooms out of the cow

pasture? Five years old and saying "penis" like it was just another word. And growing new ones in a hospital? Stem cell research hadn't gotten that far, that he knew of. (If it had, he'd definitely know. Everybody would. Guys would be lining up for miles to upgrade to porn-star size. Maybe *that* would persuade Republicans like Dad to stop opposing it!) And covens? Otherside? "Avs," whatever that was? "Sorry, buddy, I don't know about that stuff, I'm not a doctor."

"What are you?"

"I work in an office, for Duke Energy. I take peoples' calls when they want their electricity turned on or off."

"We make our own!" the boy said proudly. His sister agreed, pointing at the cabin roof. "Sun tit-ti-cy."

That might explain things, sort of. A 21st-century Modern Family, with a transgender member, Wiccan and living off the grid. Special 'shrooms from the pasture, and probably a discreet pot patch back in the woods, like old hillbillies' moonshine stills. Maybe for their safety they kept a low profile, homeschooling the kids and thus leaving them with odd notions about what the world "otherside" was like. Out here people like this would have much more cause to fear shotgun-and-banjo rednecks than he would.

Two figures had appeared on the porch, a slender black man and a stout, buxom blonde woman. They and the eldest daughter conferred, with occasional glances Rick's way. The woman hopped on a motorcycle parked by the front steps. It started with a quiet purr instead of the Harley roar he half expected. She rolled down the drive with her daughter, clutching what looked like a shoebox, riding pillion behind her. She was cheerful and friendly, with a very country accent. "Hey there, hon,

Study: Keystone's climate impact would be 4 times greater than government

ya got you some car trouble? Pop the hood and lemme have a look."

"Mama car fix."

Rick sat in the driver's seat at her direction while she and the daughter tinkered, their doings hidden by the raised hood. "Have the kids been keepin' you entertained?"

"Yes ma'am; they've been telling me all kinds of things."

"All about avatars and 'Otherside' and the Wizard and all?"

"Uh – yeah."

"It's from a online game some friends of ours are workin' on, one o' those multiple-player things only without all the violence and stuff. We're helpin' 'em beta-test it. The kids are all into it like it's for real!" she laughed. "Okay, now try it."

The engine came smoothly alive as soon as he turned the key. The toddler, delighted, bobbed up and down on her plump little legs. The woman let the hood slam shut and came round to his window. "One o' your battery cables done got loose, and your fan belt was half off track. It musta been from where you hit the gravel back yonder. It's a nasty bump."

He thanked her, and asked directions. The daughter must have gone round behind the car, for she now stood next to her siblings, all waving as he drove off.

The road S-curved to and fro. The gravel changed back to asphalt. He took the transition slowly, so as not to dislodge anything again. Around another bend, the dark skies and rain squalls came back, and gusts of wind skidding broken branches across the pavement. The temperature, or pressure or something, dropped, and he shivered again. A few miles further, the GPS restored itself, all self-assured as though nothing had happened.

"At the next intersection, turn Left…Go eleven point three miles to Interstate Forty."

There was a convenience store at the crossroads, so he pulled in for a soda. A radio speaker up in the canopy was warning of downed power lines and floods in low-lying areas. Rick hoped the Wiccan family wouldn't get washed away, cow and all. They seemed like nice people, albeit strange. That "online game" story didn't ring quite true, didn't explain all the oddnesses. And wait a minute – hadn't the daughter said something about a "temporary converter?" What was that about – was that the shoebox thing she'd been carrying? And what had happened to it? He raised the hood. Everything within looked normal. Thinking of catalytic converters, he walked round behind his car.

The last cardboardish shreds of a shoebox-sized object, honeycombed inside, hung from the tailpipe. When he touched it cautiously with a stick, it crumbled away into a powder which dissolved against the wet concrete.

*

An e-mail from Claire one morning: Hugo Baum, the Haw Court guy, had died, back in June. A lost motorist passing the Court's gates had found him sitting against the wall, eyes closed and with a smile of peace, as if he'd taken a nap in the sun and never awakened. There was a photo, but it was grainy and from Baum's long-ago years in California, so Rick's brief flash of *I've seen that guy somewhere* probably meant nothing –

"*Son of a goddamn fucking piece of –*" Leslie's cursing voice held the fiercest fury he'd ever heard from her. Before he was halfway out of his cubicle she was already storming across to Angela's office.

"I have been *doxxed*," she announced upon returning. She pointed at her screen, while gathering keys, bag and heirloom *Josie and the Pussycats* thermos. *"bitchs lik u need 2 b cut up." "pour hot battery acid up yr cunt u cunt." "Coming RIGHT NOW to RAPE yr LESBIAN ASS til u BLEED TO DEATH DONT U LOCK YR DOOR BITCH U KNOW U DESERV IT."* And worse.

"My address. Phone numbers. Passwords. License plates. All out there for the whole world to see."

"Fuck!! Goddamn – I'll drive you home."

"No. Thanks though. I have to do this myself. I can't let them scare me off."

He left a message for Mom, and as soon as lunchtime came he raced to Leslie's apartment. He knocked, and heard her distant voice call "Who is it?"

"It's Rick. You OK?"

"Yes. Just a minute," came the faint reply.

His phone rang. "Are you at my door?"

"Yeah, I'm right here."

"Is anyone else nearby?"

He looked out over the railing. "There's a lady walking her dog across the street...and a couple of little kids playing soccer; but that's all."

The locks clicked, and the door opened. Leslie was in sweats and a t-shirt. "Come in." The little apartment, dim behind closed blinds, was in its usual dishevelment. Her laptop on the dining table was surrounded by a chaos of paperwork. A slave-bikini Princess Leia figurine crouched atop the bookshelf, manacled but defiant. "I've been changing all my passwords, and my e-mail, and Facebook, and security codes, and phone numbers;

and warning my bank, and my doctor, and anybody else I can think of who has my data."

He saw that she was trembling. "Can I get you anything? Coffee or something?"

"Coffee?? If I got any caffeine I'd probably start screaming."

He phoned Mom's office again, and this time caught her. "Is she all right, kiddo?...Let me talk to her."

"Hi, Bev...Yes, I'm ok. Shaken up; but I'll be all right..."

While Mom put her through a friendly interrogation, Rick fumed. He wished he could get his hands on the asshole who'd done this, give him a good punching out. Break all the bones in his hands so he couldn't troll anybody else for a good long while. Fucking jerk. Some fat slob loser probably still living in his mom's basement, masturbating into old socks, who'd shit himself in terror if a real woman ever talked to him. But hiding behind his keyboard he could be Conan the fucking Barbarian. "Ask her, can we sue the guy if they catch him?"

"...what?...You heard?...Yeah, he did. He rode to my rescue." Leslie smiled at him. "They're sending a detective who handles cybercrime. But in the meantime I'm changing all my passwords...Yes; and I'm very careful who I open the door to...Oh, I'm sure it is. The hate mail's tripled since the Wizard story went public. And got a lot more personal...Yes...Ugh! – do I really have to?...Oh yes, I'll show him all of it...Thanks. I appreciate that. 'Bye."

"Show me all of what?"

"The cyber detective. She said to show him all the hate mail. And to save it, in case it does come to trial; it's evidence."

"When is he coming? Let me buy you lunch somewhere, before he gets here."

"Thanks; but by the time I got cleaned up you'd have to go back to work...I'll be all right. I'm calming down. I'll be back tomorrow."

"You're sure?"

"Yes. And your mom said, if I don't feel safe tonight I can stay with them...I'll call you if anything changes."

She sounded assured, but when she hugged him goodbye her grip was tight. "Thank you for checking on me. It was really thoughtful of you."

He worried about it all afternoon, and called her as soon as he got home. She assured him everything was still fine; the cyber detective, though admitting the chances of catching the culprit were slim, had been sympathetic and sensible. He read article after online article about doxxers, in chivalrous hope they might offer some clue to catching hers. He told Claire; she was more distressed by it than Leslie had been, and wanted to come stay with him that night (he obliged, naturally). He called Mom to ask her what legal recourses Leslie might have. There were laws against cyberstalking, she told him; but again, they all hinged on the slim likelihood of catching the stalker. "I was afraid something like this would happen," she said. "We thought misogyny was bad before, but now with the Wizard...You've seen what's been going on, right? They're saying we should be put in concentration camps and lobotomized and gang-raped to death, if we take the Wizard's offer. Thanks to Arlene Hooker opening her big mouth. On mainstream media they're saying this, and nobody, *nobody*'s calling them on it! God, it makes me sick...Power madness, is what it is. Every inch of empowerment we've gained, and they've gone nuts. Every bit of control they've lost over us, they can't stand it. Now we've got the possibility of complete freedom, and their heads are exploding. And they're going to take it out on us like never before. Did the Wizard think of this when he set it up? 'Here, you won't get pregnant if you're raped by some crazy vengeful nutcase; but you still get raped.'"

"Well, my head's not exploding."

"Yeah, yeah, I know. You're not the problem, kiddo. It's the bastards who think that just because they've got man parts it entitles them to our lady parts."

"Don't get too graphic on the imagery, Mom."

She laughed. "You know me. When I get on a rant…"

"I get you, though. Leslie calls it 'testosterone poisoning.' What pisses me off is the thought of that fuckhead using his anonymity to get away with it. If I was the Wizard I'd figure out a way to go back through the Internet and punch him out."

Claire arrived. She wanted to be held; and with the holding and comforting became willing to be fucked. He made it as good for her as he could. When they were finished, he still inside her, he attempted a joke about his vulgar-guy thought (could the Wizard's gift enable a woman to manipulate her, um, like… "lady parts?") She didn't think it was funny.

*

Mrs. Hooker's staff said she was in hospital with "a sudden illness," but would not elaborate. They canceled her public appearances for the indefinite future. She went home to Mississippi to "convalesce." On June 30 she released a statement: she was resigning her seat; she would not return to public life; and

strikes down "upskirt" photo ban; says 1st Amendment protects surreptitiously

she was detaching herself from any and all connection with the anti-abortion movement.

One of her staffers, an equal zealot, immediately quit in outrage, and went directly to FOX News. Mrs. Hooker, he announced, had been "brainwashed" by the Wizard. He'd attacked her in her sleep with a nightmare so powerful that it had completely destroyed her character and willingness to fight. He'd turned her into a complete apostate, who no longer cared for the rights of the Unborn but could only weep about the mothers, and parrot all their excuses for killing their babies.

Mrs. Hooker would not explain. She refused to give interviews. Her husband said only that he supported her in whatever she was going through. Anti-abortion groups requested, pleaded, demanded to speak with her; and, when refused, denounced her with utmost viciousness as a Judas. They denounced the Wizard as well. Their spokespersons challenged him to show himself; or to show them with what he'd used to take her out. Others asked too: journalists, researchers, the angry or the curious.

*

The night of July 4th, Rick went to sleep to the sound of fireworks near and far, and dreamed a Wizard dream.

He dreamed that it was Monday, that he was back at work. Two colleagues, one an Army reservist, the other in the National Guard, hadn't come in. Sending word that they'd been "called up," but not saying why. Items flitting across the Net, of North Korea accusing the U.S. of "sabotage," of Homeland Security raising the Terror Alert Level to "High." Then Angela coming out of her office saying "Oh my god, have you seen the news?" – a

taken photos...Kochs, other billionaires "determined" to buy White House in

phrase no one who lived through 9/11 has ever wanted to hear again.

Every nuclear weapon in the world had disappeared.

Not stolen, sabotaged or disarmed; they'd simply vanished. So had all stores of weapons-grade plutonium: all fissionable material that had ever gone missing due to civil war, economic chaos or ineptitude. The media had received an anonymous dispatch: "Any new nuclear weapons built will be eliminated in this same way."

The Wizard said, *I can do this, if you wish.*

He appeared, standing within a barrier like the "force fields" of science fiction: a barely visible iridescent shimmer, dome-shaped. Dark faceless figures came forward, shooting all manner of guns at him, everything from pistols to missile launchers. Every bullet and missile and bomb was caught by the barrier and held motionless, while the kinetic force of their shooting was absorbed into it, strengthening and renewing it. Now the figures lunged forward with knives, with swords, with baseball bats, with lead pipe. The barrier spread and absorbed them, like marshmallows in Jello, pushing them back with the very gentlest of pressure. They screamed the vilest, most vicious abuse that could be imagined. Not even the sound, let alone the sense, of their words could penetrate. Then they parted ranks, as a suicide bomber in an explosives-filled truck came hurtling forward. The barrier flowed out; absorbed the truck; slowed it, stopped it at a comfortable distance from the Wizard. It took in the driver's inertia as well, lest the stopping hurl him through the windshield or against the steering column. The explosives all crumbled away into a harmless powder of their basic elements.

2014...Iowa Senate candidate Joni Ernst backs bill to nullify ACA, jail

They hurled biological weapons at it. They sent computer viruses. They detonated EMP devices, designed to fry every chip and circuit within range. Nothing penetrated. Finally, a nuclear missile came hurtling down out of the sky. The barrier blossomed upwards, like the contents of a lava lamp, capturing and halting it. It didn't even detonate; just disintegrated into nothingness.

Figures, weapons, bomber's truck all faded. The Wizard dispersed the barrier with a simple thought, just as he had summoned it.

You can have this, if you wish.

There were caveats. If you willingly took up a weapon, your barrier would evaporate: you could not use it to harm others while remaining untouchable yourself. (Law officers could be armed and barriered simultaneously, but only when on duty.) Nor could you steal, shoplift, purse-snatch, from within: the barrier would become impenetrable between your hand and your intended theft. Then again, your own purse or pocket was just as unattainable. You could expand the barrier to cover your house, your property, your car as you drove. You could cover children too young to form the thought, people incapacitated by illness or dementia; even pets. It was instantaneous, so no surprise attack could catch you defenseless. Stray bullets would never reach you; you'd never be "collateral damage" to someone else's battle.

You can have this, if you wish.

*

B-ball night at Walltown. "You heard about this 'Wizard' thing?" Rick asked. Neutrally; to see what came back, if anything.

"Oh, man! – I dreamed about some kinda Wizard!" Jimmy exclaimed. "He had this invisible shield thing, that'd keep you from being shot by anybody. But if you've got a gun yourself it won't work."

"What did he look like?"

"Uh – I guess, just, you know, a wizard. Big hat, a – a staff; beard...You know; like Harry Potter."

"Rielle keeps telling me about some wizard guy," Scott said. "Wakes me up in the middle of the night going 'the Wizard, the Wizard, he's doing all this great stuff!' I'm like, 'Yeah, and it'd be great too if he'd let me sleep!'"

"You got a wizard story?" Marcus asked Rick.

They compared notes. Scott's Wizard looked like the Gandalf from Ralph Bakshi's *Hobbit*, but talked like The Big Lebowski. Marcus's was merely a calm, friendly older man; but still white, about which Marcus had some remarks to make the next dreamtime they met up. If the gun barrier was real, Rick asked, would they take it?

Jimmy goggled at the idea, open-mouthed like a fish. "But what if it isn't? What if it's, it's, ISIS or somebody, trying to get us to give up all our guns?"

"How would they do that?" Marcus was skeptical. "Get into our dreams?"

"Satellites? Radio waves. Wi-Fi. All that stuff's flying around in the air, where I bet you could hijack it if you knew how. There's all kinds of satellites up in space, that nobody even remembers what they did. And they'll be dead for years, then turn themselves back on, and nobody knows how."

Marcus was skeptical. "Only time satellites are brainwashing people's when they're transmitting FOX News."

"ISIS is gonna claim it's them even if it isn't," Scott said.

"They're always claiming they did stuff when they didn't, trying to scare us that they're more powerful and widespread than they are. And people say they're in ISIS who've never been to the Middle East, never even left the country. They want to intimidate people, you know: 'don't mess with me, I'm in the Mafia, I'm with the Crips.' But yeah: if it was real I'd do it in a heartbeat. For Rielle and especially Meghan" (his girlfriend and their daughter).

"Can't do it." Jimmy shook his head. "I'm not giving up my guns. Granddaddy'd run me right out of the house if I even said it."

"Dude – whoa!" Scott was concerned. "You've got guns in the house? With your kid running around?"

"They're locked up. And Granddaddy's the only one's got the keys. We don't take them out except when we're hunting."

"Would you?" Marcus challenged Rick.

Rick mopped himself with his shirt. "If I knew – totally for certain – that it worked…"

*

(forwarded)   *(from:)* KingR008   *(to:)* shewfly
[*Anomalist*, July 7, 2014]…Not from one of our usual sources: the ultraconservative Family Values Council claims that one of their own, Rep. Arlene Hooker, is a victim of Liberal Psychic Warfare…

*

"Oh my god," Mom said. "He thought to me, 'Do you really want to know?' I saw Dante's warning from the *Inferno*, you know; 'Abandon all hope ye who enter here,' written in coals of fire. Honestly. I said Yes; and then I – it was –" Annie lay a comforting arm round her shoulder. "Like this…immersive vision, of her forced to personally experience every last bit of pain she and the whole pro-life crusade had ever caused to every woman everywhere, forever. Piling up and piling up, stuff she'd done on top of everything they'd all done, until it reached, like, critical mass, and resonated back to blast their souls. Like people in Hiroshima seeing the shock wave coming at them. And in the center where you knew you couldn't look because your eyes would melt and burn out of your skull: there was Jesus – because she's a quote-unquote 'Christian,' of course she is. Jesus, looking right into her eyes as he gets shredded into this, like, powerless bloody carnage by the trillion shrapnel-cuts of their self-righteous cruelty. 'Jesus fucking Christ, what are you *doing*?' I asked him. He said, 'They are bullies. This is how we deal with bullies.'"

Dinner at her and Annie's. Leslie was with them, having taken up their shelter offer. Mom was in a downer mood due to a new case, a death-penalty appeal. TeShawn Williams was a black youth, a career criminal, the only child of a devout widow who worked two hard, low-paying jobs and barely made ends meet. He had broken into a house in Trinity Park. He'd seen the owners drive off and thought the house empty; but the couple's seven-year-old daughter and four-year-old son were there in the care of a babysitter, a rising senior at the School of the Arts downtown. She and the daughter, going into the kitchen, had encountered him standing at the head of the cellar stairs. He shot them both, and fled. The daughter was killed instantly. The babysitter bled to death, some time before a curious and worried neighbor, puzzled by the open front door, came to check.

TeShawn's behavior on trial hadn't helped. He denied everything. He was insolent. He threatened revenge against prosecutor, detectives, witnesses, and their families. He'd looked both sets of parents (upright, decent, progressive, well-respected; shattered) in the eye without the slightest sign of remorse. Rick knew that though Mom tried to keep things professional, some of the human pain always got through to her. She'd told how Mrs. Williams, who'd come to their meetings supported by members of her church, had said "I know what he is. But as long as he's alive there's a chance for God to touch his heart."

"He's a vicious bastard," Annie replied. She'd had to fight off more than her share of sexist crap in the Navy, and had absolutely no use for men who hurt women.

"He is a vicious bastard. And I could go into my whole liberal schpiel, you know, 'ohh, poverty, racism, bad schools, yadda yadda yadda. If we'd intervened thirty years ago this wouldn't have happened.' But it did happen; and now everybody's suffering for it, his mom just as much as those kids' parents."

Had they received any dreams about a gun barrier? Would they take it, if true? "In a heartbeat," Annie replied. "Abso-fucking-lutely," Mom insisted. "Two lesbians, living by ourselves, in a Fifties-era house that wouldn't be hard to break into, in an America where the very worst of the Fifties' sexism and homophobia and all the rest of that shit's doing its double-God-damnedest to stage a comeback." Annie still had her Navy-issue Beretta M9, but it reposed in a gun safe in the bedroom. "And that's where I want it to stay," Annie said.

"Now I'm waiting for the NRA's heads to start exploding," Mom continued. "They'd outlaw it the way Hooker wants to outlaw reproductive control. If they find him – my god, he'd be facing Second Amendment suits from here 'til doomsday."

"No, he'd be facing a firing squad before that ever happens," Annie said ruefully. "But that's *if* they caught him."

Mom sighed. "But you know – if us liberals get him first we'll lynch him for negligence. 'Why didn't you do this sooner? Don't you know how many lives you could've saved?' Like those two poor girls."

"Maybe he couldn't," Leslie speculated.

*

He picked up Claire after work. They were going to Chapel Hill, to see her friend's band play. He wasn't expecting danger; wasn't even thinking of it. Southpoint Mall was nowhere near any "bad" parts of Durham. It was miles from downtown, surrounded by car dealerships, subdivisions and upscale motels off I-40. The parking lot was well-lit, with people going to and fro. He was wondering how long Claire would want to stay out; would she be In The Mood when they got back; if she was, would he have the energy or be too tired. He didn't even hear what the guy said at first. "What?" he replied, distracted.

"Gimme your fuckin' money!"

The guy had come out of nowhere from between the parked cars. He was small and dark, wearing dark clothes: hoodie, saggy shorts, ball cap with some kind of logo on the front. Yes, that was a gun pointed at them. The man's face looked frantic and vicious, but maybe that was because he was pointing a gun at them. He was standing by the rear bumper. Claire was leaning down to get in the passenger seat, Rick holding the door open.

He couldn't think. He didn't know what to think. He could feel Claire's horror like a psychic wave. The Wizard appeared in his mind – ridiculously like Obi-wan's ghost telling Luke to *"use the Force!*" – with that "boundary" he'd been offering. "What?" Rick repeated; but now as in "what the *fuck* do you think you're *doing*, you fucking idiot??"

The gun hand jerked up. He shot twice.

The bullets appeared in mid-air, tiny dull lumps of metal. They slowed, flattened, hung motionless as if suspended in some invisible viscous liquid. They fell to the asphalt with a tiny *tink, tink.*

The robber's face was now sheer panic. He stepped back; then turned and fled. Rick screamed in rage, and launched himself in pursuit. Claire was screaming too, her phone open in her hand. The man turned and fired three more times. Rick wasn't even paying attention as these bullets also clinked harmlessly to the ground. He pushed himself in an adrenaline burst of speed, and tackled the man, knocking him down. He seized the gun arm with both hands, while the robber's other arm tried ineffectually to club at him, and bit at the wrist as hard as he could. The gun fell away. He pinned the man by the neck; and with every ounce of force he could muster, punched him in the face. He kept punching until his adrenaline gave out. He sagged, gasped for breath, staggered to his feet. He kicked the guy in the ribs. Then he jumped, and with all his weight and remaining strength, stomped him square in the chest.

Security guards came running up. Claire, gabbling, seized him and clung to him. He was sweating bullets, but also shivering. The robber lay prone on the asphalt, bawling hysterically. His cap had been knocked off, and Rick saw now that he was but a youth, maybe fifteen or even younger. He was wearing a pair of ridiculous bright orange sneakers.

"It *worked*?" Jimmy exclaimed, wide-eyed. "Fuck!"

"What'd the cops have to say about it?" Marcus asked.

"They didn't. They questioned me for two hours straight: where was I standing, where was he standing, how was he holding the gun. All around the big question of, how the fuck did I not end up dead, like anybody else would have."

"Did you tell them it was the Wizard's barrier?"

"If they'd said anything first, I would've. But if I brought it up, and they'd started looking at me like I was nuts? I don't think cops like being weirded out, and they were already weirded out that I wasn't dead. And I don't think they were too happy that I beat the crap out of the kid, either. It could make the case more complicated. Mom's worried his family'll sue me...It's a clusterfuck. I was freaked out, and probably in shock, and worried about Claire because they were interrogating her too, which was liable to freak her out...I didn't need to start telling them about a 'Wizard' and some sci-fi force field."

"But it *worked*," Jimmy said. "Man...if it'd still let me go hunting...For Darnell...Who *is* he? Does he hate guns? Why's he doing this?"

*

The robber grabbed him from behind. Pinned his arm to his side, squeezed him so he could barely breathe. He writhed. The robber's long blond hair tossed jellyfish strands in his mouth. Barrier, barrier! The gripping arms flew loose.

Claire sat up, gasping sobs.

"What the fuck!" Rick said. Then softened his tone. "What's wrong? You OK?"

It was sometime past 3 A.M., pitch black. "He was shooting at you," Claire moaned. "I kept trying to pull you out of the way. But then my arms came loose, and you – and you –"

"It's okay, all right? I'm fine. You had a nightmare."

He held her and let her cry out her fright. "He was right in front of you, and I *knew* you were going to die…"

"But I didn't."

"But *how*? His gun was almost touching you."

"I think…I think it was the Wizard. His gun shield. Have you had that dream?"

She had. "But what if it hadn't worked? Please, don't try it again! Just give them the money and run away."

"I know; that's what everybody tells you. But it happened so fast. I thought of the barrier; then he started shooting; and…You know, the police were bewildered too, why I didn't get shot. That's why they questioned me so long. Did they give you a hard time?"

"They were actually…*nice*." She cried a little more. "They asked me everything I remembered, but they were sympathetic, because they could – they said they saw how scared I was."

"We both were. Naturally. Now are you going to be all right? You think you'll be able to sleep?"

He gave her a gentle shoulder massage, keeping his hands clear of any place or motion that might suggest desire. He was not going to take advantage of her distress.

In his own dreaming distress, had he barriered himself and flung her from him? If his fear had been strong enough, could it have wrenched her arms out of joint, or even flung from the bed poltergeist-style? He'd punched the shit out of that kid, with his stupid orange sneakers.

*

Why are you doing this?

Another night. Claire away, visiting her mother. As Rick lay in bed he actively thought about the Wizard. In the coffee shop on 9th Street, communicating with him as they passed. Under a tree with Aidan, and Ava Gardner. Observing Arlene Hooker as she brutalized women outside clinics. The little boy who'd tried to rob them, bawling hysterically. *Hey Wizard – what are you doing? Send me a dream.*

*

He did not feel the pain itself, but felt its might, like the heat from a fireplace across a room. Every single instance of terror, agony, despair and death by gun. Columbine, Newtown, Aurora, and the sidewalk where Trayvon Martin fell. Every woman shot down by an abusive lover, every suicide, every innocent victim of some madman's massacre. Every heart ripped apart by a loved one's loss to *preventable* killing – for there'd also be shown how the deaths could, *would* have been prevented, by requirements for registration, waiting periods, training, insurance, or laws keeping guns from the hands of the mentally unstable. And to this was added all the frustration, rage and grief caused by those who brutally sought to crush anyone who said so much as a single word in favor of such regulations. The NRA with its coffers funding vile hate-feeding propaganda; the gun-worshippers who threatened, slandered, libeled, trolled and doxxed, vandalized and abused in person; the open-carry fanatics who loved to swagger in cruel gloating arrogance through grocery store or airport, as others ran and cowered from the big black "equalizer" at their side. Cruelty that blamed victims for their own deaths, for not being as viciously, violently armed as their killers. Cruelty so sick that on the anniversary of Trayvon Martin's murder that it sent missives of gloating delight to his mother, to sadistically break her heart still further and revel in her tears. Cruelty so monstrous that it told the parents of Newtown that their children, and their grief, never existed: it was a "false flag," a treasonous conspiracy. Parents whose only means of identifying their beloved child might have been a simple little barrette, gifted her that morning, on a lock of hair attached to a chunk of skull, from the unrecognizable, unbearable hamburger mush of bone, brain, blood and flesh that had been their daughter's face, denounced in screaming fury "YOUR KID'S NOT REAL! YOUR GRIEF'S NOT REAL! IT'S ALL FAKE! YOU'RE TRAITORS! HOW *DARE* YOU GRIEVE! YOU'VE GOT NO *RIGHT* TO GRIEVE! YOU DON'T *DESERVE* COMPASSION!!" A vision of every single instance of such merciless hurting, coalescing into a psychic blast more powerful than a trillion Hiroshimas, ready to smite the cruel and arrogant: Jesus looking directly into their eyes as all the guns they've worshiped blast Him into bloody shreds like Newtown's children, shreds not even big enough for a communion wafer; with each of their own personal cruelties being the final bullets that take Him out.

"Holy shit," Rick said, and was awake. Baxter was giving him a puzzled look. "What the fuck?!"

*

They are bullies. This is how we deal with bullies.

*

Rick looked for the hippie family's farm again, but never found it, either driving or on Google Earth. One clearing, by an old concrete bridge, seemed familiar; but it was grown up in long-undisturbed weeds, the only human signs a few burnt rafters wrapped in kudzu beside the stump of an old chimney.

Ebola...Pat Robertson: Genocide's OK if it's in the Bible...Our oil addiction

Schedules Subject to Change

2014. January; Freeport, Illinois...

The City Council is hearing public comment on a proposed gun-regulation ordinance. One man reads a prepared statement. *"My* right to protect *my* children with *my* guns, trumps your fear of my guns," he concludes, to booing and applause.

Another person stands, a huge man, built like a lumberjack. He is father to two little girls, but has lost their custody. (His ex-wife, who'd loved him for his intelligence, had divorced him for fear of his violent temper.) He confronts the first man. "You have just said that your guns are more important than my babies' safety – than my babies' *lives.* You are, therefore, my babies' mortal enemy. *I cannot allow you to live."*

He seizes the other man by the throat, and snaps his neck.

Then, with the energy of madness, he rips the man's head from his shoulders. He holds it up, blood dripping. *"So perish all enemies of little children,"* he announces. He slam-dunks it into a nearby recycling bin, with such mighty force that, horrifically, it bounces twice before landing among the empty cans.

People shout and scream. The dead man's girlfriend comes at him shrieking, fingers outstretched to claw. He knocks her unconscious with a single punch. He leaves the chamber, shrugging off all attempts to stop him as though they were no more than hovering mosquitoes. He walks out of the building, and disappears.

An intense manhunt is conducted, without success. His car remains where he'd parked it. His apartment is unvisited. His bank cards register no use. His ex-wife and children, mother, sister, neither see or hear from him. Early in the morning of the fifth day, he is found lying in a gully, grievously wounded, near the corner of Third Street and College Avenue in the southern outskirts of Milwaukee. His injuries indicate that he had been struck by a large, heavy object traveling at high speed. He was too far from the road, though, to have been tossed there by the impact of a vehicle. There were no signs that he'd been carried there, or that he had walked or crawled there himself. Flecks of paint on his clothes, green and orange, prove untraceable.

He had been living on the streets, sleeping in remote corners of public parks or in empty houses he'd broken into (where he stole nothing except food, and took care to do as little damage and leave as little trace of his presence as possible). His last memory was of walking past the intersection. Interviewed from his police-guarded hospital bed, he stands by his feelings. "It's an obscenity, and an *abomination*, to say that guns are more important than childrens' *lives*. If you say that, if you even *think* it, you are a God-damned child abuser. Every mother in that room should have risen up and torn him to pieces with their bare hands…If you think you have to carry a gun everywhere to be safe: you're a coward. If you *want* to carry a gun everywhere, you're not just a coward, you're a God-damned Christ-crucifying sadistic *bully*, who *enjoys* terrorizing people…*Our* right to protect *our* children from YOUR guns, trumps your so-called 'right' to swagger around with them, making up for your pathetic raging inferiority complex by *terrorizing* people."

(No one connected with the case is old enough to remember that the gully once carried the tracks of an electric railroad, the Chicago North Shore & Milwaukee, abandoned in 1963. Its green and orange "Electroliner" trains had traveled between Milwaukee and Chicago at speeds approaching a hundred miles an hour.)

*

March; Ballyward, County Down…

Agatha Macrae turns off the television and the electric fire. Once the late news ended, it was time for bed. Though why they even watched the news any more, she couldn't say; it was never anything but depressing. Drowning refugees, terror attacks, Americans shooting each other by the dozens…It was a ritual, these many years. She and Mary Adelaide in their dressing gowns, sharing a pot of tea – chamomile, so as to keep Agatha's insomnia away – and watching UTV, more to see what tomorrow's weather might bring than anything else. Rituals were a comfort, and at their ages any small comfort was welcome.

How would Mary Adelaide get on when she herself passed? Their two combined pensions just barely kept them. They'd divided the cottage, renting the other half to a young Belfast couple who came down for weekends. (The couple's children adored them and called them "the Aunties.") It helped a little; but taxes and the cost of everything kept going up. But Agatha kept her concerns to herself. As elder sister she'd always felt responsible to keep the level head. Mary Adelaide had always been the timid one, ready to worry herself near to death over the least little thing.

As she pushes herself up, one hand on the mantel, she hears a faint faraway sound…

…*clackatack, clackatack…clackatack*…

…a sound she'd not heard in so many years. Surely it couldn't be? Hadn't it been gone for so long there was hardly a trace left? When they'd walk out Moor Road of a nice day and pass over the old arch, they'd look down to the cutting and see nothing but half-grown trees and dirty puddles, and mattresses, stoves and shopping trolleys shameless people had dumped there…

…*clackatack, clackatack*…A sudden clear memory comes to her, as clear as if the eighty years had never passed. There they all are, on the platform at Ballyward station: she and Mary Adelaide and Dad and Mum, and Uncle Jamesie, who's all a-huff at the Great Northern of Ireland for replacing its steam locos with Diesels. "Not even a proper whistle do they have!" he says. "Just a paltry little hooter, that sounds like an angry sheep!" Aunt Maureen is there, and Cousin Tom, the handsomest boy that ever was, though Agatha would sooner have died than say so out loud. It's August Bank Holiday, and they're going down to Newcastle, to the seaside. And going First, too!   When they went up to Portadown for shopping or the cinema, they travelled Second; but Dad has declared today a special treat. Her one hand holds Mary Adelaide's, with her other safe in Dad's great paw. He's tickling Mum, and she's laughing.   And now here comes the train, *clackatack clackatack*, a proper huff-puff steamer with its sharp bright whistle; and Mary Adelaide hiding behind her, as if the great thing might leap the rails and eat her up…

They were all gone now, long gone and buried. Dad, Mum, Uncle Jamesie, Aunt Maureen; Cousin Tom lost to a stroke, his children scattered with their own families to Vancouver, Cambridge, Ibiza. The railway line was pulled up, sleepers gone to build peoples' garden beds, the metals sold for scrap – melted down, for all she knew, into more guns for the Americans to shoot each other with…

Mary Adelaide is staring at her, mouth agape. "You hear it too!" she exclaims: a statement, not a question. They go to the window, draw aside the curtain. *Clackatack, clackatack,* louder now; the steady chuffing of a locomotive; and finally, that bright sharp whistle. There, at the distant edge of the pasture, a dark silhouette hurries briskly along. Light from carriage windows reflects across the thin snow, and a plume of smoke casts a feathery shadow in the moonlight. The train's chuff and clatter echoes briefly as it passes beneath the arch and goes out of sight, towards Banbridge.

Mary Adelaide's picking up the phone. "What are you doing?" Agatha demands.

"Calling the Daughtrys up at Tullymurry, who live in the old station house –"

"You'll do no such thing. Do you want everyone to say we've gone mad?"

"Agatha, we both saw and heard it, with our own eyes!"

"And what if we're the only two who have? The Council would be knocking on our door to check us for dementia. No – here's what we will do. Tomorrow when we go to the village we'll say to people how we both had a *dream* of seeing a train. We'll spread that story round. Then if anyone else saw it too, perhaps they'll speak up."

"Ohh, we're neither one of us mad, and you know it." Mary Adelaide is showing unusual spirit, as if the strange train had spared extra steam to energize her. "If you insist on that story I'll go along; but I *know* what I saw. And I think it was a marvel!...Now wouldn't it be wonderful if they brought the railway back for real? We could go up to Belfast again so easily, without your having to drive…"

*

April; Pélérin, Argentina…

Marc Reyes trots Lolo towards the cluster of trees, already showing their autumn colors, that mark the old *estácion.* He knows he can be alone there. No one goes there any more. There's no reason to: there are no more trains. Even the rails themselves are gone, rusted away to nothingness. It's been left to itself; plaster walls slowly crumbling, bare rafters showing through the roof. The pampas spreads out all around, so flat and still in the gathering dusk that the lights of farms ten, even twenty kilometers distant can be seen.

He comes here when he needs to be alone. He's made a secret refuge in the cabinets of what had been the office of the *jefe,* the "stationmaster." There he can read, or dream, or watch videos and practice his English. In daytime he'll lie in the field that used to be the train yard, watching the clouds make endless patterns high above, and the first stars beginning to shine. Once he'd come back and told the family he'd seen an OVNI, a "UFO." This was a lie, though. He'd said it because Cousin Lucia and her son, from Carhué, had seen one, a real one. Everybody believed them and asked endless questions. How big was it? How fast was it? Where did it come from, where did it go? He was jealous of all the attention they were getting. Mama could tell it was a lie, and smacked him good. He dreams of being a teacher when he grows up. He wants to live in town, where there are lights and people and so many things to do. He wants to live in Carhué, boarding with Cousin Lucia and her son, to whom exciting things happen. Cousin Lucia had been to University and was friends with brilliant people, scientists and researchers. People who might not, just might not, laugh at him if he told them of his Curse.

His real name is Miranda, and he was meant to be a girl.

He knows this through and through. He knows it the way he knows how to breathe, the way he knows up is up and down is down and gravity makes you fall. But *Brujeras*, "witches," must have changed him while he was growing inside Mama, so no one would ever know the truth, or believe him. Why they had done this to him he can't understand, except that they took delight in such cruelties. He does the things boys like to do, riding horses, playing soccer; but he also likes to sing and dance along to videos, and draw pictures of fairy-tale princesses in their beautiful gowns. When he does, though, Papa yells at him, Mama smacks him, his older siblings mock him and call him *balero*, "Queer." More and more often he must get away. He's eleven, and soon his body will start to change. He'd watched his older brother go through it. It had made Raul even meaner than before. He'd been arrogant about his rising height, the hair growing on his body, even how he smelled different; while Papa looked on proudly.

He reins in Lolo, her hooves kicking up puffs of dust. Something's wrong – something's different. There are *lights*!

Bright lights shine down on the old platform. Golden light gleams from the windows. Silhouettes pass across them. He hears faint conversations, even laughter, from within. He sees in the dusk the shapes of horses tethered in the forecourt, and a few cars. How could this be? The last time he'd come, three days before, there had been no sign of workers or repairs; only birds fluttering out through the roof as he approached. A shiver runs through him. He tethers Lolo to the outermost tree and creeps as close as he dares.

A signal arm – signals? Where had they come from? – creak from vertical to horizontal. A strange horn blows in the distance. A little three-car train is quickly approaching from the east. New rails gleam in the light of its headlamp. It draws up at the platform with a shush of air. He recognizes it: a "Fiat-Diesel," the kind his Tatarabuelo, "Great-Grandfather," had ridden as a child, when it was the Ferrocaril General Belgrano and he'd been friends with the *jefe's* son. He'd shown Marc a picture once before he died. Figures stand and chat at the baggage door. Others emerge from the entrance, mounting horses or starting cars, and vanishing into the darkness.

Lolo nickers. She has strayed to the end of her tether to touch noses with the other horses. He dashes to pull her away.

"What a pretty pony!" someone says. "Is she yours?"

A young woman stands by the horses. She is as beautiful as a fairy princess. Her eyes are emerald green. Two men are with her, one in a stationmaster's uniform, the other a porter's. "Where have you come from?" Marc says when he finally finds his voice. "How did you get here?"

"I came from my farm to collect a package," the lady smiles, stroking her horse's neck. "I rode; as did you."

"But – are you magical?"

"No. We're no more magical than you."

"Did you need some magic?" the stationmaster asks, in a kindly voice.

"If you were magic – you could change me!" Marc cannot contain himself. He pours out his whole story to them, the *brujas* and the curse and his fear and aloneness and all the things he wants so desperately to change, to become. As he talks he starts to cry, and is ashamed.

The woman kneels and holds him. "You poor child," she says. "You poor child." She seems close to tears herself. The mens' faces are sad too. She takes a handkerchief and gently touches his cheeks. "I'm so sorry we can't change you. But in Buenos Aires there are doctors who can. They do such operations all the time."

"My family would never let me! Not until I'm grown!" Marc cries out. "What can I do until then?"

The three adults look at one another, seeming to exchange thoughts and reach a decision. "We know of someone," the woman says. "He cannot change you either; but he can and will help you. He's called *El Brujero*. He comes to people in their dreams. He comforts and encourages them and helps them find their strengths. We'll tell him about you and ask him to come to you."

"A *brujero*? Is he good? Don't all *brujeras* come from the Devil?"

"He is very good." The men nod agreement. "He's just as much of God as you and I and all of us, even your dear little pony." She strokes the blond tuft atop Lolo's head. Lolo nuzzles her. "I promise you, he will help. I know because he's helped me. In the meantime –" she places her hands on Marc's shoulders and looks into his eyes – "you are Miranda, and you are strong and brave."

"Strong and brave," the stationmaster agrees.

"Miranda's a powerful name," says the porter. "There's a play by Shakespeare, *The Tempest*. I saw it at University. It has a wizard named Prospero, who can call up storms and control spirits. And his daughter's named Miranda."

The train blows its horn again, and pulls away, a glow-worm of lighted windows trundling across the landscape, towards Carhué. The stationmaster goes back inside. The lady mounts her horse and rides off, waving goodbye to Marc. "Something else they should've told you," the porter says. "We're not magical; but all of this is. In a way." He indicates the station and the disappearing train. "We think – no, we're sure – *el Brujero* has a hand in it. So some people can't see it, and some can. And they can't always see it. You did see it, so we know you're on his right side. But I'm telling you so if you come back another time and we're all gone, don't worry. Any time you need us, we'll return."

Marc lets Lolo guide herself home. Should he tell the family? They wouldn't believe him. They'd drive past tomorrow and find it all ruined and empty like before, and he'd get smacked for lying again. Why didn't he take pictures?! He'd been too scared, too amazed. But he *knows* it had been real; he *knows,* just as much as he knew his true self and who he was meant to be.

El Brujero, "the Wizard…"

Exciting things were happening to *him*.

*

August; South Carolina…

U.S. 321, the Columbia Highway, runs twenty-four flat, straight miles from Fairfax down to Garnett across the sandy coastal plain, paralleled by CSX's Columbia-Savannah secondary line. On a Sunday afternoon, with sultry air motionless beneath blazing sun and heat mirages rippling off pavement, two cars are traveling along the road: a blue Accord, and an old white El

Camino. The Camino comes up behind the Accord; flashes its lights, blows its horn. It bumps the Accord once, then a second time. It pulls out left and alongside, as if to strike the other car on its flank...

In the Camino are two brothers, twenty-eight and twenty-five, the second and third sons of a rich man of that district. He owned convenience stores, fast-food franchises, storage facilities, trailer parks, a satellite-dish concession, and other enterprises. He gave no quarter in his business dealings, but denied his boys nothing. Their jobs in his companies were mere window-dressing, and had never really required any work. The boys were pleased to regard themselves as tough, hard-living rednecks. They have been drinking that day. The younger is driving. His three-year-old sits between them, playing with a stuffed rabbit.

They'd been speeding, until they got stuck behind the Accord. It has decals on its rear window, a rainbow flag, and a blue square containing a yellow "equal" sign. The older brother has to think a moment through his whiskey buzz, before identifying these. "Goddamn fags."

"What're they doin' here? We don't want them 'round here," says the younger.

"Oughta run the sonabitches off the road."

So the younger flashes the lights, honks the horn, bumps once and again. He roars out and alongside, preparing to shove. But the Accord slams on its brakes and swerves to the shoulder. The Camino overshoots it, and runs headlong into a Land Rover coming in the opposite direction.

The impact sends the Camino flying upwards, into a stand of trees. The car has no airbags, so both men suffer crippling injuries. The little boy is flung through the windshield and killed. The driver of the Land Rover, a student at the University of South Carolina at Aiken, also dies. She is knocked unconscious, her car landing upside down in a ditch overfull of water from downpours off the fringes of Hurricane Arthur, pinning her there and drowning her. (Her father was a state senator, arch-conservative, a protégé of Jim DeMint, and never missed a chance to heap scorn on ideas like global warming and gay "rights." The brothers and their father had all voted for him.)

There are two women in the Accord, a married couple. One is a conservator at the Savannah College of Art and Design. The other, formerly a combat medic with the Army, supervises a furniture store. They call 911. They triage the men as best they can while waiting for the ambulance. They weep in heartbreak over the little boy and the young girl, for whom nothing can be done. They tell in their accident report how the Camino had come up from behind and attacked them. They testify so in court as well; for the rich father, imprisoning his grief behind a wall of anger, sues them. His lawyer tries to convince judge and jury that the women themselves had caused the accident, by "reckless driving." He convinces no one.

The father's anger only grows. He learns the womens' address in Savannah. He conspires with his eldest son. The son brings in friends. They drive to the womens' home by night. They wear black clothes, and black ski masks. They carry a crowbar, a baseball bat, shotguns, a hunting knife. They creep across the back yard and up onto the deck. They kick the door open, and charge in…

…to an empty house.

Not a stick of furniture in the rooms, not a stitch of clothing in the closets, not so much as a toothpick in the kitchen drawers. There's nothing; except for a functional alarm system that soon brings the police down upon them. The father tries to trace the women, but never succeeds; and presently the rising costs of bail, legal fees and medical bills pull him down into bankruptcy.

The little boy's last act before the crash was to point at something which was not there, and exclaim "Daddy, a *train!*"

*

September; Meadville, Pennsylvania…

The weekend suffocates beneath unseasonable heat. Even at one in the morning, the temperature is above 90. Sally Cole lies watching the ancient fan on the dresser, thinking its weak to-and-fro might hypnotize her to sleep. (The new fan, the big square one that actually moved air, she keeps in the girls' window.) Although Zach's shift ended at eleven, he's still not home. She knows this means bad news.

She hears him climbing the steep stairs, his key scraping in the lock. She leans against the doorframe looking at him, swaying there in the dark hall, 12-pack in his hand. He stabs his finger at her. "Don't you fuckin' start on me...I don't wan' hear it." He collapses on the sofa. Waldo dashes from beneath to cower in the kitchen. "...sonabitch already gave me an earful; I told him, fucker, you don't pay me worth shit to let some customer asshole mouth off to me like that, damn sure I'm gonna fuckin' tell him where to stick it--" Hitting the remote, he gets only snow and static. "Where hell's goddamn cable??"

"Disconnected, 'cause we didn't pay the bill. Last week."

He hurls the remote against the wall. From the girls' room

beyond comes a small fearful sound - whether Ruth or Rachel, she can't tell. The light from the fuzzing TV casts ugly shadows on his face and makes his skin death-pale. "I *told* you, fuckin' don't *start*."

"You asked a question. I answered." She knows she should walk away, leave him be, by morning things'd be back to normal. She never could, somehow.

He sways to his feet. "Didn't I tell you to pay the cable? Didn't I give you fifty bucks last week, and tell you, go pay the goddamn cable??"

"Last *month* you gave me 50, to buy Rachel new shoes. She outgrew the--"

His blow hurls her into the wall with such force that her head leaves a dent. She knows she could hit back, paste a shiner on that twisted handsome face. She's done so before. Drunk as he was, he'd be no match for her. In the morning they'd both act like nothing had happened, and go on with their "relationship." There'd just be a few more dents in the walls. "*Why the fuck don't you ever* do *what I* tell *you to??! Are you some kinda fuckin'* retard?? *I tell you, pay the cable bill and you don't. I tell you, don't get on me, and you don't* not *get on me....*"

She hears more sounds from the girls' room - tiny sobs, stifled by pillow or blanket. It comes to her that they know – though Ruth can barely talk and Rachel barely walk – they already know that crying out loud would only worsen things. Her head throbs. "That's it," she says. "That's it."

She dresses the girls, then herself. Presently Zach stops pounding on the bedroom door. From the living room she hears a crash, as he trips over the 12-pack and falls flat. She seizes the opportunity and slips out, thinking *I will never see this again* – the rickety stair sheathed in green corrugated plastic; the light fixture at the bottom with its cloud of moths and the great ugly toad waiting beneath; Mrs. Chadwick's dark windows. Mrs. C. used to complain and pound on the ceiling when she and Zack fought, and sometimes even call the cops, but of late had given up trying. As Sally backs out, Waldo races down the stairs, barking frantically, and with a mighty leap manages to scrabble into the back seat.

The empty streets downtown all look alike beneath the streetlights' unnatural glow. Her headache grows worse – had Zach bounced her off the light switch this time? – and her vision keeps blurring. Traffic lights that flash at nothing....abandoned stores, blank-faced churches...the clean bright-lit Erie Depot beside Arch Street --

Sally pulls over. A train station? When had they built this? There hadn't been any trains; in fact, not even an Erie Railroad, since before her mother was born. Yet it stood now before her, solid in brick and stone and broad sheltering roofs, with a neon sign along the ridge: a logo, a bright green E inside a yellow circle inside a green square balanced on one corner, and the words ERIE RAILROAD; the only sign of life in the dark downtown. Dazedly, carrying Rachel and leading Ruth by one hand, she goes in....

....to the cool of a pleasant high-ceilinged waiting room, with sturdy polished wood benches and a carpeted floor. A handful of people scattered here and there. An arrival / departure board; a ticket counter staffed by a young man well-dressed in tie and name tag, a scent of newness and a sense of everything-on-schedule, cheerfully competent.... "Good morning; can I help you?" the young agent says pleasantly.

"....uhh, yeah; maybe. Do you have a train to Binghamton?" She'd gone to college in Binghamton, before taking up with Zach. Mary, her sister, a veterinarian, lived there.

"We do: the *Lake Cities*, in about fifteen minutes. You're just in time."

"What time does it get there?"

He runs his finger down a timetable beneath the glass of his countertop. "Just after six-thirty."

"And how much are tickets?"

"Basic coach is ten cents per mile, so…three hundred point eight miles, that's …\$30.08. We also have various sizes of sleeping-car rooms, starting at twelve cents per mile."

She tries to focus. How much money did she have, if any? Was their Visa maxed out yet? "Alright. Three for Binghamton. One adult and two kids – they're both under six, so do they -?" He assures her that yes, they'll both travel free. And Waldo too: a ten-dollar surcharge rents a pet carrier, so he can ride in the coach with them (so long as he's well-behaved) instead of being stuck in the baggage car.

She leaves the car where it'll be towed – though she pays for its upkeep, Zach insists on holding title. The train arrives on time: a two-tone green streamliner, as new as the station. A conductor gently helps her and the girls on board, and shows them to seats. The coach is dark save for tiny lights under the aisle seat edges, like in a fancy movie theatre, and half-full of sleeping travelers. Soon they're racing through the night (speeding silhouette of forest and hill against a backdrop of star-filled night sky, green-lit signal arms pointing upward)....Ruth baby-talks a question. "We're going to see Aunt Mary. She can help us." Sally repeats this to herself – "We're going to Mary, we're going to Mary" - a hypnotic mantra....

She jerks awake. Dawn had come. A station sign saying ENDICOTT flashes past. She can see the Susquehanna River. The conductor comes to her side. "Binghamton in five minutes, ma'am."

That night in Binghamton, Mary Cole dreams. She dreams of her lost sister's boyfriend, crying drunken incoherence on a long-distance phone. She dreams of her lost little sister: Sally riding to her on a Mystery Train; sitting bolt upright, eyes wide open but unseeing; her babies curled up beside her and a small dog at her feet; shepherded and guarded by a conductor who looks like the Wizard of Oz. Meanwhile, here in downtown, they've fixed up the old station, and set a clock in its tower. "6:34," it reads, and begins to cheep like a phone.

She reaches to the bedside table. A text: the DiMeolas' mare has gone into labor. She dresses quick and quiet, kisses Andrew goodbye. Andrew smiles in his sleep and murmurs something indistinct.

The mare is delivered of a healthy foal, and Mary leaves the DiMeolas' farm just as day is breaking. The dream about Sally still troubles her, and some instinct, some premonition, keeps urging her to pass by the station. So she gets off the expressway at Robinson Street and cuts over to Chenango. Crossing the viaduct, she makes a hard left on Lewis and turns into the station plaza.

It's active with cars and taxis and people carrying suitcases, a baggage cart rolling up the platform stacked with more suitcases, boxes and parcels. A PA voice is announcing "…on Track One, the *Lake Cities*, for Scranton, Stroudsburg, Dover; Morristown,

Summit, Newark and New York…" She'd never really been here before, only driven by; never seen downtown from this perspective. How different things looked when you saw them from a new vantage! The city looked alive; clean somehow, awake. The old half-empty buildings seemed to gleam, as if they once again were full of thriving businesses; shining like the foal's coat had shone in the barn lights as his mother nuzzled him to his feet.

A rumbling throb of powerful engines approaches. A green streamliner rolls in along the platform, bell clanging and brakes hissing. Mary glances at her watch. "6:34," it reads. The hair on the back of her neck begins to rise.

The door of one car swings open and a set of folding steps flops down. A woman stands in the vestibule, two children beside her and a dog at her feet. Mary runs.

Sally sets Ruth and Rachel down one by one, very carefully, on the platform. "Waldo, sit," she says. Waldo sits. Then she looks at her sister with wide but unseeing eyes; and faints.

An ambulance is summoned. Mary grimaces at the thought of EMT fees, but there's no way she's going to try to move Sally herself. She'd recognized shock and suspects concussion, knowing as she does about Zach's argument tactics. She follows the ambulance back over the viaduct. She's busy talking to the girls, trying to reassure them, and pays only reflex attention to the rear-view mirror. If she had looked, she would have seen the downtown she was familiar with: empty storefronts in dusty, dejected-looking buildings, the plaza deserted with tall clumps of weed growing through its cracked pavement; the station long unused, dead and dark.

The Urgent Care Center finds no concussion, only bruises, and the effects of poor nourishment and minor illnesses left untreated. No charge for the ambulance ever appears, and Mary presently forgets to worry about it. The Center's staff, meanwhile, occasionally wonder in idle moments about its crew, and why they'd never seen them before or since. Mary's daily activities don't take her past the station for two weeks; and when she does drive by, she's in a hurry and concerned with other things. Over a month passes, in fact, before she truly notices it again, and is puzzled at the difference from her memory. Had she dreamed it too? Or had she been too focused on Sally and the girls to observe anything else? Sally remembers little of the trip. Ruth hasn't enough language yet to tell her version; Rachel is pre-verbal, and Waldo keeps his own counsel. If the ticket charge appeared on the Visa statement, Zach never mentions it during the few lawyer-supervised conversations they have (again, the card was in his name but Sally paid the bills, as best she could). No one else in their circle of acquaintance has seen or heard anything about trains at the old station, aside from vague memories of "something on the news – five years ago, maybe?" about proposals to bring Amtrak through town, proposals that had faded away from lack of funding and eventually been forgotten...

*

November...

Hurricane Isaias makes landfall on the Rhode Island coast the night of Thanksgiving Saturday. Fierce winds and rain shake the windows of robber-baron mansions along Newport's Cliff Walk, as if the ghosts of those the barons had exploited vainly seek redress within. Shingles and shutters are wrenched from the house in Providence where H.P. Lovecraft lived his last years. In Pawtucket/Central Falls early that Sunday morning, a police officer drives slowly up Broad Street, still flooding along its gutters. She glances over, as she often does, at the old train station: a neoclassical structure of brick and stone built in 1916, spanning the tracks between Clay and Barton Streets. Amtrak expresses and MBTA locals pass beneath, but no trains have stopped there since 1981. It had been closed, then boarded up, then left to slow dereliction, a white elephant which no one wished to see torn down, but for which no sources of money could ever be found for rebuilding. After she passes, though, something different, something strange, keeps pulling at her mind, compelling her to turn back.

She thought she'd seen a building completely restored: decades' worth of graffiti swept away; windows unboarded, their glass intact and clean and warmly lit from within; brass and metalwork fixtures gleaming. She thought she'd seen people, coming and going through the doors. But when she pulls up in front, there is nothing. The station is as empty and desolate as before.

*

Boston, Sunday night, Thanksgiving Sunday; and the South Station platform is jammed, with more people coming through the turnstiles every minute. Amtrak is just in from New York, fifty minutes late due to hurricane debris; and now everyone and their luggage wants to ride the Red Line out to Cambridge. The four people involved in the incident are all there, in the security-cam footage, but do not stand out from the crowd unless one has already watched the sequence and knows where to spot them. A blond youth, looking well-fed, well-cared for, well-raised, well-dressed in a preppie way (deluxe sneakers, khakis, a Dartmouth pullover), but jittering and trembling with the electrocution energy of a heroin addict desperate for a fix. An elderly mixed-race woman, coffee-colored, scarf tied round her hair, looking lost beneath burdens of age and labor and a heavy shopping bag. A burly homeless guy, made even larger by several layers of clothing; coal-black, matted hair, his eyes rolling and showing their whites like those of a frightened animal. And an ordinary man, of nondescript features and indeterminate age, slightly plump of face and figure. He wears an old raincoat and shabby fedora, like a film-noir private eye; carries a small suitcase. The name he will give to the police is also so innocuous that people retelling stories of the incident will often not be able to recall it, naming him Sal Smith or Jay Jones or Joe Blow.

There they stand, then, in the camera footage, amongst the milling crowd.

The homeless man wanders to and fro, mouthing incoherent phrases. People edge away from him without acknowledging his presence. No one makes eye contact with him. But he catches sight of Smith, or Jones; and stops dead. He stares, in some kind of recognition; in dumbfoundedness and horror and some strange kind of hope. Smith / Jones, perhaps feeling himself stared at, turns and meets the man's eyes. The man gives a hideous scream.

It echoes and re echoes off tile and concrete and metal. Conversations stop, heads turn. Puzzlement, confusion, worry: what is happening? People are fearful of late, troubled by rumors of terrorist attacks planned for the holidays. A space clears between the two men. The homeless one reaches, imploring. He cries out. "Let us alone! What have you to do with us? Have you come to destroy us? *I know who you are!*" Jones / Smith watches him, without fear or judgment. The man crumples to the ground in a fetal clutch, crying "Help me...help me..."

Smith / Jones looks upon him. He gives a slight, gentle shrug. He sets down his suitcase, kneels by the man's side. With no distaste at all, he places his left hand on the man's shoulder, and encloses the man's right hand in his own. The lights of an approaching train, meanwhile, glow ever brighter back in the tunnel, with the roar and screech of its wheels and the rush of wind heralding its arrival. No one can clearly hear him speak in a calm, quiet voice. "In the name of God the Parent, and Jesus Christ the Son, and the Holy Spirit: demons that torment this man, come out. Leave him, and seek your healing elsewhere."

The man screams again, and writhes. But then he sits upright, head in hands, and begins to sob. They are no longer the hysterical tears of madness, but of grieving in clear-eyed sanity, at all too human sorrow and loss.

The blond youth, jittering and trembling, stands in the wavery ring of people round them. All eyes (puzzled, confused, worried) are on the strange scene. His hand, though, is reaching, then retracting, then reaching again, towards Jones / Smith's overlooked suitcase. He is in fact a heroin addict, and does desperately need a fix. His wealthy family has washed their hands of him and cut off all his resources, after multiple attempts at rehab have failed. His hand reaches...

...and is knocked aside by the elderly mixed-race lady with

her shopping bag. She seizes the front of his hoodie and pulls his face down to hers, berating him in Portuguese. She is a native of Angola, where she lost her family to the civil wars. After years of exhausting struggle she had finally emigrated to America. She had gone to Philadelphia and seen the Liberty Bell with her own eyes, and wept for joy. How *dare* he, an American boy, rich and young and privileged, abuse the many blessings his country had given him, by *stealing* from someone showing God's kindness?

MTA cops have made their way through the crowd, even more chaotic now as the train pulls in and everybody tries to get on or off. The homeless man is not unknown to them. His actings-out have caused trouble before. He's a veteran of Iraq, a veteran of bad PTSD, and of the consequences of Republican budget cuts to the programs that treat it. He has meds, but does not always take them; and because of the cuts can't always afford them. But now when he stands up, straight and calm, at their command, they look at him – then each other – then back, in surprise. His eyes, they will say later, are different now: clear, somehow, and human again. There is no more madness in them. One officer will tell another, "It was like he'd gotten himself back."

The old Angolan woman, calling her complaint to the police in broken English, tries to drag the youth forward, but he is able to wrest himself from her grasp and escape. They question her and hear her story. They question the other man. He is cooperative and his answers credible. He explains that he's from out of town, from a North Shore suburb of Chicago. His neighbors there are named Harvard; and their young daughter has recently been intrigued to learn that there's a Harvard University. He had business in Fall River, and on impulse decided to take an extra day and come up to town. He'd stroll round the campus taking pictures, so Miss Harvard back home could see what her namesake institution looked like. Then he'd catch the train back. His ticket, examined, seems to be in order: Roomette 6 of Car 2702 on New York Central train #27, the *New England States*, leaving for Chicago at 4:45 the next afternoon. They will not learn until later that the street number he gave does not exist; that the neighborhood where it would be had been leveled by tornadoes that spring; and that there had been neither a *New England States,* nor a New York Central Railroad for it to run on, since the 1960s.

"This man was having a panic attack," he says. "I tried to calm him as best I could." The homeless veteran confirms. The officers take him to a shelter. His healer is allowed to go on his way, onto the Red Line, and into night and mystery.

There will be a coda to the incident, which tellers of the story will not know. One night a week later, the veteran will encounter the youth in an alley off Warren Avenue. By then the youth's superior clothes will be filthy, and smell of living rough on the streets. The veteran will lay his hands upon him in the same manner his healer – Smith, or Jones, or Blow – did, and speak the same words.

*

As the year's end nears, as far as the Internet's concerned, "the Wizard" is still just a joke. A crackpot conspiracy theory; a laughable fantasy of pussy-ass snowflake liberals, an igniter for the sort of psychotic viciousness that fills a certain blog's "Hate Mail Museum." There are more things in earth and heaven, though, than are dreamt of in "Comments" sections' so-called philosophies. Not everyone disbelieves. They keep it offline, keep it to themselves, lest they draw down the bloodlusting fury of those who deny and vilify and curse and death-threaten, to annihilate them like Hiroshima. But they think, and talk, of certain dreams, privately, secretly. People in crime-plagued neighborhoods. Battered women in shelters, runaways on the streets. Refugees and political prisoners. People weary to their soul's depth of living in constant fear: in lands rent to carnage by civil war, or cancered by the reign of psychopathic despots, or "failed states" where civil society has collapsed beyond help and nothing but armed anarchy rules. They think, and wonder, and hope; and continue to dream dreams.

And don't come crying to *us*, motherfuckers. If you do, I want you to find that *your* doing – your Newt Gingriches and Ted Cruz-es and Paul-Fucking-Eddie-Munster-Ryans, that you voted for, that the policies you and they voted for, have annihilated us. Wiped us out like Jews in the Holocaust. Or left us so shattered and traumatized by decades of merciless persecution that we're wrecked and can't do a thing to help you. All these years we tried – *we* fought fair, *we* believed in reason and fact and science; and in *compassion*, and in *believing* people when they said they were in pain – and when we did you screamed "Traitor!" at us. You firebombed our homes. *You threatened our children.* When we tried to stop *your* racism from slaughtering black people left and right, *you* called *us* racists. You don't *deserve* our help.

Like you, Mister Billboard. Gloating at our liberal tears. *Gloating*, at our tears of grief and pain and rage and *despair*. *Rejoicing*, that our hearts are breaking, with helpless compassion. Well by God, I pray with every fiber of my soul that you spend eternity in Hell drowning in an *ocean* of our tears. Drowning forever in agonizing torture. Like refugee babies in the Mediterranean.

[*pause*]

And if you try turning to God? – oh, that precious little Republican God of yours, that supports gay-bashing, and greed and war and forcing women to be nothing but two-legged incubators for babies that you then turn your back on and let them starve – well, Mr. and Mrs. Tea Party Fascist America, I want you to see that *your* policies have destroyed even Him. I want you to see that every single time an innocent person has been destroyed by what you've done – murdered by mass shooters, by gay-bashers, by pollution, racist cops, collapsing bridges, denied health care – has blasted off a chunk of Him; over and over and over and over until there's not even a husk left. Nothing. Nada. Not shit. For as you did unto every last one of the least of these – directly or by voting for the bastards who did – you did unto Him. I want you to realize that your rampant psychotic cruelty is so huge that it's destroyed even Him; and that there is *nothing, nothing* to save you from the consequences of your own evil.

That's what we'd say to you. "We will not save you from the consequences of your own evil."

We sentence you to life imprisonment in the consequences of your own evil.

[*break*]

...A world where we'll be safe from the consequences of your evil.

...It's like I'm in this car that's being driven by a bunch of psycho maniacs. And we're screaming along at top speed straight towards a bottomless cliff. Any time I try to point out we're headed for total destruction, they beat me near to death and scream psychotic abuse. "Traitor, sissy, liberal;" just total vicious hatred. "How dare you question anything; this is God's direction!" And if I try to get *out* of the car and save myself, same thing. "How dare you try to escape what's right!"

A separate world, that I could beam myself to. And no matter how much they screamed and raged they'd never be able to drag me back in again. Hasta la vista, fuckers. You can do your Thelma & Louise shit, destroy your entire world and yourselves along with it; but not me. Not us. Not all the good and innocent and the progress we've given our lives to bring forward.

Thelma and Louise are safe here, fuckers. They landed on Wile E. Coyote and bounced.

They poison their world to death with their psychotic viciousness; but if they try to escape to *ours*? They run, BAM! into this impenetrable barrier, that's made up of every last single bit of suffering they've caused innocent people. No, fuckers, you can't get through. Not until you've lived through, and *expiated*, all the hurt you've caused. Every single last bit of pain, suffering, despair, you've caused *them*, now *you're* going to have to live through it. Even if it takes a million lifetimes, over and over and over…All the weight of all that needless suffering, on *you*, like the cell between two slides, crushing and rupturing the very boundaries of your core soul so it disintegrates out into chaos, and sears like acid every last bit of hatefulness and cruelty out of your being. And for everybody. The right-wing fascist Tea Partiers; *and* the 9/11 terrorists, ISIS, Israel bombing Palestinian children; Rwanda, Bosnia, Dominicans deporting Haitians, rape gangs in India – everybody. *Everybody* who's abused the innocent and defenseless, and –

[*break*]

How will it be for the likes of you? Like you, Phyllis Schlafly, or Randall "Mister Rescue" Terry? Ha! – women need to be rescued *from* you, not by you. And who the fuck are you to even say anything? Unless you have a vagina and a womb, you have no right to open your mouth. Or, for instance, you, Mrs. Arlene Hooker. How will it be?

You'll be all the women you terrorized in front of clinics.

All the women you screamed at, prayed at, insulted, threatened, emotionally blackmailed with "Mommy, don't kill me!" In all their minds and hearts, every woman who tried to get past you, *you'll* experience all the reasons that drove them to the soul-wrenching decision of ending their pregnancies. They were desperately poor. Their families would disown them, their lovers kill them, for being pregnant. Childbirth itself would kill them. They were lied to by the fathers – "Don't worry, I'll pull out; I've had a vasectomy; you can't get pregnant from this position." Their sex education was "abstinence only" – Ha! – or nonexistent, save for gossip in the locker room or sleepover party. They were too scared, or lacking in confidence, or trained in meekness, or craving for any kind of affection, to just say No to their hormone-hopped-up bastard boyfriend. They "didn't want to hurt his feelings." They didn't want all the other girls to call them "loser." They'd been raped, or date-raped, or plied with booze or roofied, and couldn't bear the humiliation of coming forward. Slut-shamings! And some were only there for a *mammogram*, you bitch! Now, on top of all that heartbreak, fear, shame, despair; here in their most desperate, vulnerable, bereft hour, you'll see *yourself* viciously terrorizing them, vilifying them, traumatizing them, making them fear for their very lives, so close up in their face that they feel your hot breath and see the self-righteous madness blazing in your eyes. You'll be that girl who broke down in tears and run away, so completely crushed by your psychotic anti-compassion that she felt she could no longer bear to even live; seeing every passing bus or truck as a chance to throw herself beneath the wheels, every bridge as a place to jump from.

But wait, there's more! You'll feel – you'll *be* - the pain of every unwanted, abused, abandoned child that you've forced needlessly into the world. The bitter desolation of every youth whose whole life had been spent in foster care because no one adopted them. Oh; and how about a vision of the joyful lives some of them would have had if you'd let gay couples adopt? But NO; we can only have "traditional families."

Like mine.

You'll be the little children of clinic doctors, stalked to school by protesters like you yourself, hissing and whispering to them – children eight, seven, six, five years old – all the hideous tortures their Daddy or Mommy would face in Hell. You'll be every woman who ever killed herself, or been killed, because of an unwanted pregnancy. Every woman who'd died in screaming agony from a botched abortion attempt, by some back-alley doctor or by their own hand; and the unbearable grief of those who loved them but were helpless to stop the pain. The horror and heartbreak and helpless rage of family and friends when a clinic doctor or nurse got gunned down in their office or on the street or even in the narthex of their own damn *church*! And, the dismay and despair of everyone who for decades has fought for abortion rights, at seeing them relentlessly ground away by wave after wave after wave of right-wing politicians, like you, and right-wing millions of dollars. Every last single solitary broken heart, every tear, every sob, cry, wail, scream; every measure of pain that you've ever caused, formed into one mighty force that'll hit you with a power greater than infinite Hiroshimas, searing to the very core of your soul. And then; oh, and then, my pretty…

In that searing blast you'll see the face of Jesus Christ Himself, and of God in Him, looking directly at you with infinite sorrow, as every single solitary instance of that hurtled pain like shrapnel strikes off a bloody chunk of His being; grinding Him away, down, down, smaller, smaller; and with it His power to hold and to heal, until there's not one bit left.

My god; it'll be beautiful.

And then, Miss H.; and all the rest of the vicious sexist scum like you…from then on, every, *any* time you try to trot your precious little ideologies out, try to justify them –

BAM! It'll hit you again.

You'll never be able to *not* care again, as long as you live.

[*break*]

Coincidence. Just saw a picture of that bitch Hooker. She's got a four-year-old grandson. Poor kid. He'd be better off with Cruella de Vil.

Gee, Miz H., what do you think'll happen if he looks up at you with those innocent little eyes and says "What made you scream like that, Granny?"

You'll see…You'll see…He won't be forced to feel the pain, and he won't understand the issues; but he'll see *you*, attacking vast numbers of people in desperate pain, and making their pain worse. He'll see you, his beloved Granny, deliberately breaking further the hearts of already heartbroken people. He'll see you cruelly choosing to *not* listen to their desperate pleas, to not be moved by their tears, to not care about them at all. Choosing to not care, and *rejoicing* in their pain. See you gloating that they *deserve* it – and all for some grownup "thing" that he doesn't even get, but which you still decided mattered far more than the sorrow of innocent people.

And the look on his little face is one you'd sell your very

soul to not have to ever see.

[*End of tape*]

The Reveal

The mail was mostly junk. A card from the Duke Dental Clinic reminded him of an approaching appointment. Books Do Furnish a Room reminded him they were open 364 days a year. American Express wanted to give him a new credit card, and Bank of America wanted him to load up his existing one with the enclosed blank checks. Wait a minute – "Pensmore Hughley Partners L.L.C., Attorneys?"

The letter was hand-addressed, directly to him. The envelope was heavy and cream-colored with a slight tweedy texture, like it had been custom-tailored from high-class paper out of stately old-growth trees. Was somebody suing him? An underemployed English major; whose car was a 16-year-old Subaru carrying 200,000 miles, with a broken back door lock and defunct air conditioning, whose last set of tires probably cost more than the whole car would raise on Blue Book? "Blood from a turnip, guys," he muttered.

"Notice to Heirs and Legatees. United States of America…State of North Carolina…County of Chatham. Estate of Hugo Jules Baum…You are named in the petition as an heir or legatee of the decedent."

Hugo Jules Baum?

He walked slowly round it like a cat stalking an unfamiliar object, wary of whether it should be pounced on or will pounce back. Baxter stared at him, then got up and nudged his hand. "Right, buddy, you need your walk, don't you?" Baxter barked, stubby tail windmilling. "And I need a run, so I can think."

Rick liked running. He liked feeling his lungs, heart, legs

pumping, the feel of his body working at its peak. It felt healthy and powerful and even a little erotic, with the fabric of jockstrap and shorts shifting against his cock. His shirt smelled sweaty as he pulled it over his head, but it was a healthy athletic scent, and helped psych him up. As he sat down to tie his shoes Baxter came up between his legs. He took Baxter's head in both hands, scratching and ruffling him behind the ears. "Baxter's not afraid of some old nutjob with a zillion dollars, are you, buddy?"

East Campus was only a block away. Once across the busy Markham / Broad intersection, holding Baxter's leash close, a quick climb over the low stone wall put him on campus and the running track. They set off counterclockwise, parallel to Broad Street. *How did Hugo Jules Baum even know I exist? Did he meet me at some Department reception? Did he pay his bill at the office? No; if he lived in Chatham County he'd have gone to Pittsboro. Or if he was an early-computers guy like it seems, he'd be doing it online...This is truly weird. For someone of that level of...status, to notice you? Sometimes you end up wishing they hadn't.* "Those whom the gods love die young"...*But now what if they don't? Zap you with boils, maybe. Or just let you die old and in Depends, and with no insurance.*

His usual routine was twice around East, 3.2 miles total. The sky was cloudless, the temperature round 80, high for April. (Hadn't he read somewhere that 2014 had been the hottest year on record? Back in January record-setting wildfires had burned up a big chunk of Australia.) He settled into his regular pace, half jog half run. The rhythmic soft crunch of his shoes against the gravel, and his steady breathing. Traffic on the parallel roads; breeze against his face and body, and soughing high in the trees. Baxter loping alongside, totally enjoying himself with his tongue all slobbering out. Pausing a moment at Campus Drive for a passing bus, then off again; past the main entrance with its long view down the Quad to Baldwin Auditorium. Other joggers; walkers; parents with strollers. Rick steered Baxter away from potential collisions.

When he ran he tried to not do too much complex thinking. He'd let thoughts appear, frame them in words, but then let them drift away, back into the rhythm and physical sensations. *Durham's a cool place to live...Was Baum autistic?...Maybe he should've lived here. Endowed a Chair of – something...Speaking of "endowed," Miss; need some help with your sports bra?...Sexist! Sexist! Have the Wizard zap him!... Baum would've fit right in; just another over-educated eccentric...What the fuck would I do with all that money? That I don't – that I seriously doubt I'm going to get. Why would I? Why me?...uh-oh, keep Baxter away before he licks that kid's face...Call those lawyers first thing tomorrow. But call Mom first! She should know what to do.* "She'll know what to do," he repeated to Baxter.

*

Two years had passed since Aidan's disappearance. There was still no sign of him, except a new Polaroid every few months, always mailed so untraceably that it might as well have dropped in from another dimension. The SBI agents had questioned Rick twice more, and searched his place – "procedure," he knew, but still unsettling. He'd thought of having Mom wingman him if they came back; but "lawyering up" could make them even more suspicious, and persistent.

He kept having recurrent Wizard dreams, though he couldn't always remember them. None of the details remained when he awoke, only the same themes. Imminent catastrophe, collapse, anarchy, disasters natural and man-made. Totalitarian oppression, political and religious, crushing everyone in its path; mass injustice and mass slaughter. Good and right dragged into eternal annihilation by willful ignorance and deliberate, gloating cruelty. This future was rapidly heading towards him, like a runaway train packed with explosives.

There also was the Wizard, in his separate realm, his aura of calm and comfort and welcome. It was like the lawn beneath a great oak where Rick had first dreamed of him, Aidan at his side. It was the landscapes in Aidan's pictures, the clean beaches and wide prairies and sunlit mountains. It was like Haw Court the day they'd visited, stately stability surrounded by all the trees in spring bloom. *You can awake here if you wish*, the Wizard would offer, "here" where the racing holocaust would race right by towards its own doom, but do no harm in passing.

As always, the Wizard never imposed himself on one's consciousness. He stood outside it, courteously offering contact with his own. The choice to awake "here" was Rick's to make. Details would be given only if he wished. He'd awaken knowing only that the Wizard had come near, concerning some fast-approaching crisis or climax. But since he couldn't recall the details of that crisis, its feeling of urgency soon passed. Instead he'd think *Damn, I should've asked him about Aidan*. Sometimes he'd initiate Wizard dreams to do just that. The only replies were images of Aidan, hale and healthy.

In the meantime, Leslie's doxxer had been caught. He wasn't the pathetic basement-dwelling mama's boy Rick had envisioned. He was a young man of wealth and good family; a

closer to midnight...Oil companies dumping waste into California's remaining

successful junior lawyer in Richmond, engaged to a former runner-up in the Miss Virginia Pageant. But he was also an avid Breitbart follower, and a frequent contributor to "mens' rights" websites. Neighbors had heard hideous screaming from his townhouse early one morning and called 911. When the police broke in he was found curled fetally in his bed, sobbing, unable to speak. His open laptop displayed, under all his various aliases, every one of the vicious, violently threatening messages he had sent. The Richmond police had asked Leslie if she wanted to press charges. "I should; but...will he recover?"

"From what, being charged? Fuck him," Rick said.

"No, from what happened to him. And, did the Wizard do it? He's the only one who possibly could...I'd wished that he'd catch this guy, but after what he put Hooker through..."

"Charge him anyway. Yours might be the only case they can get him on."

"Did you ever visit Hooker's dream? It's terrifying."

"Whatever; as long as it makes her stop being a hateful –" (he restrained himself from saying "bitch," knowing she disapproved of the term) – "so hateful. And these guys are way worse. Putting womens' addresses online and *encouraging* guys to go rape them, *and* their kids? They need to be taken down."

"Seriously? *Seriously?* Ask him. It's like a horror film. Yes, I want them shut down. But not like this."

Arlene Hooker still refused to break silence. Her bill had died in committee, but similar ones kept popping up in state legislatures, constitutionality and enforceability bc damned. News cameras caught Dad questioned about them by a stringer for the *Triangle Free Press.* "The 'Wizard,'" he replied, with a hint of

Lin-like smirk. "You've heard those stories too. Well: if it was true – *if* –" If the State Senate produced a constitutional and enforceable version, he could see no roadblocks to its passage. "It would protect vulnerable women from making a decision they might not understand and which might even harm them," he purred, showing the cameras his handsomest profile.

In the meantime, people continued to laugh over Hooker and her crazy bill and her panic over some crazy urban legend about a "Wizard." They laughed at social-injustice warrior Republicans like Michelle Bachmann and Steve King warning that unless this "Wizard" was stopped, the white race would make itself extinct in a generation, leaving America to evaporate beneath the onslaught of brown, black and yellow hordes. They laughed even harder when a panicked Alex "Infowars" Jones broke the story of a "gun barrier" the Wizard was allegedly offering. He and Wayne LaPierre of the NRA worried whether a barriered Evil Government would be invincible against Patriots, or would barriered Patriots would be invincible against an Evil Government? And was Evil Hillary secretly using a barrier to avoid questions about Benghazi and her other corruptions? Because Jones took it seriously, nobody else did. They kept laughing; while Bill Maher called the panicking gun lovers "ammosexuals," and snarked that maybe "the Wizard" could be appointed to chair Obamacare's "death panels."

Eunice didn't laugh. She read Dad the riot act. "You ought to be ashamed of yourself! Acting like she's a fool who doesn't know the first thing she's talking about. And after all your campaign promises about protecting values and keeping women safe, and morality; and, and – righteousness! If you knew what he's done to her…

discrimination into state law...Kansas school buses rerouted from decaying

(Hooker had awakened, it was said, screaming in infinite horror until her breath was gone, a sound that could twist knots in the deepest core of one's soul. "Eyes as empty as black holes," was one report. Trembling; unable to speak, mouth twisting into meaningless shapes. She had soiled herself. Her doctors found no signs of stroke, physical injury, poison. Reflexes functioned, but in a mindless, automatic way. When consciousness slowly returned to her face, it was with the look of someone who'd just emerged from the rubble of a cataclysm, dumbfounded to find themselves still alive. Her attempts to describe what had happened would founder into helpless sobbing.)

In the meantime, TeShawn Williams had suddenly dropped his appeal. Mom arrived one evening looking stunned. "Something happened to him night before last. Some kind of… nightmare, attack; nobody knows. The guards said he woke up screaming like they'd never heard before. Even they were freaked out – big tough guys who've seen everything. Since then all he does is sit on his bunk and cry all day. Won't talk, won't eat; he's a total wreck."

The next time she saw him he had recovered enough to talk, somewhat. He'd never been eloquent before, and now his conversation was often interrupted by breaking down in tears. His arrogance and insolence were gone, blasted away, leaving devastation behind. "I saw them girls…They tol' me 'Give us back our lives. Give us back the rest of our lives'… I hurt them all so bad; so bad…" Another wave of sobbing followed.

"The poor guy's just destroyed," Beverly said. "They've got him on suicide watch. And you know, I can't help wondering: is this like what happened to Arlene Hooker? I asked him if the

Wizard had done it, but he didn't seem to understand."

In the meantime, floods in Pakistan and eastern India drowned hundreds. Freak twin tornadoes leveled a Nebraska town. The *Ghostbusters* reboot with Melissa McCarthy, Kristen Wiig, Kate McKinnon, and Leslie Jones came out, and was vilified from pillar to post to 4chan by "mens' rights" types, with Jones singled out for particular racist viciousness by Milo Yiannopoulis and his ilk. In St. Louis and Staten Island, courts declined to indict the police officers who shot Michael Brown and suffocated Eric Garner. Texas's highest criminal court ruled that "creepshot" photos, taken up womens' skirts by hidden cameras, were protected by the First Amendment; saying that banning them would be "paternalistic." And the Supreme Court ruled that Hobby Lobby could deny its employees contraception coverage, on the grounds of "religious freedom." Twelve journalists, editors and staff of *Charlie Hebdo* were gunned down in the magazine's Paris offices; and in Chapel Hill, three Muslim students were murdered in their own home by their white, male, American neighbor.

In the meantime, N.C. House Speaker Thom Tillis, a good buddy of Dad's, called equal-pay legislation a "campaign gimmick," demanded that the Mexican border be sealed to keep out Ebola, and recommended that restaurants be allowed to opt out of requiring employees to wash their hands, as a "freedom from regulation." Despite these, he won the U.S. Senate race that fall, part of a sweep that put all of Congress in Republican hands. He left the Speakership to Dad's other good buddy Paul Stam, one of the masterminds behind the state's infamous anti-gay-marriage Amendment One, and the even more infamous anti-transgender-protection, anti-minimum-wage-raise HB2.   (Mom was livid. Annie and Leslie seethed together.)

(In the meantime, "ghost trains" hadn't even made the news, other than a couple of widely spaced sightings noted in *Anomalist*: in Charleroi, Belgium, midnights on the completed but never-opened Chatelet metro; in remote central Newfoundland along the route of the old *Newfie Bullet*, whose tracks had been pulled up in 1988…

*

Pensmore Hughley's offices were in downtown Raleigh, a block from Capitol Square. Mom went with him. They both wore their best clothes.   They were ushered into the firm's best conference room, with a corner view up Fayetteville Street to the Old Capitol. Ms. Pensmore, the senior partner, was about Mom's age, with long blond hair and an attitude of calm assurance. Mr. Hughley, a few years younger, was black and Buddha-shaped. They had also brought in the accountant who had handled Baum's finances, Mr. Collinson: thirty or thereabouts; soft-spoken, clean-shaven and balding, earnest expressions behind earnest wire-rim glasses.   Ms. Pensmore made introductions, then handed the meeting off to Hughley.

Rick was informed that he was, indeed, the sole heir and legatee of the late Hugo Jules Baum, formerly residing at 1490 Lewis Ferry Road, Pittsboro, North Carolina. As per the late Mr. Baum's direction, the Executors of his last will and testament – i.e., Pensmore Hughley Partners – had already settled all funeral arrangements (organ donation followed by cremation, no memorial service), costs of administration, taxes, and other proper charges against the estate; and pre-probated the assets, so that once various documents were signed and various logistics worked out, Rick could take possession. The assets, in addition to financial holdings Mr. Collinson would explain, included the property known informally as "Haw Court" –

"Why?" Rick asked. "Why me? I never even met the guy."

Mr. Hughley paused. His hands had been resting on the table before him, lapped over one another; now he flipped them apart slowly, like petals opening. "I'll be honest with you: we don't know. Mr. Baum was not one for explanations."

"But you talked to him, right? When you did business with him."

"Most often by phone. He only came here when necessary – for signatures and the like. When he did, he didn't say much. He was always courteous, but never open. If asked a question he would answer as briefly as possible. He wouldn't sustain a conversation."

"But you did ask him, didn't you?" Mom said. "I would think…"

"We did, ma'am. When he brought us the draft of the will I said 'Is Mr. Kingsley a relative or friend?' He replied 'He's my heir,' and nothing more. He had no living relatives, as far as we knew. We offered to do a search, but he declined."

"When was this?" Mom persisted. "Did he make any earlier wills?"

"No; this was his first. He brought it to us a year ago, about three months before his death."

Rick said "Now obviously I don't know anything about wills; but I was thinking, if I'd been his lawyer I would've tried to find out about some total stranger he was leaving everything to. To make sure, you know, that he wasn't being...coerced, swindled; whatever."

The hands unfolded again. "We're limited by professional ethics and professional courtesy. We can do very little outside of what our clients specifically request, or give us permission for. We don't want to give the impression of going behind their backs. Unless there are red flags suggesting coercion, or mental instability; or if there are individuals challenging or likely to challenge the will; and in this case, there weren't. I asked him, 'Is there a connection of some other kind? I don't want to seem intrusive but feel I ought to ask, out of due diligence.' He said 'I understand. I have my reasons. I believe he'll make the best use of it.' Ms. Pensmore and I discussed it later; and we did decide we could – I hope you'll forgive us – have a background check run on you. We found nothing to concern us."

"Yeah, I'm kind of a boring guy," Rick shrugged. Mom made a face at him.

Hughley smiled, Buddhist-ly. "We wouldn't say that. No criminal record, not even unpaid tickets; good credit, steady employment. And a father who happens to be Majority Leader in the State Senate. But we found nothing at all that might link the two of you; so to tell the truth, we're as puzzled as you are."

"There's one other possibility, though we think it's a long shot," Ms. Pensmore said. "Your brother Aidan. Mr. Baum might have taken an interest in his case, and had some idea of leaving you his resources to help with the search. But as I said, it's only a theory. There's nothing he ever said to any of us or that we found in his papers that showed he was interested."

"And in that case you'd think he'd have given it to Dad and Eunice," Rick told Mom.

She rolled her eyes. "God forbid. It'd go right into his campaign contributions. Unless they're right, and he didn't like your dad's politics. Believe me, he wouldn't be the only one," she said to the lawyers, who kept a discreet silence. "Now who's the residuary legatee? Meaning, next in line, if something happens to you."

"You, ma'am, and your spouse, Ms. Rodriguez," Hughley answered.

"No kidding," Rick smiled. "Don't let Annie poison me."

Mr. Collinson's turn came next. "I'm afraid your life won't be boring much longer," he said, opening his laptop. His voice was earnest as well. The screen began flashing charts, graphics and files, the kind that always made Rick's eyes glaze over. Math had never been a strength of his; when he managed to make his checkbook balance, he was surprised as much as pleased. If he did have good credit, like they said, it was because he was careful about spending and not letting his card balance go unpaid too long. (One of the boringly predictable things he and Claire disagreed on was impulse buying. She had – well, not made it clear; but by passive hints and sulks and overheard remarks, given him the strong intuition that she expected him to impulsively produce flowers and dinner reservations and Francesca's Ice Cream and tickets to the Durham Performing Arts Center, at frequent intervals. God help them both when she found out he was now Richie Rich.)

So: how rich was he? Please explain in as much simple English and as little Accountant-ish as possible. Mr. Collinson, looking even more earnest, stuttered a little, and Rick saw Ms. Pensmore hide a smile. The short answer was, that his new assets would be worth, approximately…and they gave a number.

"*Shit!*" Mom exclaimed, then put her hand to her mouth. Ms. Pensmore smiled at her. "Don't be embarrassed. I thought the same thing."

"Would be?" Rick asked.

Most of the financial assets, Collinson explained, were held in an assortment of trusts, which would come to Rick next year on his 30th birthday. This too had been at Baum's direction, again for reasons he hadn't chosen to give. There were Irrevocable Life Insurance Trusts and Legacy Trusts and Dynasty Trusts. There was a Charitable Lead Trust, the "Aurelia Foundation," whose yearly income was distributed in small contributions to a long list of progressive nonprofits around the country, but whose principal would also be Rick's at his 30th. There was a Qualified Personal Residence Trust, which held the actual title to Haw Court (though Rick could move in any time he wished), to keep it out of Baum's estate and thus safe from inheritance taxes. The assets themselves comprised all sorts of stocks, bonds, investment funds and holding companies, whose holdings had subsidiaries, which had subsidiaries and sub-subsidiaries of their own. "It's not as simple as Scrooge McDuck, where he just had a vault piled full of cash," Collinson said with an apologetic smile. And while his net worth did vary with the markets, it also increased every year, because Mr. Baum had put much of his income into automatic re-investment. He had taken only what he needed for his very modest living expenses.

"So besides us: who else knows about this?" Rick asked.

Black lawmakers oppose war because they want the money for food stamps

Ms. Pensmore took the question. "Only us, and the will's two witnesses, both of whom are on our staff. They've both been with us for years and are thoroughly trustworthy; and of course we have a very strong confidentiality agreement. In North Carolina the contents of wills are not made public until the estate is settled; meaning, not until you take full possession of all the assets."

"Thank God for that," Mom sighed.

"What did you tell people when they asked?" Rick wanted to know. "Like, from the media. They must have."

"We have been approached," Ms. Pensmore smiled. "We've told them the same thing: that we can't release any information until the estate's been settled. It was also part of Mr. Baum's instructions, that we not give out your name, and let you decide how to release the news."

"Thank God for that too," Mom said. "I think."

Their firm, Ms. Pensmore continued, was currently acting as administrators of the Estate; and, if he wished, would continue to do so, handling all necessary business without revealing his name. The income would continue to arrive in accounts at several different online banks, from which Baum had drawn for his modest needs, and from which Rick could electronically transfer into his existing account. Access to said accounts was a mere matter of handing over usernames, passwords, security questions and the like, once Pensmore Hughley had ascertained that he actually was himself (they'd asked him to bring driver's license, social security card and birth certificate). He could then set his own account as receiver for said direct deposits.

Documents were brought forth; explained, signed and notarized. Rick agreed to retain Pensmore Hughley Partners

L.L.C. as Administrators of the "Baum Estate," and of his legal needs thereby appertaining to, "until such time as the (hereinafter-referred-to-as) Client, with due and proper notice, chooses to terminate (etc.)" He agreed to continue with Collinson, Glenn & Associates for the Estate's accountings. He was shown property deeds and tax documents (county, state and Federal). There were contracts for security, maintenance, cleaning, groundskeeping, pool care; phone, cable and Net. There was an agreement with Duke Power: Haw Court had an up-to-date solar generation system, and on good days could sell to the utility instead of buy. Rick tried to make sure he got at least the basics of each thing he signed. When he started scribbling notes on the back of something they hastened to bring him a brand-new legal pad, and a golden pen whose ink flowed as smoothly as drawn butter.

They brought him copies of the signed documents, with the urging that he keep them in some secure place such as a safe-deposit box. (He didn't have one. He had a little office safe, hidden on the shelf in his bedroom closet, with not much in it: car title, lease, Social Security card; Baxter's adoption papers, and the will Mom had insisted he make when he turned 21.) They brought him a sturdy box holding the Court's keys, clinking faintly within like Jacob Marley's ghostly chains. They brought the list of usernames, passwords, access codes and security-question answers, printed on the same elegant paper as the original letter; and also loaded onto two brand-new flash drives. He could now come and go from Haw Court as he pleased. His hand was cramped from signing, in spite of the golden pen's ergonomic design. "You know – I never told anybody this; but I got to see it up close, once. Some friends and I were driving down to Pittsboro, and went by it. The caretaker recognized me as Aidan's brother, and let us in."

Pensmore's, Hughley's and Collinson's faces all went blank with astonishment. "There was no caretaker," Hughley said. "Can you describe this person?"

"He was an older guy; white-haired. Tall, thin; a little shabby-looking."

The three exchanged glances. "That was Mr. Baum himself," Collinson said.

Rick's turn to be astonished. "That was *him*? Damn! I thought he looked familiar."

"Had you seen Baum before?" Ms. Pensmore wondered.

"Just pictures of him in the news, after he died…"

"What did he say to you?" Hughley asked.

"Just – 'hey, aren't you Aidan Kingsley's brother?' He offered his sympathies, and said we could drive in and walk around the outside of the house. But that we couldn't tell anybody afterwards."

"Do you remember the date?"

"Not the exact date, no. It was about a month or two after Aidan left, so, early summer of 2013."

"Which would put it at, not long before he made this will," Mom speculated. "But he never said anything to you at all?" All three demurred. "And you didn't find anything in his papers or effects? – anything to do with Aidan, or Rick?"

"He didn't leave any personal papers," Hughley replied. "His personal effects were minimal. Clothes; household utensils and books; a few pieces of furniture. A computer, which we had examined by data retrieval specialists. There weren't any hidden files."

"But you searched the place; or had it inspected, right?" Rick asked. "As big as it is, they could've missed something."

"We did have it gone through. Although in fact, Baum never lived in the Court itself. He lived in the gatehouse."

Mom made a frustrated noise. "What was up with the guy? What was he thinking?"

"We've all asked ourselves that question," Mr. Collinson replied. "We don't have the answers either. I'm sorry; I wish we did."

*

In the elevator Mom said "You okay, kiddo? You're trembling."

He wanted to deny it but couldn't. "Can you blame me?"

They decided to have lunch at a fancy place on Fayetteville Street – "but I'm buying," Rick said. "Now that I can afford it." The hostess offered them a table, but Rick saw a booth in a shaded, empty corner and asked for it instead. The waiter took their orders and departed.

"You know what I'm most afraid of?" Mom said. "I'm worried you'll be so busy dealing with everything that's gonna come at you that you'll be miserable. You won't have any time for yourself; like for instance, to take Baxter and go for a run. Like these celebrities who can't walk out their front door without a mob of paparazzi chasing them."

"I don't think it'll be that bad. I hope it's not. People like Justin Bieber get that, not Bill Gates. And I'll keep everything low-key as much as I can. I won't try to be famous."

"You're going to see a lot of ugly human nature."

"Like I do at work every day?" he laughed.

"There you've got Duke Energy to back you up. If you can't deal with crazies you can pass them up to Angela. Pass them up the chain. But now you'll be the top of the chain. People are going to sue you just because you have money, total strangers out of nowhere. Because somewhere you own some shares of an appliance company, and they burned their finger on one of its stoves. Trust me, Bill Gates has lawyers whose sole job is to fend off nuisance suits like that. Oh shit! – or that kid you beat up who tried to rob you." (The boy had pled guilty, so there'd be no trial, only a sentencing. Rick was relieved. He did not want to testify; or have to see Claire testify and be re-traumatized by the memories.) "Now you're rich they might try it. And people who start turning up claiming they're Baum's long-lost relative or something, with forged wills."

"But now I've got lawyers too." He pointed upward in the general direction of Pensmore Hughley's offices. "And I can afford them."

The waiter appeared, respectfully demure with downcast eyes, and refreshed their water glasses. Rick paused. "What I'm not looking forward to is,…I'm going to have to say No to a *lot* of people. Family; and friends too. People like, someone I've known for years; that I'm cool with, that I care about. They come to me saying 'I've got this project, this dream, I've wanted all my life, all I need is the money'…But their idea is, like,…"

"Completely crazy?"

"No, no; it's…*almost* do-able, but not quite. Almost plausible. They think they've planned for all the drawbacks but they haven't, or not enough. Or they're the 'build it and they will come' kind of…believer. Eunice and 'leaps of faith' kind. It's going to be hard as fuck, for me to say No and see the hurt and disappointment, and *anger*, on their face."

She touched his hand. "It is hard, kiddo. It's the toughest thing in the world sometimes, to say no. And often the times it's hardest are when it's most important. For your own survival."

"It's because I hate hurting people. I still cringe over shitty things I did to people in middle school. Things I said to you when I was mad."

"Nothing I couldn't handle. I knew where you were coming from. And you had just as much right to be mad at me, as I did to do whatever it was that pissed you off."

Another waiter appeared, one hand upholding a loaded tray, the other clutching a foldout stand. She flipped it open with practiced ease, set down the tray and presented them with their plates. Mom pounced on her salad straightaway. Rick paused again until the waiter had gone. "And I hate to…disappoint people. The guy asks me but I shoot down his dream; and he says 'I thought you were my friend.' Like that, you know: more hurt than angry."

"God. Emotional blackmail. I'm telling you, it should be actionable as a form of abuse. What you oughta do is," – she pointed with her fork – "say, 'If you were *my* friend you wouldn't say something like that.' Call them on it."

"I know that's what you would do. But you've got all that experience from being in court. Standing up to judges and prosecutors, and cops; and all the times your clients still went to jail and you had to face them, and their families."

"It was tough. But you know what, a lot of the time they

were thankful that I did stand up for them, even if I failed. You have the right to stand up for yourself. They *don't* have the right to emotionally blackmail you. They don't have the right to piss you off. I do because I'm your mother" – a wicked grin – "but they don't."

He matched her with his own evil smile. "You, blackmail me. Yeah right."

"There ya go," she said firmly. Her fork pointed again, now with lettuce and feta impaled upon it. "You can stand up for yourself. You always could, from as soon as you were able to talk. You do, and you don't even realize it. Like here: the maître d' wanted to put us in one spot but you said 'No, I want that one.'"

He kept the smile. "I thought that was just White Male Privilege."

She raspberried him. "A lot of people – like Eunice, she'd be so intimidated in a place like this she'd let them put her anywhere."

"I don't know. She and Dad go to a lot of five, ten-thousand-dollar-a-plate fundraisers, in places a lot swankier."

"And who's telling her where to sit and what to say?...You've got more strength than you realize, honey. You can use it. I know you can. And, you know you'll always have us in your corner...You'll tell them, 'Yes, I *am* your friend; but I can't get behind your idea. Here are my reasons why; and here are the facts behind those reasons; and here are the accountants and lawyers and business consultants who gave me those facts.' Because naturally, when they first bring you the idea you'll say 'Let me talk to my accountants and lawyers and whoever.' Right? Now eat your soup before it gets cold."

Marriage in decline due to "horny immigrants and feminists who have sex like

"Or what? I don't get any dessert?"

"Ha! No – you're buying *both* of us dessert."

*

He'd taken the day off, not knowing how long becoming a super-billionaire would require. Should he tell Dad? The Legislature was in session, a short walk away. He'd have to get it over with sometime.

He'd never felt comfortable in Dad's office. There was always a crowd of people hovering round Dad like he was some kind of rock star, with him seeming to bask in it. He'd introduce Rick with risqué comments – "my Youthful Indiscretion" – to show that although he supported Family Values he wasn't going to hide the fact he'd had a kid out of wedlock (and as if implying Rick wasn't a full-grown man fully equipped to produce his own indiscretions). His staffers were always really youthful and wholesome-looking in a creepy, unwholesome, too-good-to-be-true, pod-person way, perky and annoying like little Young Republican chipmunks. He'd joke with visiting constituents about how he hoped to see the Social Services Building across Salisbury Street torn down before he left office, once he and his fellow Republicans had eliminated the Department of Social Services. (To far too many of Dad's supporters, "Social Services" meant Welfare, which meant taking the hard-earned money of good upstanding Christian citizens and giving it to lazy-ass welfare bums. The specific of "nigger," between "lazy-ass" and "welfare," was not left unspoken anywhere nearly enough.) There were photos of Dad buddying up to liberals' bogeymen like Jesse Helms and Newt Gingrich; and plenty of family pictures of Dad with Eunice, Lin and Aidan in prominent view, but only a couple of

men"...*Wall St. Journal* columnist: More progress occurred when "whites

Dad with Rick.

He phoned. Dad was "in committee," his secretary said, something to do with the Ag Department and "hog waste mitigation,". *Mitigating the waste, or the environmental regs against it?* Rick wondered. *Knowing Dad, probably the latter.* Grant County harbored a number of factory-scale pig farms. The pigs' shit and piss was corralled in man-made lagoons, because it was supposedly so toxic that to fall into one meant certain death. Some people naturally thought that keeping it out of the water table was a good idea, and wanted regulations requiring same. Many of the factory-farm businessmen just as naturally felt that such regulations were an unnecessary, unjust and unfair burden and a threat to their profits; and naturally turned for support to the kind of Republicans Dad had hitched his career to, who believed that environmental regulations of any kind, no matter how much they claimed to benefit public health, were part and parcel of an unnatural, un-American evil plot by treasonous "liberals" to bankrupt and oppress those same good upstanding Christian citizens. This in turn got the environmentalists, the ones who knew the science, knew the dangers, knew what they were talking about, so hopping mad they'd want to force the hog-industry magnates and their boughten politicians at gunpoint to drink hog-waste-poisoned water (oh, and fracking waste too), or even drown them in it. An Earth Firster he'd known at State had actually wished that, surprising him with her murderousness, since everything with her before had been about saving and protecting life. (Debbie Something – Deborah Vergara. They'd called her Debbie Vespa, because she rode one. He wondered where she was. The summer before he graduated she'd gone out to Burning

were still lynching blacks"...ALEC threatens lawsuits against groups calling it

Man and not been heard from since.) The kind of issue that'd get people like Mom, or Aidan, so mad they were spitting nickels and with steam coming out of their ears – though Mom would be the one doing the nickel-spitting and steaming. Aidan would be all in hysterical tears. But they'd both be coming from the same place: "How *dare* you not give a fuck that what you're doing is *hurting innocent* people? How DARE you make *your profits* more important than their *lives*?!" With Aidan sobbing in fury and despair, "How can you not *care*??" The key trigger for both of them was, *you have the power to do what's right, but you've* chosen *not to.* How much power would he himself have now, once all of Baum's investments became his?

Maybe he should go out to Haw Court and explore, now that he had full access; see what it looked like inside. Then again…it was an hour's drive or more; and the house, the whole estate, was empty. There'd be nobody to know if something happened to him, say for instance if Baum had been even more unstable than anyone knew and had left lethal booby-traps behind. The thought of that huge building with all its empty windows watching him, all those empty rooms with nothing but the sound and echoes of his own footfalls, made him uneasy. He could go home and give the apartment a good cleaning, since he hadn't done so for several months; although if he soon was going to move out to Haw Court, why bother? Yes; but *was* he going to live there? He'd need to in order to sustain his "caretaker" cover story. But he realized he'd miss living in Durham, in his neighborhood. He'd miss the activity; the presence of people all around, neighbors he'd not met but knew by everyday sight: walking with their kids in strollers and dogs on a leash, working in their gardens, coming home from work at Duke Hospital on their bikes. East Campus's running track, Ninth Street's stores, the fire station, the elementary school where he voted in elections. The plaintive horns of trains rumbling through, day and night, on the tracks paralleling Main Street. Maybe he could keep the apartment – shit, now he could afford to, in spades. Have his "Town House" and his "Country Estate," like some British nobleman...Maybe he'd just chill the rest of the afternoon; re-read some Lord Peter Wimsey, *The Nine Tailors* or *Thrones, Dominations. I could afford to buy autographed first editions, if I wanted to; to throw away all that money*...Lord Peter, as Dorothy L. Sayers had portrayed him, had a conscience about his inherited wealth and title; it was what drove him to solve crimes. He used his wealth and power to pursue justice, to right wrongs; to protect society on behalf of those who didn't have wealth and power (and impeccable valets like Bunter) to defend them...

*

"Did one of those teaching jobs come through?" Leslie asked, with some excitement. He'd given his notice that morning. They'd gone to lunch at Satisfactions in Brightleaf Square. "No. It's a weird situation."

"Now you've got me curious."

"Remember when we went to Haw Court, and the caretaker guy let us in? And he recognized me? He wasn't the caretaker. He was Baum himself. And...he left me the estate; and all – and everything."

If computers had human expressions, hers would have been that of one which had locked up from receiving data way beyond its processing power. "Why?" she finally said.

Christian, neither are his supporters...Wisc. GOP bans state officials from

The Reveal / 223

"I don't know. Nobody does. Not his lawyers – He didn't leave any explanations…He made the will a couple months after we met him, and we – me and the lawyers, we wondered if it was because he had some kind of sympathy for Aidan; but he never said so."

"Wow." Another pause. "What did you tell Angela?"

"I told her I'm going to be caretaker at the Court, working for the 'Baum Estate.' That's the story I'm going with, until I can figure out the best way to tell the truth. Mom and Annie know, but they're the only others, so far."

"What about Claire?"

He grimaced. "Yeah. I know I'll have to tell her too, but…I'm worried she might not be able to keep the secret. You know. She'll be so thrilled; she'll light up like a Christmas tree…"

"If you explain it clearly she should understand."

"But the other thing that worries me…" He wanted to choose his words carefully. He was uncomfortable telling Leslie possibly critical things about Claire. Besides being Claire's cousin, she, like Mom, seemed to hold him in good regard as an enlightened Male aware of Male Privilege and its abuse possibilities, but for the same reason held him to a high standard of behavior. "I'm afraid she'll want me to start living like a billionaire. Buying extravagant stuff and having huge parties. And I don't want to do that."

"I could see that," she agreed. She'd taken the ketchup and mustard squirters and was making little dollar signs on the plate: a ketchup "S" with mustard crossbars, then the reverse; then a ketchup "Euro" symbol. "But like I said: explain it. Be honest. Say 'this is what I want, and what I don't want.'"

"Which'd be a lot easier if I knew myself."

*

"I've got something important to tell you."

Claire looked worried right away, and hurt. *Uh-oh, she thinks I'm going to break up with her.* "It's good news, in a way. A totally weird way..." He explained. "...he left me Haw Court, and all his money. I've inherited it."

"Be serious. Don't freak me out."

"I am serious. I wouldn't make up something like this."

She tried to take it in. "Seriously? – you're not teasing me?"

"Seriously. I can show you the paperwork."

Seriously indeed. In all their two years he'd never had to tell her anything this serious. He'd seriously had no idea how she would react. He feared the unknown and un-deal-able-with. Would she have hysterics; faint; squeal with glee and then start making shopping lists? If she'd been a Victorian lady she could swoon; although once she was on the floor Baxter would start licking her face. He felt a breath of guilt at never having tried to have serious conversations with her. But she hadn't tried either. He wouldn't have shut her down if she had. He hoped it wasn't one of those things where she expected him to, but wouldn't tell him, but still thought he should do so anyway, instinctively. Where did that notion come from, that good boyfriends were mind-readers?...The closest they'd come to serious discussions was over Aidan, and about the Wizard's birth control.

"Oh my god...But; how did he know to give it to you?"

"I have no clue. The lawyers don't, either. Nobody does."

"Oh my god. This is so weird."

"Seriously."

"Are you going to live there?"

"Yeah; eventually, I suppose…You know it turns out Baum never really moved into the main house. He lived down at the gatehouse the whole time."

"Will you have servants?"

"Whoa, I haven't thought that far yet. I don't think I'll go full-on 'Downton Abbey;' but I'll have to have at least a cleaning service."

"You should. And guests. People around you. Or you'll turn into a hermit like he did." The thought clearly pained her.

"What I'll do first is get a concierge. That's what big estates have now, instead of butlers. Then he or she would work with me on figuring out what I need. Need or want. But that's in the future. For right now – And you understand, this is all way confidential."

"Ohmigod, yes. It'll be insane when everybody finds out."

"For now I'm telling people I'm going to be the Court's new caretaker. Next Wednesday's my last day at Duke Energy. Then I'll try to figure out how to make the announcement; and where I'm going to go after I make it. I'm walking on eggshells hoping nobody breaks the news before I'm ready…I told Mom, she went to the lawyers with me; and Annie naturally; Leslie; but that's all…"

"Leslie? Why?"

The question stopped him, with another faint breath of guilt. Was she jealous? "She's a good friend. She's sensible and sometimes I ask her for advice. Also she'd be really curious and ask all kinds of questions, like 'how did you find out about a job like that; aren't you going to still try for a teaching job?'…I'd have a hard time lying to her."

"I wish you'd told me first."

"Honestly: I had to work up the courage to. I didn't know how – I was afraid you'd – I was just afraid. This thing's got my thinking all screwed up."

"Don't you trust me?"

"I –"

"I'm not going to run around blabbing to everybody. It's too important. But see? It's already making you act weird. I don't want you to get like he was. Hiding from everybody and living all alone."

"He didn't have any family or friends to bring him out. I've got you; I've got Mom…I've got Baxter," he added, reaching to scratch him on the head. Baxter's rear half wriggled in delight. "I'm sorry I didn't tell you first. I should've…You want to come out with me this weekend? You can see it from the inside…"

She couldn't, because of work. She stayed the night, but they didn't fuck. She didn't suggest it, and he got the sense she was still hurt at his delay in telling her, so he didn't suggest it either. In the morning they talked of innocuous things.

*

Dad quickly eyeballed the documents, laying each one face down on his side of the desk. He and Rick were in the den of the Raleigh house. He drummed fingers on the desktop and stared into space. "I'll be damned. And they didn't tell you why?"

"They asked him, but he wouldn't say. He said he 'had his reasons,' and thought I'd make the best use of it."

"You never met the guy?"

"That's part of the weirdness. I actually did, but I didn't know it." He told of the visit to Haw Court.

"He offered you his 'sympathies.'" Dad said it sarcastically. "He could've offered a big chunk of money for the reward; but uh-uh, he just gives you a tour."

"I could. If it'd actually help." He was strangely reluctant to make the offer. It felt sordid.

"And why wouldn't it?"

The reluctance and sordidness hid themselves from easy explanation. "You'll get all kinds of sick greedy assholes trying to con you. Who don't care about...about anything but the money. Who don't even know where Aidan is, but just see dollar signs. Or possible fame. I know you're getting that already. I don't want to make it worse." *And because...because if someone who did know came forward, they'd be someone he'd met out there and maybe even trusted, who'd be selling him out because the price was high enough. And since it's my money, I'd be part of that betrayal. And;"* – this last thought was small, but feral – *"and because I don't like your politics or your meanness or the way you treated him, I don't want your hands on* my *money.*

"The SBI can handle it," Dad said. "It'd give them more to do than keep telling us they got 'no new leads.' And you know that soon as Eunice hears about this it'll be the first thing she asks you. You want to be the one to tell her no?"

"No sir."

"Me either...He never knew you; never met you but once," Dad mused, frowning. "Now who else knows?"

"The lawyers; the accountant; Mom and Annie. That's all."

The fingers ceased drumming, and the palm went flat against the desk. "Alright. Here's what we'll do. Soon as you leave here, go straight to Grantsville. Don't go home. Cal'l have somebody get your stuff. I'll tell Eunice to – no, better, go to Cousin Mason's, it's more private. Cal's in Greenville today, so he can be down there in a couple hours. He can start setting up a press release for Monday, and field interview requests."

"No, wait – I don't want to announce it right away. I may not have to at all. They said there's no law that it has to be made public."

"A will's a public document."

"Not until the estate's been settled and I've taken full possession."

"Which you have."

"So for now – and I asked them and they agreed – I'm going to say I got a job as caretaker for the Court, that I'm employed by the Baum Estate, which is a legal entity in its own right. It doesn't have to tell anyone that the 'Estate' is me."

"People don't need to be told, to put two and two together and bring the shitstorm down on you."

"I know there's liable to be a shitstorm. That's why I want to go slow, so I can think through the best place to face it from."

"And I'm tellin' you, you may not be able to. You have to hit it before it hits you."

"No, this is the way I want to do it. I'm not going into hiding like I'm a fugitive or something. I asked them, can I do it this way, and they said it'd work. I mean, they have to – I'm paying them to. To make it work. And they did it successfully with Baum for twenty years, so they must know what they're doing."

Dad raised his hands. "All right, all right; do it your own way. But if you don't want my help I don't know why you came to me at all."

"You need to know about this. I mean, you're my dad."

His father was stumped for half a moment. "Thought when you came in you were gonna tell me something like you got AIDS or knocked up some fourteen-year-old."

"Come on now. Fourteen? Not even. They've got to be college-age at least, so I can talk to them."

"You've got that much sense…Congratulations, by the way. Shoulda said that earlier."

"Thanks."

"I won't tell anybody until you give me the go-ahead."

"Including Eunice, and Lin?"

"Including them. Now I am going to tell Cal. I trust him, and he's never steered me wrong. When you do announce it it's going to affect me too, and we need to plan for it."

"That's fine."

"And if you do need to run, go straight to Grantsville. You don't even need to call."

*

Leslie laid on a going-away party Wednesday, complete with cake, at Bull McCabe's. After dinner they hit the Atomic Fern, then Fullsteam Brewery. She drove him home. As they passed the old McPherson Hospital, his phone burred. It was Mom, sounding urgent. "Rick – where are you?"

"Heading home, with Leslie. What's wrong?"

"Eunice –" She took the kind of deep breath she used when

trying to keep her temper from exploding. "She's outed you."

"What?"

"She's told the media about your inheritance. *And*, get this, she says you've promised to spend it all on getting Aidan back."

Investiture

He checks himself in the mirror, tugging at cuffs and collar. He's wearing his one good suit, and the silk Dolce & Gabbana tie Claire gave him for Valentine's Day, via her Macy's employee discount. The hotel manager will soon arrive, to escort him down in the service elevator and through the kitchens to the meeting room. "Doors at 8, press conference 9 to 12," he'd had his press release say. He hopes the reporters are eating themselves into a friendly mood at the breakfast buffet he'd had the hotel lay out. A decent spread, too: fresh hot biscuits, an omelet station, a selection of gourmet coffee and tea. He'd considered Bloody Marys and mimosas too; but decided that between professionalism and piss tests, few would want them.

Dad and Mom both had offered to join him, but he'd said No, I have to stand up to this myself. Mr. Hughley and Mr. Collinson would be on hand, though, for answers needing deep detail. "Billable hours" for both of them, of course; but that's how things worked on this new playing field he'd entered. He could hire lawyers and accountants by the hour. He could, in the short time between Thursday afternoon and Monday morning, summon up a conference room at the downtown Durham Marriott, complete with deluxe buffet; a press release, FAQ packets; a hotel room he could take incognito the night before, and the hotel manager as personal escort. When you were the Master of Haw Court you could pull off stuff like this.

*

"*What?!* No fucking way! How'd she even find out?"

"Don't ask me," Mom sighed. "You told your dad about

higher salaries: "They don't want to lose the free stuff from the government"...

Investiture / 232

it?"

"Yeah; but he said he wouldn't tell her until I gave him the go-ahead."

"Yeah well...Look, come over here instead and hide out, if you need to. They aren't ringing the doorbell. Yet. God, I'd like to wring her neck."

"If Dad and Cal don't beat you to it." He turned to Leslie, her face pale in the passing streetlights. "Eunice has ratted me out."

"I heard."

"Go by my place anyway; maybe it's still safe."

It wasn't. At Broad and Markham, they saw a strange bright glow against the night sky. It seemed to be emanating from somewhere behind the Fast Fare and the used bookstore; from somewhere on his street. They turned the corner. Iredell was clogged with TV news vans, their towers up; with klieg lights; with milling people. They were all gathered round his house.

"*Shit!*"

"Get down and cover your head," Leslie hissed.

He slouched down and pulled his jacket over himself. Patterns of blackness and blazing light filtered through the fabric as the car rolled forward. He heard gabbling voices, buzzing generators, police sirens approaching from somewhere, a frantic dog barking. It might not work. They might see him, and pounce. He was tense as a steel wire; as tense as on the night he and Claire almost got robbed, the night he'd used the Wizard's boundary. The poor dog kept barking, barking, its voice near to breaking in hysteria.

(*The bullets slowed, flattened, hung motionless as if*

suspended...)

Baxter was the dog barking.

"Stop!"

The car rolled to a halt. He looked out from under his jacket. They'd crossed Green Street, leaving the chaos of people and lights behind them. "I gotta get Baxter. He's losing his shit."

"Are you nuts??"

"I'll use the Wizard's barrier."

"The *what*?" But he was already out of the car.

He envisioned the barrier around him: an invisible bubble, enclosing calm and quiet. Would it work here? He was trembling. But nobody recognized him; they didn't even seem to notice him. He slipped through the knots of people as if he were invisible. Reporters talked earnestly to the cameras, clutching their mics; talking about him, probably, but their voices were an indistinct blur of sound. They didn't spot him until he crossed the lawn to his front steps, half a dozen iterations of his shadow looming up before him in the blazing white lights. His neighbors in the duplex – the Govindas, a young couple, grad students, recently arrived from Pakistan – were cowering on their porch.

He stepped up, turned, faced the crowd. Their excitement skyrocketed. Cameras flashed, voices shouted. "*Mr. Kingsley! Mr. Kingsley!* –" They were about to surge forward at him. He imagined the barrier expanding outward, enclosing his house, keeping them at bay.

They stopped.

They shifted back.

Fuck, it *was* working!

He'd spread his arms without thinking. Now he raised

them for quiet. He used his best front-of-the-classroom voice. "I don't have anything to say right now. I'll let you know when I do. Now please go home – you're scaring my neighbors." Amidst their staring faces he glimpsed Leslie, watching him in astonishment.

He slipped inside, double-locked the door, drew all the blinds, hurried to the back and let Baxter in, locking that door as well. Baxter jumped up and slobbered on him, nearly beside himself with distress. He sat on the bed and held Baxter to calm him; and to calm his own nerves too. "Buddy, The Shit has hit The Fan."

The Wizard's barrier *worked.* He could sense it at the edge of his thoughts, steady and reassuring, a sort of mental white noise. Turning it off would be a simple matter of thinking so…or would it? When he wondered about doing so he got a detailed image, almost as if it was warning him, of the crowd outside. They were dwindling, the media people turning off their lights and packing up their vans one by one; but they were still there. The police had now arrived. They might want to talk to him. Would the barrier let them through? Did he want it to let them through, it seemed to query in reply, not in words but in the thoughts themselves, flashing quicker and cleaner than words could frame them. Well, sure, cops shouldn't be a problem (unless of course you were a young black guy). He imaged a couple of policemen crossing his lawn.

There were steps on the porch. Someone knocked. "Durham police…Everything all right in there?"

He stifled Baxter from barking and held his collar; peered out between the blinds (yes, it was a pair of cops); turned on the living room light and let them in. He explained, briefly, who he was and why the media was after him. No, he didn't think he needed protection; though thanks for the offer.

He called Leslie, then Mom, to reassure them. Claire didn't even know what had happened; she'd had to work late and miss the party. Once informed, she got all worried, and it took nearly ten minutes of repeated assurances to calm her down. When he tried to call Dad he got patched over to Cal Boulware instead, who explained that Dad was at a meeting in Edenton, and would be back in the morning. Mr. Boulware already knew, as video of Rick's front-porch dismissal had gone viral almost instantly. "You handled that quite well."

"I had some help from the Wizard."

"The *Wizard*?? How?"

"I used his barrier to keep them off."

Boulware was full of questions, but Rick was tired and put him off. He passed out almost as soon as he hit the bed. The Wizard's barrier shimmered along the edges of his dreams as he slipped into sleep.

*

The barrier was still there, discreet at the edge of his thoughts, when he woke up. A look through the front blinds showed the street quiet in the sunshine; but there seemed to be more parked cars than usual, some occupied. And was that movement he saw behind the back yard hedge, when he let Baxter out? But Baxter didn't start his "stranger" bark.

He online-searched himself while coffee brewed. There he was on the front porch telling them to go away, looking small and vulnerable in the blazing light, like something nocturnal dragged

of another Civil War; calls for mass right-wing civil disobedience to Supreme

out into the open. There too was Eunice, in the living room of the Raleigh house. "Mr. Baum gave it to Rick in compassion for what we've suffered. And Rick has promised that he'll give every penny of it to anyone who brings Aidan back to us." He wanted to reach right through the screen and shake her until her teeth rattled. Was there any way the barrier could have thwarted her?

He packed some clothes and Baxter into the car, surrounding themselves with the barrier. None of the watchers in the cars seemed to notice, and nobody pounced. He drove straight to Raleigh, met Dad at the house. They confronted Eunice. "How'd you find out about this?" Dad demanded.

She put on a look and body language of stubborn martyrdom. "I overheard you and Cal. You said something about Aidan. So I listened at the door."

"Now Eunice, you know there's some things that are my business and my business alone. If I don't tell you it's because I have good reason."

"I had to. You were talking about Aidan. I had to know. *Nothing* is more important than bringing Aidan back. I prayed and prayed over it, and I know it's what I need to do."

"What you need to do is not tell everybody my business," Rick answered. "And not go spending my money behind my back."

"But you don't need it! You'll never need it; we'll never let you want for anything. We'll always take care of you, you know that."

"It may not even be practical. There's taxes, and the house itself. Let the SBI decide. They're the professionals."

"*But they're not his mother*! They don't care. It's just a

case to them. They don't care what I'm feeling. They don't care if he's alive or dead. To them he's just a statistic." The tears were starting. "If I was your mother, you know I'd spend every penny I ever had to get you back. I wouldn't care if I was begging on the street, as long as I had you home safe!"

"They do take it seriously, babe," Dad said. "It's just as important to them. They maintain a detachment because they're professionals, like he said."

"Then why haven't they found him? With all your money, *surely* somebody would do something."

"Somebody greedy and vicious, who really didn't care about Aidan, or you, or anything."

"I wouldn't care what they were, I just want him back."

"He doesn't want to come back." Rick realized as he spoke that this idea had been growing in his mind for some time, only now reaching coherence. "Every picture he's sent, he looks totally safe, and totally happy. He's always smiling. He looks like he's having the best time ever. He's the happiest in those pictures that I've ever seen him, and I've known him his whole life. You can't fake that kind of happy. Remember what he said when he left? That he wasn't going to come back until he felt ready."

"It doesn't *matter* what he wants! *I have to know he's safe!*"

"The pictures –"

"They're faked! They have to be! He *can't* be happy! He'd *never* do this to me! Who's taking those pictures is *forcing* him to *pretend* he's happy, to keep him from me!...And you won't pay a *penny* to catch them?" She sagged into a chair. "Is this how that so-called 'mother' of yours taught you, to be hard and cruel, and *selfish*?'"

"Eunice, that's enough," Dad warned.

Rick spoke simultaneously. "*Out of bounds*, Eunice. Mom taught me to be honest and stand my ground. What if you did force him back, and he didn't want to? He'd just run away again. Unless you locked him up –"

"Is your money more important than your own brother's life?"

"*He's not in danger!* He's *fine!* The pictures show it!"

"*I'm* not fine! And I won't be until he's back, and I can see for myself. And I don't care about your money. You're a member of this family – we didn't have to take you in but we did – and as part of this family it's your *duty* to do everything you can to save him."

"Goddammit, it's *your* duty to not tell *lies* about me!"

"It'll only be a lie if you make it a lie. If you want to go out there and tell them you're not going to help, if you want to show the world you're the *cruelest, meanest* man that ever lived, who'd deliberately keep a mother from her baby –"

"Dammit, *you're* a big fucking reason he *left*! You treated *him* like this, going holier-than-thou on him instead of fucking *listening* to him and having some compassion for what he was going through. He ran away from *you* as much as those bullies!"

"I won't listen to a word –"

"And don't give me that 'Oh, we're so holy' bullshit about taking me in. I didn't *need* you to –"

"Then go, then. Go back to your, your – that –"

"My lesbian feminist Democrat *real* mother, who raised me just fine and I didn't *need* to be rescued from? Tough shit; you're stuck with me. Because you blabbed to every damn body about my inheritance, you're stuck with me, until I figure out how to fix this fucking clusterfuck you caused, because you won't face the *fact* that Aidan doesn't *want* to come back until he's damn good and ready!"

She fled the room in tears. "Shit." Rick told Dad. "I hope she doesn't take this out on you."

Dad sighed. "It's gonna be what it's gonna be. If it wasn't you it'd be something else... Something I never told you. Never told a lot of people, and I want it kept that way. All right?"

Rick nodded.

"Round the time Aidan got his hematoma – she had a miscarriage. Bad one. She had to spend a week in the hospital...Afterwards her grandmama and aunts all told her, if she tried to have another baby it'd kill her. The doctor said no but she believed them...She always wanted a daughter, after the two boys... Addelie'd just retired, and Lin was being a little shit, talking back every chance he got; and then there was all that screaming and fighting when we had to change Aidan...That was your first year here, so maybe you don't remember."

"I remember her being all worried because with Addelie gone, she had to learn to cook. But she got pretty good at it."

"Better than Addelie, to tell you the truth. I was surprised... You know Mason was saying the same thing the other day – about Aidan not wanting to come back."

"It's this really strong hunch I've got."

"But however bad he felt, he still shoulda manned up and come told us, instead of putting us through this."

"He couldn't because he couldn't. It wasn't who he is.

Everybody deals with serious shit differently."

"That's what you would've done."

There was a subtle compliment in the phrase. Rick blinked. "Maybe. I hope so. And it'd depend, maybe, on if I'd grown up with you. Maybe he was scared of you."

Dad looked at him speculatively. "Are you?"

"Ehhh –" Rick wavered a hand. "I'm…wary of you."

"But you don't hate me."

"I hate your politics. I keep hoping you're better than that, that your constituents are forcing you to so you don't get primaried. But you – and her; no. I've got no ill will towards either of you."

Dad toyed with a pen. "Sometimes I think you're the only one of my kids who's got any sense."

*

There's a podium with a microphone, but he stands next to it instead of hiding behind it. TV cameras and lights are ranked across the back wall. The buffet has been well-plundered. "Good morning, everybody. I'm Rick Kingsley. You all got the handouts? They outline what the estate's comprised of, and also a list of FAQs. Questions *I* asked when this first happened. Now I want you all to get a turn, and if we keep it moving we'll all get out of here in time to make your deadlines. Okay. Last row, first person on the – on my right." His plans for a teaching career may have wandered off track, but this shouldn't be too unlike leading a classroom.

*

He'd had occasional fantasies of being ridiculously rich. Hadn't everyone? If he won the lottery, for instance, even though

to gain foothold in Texas town...*National Review*: Bernie Sanders a "Nazi,"

he never bought a ticket. (Mom and Leslie never did either. Claire sometimes would, if the payout had gotten up really high and she was feeling optimistic after a few drinks. Annie bought one ticket a month, even though she'd be the first to tell you that you were more likely to get struck by lightning than win. Rick asked why, then? She hemmed and hawed and looked embarrassed, and finally admitted that she couldn't really explain. It was a habit she'd gotten into long ago; it was a kind of superstition, kind of an ass-backward good luck charm.)

Fantasies like, being in a James Bond adventure. He'd be at the sort of lavish black-tie party where Bond and his martini tended to hang, when a flock of the Bad Guy's minions try to take Bond out. Bond clobbers them with his usual *savoir-faire*. Richie-Rick keeps calm, and maybe even clobbers a couple minions himself. (Which Bond? Oh, Roger Moore. The others were all too serious. Moore played him with a twinkle in his eye, like he knew that if you dug down past the camp, past Q's gadgets and the beautiful but sometimes lethal babes, you'd find foundations resting on a bedrock of Silliness. I mean, come on: remember Ian Fleming also wrote *Chitty Chitty Bang Bang*.) Or he's in his private jet at an airport, sees Bond pursued by more minions, rescues him and offers a lift. Telling his pilot, "This is Mr. Bond, he works for MI6. He needs to be in," let's say, "Mogadishu, ASAP." Then again…the minions would know Bond is trying to get to Mogadishu. If a plane suddenly changes plans and heads that way, they might have suspicions; along with surface-to-air missiles. Maybe take him elsewhere, some innocuous European capital. "I'll be a little late getting home; I'm stopping in Istanbul for Turkish coffee."

(Even if he did get ridiculous rich, though, he couldn't see himself shelling out all that money for a private jet. Business class, or even high-end coach, was good enough for him.)

Or, he's become owner of a pro basketball team. At his first press conference they ask "Will you hire gay players?" (This was around the time Michael Sam got drafted by the Rams.) "If I do," (he'd answer) "it'll be because they're good players, not because they're gay. Finding and hiring good players is Mr. A's" (the head coach) – "Mr. A's department. I'm not gonna interfere. We may already have some gay players, who've kept quiet about it."

One player voices his doubts about gay teammates. He appears in Rick's mind as a hulking black man, with dreadlocks and a deep voice, and a hard life in the projects as his backstory. He meanders about feeling comfortable in the locker room and being able to trash-talk after a tough game and divisiveness instead of team unity. "On any team," Rick answers, "there'll be people you connect with, and people you don't connect with. But because you're a team, you learn how to work around that, and how to work with them anyway, to get the job done. If someday we do get a gay player – or like I said, if one we have already comes out – I'll expect you to learn to work with him to keep playing your best game, which is what matters."

There's a tragedy. The young brother of a team member, perhaps the dreadlocks guy, is shot by the police, in controversial circumstances. Rick flies to the city (high-end coach) and attends the funeral, sitting with the team. Afterwards if people call him "reverse racist" or "enemy of the police" or shit like that, he says "A man who works for me has lost his brother. I came to show my sympathy. Where's the problem?"

Another idea: he holds a stake in a new building in, just for example, Evansville, Indiana. Storefronts at street level and condos above, in a neighborhood that everyone expected would gentrify but didn't, due to the recession. Evansville's market for deluxe condos and Class A Retail Space was saturated. Only a few units were sold, to people who didn't even live there but just kept them for rental income. Most of the building was still sitting empty. Hercule Poirot had lived in a place called Whitehaven Mansions; well, this was White Elephant Mansions.

It didn't have to be, though. The high-end housing market might be full; but if Evansville was anything like the Triangle, the market for apartments affordable by, for instance, Macy's salesclerks, tow-truck-driving teen single dads, and Duke Energy customer-service reps, was going begging. Not even to mention the homeless, and single moms trying to get their families out of the shelters. So, buy out the other investors. They probably didn't care about the building itself; to them it's just a lever they'd hoped would tilt a flow of money into their laps. Make sure all the contractors get properly paid, particularly the construction workers at the bottom of the pile, since they're the ones who might be living out of their cars otherwise.

Then he goes to Evansville and says to whoever's in charge of the main shelter, "Look, I've got 150 apartments here and want to put them at your disposal." He'd charge rent, but not a fixed amount: it'd be a percentage of the person's income, whatever percentage was considered reasonable and fair by the kind of progressive experts who did such accountings. X per cent of whatever they made, even at part-time minimum wage, so they'd

candidate Rick Perry: Americans should carry the guns they are "legally

have Y and Z percent left over to feed the kids and pay utilities. Or would he bundle utilities in with the rent? And hope nobody left the water running or set up a pirate server farm in the living room. Basic cable; if they wanted premiere channels it'd be extra. And Internet – you couldn't not be online and look for work. Cable, Internet and phone: bundle it all; with 150 units, plus the shelter people putting public-relations pressure, maybe they could arm-twist Charter Communications into a good discount. Oh; and rent the storefronts on a similar fair-pay basis to small start-up businesses, mom-&-pop places, like Claire's aromatherapy shop.

And maybe some Tea Party type would get enraged about "giving away free apartments to People Like That" – which everybody knew was their dog-whistle code for "Lazy Niggers." Put a private detective on the guy, with one of those micro-cameras Aidan had used, and see if they could catch him actually saying "Lazy N-Word." Once *that* went viral, that asshole'd be wiped off the face of the earth. And Claire could dress up and do the Good Fairy bit from *Wizard of Oz* on him. "Away with you; you have no power here."

Dreams of glory, dreams of fame…Well, now he *was* ridiculous rich, in the real world. One good thing about daydreams was that they *were* dreams. They were like your own private Narnia, when you needed a vacation from reality. In daydreams everything ran smoothly. Then after you'd rested your mind a while, you came back to reality and all its complexities, grabbed a cup of coffee and went back to work.

Thinking through what he did and didn't want himself invested in was easy in principle, well-raised liberal boy that he was. No sweatshops; no arms manufacturers, regardless of who their customers were, not even if their dividends included his own personal Iron Man suit. It wasn't the manufacturers, though, so much as the black-market dealers who provided terrorists with weapons. No arms traders, dealers or facilitators, then, of any kind. And no banks, either, who handled terrorists' money: he'd read someplace that ISIS was funding itself by selling oil from its captured territories. Or if the banks took deposits from dictators like Mugabe, deposits from their plundering of their countries, living like kings while their people starved – or turned to terrorism in their despair and rage. Those banks were just as morally responsible for that suffering as the dictators themselves: they were enablers. Speaking of oil, there were companies like Shell, with an ugly reputation for colluding with murderous regimes in places like Nigeria: innocent people butchered, and survivors forced to exist in environments poisoned beyond repair by the side effects of oil drilling. (A hundred years ago it was King Leopold and rubber in the Belgian Congo; now it was Shell with oil in Nigeria. The things that should change, never did.) Then, of course, those same oil companies took all that bloody profit and fed it to the politicians, lobbyists and paid pseudo-"scientists" who conspired to deny the proven truth of global warming and sabotage attempts towards renewable energy. (Hadn't they said that Haw Court was 100% solar-powered? Maybe Baum had already done the right thing in terms of his energy investments.)

So, what else? Minimum wage. All his companies would start base pay at $15 per hour. With 40-hour weeks, regular scheduling, benefits, full cooperation with Obamacare; not like that asshole pizza magnate – was he Jimmy John's or Papa John's? – pitching shit fits because giving his employees health care would make him have to raise his prices by ten cents. No cutting corners, either, no using temps or shortening hours to escape having to pay benefits. Claire was always worrying that Macy's would cut back her hours. Her rent took half her paycheck, for a tiny apartment in a complex whose buildings were no sturdier than chickenhouses. She got nervous any time there was a tornado watch. No; anybody who worked for him was going to get paid decent wages.

What else? "Diversity," naturally. Equal treatment for everybody regardless of gender or sexuality. Who and how his employees fucked was none of his business; unless of course it was children or goats or something. And of course, gender parity. Equal pay for women and men. Mom and Annie both would rip him a new one if he didn't put that in.

He had the feeling that Baum had been a "savant" about all this financial stuff, the kind of mind that had an intuitive, rather than an intellectual, comprehension of something. He himself didn't, which left him kind of screwed. "Rich and powerful," went the phrase; but the former didn't necessarily confer the latter…

*

It's on the FAQs but they ask him anyway: when, where, how and why did he become Baum's heir? "I don't know, and don't think I ever will." Would he use the whole fortune to find Aidan, as Mrs. Kingsley claimed? Why had his father retracted that claim?

Diplomatic reply needed. He's still pissed at Eunice but isn't going to trash her publicly. "I think she misinterpreted things I said about the inheritance. She's totally focused on finding him. Naturally. Of course I'm willing to spend what I can, in any way the SBI thinks will work."

Do you think he's still alive?

"Yes. You know he keeps sending pictures of himself every couple months. He always looks healthy and happy."

You've seen his video. Do you think he had reason to run away?

More diplomacy required. "I can sympathize with him feeling like he did. But no, I don't. There's other people, other relatives, he could've asked. Like me and my mom."

Did your father treat you like he treats Aidan?

Not exactly friendly. A little Philly creeps into Rick's voice. "No. But I was raised by my mom, and didn't start seeing him regularly until I was fifteen. But I have no complaints about how he's treated me, then or now."

You're a registered Democrat, but your father's a Tea Party Republican. Will you support his campaigns? What are your opinions on his policies?

"I don't agree with them. He knows that." (Now how did they find out his registration?) "But we respect each other's political...space, boundaries; whatever. We don't talk about it. I don't plan to donate to any campaigns. It's a gamble. The Koch brothers threw millions against Obama and he still won. I want to do things I know will work."

*

He'd had a dream, though he couldn't remember when, of the Wizard being interviewed by Rachel Maddow. Again, looking like Frank Morgan: white-haired, though not quite elderly yet; mobile facial features, full of lively expressions; a bit dithery at times, but cheerful and endearing. A tendency to grandiose bluster, but blustered with a twinkle in his eye, showing that he

...Trump's immigration plan: Overturn the 14th Amendment, round up

didn't – and that he knew you didn't – take himself too seriously. They were talking politics. "Ever since the Second World War," he was saying, "the Republicans have…de-evolved, as it were. Before the Thirties, their party could still be proud of having Lincoln in their political bloodlines. But since then…They've made themselves the unrepentant champions of everything sick and evil in America's soul. Racism, sexism, homophobia; war lust, gun worship; religious extremism – not Christian, mind you, not at all, no matter that they call it such; it's no more true Christianity than ISIS – or ISIL, or whatever they're calling themselves this week, is true Islam. Religious *fascism*: anti-abortion terrorism, psychotic greed, ruthless ecological genocide, pathological denial of *proven* facts and science; *deliberately* heartless *cruelty* towards the poor…" Ms. Maddow's queries didn't seem to be spoken at all; they came as thoughts in Rick's perception. "And voter suppression – oh dear me, don't get me started. Voting is the very lifeblood of democracy; and any legislator who works to hinder or prevent American citizens from voting is a traitor and should be shot."

Ms. Maddow looked concerned. Her query wondered, *meaning / encouraging assassination?* "Oh my goodness, no. They should be arrested, tried and convicted, by due process of law. Then we can shoot them," he twinkles.

…violence / revolution / innocent bystanders…?

"Oh yes; I know how badly wrong that can go…It has the same kind of vigorous macho appeal that ISIS has for troubled young men. The vision that 'if we kill enough of the right people, the world will at last be perfect.'…Have you ever seen *Ninotchka*? Greta Garbo as a Soviet commissar, in Paris checking up on some comrades. They ask her, 'How did the show trials go?' She replies, 'Very well. There will be fewer but better Russians.'" He chuckles; then grows serious again. "It's the same sort of...passion, that lead the likes of Timothy McVeigh to commit their terrorisms."

*

Because of billionaires like the Koch brothers – and politicians like your father – our country's at a critical tipping point. Civil rights, workers' rights, human rights; environmental protections; free speech, freedom to vote, are all under attack. Do you feel any obligation to use your wealth to fight this?

That "any" definitely has a hostile edge. "Don't worry, I'm going to. Baum already started: you've got a list in there of like, four dozen organizations his 'Aurelia Foundation' already donates to. And when I get full control of the assets next fall, I'll be able to do more."

What created and drives his "values," they ask; what are his spiritual or religious views? "It's how I was brought up. Mom's a progressive activist, and worked the Public Defender's office back in Philadelphia. We've seen firsthand how injustice and inequality, and prejudice, can wreck peoples' lives. And then there's all my friends and people I know, a lot of whom are living paycheck to paycheck, if they can even find a job. Religious beliefs? I don't have any to speak of. I accept whatever's good in any of them...Abuse of power is wrong, and anything that needlessly hurts people."

*

(In that dream – or was it another? – the Wizard's own spirituality was queried. In answer, the scene changed to an old

for brutal attack on homeless Hispanic man...FOX News: Black Lives Matter

1930s cartoon. A country church, swaying to the rhythm of the music within, its bell swinging gaily in the steeple and musical notes floating out to take wing in the sky. The congregation inside was all of the famous cartoon characters. Together they sang old simple hymns; and as they sang they were so moved they began to weep with joy, and the tears they wept were so copious that soon the whole scene was flooded and everything afloat: pews and pulpit and puffing, tootling organ; a white-robed choir of church mice harmonizing atop a bobbing hymnal; until Noah came steaming along in his Ark to take them all aboard: an Ark the size of a cruise ship, with room enough even for dragons and unicorns. "Yes, it's kind of cornball," the Wizard said; "but…it is what it is.")

*

Do you believe in the Wizard?

Blindsided. Oh boy. "The Wizard?…I've heard the rumors…I guess I believe in the possibility of him; but, like, in the way I believe in the possibility of Bigfoot or parallel universes. Like, it'd be great if it was true, but I'm not going to bet on it. Why do you ask? I mean, how does that connect with my inheritance?"

Because if he does exist and has the powers he claims, would you use your assets to find him and stop him?

"Well, like with Aidan, I'd put up money if I was convinced it'd help. I wouldn't write checks to every person who came along claiming they had some foolproof scheme to catch him. I'd be flat broke before I knew it. But I've got this hunch money wouldn't help. We're talking about somebody who only turns up in dreams. And who might not even exist in the first place."

There are claims that the Wizard also has a barrier against physical attack. You were the victim of an attempted robbery last year. Your attacker shot at you several times, at point-blank range, but you were unharmed. Did you use that barrier?

"I don't know. I'd heard about it too; and it crossed my mind at the time – along with a lot of other things, like, 'Oh shit, this guy's trying to kill us!' But was it the Wizard? – and again, I'm still not convinced he exists. I do know I'm glad as fuck we're still alive."

Would you, or have you, used this barrier to keep the press away from you?

"Wait, can it even do that?" Yes it could, he was sure; but he didn't want to admit it. "But if it did: can you blame me? When the story broke you totally Benghazi'd my house. If I hadn't – if the cops hadn't come you'd have been pounding on my door all night long. My dog was completely freaking out."

Do public figures like yourself have the right to barrier yourselves against the media? You realize it could be a weapon against freedom of the press. Politicians who don't want to face their constituents, or who are under investigation?

Wait, wasn't this the same guy who'd asked him about the Kochs? No, he was still over there by the News 14 Carolina crew. "Again; again; you're assuming all kinds of powers to something that doesn't – that we don't know is even real. Maybe I am a public figure – and I'm going to be as little of one as possible – but I'm also still a person, with the right to privacy in my own space…And you know: Baum didn't bequeath me the Wizard. They've got nothing to do with each other. He left me his estate, which is what we're here to talk about. Next?"

*

The dream had shifted to the old *Tonight Show*, the Wizard seated at Johnny Carson's right hand, Ed McMahon a jovial aura off to the left. Why, with all his magical powers, did he not want to be famous, Carson wondered. "Well, as a child I used to fantasize about being here," the Wizard joked, "but you retired before I got the chance." Carson made one of his wry, bemused expressions, and the invisible audience chuckled. "But in all seriousness..." – and a scene appeared, of the death of Princess Diana, the media pursuing her like a buzzing plague of monstrous wasps with deadly poison in their stingers.

*

How do you see your lifestyle changing, now that you are a public figure?

"As little as possible. I never wanted to be famous. I plan to keep as low a profile as I can."

With your inheritance, are there still things you want to do but can't?

"I can't change human nature. None of us can." He indicates them all, gathered before him. "I can't stop people from making stupid decisions or hating each other, or hurting each other."

*

Another of Aidan's photos arrived the following week. He was swimming in a mountain pool fed by a waterfall. There were towels and rustic furniture. The surrounding trees looked like those found in Pacific Northwest rainforests; but the postmark said "Athens, Ohio." This time there was a note on the back, in

Scott Walker fires 57 environmental employees on Earth Day...Thousands of

Aidan's handwriting.

Leave Rick out of this. All the money in the world won't bring me back until I'm ready.

*

They are bullies. This is how we deal with bullies.

The dream faded, becoming misty. "It'll be an interesting sociological experiment," the Wizard was saying, to Oprah or Jon Stewart or the women of *The View*, "to see what the bullies do when there's no longer anyone they can bully."

walruses forced ashore by melting Arctic sea ice; earliest haul-out on record...

Lush Life

Mid-September, 2016. He wakes around 8:30, as usual. The view outside predicts another hazy, hot day. The AC system will get a workout, even with the eight big attic fans pulling cool air up from the cellars; and even though the Court seems to have its own microclimate, always feeling a few degrees cooler when he drives through the gates.

He gets up quietly, so as not to disturb Claire. Pulls a towel off the rack and, in just his boxers and with Baxter trotting alongside, goes out through the screen porch to the pool.

By the pavilion, he drops the shorts. He's got morning wood, half-erect. (Claire was too tired last night, and most mornings is too sleepy.) He could beat one out here by the pool if he wanted; or into the pool, or even in the pool. It's his pool, after all, with professionals on call to regularly clean it. *Droit du seigneur* and all that. Still, though: *ick.* The pavilion blocked only a small part of the pool from the house's rear windows. If David was up and about and saw him doing the nasty…well, David's so Professional that just talking to him made your asshole tighten up; he wouldn't say anything, but you'd see behind those designer glasses a look hinting that he was filling in his dossier on you. *If I ever write my memoirs…* it hints.

He dives in, swims his usual laps. The shock of the water lowers his woody back to normal. (If he feels like a run, or the weather's too cool for the pool, he'll run the drive to the crest of the hill and back. If it's raining he'll do a circuit of the corridors and stairs.) He climbs out behind the pavilion's shelter, dries off; wraps the towel round himself and heads back inside. In passing he tosses his shorts on Baxter's back. Baxter spins round and round, trying to see what landed on him.

Claire stirs, stretches. "You want breakfast?" Rick asks. She nods, with a sleepy smile. Chris will also be up, working in the big basement kitchen, proud in his harlequin-check chef pants and white coat, hair tied back in a samurai knot. He'll fix breakfast for anyone who's awake and hungry. Rick takes up the house phone. "Hey Chris. What you got this morning?"

"Another experiment, if you're feeling adventurous."

"Oh lord. What's in it this time?"

One of Chris's specialties is breakfast soufflés, which Rick's happy to let him experiment with, trying new ingredients: maple sugar (bad idea); Spam (edible but peculiar); Cuban ham with shavings of green chile (awesome). Back when he worked for Amtrak, he'd asked if he could put his soufflés on the dining car menu, but the proposal got lost in the jungles of Amtrak's upper bureaucracy and presumably perished there, for it was never heard from again. "Very mild goat cheese," his voice now answers, "minced fresh collards, crumbled bacon; and I don't know, *maybe* a little teaspoon of Southern Comfort, for that kind of glow-y taste?"

Rick laughs, tells Claire. "We'll risk it. And biscuits."

"And biscuits. The usual orange juice, and coffee?"

"Yes please; both." Soon, even before he's finished shaving, he'll hear the "ping!" from the other end of his suite, announcing that breakfast is coming up on the dumbwaiter. After eating, check the Net, brush teeth, get dressed (including fresh boxers; the least the Master of Haw Court could do was buy enough underwear for a clean pair every day). See if David or

Chris have any issues needing his decision. Then down to the "home farm," to talk greenhouse plans with the Germains. From there to Durham, for his weekly office time with Sarah. Dinner afterwards with Claire and her business partner Andy. She'll have come from a meeting with Duke Hospital boffins, seeking to get her aromatherapy store, "Aromamora," on their approved list of outside consultants. (The meeting's outcome may have influence on whether he Gets Some tonight. It's not a crucial need, though.) And after that, finally, Walltown, and the relief and release of b-ball with the guys.

*

He'd never had so much on his plate as he did that previous May. He needed a staff. He needed a plan of operation. He needed a book like *Stately Home Management for Dummies*, but the Durham County Library didn't have one. He needed a fuck-ton of furniture, as his own would barely fill the "master suite." (A nice suite it was, too: bedroom, study and private sitting / dining room, all with fireplaces; spacious bathroom complete with tub, shower and bidet; equally spacious closets; a private screen porch off bedroom and bath; the whole opening out onto the back lawn.) He'd make day visits to the Court, walking around inside and trying to acclimatize himself to it, with all its rooms and corridors and stairs.

There at least he didn't have to worry whether or not he'd left the Wizard's barrier on. In the outside world he kept it going 24-7, feeling when he didn't that people were starting to point, whisper, and converge on him like lions towards a wildebeest. He'd alternate randomly between staying at his own place, at Mom's, at Claire's, not knowing from day to day which would feel

to form militias..."Patriotic" treason: Poll reveals many Republicans favorable

safest that night; like a homeless guy with paranoia issues. When David said in his interview, "My job would be to leave you with as few things to worry about as possible," Rick was sold, listening to the rest of Hughley's questions as mere courtesy.

David Macalvie came bearing a degree from concierge school, and experience at estates in Florida, Arizona and Colorado, and at an extremely discreet, extremely expensive rehab resort in Malibu. He returned to North Carolina because of elderly parents in Burlington. He always wore a coat and tie, was always clean-shaven, his blond hair always flawlessly styled and producted. When he smiled it was always with thin-lipped politeness, at least when on duty. What he was like in his down time, Rick had no idea. He was also 36 to Rick's 29, and taller; plus, one day Rick had discovered that his car – a Fiat convertible gifted by a previous employer – had Republican bumper stickers.

Despite unnatural perfectness and suspected Republican sympathies, he proved to be an able administrator. He set up an office in the staff wing, hired a housekeeping crew, connected with all the entities dealing in supplies, security, maintenance, utilities, taxes and other bureaucracies. He started on the furniture issue, bulk-ordering bedroom suites for the staff wing from a company that supplied hotels. ("Is it American-made?" Rick ventured, when David showed him the estimates.)

Sarah Goss, his business manager, was another applicant who gave him the sense she could lift some of his headaches. He'd rented space in the Snow Building downtown (old, Art Deco-cool and still with human elevator operators) for a "Baum Estate / Aurelia Foundation" office. A healthy, plump brunette in her late 30's, she had degrees in finance and nonprofit management, a

to idea of military coup against Obama...1 in 3 Iowa Republicans think Islam

husband teaching at the School of Science and Math, and two little girls. She'd been recommended by Ms. Pensmore, who'd met her at Planned Parenthood fundraisers. She was competent like David but without his starched-uptight air. She set up an Aurelia Foundation website and a grant-application process, and each week they confer over the latest requests. Appeals from every nonprofit and lobbying group and Save the Children / Whales / Rainforests / Etc. crusade imaginable. Companies wanting to sell him yachts or Porsches or Learjets or ski chalets in Gstaad. Ominous militia-ish groups, convinced the Wizard exists, wanting funds to find him and take him down. Proxy forms and booklets from companies in which the Estate has holdings, many with measures he's proposed: pushing for raised minimum wages or transparency on political contributions; family leave, paid holidays for election days, renewable energy conversion, in-sourcing back outsourced jobs. Weirdnesses: on paper torn from a spiral notebook, a letter handwritten in tiny intense printing that winds out to every corner of the page, repeating over and over an incoherent rationale for needing $5000 and a ticket to Nepal. Hate mail, of course: persons enraged that the Foundation donates to some cause or doesn't donate to another. "I hate that you have to see these," he told her soon after she started.

"Thank you; but I think I can handle it."

"Seriously?? – I mean, this bastard knows your kids' names, their school, where you live, where Mark works…" The e-mail threatened rape, butchery and home incineration, because a prior request to fund an anti-Hillary crusade had been declined. "This is the kind of stuff they did to Leslie. I hate having to inflict it on you."

should be illegal…Dallas 9th grader taken from school in handcuffs because

"Oh, I had to see much worse at Planned Parenthood. This is nothing. Anyway, it's part of my job to see everything that comes in. Somebody might write four pages of craziness before they can get to their real need on page 5. As for this guy, don't we need to know they're out there? I forward them to the police and SBI, so they can keep an eye on them."

*

He wasn't sure he needed a Personal Chef, until he saw the size of the Court's kitchen. David posted the position; but Claire produced Chris Oelrichs's résumé, an actual paper one, with grease spots in the corner. (He was a friend of her friend who was in a band. His résumé mentioned as an afterthought that he could "also operate guitar, mandolin and banjo.") He'd studied History and Philosophy at Virginia Tech, graduated from the Culinary Institute of America; then worked at Richmond and Raleigh-area restaurants, with a stint on Amtrak in between. He had hippie-shaggy brown hair, a hangdog posture, and an embarrassed grin, but an open, easygoing persona that Rick quickly connected with at their interview, despite David's sitting like an unsmiling conscience at his left shoulder. Chris did ask one favor when hired: the privilege to bring in his buddy and assistant-slash-apprentice Jésus "Osito" Alvarez, who had been dishwasher at Chris's last restaurant job but wanted to become a professional chef too. Chris offered to pay Jésus out of his own salary, but Rick said No, he'd get the standard Court part-time package: $15 per hour, medical coverage for on-site accidents so long as they weren't the worker's own fault, benefits after a year or if the job became permanent. The look of delighted awe on Chris's face warmed Rick down to his bones.

The "home farm" was a project Baum had been working on in the last year before his death, another step towards making Haw Court self-sufficient. It had several acres of good gardening land along the river; a fruit orchard; pastures and fields; a barn and assorted outbuildings; and a small, sturdy farmhouse. It had its own entrance to the property, a gravel drive that emerged, barely noticeable amidst the kudzu, at Lewis Ferry by the ruined mill, and in the other direction linked to the main house's service road. There was a view of it from the drive, just before cresting the hill: a vista down green fields to a distant pasture where ordinary brown cows grazed, with gentle rolling hills beyond hazy in the sunshine. Rick liked the idea, and had David advertise for farm managers. Most of the applicants, though, were from "agribusiness," and expecting the kind of factory farm Rick knew from Grant County, which mass-produced hogs or chickens or peanuts (and whose industry lobbyists were all financial Good Friends of his father's). When Rick told them his concept, an all-purpose operation producing whatever could be reasonably grown, raised or gathered, to fill the Court's larders as well as be sold at the Pittsboro farmers' market, they looked puzzled, dubious, or flat-out uncomprehending. Nate and Linda Germain were the only ones who "got" it.

The Germains looked nebbishy and urban, like if they opened their mouths dialogue from *Portlandia* would come out. Nate had curly black hair, five o'clock shadow, and horn-rim glasses. Linda had frizzy black hair, a hint of moustache, and tattoos (the spaceship from *Firefly* on her left shoulder, Doctor Who's TARDIS on her right.) They were short and portly like teddy bears. Both were farm kids, born and raised on farms their families still owned. Nate had one degree from vet school, another in craft-beer brewing, and was considering a third from a marijuana-growers' seminar in Colorado. Linda had raised her own cow through the 4-H Club, rejecting out of hand any suggestion that it be turned into beef. Her degree was in Sustainable Agriculture and Food Systems. When Rick showed them the farm they were immediately enthusiastic, running all about and calling to each other. "Check this out – this is perfect!" "Look at this – it's just what I wanted to do!" Once moved in, they bought a flock of chickens, a family of goats for cheese and yogurt, and a gaggle of weed-eating geese. They knew a beekeeper who needed a place for his hives. There was already a small herd of dairy cows on site, whose owner leased pasturing privileges from the estate. Nate bought three of them, to supply the Court's dairy needs. (Rick was amused to find that one could acquire a cow, approximately the same weight and size of his old Subaru, for around $3000.) There was a crippled sheep, whom Nate had saved from being put down; he named her Hoppyum, and she served no practical purpose, but the goats enjoyed her company. Nate even got Rick to invest in a pair of mules as draft animals, the Germains wanting to use as little internal combustion as possible. These received the names Bubba and Cooter. Claire adored them, and fed them things: apples, pears, Chris's maple-sugar soufflé. She also named the three cows: Maisie, Daisy and Lazy. The Germains were musicians as well; they and Chris took to one another spontaneously. There were frequent jam sessions at the farmhouse.

*

June. He'd started to feel more comfortable at the Court,

and less likely to get lost inside. (Seventeen bedrooms, each with its own bath, with space for more in the attics, plus twelve in the staff wing. The staff kitchen, dining room and lounge. The Tudor "baronial hall," the dining room, the "Bavarian tavern," with a plush screening room adjacent. The glass-roofed, greenhouse-warm north courtyard. Spacious parlors, opening onto one another and the ballroom.) Leslie had taken a particular interest in the mystery of Baum's bequest. One Monday she took off work and delved into the Chatham County archives, unearthing the Court's blueprints. She brought copies to Rick. David was in Burlington on family business. The day was summer-hot. They walked out to the back lawn, by the shimmering clear pool.

"Let's go swimming," she said.

"I don't have swim trunks."

"I don't either."

He looked at her. Her expression was completely everyday normal. "Well, okay; if you're cool with it…"

They stripped, and dove in. The water was just cool enough to be refreshing. Baxter frolicked along the edge, before lying down in the shade of the pool house. "I'd wondered if you were a ginger all the way down," Leslie said. "I figured you were."

"You could've asked."

"I never had the right opportunity."

They lazed in the water a while, then got out. Rick waited a respectful few minutes, so he wouldn't be looking right up between her legs as she climbed the ladder.

They lay on the grass. Baxter had gone to sleep nearby, muzzle pointing upward like he was trying to scent things in his dreams. The lawns gleamed brilliant green in the sun, and the pool water sparkled. There was no movement and almost no sound, only the faint white-noise buzz and hum of nature.

"I wonder what it would be like to grow up here?" Leslie said. "As a child."

Rick considered. "Tell you the truth, I wouldn't want to. I'd want to raise them in a neighborhood like mine, in Durham. Out here they'd be isolated. Especially before they could drive."

"How so?"

"Back in Philly there were always other kids around, other families. And stores I could walk to. Or I could take the bus or trolley and go places. Mom got me a transit pass when I was eleven and let me go by myself. I learned to be independent...Out here they couldn't get independent unless somebody drove them."

"They could learn to be independent in different ways. They could play everywhere. Swim, camp, climb trees...It'd be like having their own state park."

"I want them to be independent around people. Who're their...their equals, you know? Not family, or on the payroll."

"Yes. But I was thinking of all the outdoors adventures they could have."

"I'd have them spend summers here. And holidays."

Another stretch of quiet. *This is...unusual*, he thought; *but not in a bad way. Naked, sitting outdoors on a beautiful day, next to a naked woman who's nice to talk to. You never see bush and boobs outdoors, except in porn. She has a nice pair, too: shaped like...like exactly the way breasts are supposed to be shaped, and hanging with just the realistic right amount of resistance to gravity. Not as big as Claire's, but then half the time Claire's*

"aggressive secularism"...Floods after "1000-year storm" in SC kill 12, burst 9

worrying hers are too small and the wrong shape.

His dick was beginning to express an interest in these thoughts, so he raised his left leg up to obscure it.

"Do you have a boner or something?"

"Yeah...It's this weird reaction I get around naked women."

"You don't have to be embarrassed. It wouldn't be the first one I've seen."

He tentatively lowered his leg. Leslie said nothing. She lay back down with her eyes closed and a slight smile. She seemed as still and quiet as the day itself. But then he noticed, almost doing a double-take, that her nipples seemed to have stiffened. And was it his imagination, or was that just the faintest scent of...feminine arousal? His boner grew even more boned.

"Have you ever been with another redhead?" she asked. "I'm told they taste different."

Would you like to find out? "If you want to...test that theory; you can..."

She did. "How's the taste test?" he asked.

"No difference," she smiled.

"Like me to return the favor?"

He worked what he hoped was tongue magic. She seemed to like it. So he made his way up across her belly and between those lovely real-world breasts, to kiss. She shifted her hips to let him slide up and in. "I've always had a thing for redheads, " she said.

He grinned. "I'm finding that out."

"Damian Lewis as Henry VIII in *Wolf Hall* – did you watch it? Not really handsome; and Henry was an uber-jerk, but every time he was onscreen I was fascinated."

Why am I doing this? Why are we? It's not like I had to talk her into it; I didn't seduce her. We both had the same idea, she just as much as me. It just kind of happened. But no way will Claire buy that excuse, if she finds out..."I couldn't help it; I was possessed by the spirit of Henry VIII." Only she'd be the one saying "Off with his head!" Or Leslie's head, or both ours. Or even Baxter's, for not being a good chaperone!

They lay still; his head against her chest, her hand lying half-forgotten on the small of his back. They listened to the quiet summer-sunshine sounds, watching the occasional pale shadows of small cotton-puff clouds drift along the grass. "Can I ask you something like – really intimate?" he said.

She giggled. "I don't see why not."

"With the Wizard's – patch, upgrade, thing, would you know right away if you were pregnant?"

"Yes; I would. And no, I'm not."

"You did get it, then."

"Not without concerns. Are there side effects, for instance?"

"They haven't found any."

"Long-term ones. Mental ones...And also: everybody's been saying 'Oh, now women are completely free, and empowered!' But do you know what else is happening? Men are saying, 'Now I can fuck all the women I want and not even have to think about being responsible!' It's letting them be even more sexist. Frats are already telling girls they can't come to their parties unless they've been 'Wizard-ized.' So girls who haven't but don't want to be ostracized will lie and say they have, or feel pressured into doing it before they can really decide for themselves."

"Ahh, fuck. No matter what, us guys are still to blame," Rick muttered.

"Another thing: why does he always appear as a man?"

"Maybe because, he is one?"

"We don't know that. We don't know what he is, or what his motives are."

"Have you asked him? Because for what it's worth, I believe him. And I think what he's done is amazing. It feels like for the first time you and us, men and women; you've finally got – " he sat up, both palms facing her, moving them separately forward and back as he sought the right balance of words – "equal...*power* with us. No 'pro-life' assholes can force you to have a kid you don't want. Every time I talked to a girl before, part of me felt like I was walking on land mines or something, because I'm a big scary dangerous MAN, meaning a loose cannon, and I have to be careful I don't go off and hurt her. I know a lot of us *can* be assholes. Some guys always will be. So; *tell* him. Say, 'Hey Mr. Wizard, you did this one part, now here's another part you need to do: show us how to shut down the, the Alpha Drunka Jerka Fuckas who want to abuse this – this privilege.'" He shook his head. "I still feel like that sometimes, talking to Claire."

Leslie sighed. "Let's not talk about her. I'm already feeling guilty."

"That's why I asked, about pregnancy." He was feeling defensive, though he couldn't explain what he was trying to defend. The Wizard? The fact that they'd had sex (good sex, too), even though they really shouldn't have, and already now she was having buyer's remorse? "Wizard or not, I wouldn't want to get you pregnant unless you wanted – unless we *both* wanted it. I'm sorry some guys are assholes, for what it's worth. But here's the thing: now neither of us has to worry about asking, have you got any condoms? The man doesn't have to feel like a shit for not asking, and the woman doesn't have to feel, like – oppressed, or weak, if she doesn't want to ask. If she's afraid to, for instance. See what I mean?"

"It still doesn't solve the problem that men are mostly larger, stronger and more *assertive* than women. They're conditioned to be. And women are still conditioned to be less so. It's endemic in our culture. I don't know if it'll ever change. There'll always be some imbalance of power. And as long as there is, the side with more will have the more responsibility to use it fairly."

He flopped back on the grass. "Fuck it. I should just go gay."

She giggled again.

"What?"

"*There was a young man of Khartoum,*
Took a lesbian up to his room.
They argued all night, as to who had the right,
To do what, and to where, and to whom."

He snickered. "I thought, you think gay sex doesn't have power issues?" she explained. "Top, versus bottom, versus power bottom? Imagine those negotiations."

"Can I ask you a favor?" she said as they came down the drive. "I want to rent the gatehouse and live there. It's silly, but it's cute."

potentially execute Obama...Bill O'Reilly: Time to start arresting "subversive

"Well, sure, yeah. Though you didn't have to fuck me to get it." She laughed.

*

He solved the furniture problem after a pub crawl with some old N.C. State friends, Interior Design majors. He got the idea of offering new young local designers a budget and a room at the Court to spend it on. They'd all get a classy prominent job for their portfolios, and he'd get a fully furnished mansion. (When he woke the next day he was abashed at the idea's drunk generosity, thankful he hadn't been so lagered up as to blurt it out to his companions. It still seemed a good idea, though; besides, he figured, if the Master of Haw Court made a point of following through when sober on promises made when drunk, it'd teach him to be more careful with said promises.) He brought the idea to David. David didn't flinch. He rounded up dossiers of candidates, contacted the ones Rick chose, oversaw their work; and sat in on the occasions when Rick had to tell them their proposals needed a makeover – like the girl who offered a Goth / S&M room, completely black, with a bed hung on chains like a giant sex sling, and a portrait of Marilyn Manson staring at its probably sleepless occupants. Rick and David looked at the pictures, then each other, and laughed "*No!*" simultaneously.

*

July 1st, he and Claire moved in; and Leslie to the gatehouse. (She still worked at Duke Energy's Durham office, but was angling for a transfer to Pittsboro. She was often up at the main house, often alone with Rick, but they didn't fall into bed again, even though some rooms now had beds to fall into. They didn't talk about it either. She seemed content to let their

office holders" who disagree with him – "Things are officially out of control"...

Lush Life / 269

friendship go on as before. He was thankful for this lack of drama.)

"You ever get the feeling Baum's haunting the place?" he asked her.

"Oh, no. It has a contented feel. I think he died happy."

People had already started waiting for him outside the gates: reporters and photographers; protesters angry because he wouldn't use his wealth for this or against that, or just because he had it, and was therefore responsible somehow for too many people not having enough. Fans of Aidan. Gawkers. Desperate souls hoping to flag him down and beg his help, bearing long tales of catastrophic tragedy or injustice they had suffered, or would suffer, unless he used his wealthy might to intervene; making clueless, absurd, insane or outrageous demands. Sometimes they'd wait all day. The Wizard's barrier seemed to keep them from chasing him when he passed through, and from pounding on Leslie's door at all hours; so they'd leave messages: handwritten appeals, with awful spelling and grammar, stuffed in the mailbox. Or hold up signs: RICHARD KINGSLY IF U IGNOR ME U MURDER MY BABIES, from a porcine unsmiling woman with blond hair pulled painfully-looking tight in a ponytail. Leslie called out the sheriff and a social worker to see what the woman's problem was. (Her problem turned out to be mental instability plus a bitter custody fight, along with the delusion that Rick owned the company her ex worked for, and thus had some vague, incoherently explained Moral Responsibility to rescue her children before – another delusion – before her ex could poison them to spite her.) One night coming home he absently turned the barrier off too soon; and as he approached the gates, a wild-haired wild-eyed man leapt out of the woods and hurled himself at the car. He pounded on the hood and even tugged at the door handle, all the while babbling some desperate news of space-alien lizards stealing human body parts through portals to alternate universes. Rick threw the Subaru in reverse and floored it backwards, thinking the barrier back on and calling 911. The man staggered about in his headlights like someone struck blind, wailing. Rick drove carefully past him, as far away as he could, and through the gates. He was still shaken when he got back to the house, a void in his gut like one of those alternate-universe portals.

He wondered if letting the general public see the place, like a historic-home tour, might satiate some of their curiosity and get them off his back. The designers' bedrooms would be finished in late August, so he decided to hold "open house" over Labor Day weekend. He didn't want to be there, though, like he was one of the exhibits, so he left all the planning in David's hands and took Claire to England for a tour of Stately Homes, including Highclere Castle where *Downton Abbey* was filmed. The trip didn't go as well as it could have. It rained a lot. She fussed a lot. She was convinced that her clothes were getting mildewed. She said the hotel rooms were all too cold, and that jet lag wasn't letting her sleep right. She fidgeted and sighed while Rick asked tour guides detailed questions about estate operation. "Couldn't you pick a month when it doesn't *rain?*" she complained one night.

The irrationality exasperated him. "It's England. It rains every month…You know I can't buy good weather, right? Not even Lord Grantham could do that."

"It doesn't rain in *Downton Abbey!*"

"Because they shoot the exteriors on sunny days!"

college professors who teach "propaganda"...Trump's version of "religious

The next day she accidentally jabbed him in the eye with a mismanaged umbrella, leaving a garish bruise that drew curious and concerned sideways looks. They'd fucked on the first excited night they'd arrived, but by the end of the ten days they were barely touching each other. As they sat in Heathrow waiting for the flight home, Rick reached out tentatively to stroke her arm. She didn't pull away; but didn't respond either, just kept on texting messages about her shop plans.

*

In September he finally quit dragging his feet and threw a housewarming: a weekend "house party," Stately-Home style, for family and friends. Planning it had required a whole morning spent with David. David was used to lifestyles-of-the-rich formality. Rick didn't want that; he wanted everyday-guy egalitarianism, a sized-up version of your typical twentysomething kegger. They'd had to do some negotiating. So, no flotillas of waiters circulating with stuff on trays; no string quartets, ice sculptures, chocolate fountains. Chris served dinner buffet-style, with Jésus in the kitchen to send up refills in the dining room dumbwaiter. The bars in the "Bavarian tavern" and pool pavilion were stocked with liquor, mixers, plentiful beer and plentiful ice, with guests welcome to barista themselves. Rick did agree to a pair of security guards at the gatehouse, to check people in, but insisted they dress casual and be armed with nothing more than a guest list. (Rick also made sure they got fed too.)

He hoped none of his friends would be put off by the grandeur. The "Master of Haw Court" and all its wealth was the same plain old goofball Rick Kingsley they knew, over-degreed and underemployed and looking forward to his first beer, feeling not so much like Lord Grantham as Jed Clampett. "We've even got a Cee-ment Pond for y'all to swim in."

Dad called at quarter to seven. "Rick, we're having trouble finding it. We've gone past where GPS says it is a couple times, but can't never see anything."

"Really? That's weird. What are you driving? I'll have the guys at the gate flag you." Twenty minutes later maybe, during which Cousin Mason and Danny, followed by Annie and Mom, turned up without any difficulty, Dad called again. "I think we're here...We're at the end of a driveway at a four-car garage..."

"You must've missed the turn to the front entrance. Hang on; I'll be right down."

"Man, is that yours?" Lin asked, admiring David's Fiat. "That thing is *sweet.*" In the dining room, Mom encountering Eunice for the first time, an event Rick had concerns about and watched with some wariness. "It's *so* nice to finally meet you," Eunice said, introducing herself. "Such a funny name, isn't it? At school they used to tease me something awful."

"God, I know; kids can be so vicious. I wonder how any of us survived junior high."

"I had a chemistry set and threatened to blow them up," Annie grinned.

"And I'm so sorry for all you've had to go through, not just with Aidan but all that online harassment. There should be better laws against that crap. Has Lin ever thought about asking the Legislature to work on it?"

"Thank you so much. I keep praying for Aidan every day." She still wouldn't say what she'd seen in her nightmare, but she no longer set a place for Aidan at the table or kept his bedroom light on. She did still carry copies of all the pictures he'd sent and showed them to any who were curious, in case they might recognize the locations.

After dinner, a house tour, Rick conducting the group with the fork he'd been using to eat dessert (a sheet cake depicting the Court's front façade). "This sweet life's already got you putting on weight," Marcus smiled.

"Am I? Fuck. I'll have to put in a gym someplace."

"You know I got a friend who's a personal trainer at Crossfit –"

Rick waved his fork. "Now this here was *almost* the 'Goth Room'..." (He'd agreed to the designer's second-string idea, "Seventies stoner," with blacklight posters and a lava lamp).

The ballroom awed them. Angela mentioned her younger brother back in Charlotte, who was a DJ; if Rick ever wanted to throw a dance party...The "Outpost of Empire" billiard room, next to the "Bavarian tavern": cream plaster walls above bamboo wainscoting, rattan furniture, tall dried-grass arrangements in ceramic jars, engravings of British colonial scenes. Aaron, Rick's old UNC roommate, who was in a darts league, said maybe some night they could do a charity competition there...The balcony above the Tudor "hall." Down below, Eunice stood near Mason and Annie as they traded stories from their military days. "You remember when she told everybody I'd give it all to get Aidan back?" Rick murmured. "That seriously, *seriously* pissed me off. Because first, she didn't ask me; and second, I *can't*. Because of the way Baum set it all up. Most of it's not even mine until I'm thirty. Anyway...that's one of the headaches: everybody wants a piece of you..." He told them about the sign lady and the alien-lizards guy.

Lin took him aside afterwards, holding a tumbler half-full of whiskey. "Hey listen: your butler guy – he buy that Fiat on your dime?" He was nineteen now, still too young to legally drink. Rick wondered what would happen if Dad saw him.

"No, it was a present from his last boss."

"How much are you payin' him?"

Rick waited for an *if you don't mind me asking* to accompany the question, but didn't hear one. "It's six figures. Estate managers don't come cheap."

"Low six or high six?"

"Between one and two hundred. That's all I'll say."

Lin lowered his voice. "'Cause look, tell you what: for a hundred K even, I'll run this place for you. I'll take care of everything. I'll get you some parties up in here like you won't believe."

"It's a lot more than parties. He handles all the employment stuff, the W-2s; all the property taxes, the utilities, ordering, maintenance – He has an MBA and special training, and experience. That's why they get paid a lot."

Lin looked at him like he was a nerd. "You don't got accountants to do that shit?"

"For the money, yes. For this, the house and estate, no."

"'Cause I'll tell you, I can see in his eyes, he's the kind that'll stab you in the back first chance he gets."

And you wouldn't? Rick kept his voice pleasant. "That's why I had him sign a contract, that my lawyers supervised. Does Dad know you've gotten into my whiskey?"

Lin gave a half-smirk. "If you didn't want people drinkin'

it you shouldn't have put it out." He downed the rest of the glass.

Jimmy Womble chased a happily shrieking Darnell along corridors. Linda buttonholed Dad with intense explanations of how hog farming could be made ecologically safe but still profitable. Scott's daughter Meghan buttonholed Nate and requested personal introductions to the farm animals. Claire's singer friend enthused about the north courtyard, which Rick had filled with a bunch of tropical plants, orange and grapefruit trees, and even a couple of palms, which he'd got cheap from a greenhouse going out of business because it lay in the path of the Outer Beltline extension. She asked, had he ever heard of Flying Colors Bird Sanctuary in Haw River? They rescued parrots, cockatiels and other exotic birds; they were always looking for places for them...Lin and some sports-fan guests took over the screening room, switching between baseball (Braves vs. Cubs at Chicago) and one of the *Terminator* movies, each chair surrounded by little mushroom-clusters of empty beers.

By one A.M., his guests were in their rooms or departed. He found Claire already in bed, but not asleep. He brushed his teeth, undressed and joined her. She remained silent. "You okay?"

"I just wish you'd gotten here sooner."

"You could've come found me."

"You were too busy talking to everybody else."

She didn't sound like she was okay. He suppressed a sigh. "Is something bothering you?"

"You're changing. Already." She lay on her side, facing away from him. He reached an arm round her, carefully, waiting to see how she might react.

"Changing? How?"

When she was unhappy like this it took her a long time to answer questions. "All you seem to think about is this place, and your money."

"They take a lot of thinking about. I have to learn a lot and make a lot of decisions. It's like you and Andy having to do all the stuff to start your store."

"It doesn't take up my every day."

Neither does the Court take up mine. But... "Is there something I'm not doing that I used to do? Or vice versa?"

Another long pause. "You're changing," she repeated. "You're starting to act like, 'I'm Mister Rich, look at me.' Like it's okay...You pay people to do stuff you used to do yourself. 'See what I can do with my money.' Like it's normal."

"I've always been careful about money," he replied. "Before now, I had to, because I didn't have any. Now that I do, I feel like I have to be even more careful. Because there's so much of it...If I use it the wrong way, I could do real harm. Or give it to the wrong person. Lin wants me to hire him as a kind of party planner. He wants to turn this into the next Playboy Mansion...That's why I have accountants and lawyers, and Sarah fending off all the people wanting contributions, and why I have to spend so much time with them...Look; anytime you're feeling deserted or something, just come find me. Okay?"

Long pause again. "Okay..." in a small voice.

"Or if you want dessert. Or just deserts." He continued holding her, but not too close, lest his dick got the wrong idea. He doubted she was in the mood.

*

Morning, a week later. "I need to see you," David's voice

said, in a tone that always gave Rick an *oh, shit* feeling. It meant there was something he'd have to adult over, that might not be pleasant.

One of the maids – Ana Anzora, her uniform said – was in a chair before David's desk. She looked terrified. Wasn't she the one who had to flee El Salvador because gangs threatened her? A boy, also Hispanic, maybe thirteen, stood behind her. He gave off truculent vibes, glaring at Rick, hands half-clenched. The first traces of moustache showed on his upper lip.

David handed him a phone, with a paused video. It showed the pool, early on a sunny morning. Rick watched himself appear from behind the pavilion, Baxter gamboling at his side. He stripped off t-shirt and boxers. Morning wood again: his dick sticking straight out, even casting a little shadow on the cement below. He scratched round it, and stroked it a time or two. Then stopped, with a half-amused look; shrugged and dove in.

Ana poured forth rapid agitated Spanish. The boy rebuked her, a hand on her shoulder. "That's mine," he pointed at the phone. "Don't you be messing with my mama."

All Rick could do was laugh, because the whole thing felt absurd. David frowned. "Where'd you get this?" Rick asked the boy. "Where were you hiding?"

He was reluctant. "That room next to the big living room," he admitted.

"This is Ms. Anzora's son Rico –" David began.

"What were you gonna do with it?" Rick interrupted.

"Nothin'," the boy replied after another sullen pause.

"Show it to your friends, I bet."

His mother remonstrated and reproved him, calling him

Frederico. He talked back, with words whose consonants sizzled and spit like firecrackers. Rick wished he'd learned Spanish, like Baum had. But between all the Court's duties, and all its opportunities to be lazy, he hadn't pushed himself to. David overtalked their squabble. (He spoke fluent Spanish. Rick wondered what kind of accent he had: Spain Spanish, the equivalent of British "posh;" or vernacular Southwest / Central America Hispanic? Maybe he spoke Chinese, Japanese and Russian too. Rick would not put it past him.) "This is a breach of the Court's confidentiality agreement. He says he hasn't put it online –"

"I have confidentiality agreements?"

"For your staff and subcontractors."

"Oh; right. Can I see one? I want to see what it says I'm supposed to do."

David handed him a blank form. He traced the lines with a finger. "Failure to abide…result in penalties…termination, civil suit; monetary damages, criminal charges? Yikes."

"Fuck you," Rico exclaimed. "She doesn't have to work here. She can get better jobs. She's not a maid! She went to college. She used to be a librarian!"

Ana pleaded and argued with him. David tried to interrupt. Rick waved both hands for everybody to stop. "Nobody's getting fired, okay? Just chill. If it hasn't been leaked, we just erase it and give them both a warning. You didn't post it already?" he asked Rico.

"Wouldn't upload."

(Had the barrier not let it? He wondered how it decided what you could and couldn't upload.)

wanted to burn Black Lives Matter activist alive: "Light the motherfucker on

"All right then. It gets erased; David, you tell everybody else not to do this. Just make it a general announcement; don't single her out. Why were you here?" he asked Rico amiably. "Just wanted to see the place?"

Ana tried to explain, in mixed languages. "Some guys in our apartments," Rico answered. "Trying to start stuff with me. She thinks they're gangs and are gonna kill me. So she makes me stay here. But I can take care of myself." His mother had sharp words for him, probably the Spanish version of "like hell you can."

Rick wondered about asking the county sheriff, whom he'd met a few times, for suggestions about Rico's bully problem, and the county library if they could use a degreed ex-librarian who spoke more Spanish than English. *Lord-of-the-manor fantasies*, he thought with a smile.

The two were excused. "That was a narrow escape," David said.

"You were afraid it was gonna end up on *TMZ*?" Rick grinned. "I'm not *that* famous."

"You're still of interest to the media. A skilled interviewer could lead someone – a hothead like Rico, for instance – into revealing confidential detail." Ever since he came on board, David had been pushing, soft-spoken but persistent, for Rick to hook up with a PR firm. He'd talk about Rick's "image," his "brand," which gave Rick a mental picture of walking around with corporate logos stuck all over himself like a NASCAR racer. David said PR would enable Rick to present himself to the public the way he wanted to be seen. Rick wanted to be seen as still a regular guy, who despite now having money out the wazoo, didn't get into pretentious things like having a public-relations "image."

fire!"...Flint, Michigan city water found to contain dangerous lead levels after

You don't wish to be a public figure now, (David would explain). *But if you do in the future, if you wish to take a prominent role for social or political issues that interest you…When you take full control of your assets, next fall…The groundwork would have been done, for your efforts to be maximally effective.*

But when he thought about that, he thought of all the appeals he and Sarah had to sort through every week. Which one would he choose? And what if he chose the wrong ones? Like if they turned out to be run by bumblers and failed; or if the Catastrophe That Destroys Civilization came from some other danger he'd decided to not throw money at? *Well, shit, I fucked THAT up big time. Smooth move, Lord of the Manor.*

*

October, and the Grand Opening of "Aromamora," at Brightleaf Square. He had to attend, of course, as Claire's boyfriend; and as the Master of Haw Court, whose rumored presence, Claire insisted, could draw in more potential customers. "So I'm an Extra Added Attraction," he ventured.

"You know everybody's curious to see you. You only gave that one press conference. I wish you'd do more interviews. People are already saying you're turning into a recluse, like Baum."

"'People,' quote unquote, are always going to say all kinds of shit. But you know it's not true. We go out all the time; I have basketball night."

"But you're always nervous, because you're afraid people are going to ask you for money. You don't have to be. When they do ask you're always nice about it. You tell them to write a business plan or something and give it to Sarah. You don't *need* to worry about it." She opened his side of the closet. "Why do you *still* only have one suit?"

*

New Year's Eve. He and Claire went to various friends' parties. (The Court staff, meanwhile, were throwing their own bash, under David's watchful eye.) There was much talk about weather; as in, "Hasn't this been some of the craziest ever?" Summer 2015, according to the NOAA, had been the hottest on record, with heat waves killing thousands across India and Pakistan, and rampant wildfires in California. That fall a "thousand-year storm" had burst nine dams and drowned twelve people in South Carolina. On its heels came Hurricane Patricia, the strongest the Western Hemisphere had ever seen, flattening Mexican villages with winds of 215 m.p.h. Half the trees in the Amazon rainforest were said to face extinction, and Beijing issued its first pollution Red Alert. (A party guest made *Star Trek* sounds and jabbered warnings in a non-PC Chinese accent.) "And God, don't get me started on Trump..." The bastard had proposed banning all Muslims, enforcing it with a Wizard-barrier if necessary. (Rick, in Grantsville over Thanksgiving, had barely managed to not throttle Eunice for saying this was a good idea.) Then no sooner had 2016 come staggering in than David Bowie, Alan Rickman, Glenn Frey and Paul Kantner all dropped dead, along with (but not due to – thanks for small blessings) the Zika outbreak.

Aidan, and the Wizard, still could not be found. Aidan's untraceable Polaroids continued to arrive every few months. The Wizard, meanwhile, was still regarded in public comment as something between a myth and a joke to troll right-wingers with.

bought 2 guns per second on Black Friday...Ryan, McConnell confirm no real

He seemed to be doing random individual takedowns, like Arlene Hooker, Leslie's doxxer, TeShawn Williams. ("Seemed," because there was no way to prove him the culprit. Questioned in dreamtime, he gave no answer. His victims couldn't recall sensing his presence at their attacks.) There was no discernible pattern. A Fundamentalist from Florida traveled to Uganda and urged its government to make "holy war" on all its homosexuals; he shared and screamed in the agony of gay Ugandans doused in petrol and burned alive because of his words. A serial child-killer in rural Oklahoma turned himself in to the police, crushed by the agony of his victims and the trauma of their families. A refugee trafficker in Sicily, who'd take from desperate families every penny they had and then abandon them to drown in unseaworthy boats, was driven mad by nightmares of his own endless drowning. But when Trump made filthy remarks about Megyn Kelly's period, or Martin Shrekli raised Daraprim's price five thousand per cent and then smirked at his economic brilliance on national news – nothing happened. The Wizard had no answer to queries, pleas and vilifyings over his actions or inactions. In Rick's own dreams he was a strongly felt presence, somber and watchful.

*

April 3^{d}, a Saturday. The air felt chilly. Rick turned on the fireplace before letting Baxter out, then quickly climbed back in bed with Claire, but a moment later his house phone beeped. David. "Good morning. Ah – you need to know that your brother Linwood is in the Chatham County Jail."

Rick couldn't quite process things that early. "My brother?" Claire, overhearing, sat up suddenly and grabbed his arm, asking "Is it Aidan? Have they found him?"

"What for?"

"Public intoxication; property damage, resisting arrest, and possible assault."

"Shit. What the hell was he doing there?" He put the phone on speaker so Claire could hear. ("Lin, not Aidan,") he asided to her.

"He brought some frat brothers to Chapel Hill yesterday, for the NCAA semifinals," David's voice continued. "Carolina won, eighty-three to sixty-six against Syracuse. They went to numerous parties afterwards. Around two A.M., they decided to come here. They got lost and couldn't find the entrance, nor could they get through on the phone. They ended up in Pittsboro. There was an argument about directions. One of the other men pushed past the driver and tried to grab the wheel, causing the limo to knock down three street signs."

"A limo? Where'd they find a limo at 2 A.M.?"

"They chartered it in Greenville."

"From *Greenville?* Argh. That dumbfuck...Is the driver okay?"

"Yes. I offered him a room here, which I trust is all right with you. He's eating breakfast right now, if you'd like to speak with him."

"No, not now, not unless he needs to. Yeah, that's fine, giving him a room. When does he have to get back?...Okay; once he's eaten he can go, unless the police need him. If he needs anything for the trip let him have it; but make sure his company knows Lin gets the bill. Was he asshole-ish to you? Lin, I mean."

"I haven't spoken with him. The deputy sheriff called me.

water companies like Flint's charge average of 58% more than public ones...

Lin couldn't reach us on the jail phone either. I've put in a call to Time Warner to check our system."

"Yeah, good. All right…do they need bail or something?"

The police plan, David replied, was to release them on "recognizance," meaning they would sign a promise to reappear in court when summoned. They would be let out around noon. Rick, muttering "Dad's gonna love this," texted Cal Boulware. *Lin in jail here. Drunk; several charges. Recommend?* Claire was ticked off. "He's the one who was so hateful to Aidan. Now he thinks he can bring his drunk friends and crash here, without even asking first! That is *so* rude."

Dad called back as they finished breakfast. Neither he nor Cal could get away. "Sorry to dump this on you. Just ship him back to Greenville any old way you want. Rent him a car or put him on the bus. And send Cal the receipts. I'll deal with him later. And I'll make sure he's there for court."

Lin's party posse, shambling bleary-eyed from the cells, comprised two guys and three girls: Reece and Tyler; Jerri, Katelynn, Marla. The boys looked like hung-over football players and smelled of stale beer. The girls were probably arm-candy beautiful yesterday, but a night in jail had abraded off their glamour. Lin hustled among them, confronting the officers. "See, I told you! I told you who you were dealing with. Here he is," – waving at Rick. "I told you, you better not fuck us over. You need to tell your goddamn butler guy to pick up the goddamn phone when people call. What if this had been an emergency? And how come the fuck you're not on Google Earth? We drove up and down that damn road a dozen times and couldn't find it."

"We passed it," Marla said. "Twice. I saw the gates, but

you wouldn't stop."

David had miraculously, on this Sunday morning, found a shuttle company willing to haul them back to Greenville. They would stop by the Court first. "Do they have to?" Claire had argued on the way to town. "You know what he was doing all night long was, hitting on women, saying 'I can get you into Haw Court!'"

"No doubt. Don't worry, I'll tell him it's not cool. And that he's getting the bill. The others – he may have been the ringleader and they were along for the ride. If I woke up in jail hung over, I'd be glad for a shower and some good food. You know Chris'll love it, a challenge like this. 'Give me lunch for nine on a couple hours' notice!'"

"Don't let him talk you into stuff. He's a con man! Just because he's your brother. I don't want people to exploit you."

The others climbed into the shuttle, but Lin took shotgun in Rick's car without invitation, and without noticing Claire's hostile looks. Rick thought about making him move, but decided to pass this small infraction for the large one. "Now what gave you the idea you could show up drunk at 3 A.M. with a crowd of people, without even asking?"

"I told you! I called but your guy wouldn't answer!"

"What time did you call?"

Lin hedged. "Sometime last night. Early."

"Six, nine, midnight? There might've been a problem with our phone lines."

"But still" – Claire interrupted. Rick warded it off. "Was it before you left Greenville? When you got to Chapel Hill? After the game?"

GOP exit poll: Trump the candidate of voters who resent African-Americans,

"Last night. I don't remember. Carolina won and everybody went apeshit. The whole damn town was a party."

"And one where not everybody checks IDs. I know what Uptown's like when the Heels win."

"You gonna bust me on that too? Like you didn't never party with your friends."

"I'm just sayin'. My point – our point," (Rick glanced at Claire), "is, you plan visits in advance. Not at 3 A.M. the night of. You ask, in advance, if it's okay. Like you'd do with Dad and Eunice."

"I *tried* to call you but you *wouldn't answer!*"

"Then the best thing to do would've been to go back to Greenville and say better luck next time."

"And all my friends saying 'Yeah, look at Mister Connected; says he can do this, can do that; but his own damn brother won't take his calls!' If it was *me* had more money than fuckin' God and a house big as the damn Deandome, I'd let anybody stay there any damn time they wanted."

"And pretty soon you'd have a houseful of freeloaders claiming to be your friends and burning through all that money."

"I'd get me some decent cars too, not ride around in this piece of shit." (Rick was still driving "Old Blue the Subaru," although now he'd been able to get all the broken stuff fixed.) Rick's fine-tuned girlfriend-listening abilities caught Claire's muted "Then you can get out and walk." He winked at her in the rear-view mirror, while making sure the van was following him through the maze of back roads. "Did you promise them you'd show them the Court? They're still going to see it. And with a free lunch."

"All this damn money and you're not doing shit with it," Lin muttered, face turned away.

"Do you know how many charities he gives to?" Claire demanded. "And how many people keep asking him for money? Most of them are crooks. Swindlers. Like those Nigerian e-mails."

"He's giving you everything *you* want."

"But in the right way. He made me get a business plan and everything, and talk to banks and get loans. And I'm okay with that. I know I'm not a business person; that's why I got a partner who is. And tell him what you're always doing with those, those ballot things when you vote with your stock? Proxies. He's always trying to get his companies to do stuff, like raise minimum wage or provide family leave. He's not just having wild parties."

"If there's something you want, you can ask me," Rick said. "Whether it's starting a business or bringing friends over. You just do it through the proper channels."

They passed through the gates. Lin suddenly looked queasy. They had to pull over and let him throw up.

Bedroom suites were ready, for those who wanted showers, and Chris had prepared a "hangover remedy" lunch (chicken soup, spinach salad), including stuff Rick didn't even know he had in the house, that he'd never think to request: Gatorade, blueberry yogurt, cocoanut water. (Cocoanut water??) "Could I get a Bloody Mary?" Tyler asked. "Sure, man," Lin beamed, and turned to David. "Double Bloody Mary for my man T-Dog here. Wait, make it two."

"Hang on," Rick said. "Hate to bring it up; but are you over 21?"

The boy wouldn't meet his eyes. "No sir."

Lin threw up his hands, seething. "What the fuck is your *problem?*" Disdainful looks from the girls, the kind that in middle school would've withered Rick's soul like a salted slug. They had no power here. "It's the law," Rick shrugged. "You know that."

"Fuck this. Go get him a Bloody Mary," Lin ordered David. David's eyes cut to Rick for a split second. "No," Rick said. "House rules."

"It's your own goddamn house, you can do whatever the fuck you want! This how you treat your guests? With your Mister Snooty-Ass butler who you pay too goddamn much to not do what you tell him to?"

"Lin – first of all, do *not* be a dick to my employees. *Don't.* I am *not* going to order them to break the law. Second; it's *because* this is my house, because I've got all this, that I'm going to go by the law. It's my job as a grownup. If I do something illegal, people are gonna notice. And they'll say 'Look at that rich asshole, he can do illegal shit and get away with it.' Like Trump."

Claire butted in. "I mean, excuse me, have you ever worked in retail? Have you ever worked in anything? Do you know what it feels like to *have* to be polite to people who're so totally rude that you – that treat you like you're, you're, dog poo they stepped in?"

Tyler was abashed. "Sorry, sir; I didn't mean to cause trouble."

"No problem," Rick assured him. "Ask me again when you hit the big two-one and you can have all the Bloody Marys you can handle." He opened the dumbwaiter doors and called down the shaft. "Hey Chris – can you think of something that's like a non-

to patrol Muslim neighborhoods; another 45% call for return to waterboarding

alcoholic Bloody Mary?"

*

Three days later, Merle Haggard died. Two weeks later, Prince followed him. In May, Guy Clark expired. In June, Muhammad Ali, Anton Yelchin, Ralph Stanley, and Elvis's first guitarist Scotty Moore all passed. "What's going on?" Leslie grumbled. "Do they know something we don't? Are they all escaping the planet like the dolphins in *Hitchhiker's Guide*?" Also in May, Trump secured the nomination. Rick worried Mom would die, of outrage. Annie said "You watch: if he wins, half the military's gonna resign. I'd re-enlist just for the pleasure."

In May, too, gigantic three-day forest fires in Alberta forced the evacuation of Fort MacMurray, a city of 10,000. In June, the same week England voted to make its Brexit, catastrophic floods fed by massive rains hit West Virginia. (Rick saw surreal news footage of a house not only floating downstream, but engulfed in flames as it floated.) The summer had been so hot that in Vermont, a manure pile at a horse farm had spontaneously combusted – resulting in a forest fire that burned not only half of the Green Mountain National Forest but also the hippie "Rainbow Gathering" being held within. There were stories of forest roads lined with burnt corpses, where the flames had overtaken those trying to escape. Then at the end of August (following Gene Wilder's and Kenny "R2-D2" Baker's demise), the Burning Man Festival in Nevada was struck one midnight by a massive freak windstorm that ripped the camps to shreds, with scores injured or killed by wreckage, in some cases actually sandblasted to death.

There were also stories from the Green Mountains fire, of glimpses through the acrid smoke and chaos, of trains which should not have been there, had not been there for a hundred years, carrying Rainbow Gatherers to safety. Likewise at Burning Man, rumors claimed, an Art Deco silver streamliner had appeared on nearby tracks – which had carried only freight since 1970 – and rescued many; then disappeared into the night. There were even tales of people known to be dead at either place, their bodies found and identified, sending friends messages later about their escapes by rail. A bullied middle-school girl in east Tennessee, told by her tormentors that the Wizard was about to drop a new scan which would expose lesbians, had fled, but not before posting an Instagram from the "Knoxv train sta." It showed a round, high-ceilinged, clerestoried hall, bustling with travelers; lined with ticket counter, baggage claim, coffee shop, newsstand; and portals marked "TRACKS 1-2-3-4 (Southern Railway Trains)" and "TRACKS 5-6-7-8 (Louisville & Nashville Railroad Trains)": a Knoxville station that did not, and had never, existed.

Even this mystery didn't get "ghost trains" mentioned in the mainstream media. They were too absorbed in the Republicans' umpteenth attempt at Obamacare repeal, Trump's promise to un-sign the just-signed Paris climate accords as soon as he could get his short-fingered hands on them, and the death of Phyllis Schafly (at which Mom exclaimed "GOOD FUCKING RIDDANCE!")

The rich, vicious Raleigh right-winger switched his anti-Obama billboard to anti-Wizard. "No Wizard!" signs, a red barred circle across a sorcerer's hat, were appearing in ever-larger numbers on front lawns and roadsides, usually – but not always – beside TRUMP placards. (The Wizard's appearance, it was said, was taking more and more diverse forms. A lesbian couple from

they're "oppressed" if they can't oppress...3-day Canadian forest fire forces

Savannah. A single mother in upstate New York. A transgender youth in Buenos Aires; a pair of retired Irish schoolteachers. Recovering addicts, a black vet and a white Dartmouth student, from Boston. Runaways in Aidan's mode from all over the world.)

*

So; mid-September 2016, and up to Durham. He always feels a little smug seeing BAUM ESTATE and AURELIA FOUNDATION on the lobby directory. Sarah has the week's work ready. They look over the latest proxies, with his latest progressive measures up for voting. "'The Board recommends AGAINST this proposal,'" he reads, "for the following ass-covering reasons. 'AGAINST; AGAINST, AGAINST.' Batting 0 for 8. Dudes, how am I supposed to save the world if you keep blocking me?" He votes "For," in defiance of all those faraway Boards. His holdings are so diversified that he doesn't own enough stock in any one place to carry the day; but when he takes full control in two months, some serious divesting and re-investing will go down. He approves some requests for Foundation grants, signs the checks once Sarah's typed them up. He looks at plans and phones people about Baum Estate properties. He's been quietly buying land round the Triangle and putting in mobile homes, then offering them at modest rents through local property-management companies. The Estate didn't own any failing "mixed-use" developments, in Evansville or elsewhere, but he's still doing what he can to increase affordable housing for the salesclerk / Customer Service Rep / tow-trucker single dad types out there.

Claire reports over dinner that the Duke boffins still aren't ready to commit. She remains optimistic. Aromamora made a small profit in the summer quarter, always a slow season, and now business is picking up with the students back and Christmas shopping on the horizon. At Walltown he stretches while waiting for the others. Jimmy rarely brings Darnell now because at almost three, he's both able and eager to get into things, such as Daddy's basketball game. Jimmy is on tense ground with his own Daddy and family, all fierce Trump champions and Hillary-haters. He doesn't trust Hillary but doesn't hate her, and cannot ignore the fact that Trump "acts like a total asshole." He doesn't know who he'd vote for and it worries him, even though he won't be old enough to vote until next spring. "I don't much care for Hillary myself," Marcus says. "Her and Bill didn't do us any favors. But if that man's the alternative…"

"Man, Bernie should've gone independent," says Scott. "He'd've wiped them both out. And Jill Stein too. Libertarians -" he gives a raspberry and a thumbs-down. "They're all batshit. 'Don't regulate anything!' they say. Know why prescription meds cost so damn much? 'Cause they're not regulated."

"How come you never talk about stuff like this?" Jimmy asks Rick. "Like, on the news. People'd listen. I bet you could get an interview on any show you wanted."

"I'm not interested in being famous. I don't feel I've got anything special to say. I'm just an ordinary guy with ordinary opinions. Yes, Trump's a walking disaster. Libertarians are too far out there. I voted Bernie in the primary. I don't like or hate Clinton. But she's smart and experienced, and I think she'd do the best job she could."

"Bet if you asked, she'd put you in her Cabinet."

"No doubt. If I made a big fat contribution."

hopes he deports "all you terrorist Muslims;" man on plane yanks off Muslim

"You suppose that Wizard barrier would keep off people hitting you up for money?" Marcus wondered.

Rick hid his double-take. *How did you know?* "Would it? I thought it only worked on guns. If it did, that'd be great. But I haven't had any real problems so far." He's developed a sense of what the barrier can do. It keeps at a distance people he wants kept at a distance. Right now it covers the building as well as himself, so he won't look up to find the upstairs walking track suddenly crowded with spectators, TV cameras and petitioners for money, all watching his every move. It keeps his private e-mail, phone numbers and social media private. But it won't keep his real friends, like his b-ball crew here, among whom he now dodges, weaves and feints, from – (*damn!* – from Marcus capturing the ball, which always seems to fly into his hands as if by magic, and cutting it over to Jimmy) – from mentioning to their friends or spouses some remark he's made in passing, about some issue like the election. The remark is free to pass on, person to person, until somewhere, somehow, it's noted by someone in The Media. They turn it back to him as questions. *Did you say this? What did you mean?* They contact the Court's web page, the Aurelia Foundation, the Baum Estate. *Can we confirm...?* David and Sarah, though, are his reliable barriers there. "Mr. Kingsley respectfully declines to comment on private conversations with his friends," they say, as per his instructions. And if The Media says snide things about him for not confirming? – well, tough shit.

No one pursues him or lies in wait by the gatehouse. But just as he turns into the drive, his phone rings. Dad. "We got another photo today. With a note. Aidan says he's coming back."

woman's hijab: "Take it off! This is America!"...Rampant racism forces FOX

Prodigal

Eunice shattered the stillness, and Rick's nerves, with an uncanny banshee scream. She ran the length of the building and up the steps to throw herself upon Aidan and clench him tightly, bawling in hysterical sobs that seemed never to stop for breath. She kissed and pawed and stroked him, rocking the both of them side to side like a ship's mast in heavy seas. "All right, Mom, that's enough," Rick heard Aidan say, and saw him try to pry off her clutching arms; but she screamed even louder – *"No, no, no!"* – and clutched more fiercely. Then suddenly she gave a shriek of pure agony, staggering back against the wall with a hand to her shoulder, staring at Aidan with horror.

"Mom, when I say *enough*, I mean *enough*."

He was wearing a dark overcoat and a grey ball cap with "MISKATONIC" in Gothic lettering; flannel shirt, jeans and hiking boots. He carried a small duffel bag in one hand. He was a foot taller; no longer chubby but still big: big like a football player, with the same broad fireplug solidness of Cousin Mason. Like Cousin Mason, he now moved with the ease of someone comfortable and assured in his own physicality. He faced them with a noncommittal, rather resigned look.

"What'd you do to her?" Mason demanded, going to Eunice's side.

"A quick pinch in a vulnerable spot. She was suffocating me."

They'd all come up to surround him. Rick, not quite sure what to do, offered him a handshake. "Welcome back – I think."

Aidan accepted his hand, with a slight smile at the humor.

"Thanks." His grip was strong. Rick pointed at the cap. "Miskatonic?"

"Oh that." Aidan grinned, removing it. "Friend who's into H.P. Lovecraft gave it to me." His hair, now a shade darker, was close-cropped. Eunice startled everyone with another despairing wail. "Oh – oh – oh, your *hair*! Your precious *hair*! What have they *done* to you!?"

"Nobody did anything. I got it cut myself. You saw it in my first picture. One of the first things I did."

She stepped back, her face falling onto her palms and her cry plummeting down into heartbroken sobs, between which words gasped out like tiny drowning figures. "But – it – made – you – look – so, so–"

"It made me look like Krusty the Clown, is what it did."

Mason took her by the shoulders, trying to calm her. "Come on now, Neece, get hold of yourself…"

"Get in the cars," Dad ordered. The mist was nearly gone, and they could see distant figures turning, looking, walking their way, attention probably drawn by Eunice's shrieks. Mrs. Pinyan was peering out the door of her coffee shop and talking on her phone. Dad, Lin and Mr. Boulware took Dad's car while the rest of them rode in Cousin Mason's SUV. Mason drove, with Rick shotgun, Aidan and Eunice in the back, she sniffling and dabbing at her face with a handkerchief. Aidan settled into his seat, placing the duffel bag between them. He unzipped it and pulled out a thick paperback with a bookmark. But Eunice, looking at him, dissolved into sobs again. She grabbed him, toppling him over with one arm akimbo, to mash him against her chest.

"Mom, let me go, *now*." His voice was stern but calm.

"I'll never ever let you get away from me again –"

"I said, *let me go.* Don't make me ask again."

His free hand grasped for her neck and shoulder. She gave another agonized shriek and jerked away. He sat back upright with the force of a taut spring released. He clicked the seat belt across himself and opened the book.

Cousin Mason turned round sharply. "What in the *hell* d'you keep doing to her?"

"Pressure in a vulnerable spot, like I said. One of the things I learned while away. When she gets hysterical," (the briefest look at Eunice) "the only options are to leave the scene until she calms down, or some kind of physical effect. I wasn't going to jump out of a moving car."

"'Cause I tell you, if you hurt her I'll get right out of this car and kick your ass."

"Don't worry, it wasn't serious. Just enough to make her let go. I'd rather have dumped a pitcher of ice tea or something on her, but there wasn't one handy." A faint smile flicked across his face. "The numbness'll pass in a minute," he told her. "Remember, though: I asked you twice, and you still wouldn't let go."

His voice had matured along with his body, no longer the reedy trembling of puberty. His quiet self-assurance was also new, and an astonishment. There was no sign at all – yet – of the passionate rages and despairings that had made even Rick want to dump a pitcher on him once or twice. "Was that some kind of martial-arts thing?" Rick asked.

"Some kind," Aidan replied.

Eunice was waggling her arm and fingers with a

bewildered look. "You OK, Neece?" Mason asked her, then leaned his head back in Aidan's direction. "Now I mean it. You do not hurt your mama like that. Or any woman."

"I couldn't breathe, and she refused to let go even when I asked." His tone held no defensiveness. He was stating rational facts.

"What the hell'd you expect? Three years she doesn't know if you're alive or dead. You come back in one piece; she's going to be…You knew she was gonna be like this."

"She's known all along I was alive and well; she knew from the pictures. That's why I sent them. I know she knew, because I know she received them. I kept informed."

Rick could see Mason's eyes darting between the road ahead and Aidan in the rear-view mirror, their expression reflecting Rick's wary surprise at this new model Aidan. Would the old version come bursting out unexpectedly? Mason's next question seemed like a flanking movement. "What kind of martial arts; what discipline? Karate, aikido –?"

"No specific one. A combination of all of them; like, the most useful parts. Karate and aikido; tae kwon do, judo, capoeira; some others. And the kind of simple things they teach in basic self-defense classes."

"You should've told me you wanted to learn that. I would've been glad to show you."

"I appreciate that. If things had been different, maybe I would have."

"You could've come stay with me, too," Rick added. "If you'd wanted some, like – neutral time, away from the family."

"I appreciate that too. But you're an honorable person, and

sooner or later you would've told them I was there. BTW – congratulations on the inheritance. I think."

"Thanks – I think. You should come check it out."

"But you need to show your family a little consideration," Cousin Mason interrupted. "After all they've been through over you."

"Everyone thinks I'm a *bad mother!*" Eunice cried out. "They say I'm a *monster!* Saying I'm selfish, neglectful, that I didn't care – They *call* me in the middle of the *night* and tell me I should *die!* When night after night I couldn't sleep, crying and crying and *crying,* praying and *begging* God, '*Please* bring my baby home!' When I would've done *anything* to get you back!...And now you won't even let me *touch* you!!" Aidan ignored the histrionics and kept reading his book.

"You got anything to say to that?" Mason asked him.

Aidan didn't look up. "No."

"No. No what?"

"No sir, I do not."

"Nothin' like 'Mama, I'm sorry I caused you all that?'"

"No, sir."

"Because I *could* pull this car right over and let you walk back to Raleigh."

"Mason, no!" Eunice wailed.

"I could hitchhike. I've done it before. I don't have to go back to Raleigh either – I could go back to my friends. But if you put me out, you know she'd go with me, and we'd both be hitchhiking. I wonder how that'd look on FOX News? Dad wouldn't be pleased, that's for sure."

Mason took his hands from the wheel in an exasperated

gesture. "Aidan – look. I'm not trying to be an asshole. I want to help you if I can. If you'll let me. But – I can *not* figure out what the hell has happened to you."

Aidan lay down his book. "What the hell happened is, I'm now someone who won't be bullied, or threatened, or guilt-tripped, or manipulated. In any way. The sooner everybody realizes that, and deals with it, the easier things'll be."

"What 'friends' are these?" Eunice demanded, dabbing and sniffing again. "Who are they? Where are they? Do your father and I know them? Did they lie to us about knowing where you were? If they did they're a bunch of..." (she had to pause for courage to utter the blasphemy) "of God-damned kidnappers! Do you know how it feels, that you'd trust some *strangers* instead of your own *mother*?"

"Don't get me wrong," Mason went on. "We're all glad as hell you're back. We just want to make sure you don't ever do this again. Did you stop to think for a moment how it'd affect us? The cops as good as told us, your daddy and me, that if they hadn't found you within forty-eight hours the odds were you were dead." Eunice's sniffling increased in volume and pace at this statistic. "(Ssh, Neece, it's OK)...What I'm trying to say is, we *would* have helped you if you'd told us. You didn't *have* to do this."

There was a long pause, while Aidan continued reading. Finally Mason turned around and glared at him. "Aidan, you do know I'm talking to you, right."

"Yes. And I'd feel safer if you kept your eyes on the road. Whether I didn't have to or not, I did. *I* felt I had to. Now I'm back. End of story. I don't feel any need to dissect it."

"Well, I do. You really believe we wouldn't have helped

you?"

"Yes."

"Alright; why?"

"Because I asked for help, and didn't get any. I know you've seen the video."

"That video!" Eunice burst out. "That horrible thing, they're *still* playing it *everywhere*! All over TV, all over the Internet – I can't go anywhere or do *anything*, without strangers or even my *friends*, *asking* me about it! How could you *do* that to me?"

"So what should we have done different?" Mason demanded.

"You should have *believed* me. You should have taken me seriously. When I told you, and Mr. Johnson, and Chief Laney, that Randy Hewitt had sworn to murder me, for no reason at all except that he hated me, and that I was in mortal terror of my life, *I meant it.*" He'd put down the book again. There was now heat in his voice. "But you didn't *believe* me. None of you did. You brushed me off. You *laughed* at me. *I was in fear for my life*, and you *chose* to not care! –"

Eunice interrupted. "Aidan, do you know what happened that very day? Chief Laney brought Randy right to our house. He was going to tell you himself that he was sorry and promised never to do it again! Did you know that? –"

"Of course he did. He'll say whatever the grownups want as long as they're around to twist his arm. But as soon as he got me alone he'd be beating me even more viciously, for 'telling' on him. I told you that too, for years, and you wouldn't believe me then, either."

"Daddy would've made –"

"Daddy was campaigning, like always. And if he had been there he would've called me a 'pussy' and told me to fight back. Fight back, against a fucking sadistic psychopath twice my size, when I had no physical strength and no fighting skills. You *know* that. You *know* that at least once a month he gets in trouble for beating somebody up, somebody like me who he *knows* can't fight back. Dad'd say 'His kind are all bark and no bite, hit him a couple times and he'll back off.' Bull fucking shit. That's what he'd *want*. The minute I lifted a finger against him, that'd be all the excuse he needed to slaughter me. Along with his gang of friends who're all just as vicious and mean as him, and'd be glad to help him do it. Then what? Oh, there'd be all kinds of fuss, and a trial; and they'd pretend they were sorry; and they'd spend a few years in juvie jail and probably get out soon as they turned eighteen. And gloat about it the rest of their lives; and *boast* about it, to show how tough they were – 'Yeah, I killed a guy when I was only fourteen!' And what would *you* do?" He turned on Eunice. "You'd raise hell at the trial and cry enough tears to float the whole fucking courthouse out to sea; but you know what? – you'd enjoy the attention. Maybe you'd even say you were sorry you hadn't listened, when somebody pointed a TV camera at you; but you could spend the rest of your life playing the most tragic martyr in the county. And Dad'd use it for sympathy votes. I'd be more use to you as a dead tragic victim, than a live person you'd have to listen to and maybe even respect."

"Aidan, Aidan, he *promised* to not do anything! He *promised*, to Chief Laney and me!...Aidan: I have been persecuted, and vilified, and cursed at, and humiliated, for three

supremacist phrase: "Demographic transformation must end"...Parent to

years, because of you! I can't ever show my face again. They'll say 'She's that *monster*, she's that *bad mother!*' Don't you care? Do you care that I've been *disgraced, for the rest of my life*, because you wouldn't *listen*? You wouldn't trust me; you'd listen to everybody *but* me, saying 'Run away, cut your hair, listen to the whole *world* instead of your *own mother*,' when all I've always told you is that you're *beautiful* just as you are! Don't you care? That I'm a *joke* all over TV?" She made a sobbing gasp for air. Aidan had returned once again to his book and was paying her no mind. It felt like he'd drawn the genie of his old self back into a bottle and corked it with practiced ease. "Aidan...Aidan, *look* at me...Please –"

Whatever she'd been going to ask was cut off, as Mason shouted "*Jesus fuck!*" and they all were hurled against their seat belts. A battered old Camaro had cut in front of them and slammed on its brakes. Mason tried to swerve past but it slalomed across the lanes, blocking him. He headed onto the shoulder; it anticipated him, pulling over and stopping, forcing them to also stop, barely inches from the Camaro's rear. Two men and a woman leaped out, with smartphones and a camera, taking pictures. They were tapping on the windows, calling out questions. "Mr. Kingsley! Mrs. Kingsley! Aidan, Aidan! Where did you go? Did you have help? Were you kidnapped?"

Mason threw it into reverse and roared backwards, throwing them all against the belts again. Dad and the others, following close behind, had seen everything, and now pulled up in front of the reporters' car. The attackers were briefly nonplussed, unsure which victims to pursue, so Mason seized the opportunity and zoomed out into traffic again, nearly sideswiping them against a passing semi. Eunice screamed. "Goddamned fucking assholes, fucking near killed us," Mason snarled. "Call your daddy," (he ordered Rick), "tell him to get us some state troopers up here. We need an escort."

Rick thought his barrier on, for both cars. Looking back, he saw Dad's car race away from the pursuers. It drew up parallel to them, Cal driving. He and Mason kept the two cars in pole position on up the highway so nobody else could sneak past, with Rick as radioman relaying phone messages back and forth, until the requested escort joined them at the Faison exit, three cruisers with lights flashing.

The news of Aidan's return was obviously loose. Dad had had to cancel several campaign appearances to make this trip; somebody must've been tailing him the whole time and witnessed, or heard about, the scene at the depot. Rick thought about offering the Court as an even better refuge from prying publicity. If the family came there, though, Dad would bring his campaign with him; and the thought of Dad's typical supporters swaggering around the place – *my own refuge*, he realized – all arrogant at having gotten in, like Hitler in Paris, made him half queasy and half pissed off. *It's a white elephant I'm embarrassed to own; but when it's threatened – when my feeling of possession, of safety, 'this is MY comfort zone' – feels endangered, suddenly I'm Mr. Earl-of-Downton-Abbey, Mr. 'My-Home-Is-My-Castle.' WTF. That place keeps making me surprise myself.* Aidan could stay if he needed to. Cousin Mason could visit. If Eunice came, he'd want Mom and maybe Leslie there to buffer her, or at least Claire to keep her talking. *No, not Claire – before I knew it she and Eunice'd have our wedding all planned out, and they'd be breathing down my neck for me to propose!* And Dad could come only if he came as himself, not as State Senator Kingsley the Radical Republican. He'd have to absolutely leave all his politics down at the gatehouse, so they couldn't get in and poison Dreamland. Rick hoped that if push came to shove he'd have the strength to hold this policy.

"See what you've done?" Eunice demanded tearfully. "It's like this *every day!* They phone, they e-mail, they pound on the doors and windows – I haven't had a moment's peace, because of *you!*...Aidan...Don't you *care?*" Aidan calmly turned a page. *"Aidan Stephenson Kingsley,* LOOK AT ME!" He slowly turned, with a weary resigned expression. It seemed to crumple her. "Don't you care for what you've done *to your own mother?*" she whispered.

"No."

She stared in horror.

"Not since you chose long ago to not care about what you were doing to me. Or not doing. Anyway, you're exaggerating; which you always do when you're freaking out like this and trying to get everyone to feel sorry for you. It may have been like that for a month maybe, until some other big story attracted them. That's how media cycles work – hasn't Mr. Boulware told you? This now, it'll be crazy, but only until Trump opens his mouth again. So, *no,* I don't."

Cousin Mason tapped a clenched fist against the wheel several times, with the vibe of dangerous anger diffusing itself for safety's sake. He opened his mouth, but couldn't seem to decide for a moment what should come out of it. "Eunice...if he's gonna be a hard-hearted little shit, we'll just have to leave him to it."

Trump's treatment of women 10 times in one day...Ohio Trump campaign

Eunice lost it. She collapsed in on herself like a balloon deflating, into maudlin bawling sobs. She cried and cried and cried, until the cries dried up into gasps for air. "How can you *bear* it?" she whimpered, in the tiniest, most piteous voice imaginable. "How can you *bear* to be so cruel?"

The scene at the Raleigh house would be chaos, Rick knew; and possibly outside Haw Court as well. He texted Leslie a warning. He wondered how long he ought to stay and show family solidarity. He wanted to go straight on and let them sort things out privately; to slip strategically away back to his own life and out of range of possible explosions; but he was just as hungry as everybody else to find out where Aidan had been and what he'd been doing all this time. (How *had* he vanished so untraceably; where *had* he gotten Polaroids from? And was there anything, by freaky far-out chance, in what that psychic had said? Thanks to the Wizard, that concept called "the realm of possibility" had gotten a hell of a lot bigger.) Aidan hadn't yet faced off with Dad, either. Dad was a whole different, scarier, kettle of fish than Eunice. That match could be interesting, in the same ghoulish queasy-guilt way videos of bad accidents were "interesting." Explosions could be fascinating, from a safe distance. He decided to stay if Aidan indicated that he wanted him there, for support. "What's that book you're reading?" he asked.

Aidan held it up so he could see the cover. "It's a novel about Chapel Hill's music scene. I found it at a free market in Montana. It's long and kind of dull, but it's good for long trips."

"You were in Montana? I was in Bozeman a couple years ago, for a job interview. It's beautiful out there. What were you doing?"

"Passing through."

"Where were you headed?" said Cousin Mason, pretending to make conversation.

"To somewhere else."

"Somewhere else east or west? North, south?"

"Somewhere else." Aidan's voice was as casual as Mason's was pretending to be. "I'm not going to give anyone specific details about where I was or when. I don't want to say anything that could expose the friends who helped me. I don't want them harassed, or worse. And I might need them again someday."

"Now why do you think we'd harass them?" Mason asked.

Aidan made that small resigned smile. "I know my family."

"Did you hear about the Wizard while you were out there?" Rick said.

Aidan looked up. "Oh yes."

"What have you heard?"

"What everybody else has, I guess. Pregnancy self-controlled, the gun barrier. And taking down conservative assholes, who totally deserve it. So FOX News and all those types are totally shitting themselves. Naturally. Did he do something new?"

"No, not that I've heard. But what do they think of him?"

"They who?"

"Your friends. Or you, since you don't want to incriminate them." Rick ventured a smile.

Aidan returned it – a brief flicker of mutual trust. "He seems like he wants to do good. I like what he's done so far."

"I dreamed once that you and he were hanging out. Right about the time everybody started hearing about him. He was with you and a bunch of famous women, like Ava Gardner and the Narnia girls."

Aidan was amused. "What were we doing?"

"Nothing; you were just there. He said you were 'doing a good job.'"

"At what? I hope it wasn't, like...stud service for the girls so they could test the pregnancy thing." Eunice looked mortified.

"But here's what's really wild: right then I woke up because the train was stopping suddenly..." He told about his Ghost Train, his interrogation the next morning, and the other sightings he'd found online. "They're still happening, too; and now some people are saying they've even ridden on them. One right up in Chapel Hill – a couple of Duke students say they took it back to Durham. And Rainbow Gathering, Burning Man this summer – you heard about them, right? There's stories that a lot of the missing people escaped on 'ghost trains.'"

Mason asked Aidan if he'd ridden any trains while he was away. Yes, some; he replied, but wouldn't say when or where. "Do you think the Wizard might be connected to the ghost trains?" Rick said.

"I wouldn't be surprised. Has anybody asked him?"

"This is a long shot, but – have you met him?"

"No." Aidan hesitated. "I mean, not that I know of. Because they say he could be anybody. I saw him in dreams, like everybody does."

*

The mob at the Raleigh house filled the whole block. The

troopers and a bunch of State Capitol police cleared a way for the cars. There were fans of Aidan's, mostly teenagers but a fair number of adults too, with signs like AIDAN RULES or BULLY THE BULLIES; supporters of Dad's and protesters against him; TV cameras moving through the crowds like shark fins above water. The crowds pressed against the restraining officers, applauding, cheering, calling questions, taking pictures. Rick saw one cop flush a covey of girls from the bushes by the garage; they looked barely twelve but were dressed as much older. *"I want to marry you!"* one shouted. Aidan paid no attention to the uproar.

A catered breakfast was set up in the dining room, the curtains drawn for privacy. Agents from the SBI and FBI awaited them. Dad took Aidan aside and instructed him. "Get you something to eat right quick and come into my office. You don't have to talk to these people if you don't want to; but if there's any reason you think you might need a lawyer, you can tell me first in confidence."

Aidan looked back at him full on, equal to equal – another change; the little Aidan who'd run away would never meet his parents' eyes, looking downward instead with an attitude of sullen martyrdom. "There isn't. But I appreciate the offer."

Dad seemed taken aback. "You're sure now?"

"Yes."

"The press'll want to talk to you too, you know. Think you can handle that?" At the word "press" Mr. Boulware came over, plate piled with food. "If not, Cal or I can speak to them for you. Just tell us what you'd want to say."

"That's fine. Might as well get it over with."

Aidan loaded a plate (hard-boiled eggs, pineapple, one

small piece of ham, half a biscuit with blackberry preserves) and crossed the hall to Dad's office. Dad motioned the agents to follow. Eunice sprung up and hurried to join them, but Dad, standing in the doorway, shook his head. "Sorry, honey; just us."

"But –"

"The fewer people round him, the more he's likely to tell."

"But Lin – I *have* to know what happened to him."

"I'll tell you everything afterwards, I promise. But this is how they work. They're the top guys at this kind of thing. The FBI didn't come all the way from Washington just to be social. I'm doing it the way they say."

"Lin, *please.*"

"Babe, it's not a choice. They don't want everybody prompting him. And you know how he gets if he thinks we're ganging up on him."

"Lin, they've *done* something to him! They've *turned* him! He's hateful and cruel, and he won't even let me *touch* him!"

"Eunice – Eunice – look. Who's the lawyer in this family? Is it you, or me?...I need you to calm down. Get a drink and lie down if you have to...It's gonna be OK, I promise." He shut the door.

Eunice trotted back and forth between the hallway and the living room. Lin was sprawled in an armchair, texting; Cousin Mason in another, leafing through an issue of *Garden and Gun*; Mr. Boulware at the dining table pulling papers from his briefcase; and Rick on the sofa, trying to eat without making too much noise. The curtains were drawn, leaving them in an uneasy dimness, and a faint atmosphere of the room being embarrassed to be hiding itself from the bright friendly sunshine outside. With the sea-green

The19th: Trump supporters tweet new anthem after Nate Silver poll shows

color scheme Eunice had paid some designer a lot of money for, it was a jungle-like dimness – a Jurassic jungle, Rick thought, with Eunice fretting around like one of those dinosaurs with the useless little forefeet. "They've *done* something to him!" she repeated. "They've *programmed* him, those 'friends' of his. And the Wizard, too! I just *know* it. The minute we began talking about him he shut up tighter than a turtle and wouldn't tell anybody anything! Didn't you see?" Nobody ventured an answer. She plopped down on the edge of the sofa, then got up again and went to pick through the remnants of breakfast.

After a few moments, while the voices from Dad's office murmured, Cousin Mason looked up at Rick. "How's things going out at your place?"

"Pretty good. My estate manager keeps the household running smoothly. The farm's producing so much that I've got more than I need We cleaned up an old store in the village and sell it there. We get interns from N.C. State to help out, from the Ag and Vet Schools."

"Interns're the way to go," Lin said, half-paying attention. "Work for free."

"Free? No! I pay them fifteen bucks an hour and put them on the insurance like everybody else."

"Must be nice havin' that kind of money to waste."

"I'm not going to ask people to do free internships. They suck. You have to have another job to live on, or two if you're someplace expensive like New York – or Chapel Hill – and the internship's like a second or third job you don't get paid for. You're tired all the time and still don't have any money."

The voices from the office rose a little. They all listened, but could not tell who was speaking.

"We saw one of your decorators at the Southern Home Show," Mason continued, "when me and Danny took Eunice. She had a booth – the little Asian girl and her partner. Neece, you remember what her name was?" Eunice wasn't listening. "While we were talking to her this editor from *Southern Living* came over, and when Eunice said 'Haw Court' you should've seen his eyes light up. They'd do a story on you in a heartbeat."

"No doubt."

"You ever get bored? With nothing to do?"

"Not often. I've got David teaching me all the paperwork, taxes and employment filings and stuff. I've got the accountants teaching me how all my trusts and funds are set up, which is *hard*. Business *and* math. I go to the Durham office and help Sarah sort through all the appeals. I run; swim, play basketball with my same friends; do a lot more with Claire, now that I'm able to. Sometimes I take Baxter and go hiking round the property, exploring it."

The voices rose again, with a note of anger or frustration. "Give 'im hell, Daddy," Lin muttered. "Little shit thinks he's better'n all of us."

"Linwood Ervin! – shame on you. Aren't you glad he's home safe?"

"Reminding everybody he thinks I'm a perv."

"Then why did you say those awful things to him?"

"Mama, everybody but you and him could tell I was just messin' with him."

"Not everybody," Mason remarked, looking at the ceiling.

"I don't care. It was horrible of you. It's one of the

reasons – *you're* one of the reasons he ran away."

"You sayin' it's my fault, huh. My fault that anytime anybody even looks at him funny he starts bawling like he's being abused? And you fall for it every time. You fall all over yourself to pet him down and say, Oh, he's special, he's sensitive. Everybody's gotta treat him like he's a antique or something. With gloves on. If I acted like that you think Daddy wouldn't beat my ass?"

"Linwood, you *know* he never did that to you. Not once."

Maybe he should've, came the disloyal thought. Rick caught Mason's eye and suspected he'd been thinking the same thing.

"He told me enough damn times he was going to. But don't nobody lay a hand on precious little Aidan, he might break. Let him call me a incestuous pervert all over the damn Internet, and make us spend shitloads of money on CSI teams and search dogs and private detectives, and goddamn goofball *psychics*, for Christ's sake, because he's run off to sulk someplace."

"Linwood Ervin Junior, don't you *dare* say another word! Don't you *dare* be so hateful. He could have been murdered, or forced to work for some drug dealer, or worse. He could've starved, or had to sleep under bridges, or in shelters with all those awful crazy people."

"Or he could've been hiding with you guys," Lin said, turning on Cousin Mason.

"If he'd come to us we would've let him stay, as long as he needed to. But we would've told your mama and daddy he was there. You know that."

"Same here," Rick added.

25,000 voter registrations...Kentucky GOP Gov. Matt Bevin hints at violent

"Yeah, or at your damn mansion."

"Before I got it? Before anybody even knew I was going to?"

"Hidin' in the attic or something."

"Like Mrs. Rochester." Lin didn't seem to get the *Jane Eyre* reference. Maybe his frat brothers had told him it was the book version of a chick flick. "I had the whole place inspected top to bottom; they would've found him. And then everybody had instructions that if he turned up they were to call me."

"If you went missing you'd want us to spend the money looking for you," Mason told Lin.

"I wouldn't run away. I'd stand up and fight."

Cal Boulware's phone kept sounding, no doubt with calls from the media. Mason leaned back in his chair and closed his eyes. Lin fidgeted, texted and made occasional raids on the buffet. Eunice just fidgeted. Rick checked mail again (Leslie had reported back that all was still quiet at the Court), sent a few replies, and wished Eunice's decorator's scheme had included readable books.

When the office door opened, they all sat up as if electrified. Eunice rushed over to the SBI agent who emerged. "Beg your pardon, ma'am – where's the restroom?"

"What has he said? Please tell me! What have they done to him?"

The agent was a bit overweight and looked peevish. He ran a hand through short sandy hair. "He won't say, ma'am. We haven't been able to get much out of him."

"Couldn't I talk to him, just for a little? He's – His father intimidates him; he doesn't understand how sensitive he really is – "

Lin made an upchuck noise in his throat. The agent shook his head, apologizing, and slipped into the powder room. "Why won't they *tell* me anything?" Eunice fretted. "What are they *doing* in there?"

Then Dad appeared, followed by the other agents. Dad was furious. The second SBI agent was shaking her head in an "I don't believe this shit" way. The FBI man, while not as angry as Dad, was definitely pissed off, as if all the interrogation tricks he'd learned at Quantico had conspired to fail him. Aidan, still the picture of calm disinterest, came last. Eunice confronted them. "Tell me everything," she demanded. "Tell me right now, everything that happened. I'm not moving from this spot until you do. You've shut me out and treated me like I'm *useless*, but – For heavens' sake, *I am his mother*, and I have the *right* to know! And it's your oath before *God* that it's your *duty* to tell me!"

"He won't tell us a thing," Dad replied. "Not one single God-damned thing. Not where he went, how he got there, who helped him – Sat there wasting all our God-damned time saying 'That's all I'm gonna say. I traveled. People helped me. I studied martial arts.' And not a damn thing more."

"Aidan –" Her voice almost broke. "Aidan Stephenson Kingsley, listen to me. You are going to *tell* me what happened to you! I am never ever *ever* going to give up until I know *every single thing* they did to make you like this…Yes I should've listened, I should've believed you; but *you have to tell me what they did*!! Did they *hurt* you –"

"Dad and the agents, or my friends?" Aidan interrupted. His calm was almost like a mantle of power. *Damn, he's enjoying this*, Rick thought. "No…Although I did have some bruises from judo, learning how to fall; and a black eye in tae kwon do. That was when I went four months between pictures instead of three. I got knocked out for a few seconds in karate, when I got distracted and let my guard down; which is how I learned to not let my guard down. And I sprained a wrist in capoeira. But –" he shrugged – "that kind of stuff happens when you're learning martial arts."

"*Knocked out*?? Oh God. Lin, he has a *concussion!*"

"No, I don't. They checked."

"Who did? How?" Dad demanded.

"Our sensei first, and the guy I was sparring with. Then a doctor, in a hospital, with an MRI."

"What hospital?" "When?" "Have you got the scans?" Dad and the agents all spoke at once. Aidan went to his duffel bag, which he'd set by the office door, and produced a manila envelope. The SBI lady snatched it first, pulling out an assortment of ghostly-grey-imaged mylar sheets. She glanced at them, then stared in astonishment. Rick saw that on the margins, where information had been printed, there were numerous neat rectangular holes. Everything except dates, medical data and Aidan's name had been cut out. "They're redacted?" the FBI man exclaimed. Dad grabbed them. "Who did this?"

"I did," Aidan said.

Dad was flummoxed for a second. "Why?"

"I told you. No information that'd help you track my friends, so you won't persecute them, and in case I need to go back."

Eunice was whimpering again. "What did they *do* to you? I don't *care* how ugly it was, you can *tell* me!"

"Nothing. I bet you're thinking molestation; and no. The

They want to "carpet bomb," "bomb the shit out of them," "make sand glow"...

Prodigal / 316

only person who tried that was Lin." A contemptuous nod at his brother. "No. Nobody did anything to me that I didn't want them to." Rick wasn't a lawyer, but even he could see what a big loophole that statement left open.

"You're not yourself any more! You're not yourself..." Her voice trickled into weeping.

"I'm more myself now than I ever was before. You're gonna have to deal with it."

Mason spoke up. "Okay. If you want to keep it a mystery where you been, I guess I can live with that. You're back, and you're okay. But can you tell us, what can we do to make it – to make you not want to run off again?"

Aidan seemed, ever so slightly, to appreciate the attempt at honest dealing. "There's a lot of things, and not all of them you can control." He indicated the "you" meant the whole family.

"Like what?" Dad charged.

"Um...political, religious, social, environmental...Just, listen to me, *believe* me, and respect me. *Don't* try to bully me or threaten me, because it's *not* going to work anymore. Don't expect me to know things you never taught me – I'm not a mind reader. Don't put me in impossible situations. *No* emotional blackmail." A glance at Eunice. "So when I tell you you're doing that – and I will – I always did before but you never gave a fuck – when I tell you that, *believe* me, and *respect* me. When I say No, I mean *No*."

"Aidan – if you run away again, you'll *kill* me. You will *kill* me. I couldn't *bear* it again; I *couldn't*."

He let slip a classic exasperated-teen sigh and eye-roll. "I don't see what's the big deal. I a couple years when I'm eighteen I'll move out anyway."

"Promise me something. Will you promise me?"

"What?"

"Don't ask; I can't bear it. *Promise* me…*Look* at me and say 'Mama, I promise!' *Please!*"

"I don't make promises I can't keep. And I don't make them until I know what they are."

"Promise me you'll never do this again. Promise me. Look at me and say 'Mama, I'm sorry, I promise I'll never leave you again.'"

"No."

"*Aidan –*"

"*No.*"

"Can't you give her just a little?" Mason insisted. "Say you'll talk to us at least, next time. Give us a chance to get it right."

"Aidan…if you love me…if you *love* me; you'll say 'Mama, I'm sorry.' If you *love* me…"

"If you loved me, you wouldn't try to emotionally blackmail me."

She let out another banshee wail, this time of frustration. She charged at him. "HOW DARE YOU! HOW DARE YOU! TO BE SO CRUEL TO ME!" Mason grabbed her in both arms and she sank to the floor. Lin slammed his hand against the wall. "Fuck this, you lyin' sack of shit. You didn't do no MMA, you little shit, you hid out with somebody you gave your boohoo poor me stories and they believed your lyin' faggot bullshit. I'm goddamn gonna make you tell us " Aidan watched his approach with a single raised eyebrow; but his posture seemed to change; not with any movement, but as a transmitted image might shift with a change in pixelation. His feet were shoulder-width apart, hands loose at his sides, body poised, not tense with apprehension but loose, fluid. Lin struck at him. There was a flash of motion, and Aidan had Lin pinned in a vise-tight headlock, the two of them crashing to the floor with such force the house shook. Eunice shrieked. The catering staff was peering fearfully round the dining room archway, Mr. Boulware clutching his briefcase to his chest. The shock set Great-Grandma Bates's heirloom clock teetering on the hall table, rocking and then toppling over. Rick leapt forward and managed to catch it just before it could shatter on the tile floor.

"*Get off him, NOW!*" Dad was shouting, and Cousin Mason yelling "What the hell d'you think you're doing?" though to which of them nobody could tell. Lin was motionless in Aidan's grip, eyes wide with dumbfounded shock as much as rage. Aidan looked right back, unblinking. When the shouting stopped, they all heard his quiet voice. "Don't *ever* try that again." Lin raged vicious obscenities at him. Aidan did not flinch, did not blink, did not loosen his grip by so much as an ounce of pressure. When Lin ran out of breath, he repeated in the same calm tone, "Don't *ever* try that again." There was mighty power latent in his voice.

"Will you *get off him?*" Dad demanded.

"If you guys'll restrain him first." Aidan's eyes never left his brother's.

Dad and Cousin Mason each grabbed Lin's arms. Once their hold was secure, Aidan let loose, springing backwards to his feet with ballet grace.

The agents were all attention. Dad looked ready to explode. He pointed at Aidan. "*Go...to...your...room.*" Aidan shrugged. He took his bag and headed for the stairs.

"You see? You see? They've *perverted* him into this hateful cruel –"

"Daddy, let me have him for five minutes. Five minutes. I swear to God –"

"Cal, get those doctors over here ASAP." Dad turned round to glare at Aidan on the landing. "We're going to get you a full physical, and an evaluation. Is that going to offend your privacy?"

Aidan shrugged again. "Fine by me." He went upstairs.

Rick decided this was a good time to slip away. The officers outside cleared a path for his car, so he was able to leave without running anybody over. People shouted questions and took pictures, but without the same energy as they'd shown for Aidan. Heading west on 64 he caught glimpses of Shearon Harris's steam plume off to the south, hanging thin and motionless in the bright sky like a giant exclamation point.

shoot up Muslim civil-rights group after week of watching FOX News...Florida

Leslie came up to the house that evening, for dinner and the Aidan news. "He took down Lin," she mused. "Can't say he didn't have it coming. Good on him."

She had news of her own, she said, producing an old shoebox she'd found in the gatehouse. It contained a handful of tiny cassette tapes, no bigger than a business card. Aside from the manufacturer's markings, there was nothing written on either the cases or the cassettes themselves. "They were hidden on the top shelf of a closet. And I thought, what if, maybe, they're Baum's, and there's something on them to explain why he left you everything? I want to see if I can get them transcribed somewhere."

"Yeah, do. I'll pay for it if it's pricey."

*

Reports from Dad told how Aidan persisted in refusing to give up any details about his absence. Neither the best therapists money and power could gather, nor the SBI's best interrogators, were able to draw out a single specific. "He just sits there smiling like butter wouldn't melt and says 'No,'" Dad related. "Says all we need to know is, he's back safe, sound and upgraded."

When not frustrating his inquisitors, Aidan maintained his "upgrades" with workouts in the Raleigh house's little-used exercise room, and on the back lawn when weather allowed. Paparazzi videos showed him practicing martial-arts moves, with notable speed and power. (He also used the moves on Lin, who tried to jump him a few more times. Lin ended up either pinned to the floor again, or unconscious for a near-minute from a well-placed right hook.) He said he'd be okay with returning to school, or getting a job. He hadn't gone back on social media; or if he had, he'd done so with such subterfuge that no one could find his new pages.

Dad allowed one on-camera interview with him. It was filmed in the office of the Raleigh house, with Dad sitting in, glowering and wary. Aidan was smiling and amiable. *Since you left,* he was told, *many children have followed your example, running away from home and leaving behind video diaries. Do you feel any responsibility for this?*

"No, ma'am. Except for the video part. I'm not the Pied Piper. The average number of runaways hasn't jumped since I left – I checked. You all just started paying more attention."

But many families still blame you for encouraging their children to run away. What would you say to them?

"I'd say 'You want to know why your kids ran? Look in the mirror.' Most runaways run away from hell in their own families. Abuse; alcoholism, drugs…And some, a lot in fact, are kicked out. Mom's new meth dealer boyfriend doesn't want them around, and turns out Mom never wanted them either. Or, they're gay, and their family's all hardcore Trump-worshiping religious fascists. That's one in three runaways right there. They don't need my encouragement."

Do you have any regrets over the effect you had on your own family?

"No. I stand by everything I said in the video. Every phrase, every word, every single syllable." He cocked a thumb at Dad. "They've given me an earful; but I said 'Too bad.' I asked them to protect my life, and they refused. They had the power to

about Medicaid cuts…Trump advisor on CNN discusses waterboarding Hillary

protect and defend me, and they *chose* to not use it."

What about the things your brother and classmates have faced, the death threats and online harassment?

"You have seen the video, right?" Aidan deadpanned. "I have no sympathy for them. They brought it on themselves."

If you felt endangered again, would you run away again?

"Not unless I have to."

What would cause you to?

Aidan thought. "The most likely scenario is, if Trump wins and makes life here unlivable."

What do you think might happen under a Trump presidency?

Aidan gave the interviewer an "are you really that stupid?" look. "Ma'am, look around – it's already happening! People are being *brutalized*. Black people, women, Muslims, Hispanics – Thugs are running around ripping hijabs of Muslim-American womens' heads. In New York they tried to push a pregnant Muslim woman down the subway stairs. All over the country kids in schools, and even teachers, are terrorizing Hispanic kids saying 'Trump'll deport your mom and dad and you'll never see them again; hooray and ha ha ha!' Right over in Greensboro you've got Trumpites telling their children, their *children*, 'Immigrants aren't people!' If that fucking orange retard psychopath wins, every kind of racist, sexist, gay-bashing, *everybody*-phobic *hatred*, that ever infected this country, will be set loose and given full power, from sea to shining sea. And they will *slaughter*, and slaughter and slaughter and slaughter, until those seas are red with blood. You're a reporter, you *know* it's true. You've seen it. You've seen the militia types like Bundy swearing that if Trump doesn't win –

Clinton...Armed Trump supporters plan open-carry demonstration outside

or even if he *does* – they'll take up their arsenal of uncontrolled guns and start shooting every liberal in sight. Everybody that's ever said a word against them. John Stewart, Rachel Maddow, Robert Reich? *BLAM!*" He mimed with perfect accuracy the firing of a pistol. "Reverend William Barber and the Moral Monday people? *BLAM!*" Each shout louder and angrier. "Him they'll get with a 'Stand Your Ground' law, like Dad supports. Though of course its real name should be the 'George Zimmerman Memorial Kill All the Niggers You Want and Get Off Scot-Free' Law."

Dad was standing up, saying "All right, that's enough; he's too worked up right now; we'll finish this some other time…" Aidan pushed him back onto the chair. Muscles outlined themselves in Aidan's arms. He looked Dad dead in the eye and spoke, clearly and carefully and slowly. "I – am – not – finished." Dad was wide-eyed, jawdropped, dumbstruck. Rick had never seen his father put down so firmly, and was as astonished as Dad had looked.

"Meanwhile," Aidan continued, "they'll also slaughter every law and regulation that holds them back. Every civil rights and human rights victory – gone baby gone. Every law that's kept them from carrying as many guns as they want, wherever they want, and shooting whoever they want whenever they want – *BANGBANGBANGBANG BANG!* Gone." His hands now shaped an assault rifle. "And every environmental regulation that's kept them from polluting us to death while they gorge themselves on profits – they won't show Mother Nature any more mercy than a serial killer shows his victims. Try to reason with them, give them facts – like I tried to give my grownups here facts" – (another thumb Dad's way) – "and they'll slaughter you even harder. They *hate* facts. And try to 'go high,' turn the other cheek? They'll gang-butt-rape you between both cheeks without even spit for lube, and do a vicious whooping end-zone dance on your body while you bleed to death."

"Aidan, calm down, you've –"

"Know what it feels like? What it's felt like my whole life? Like we're trapped in this car that's going fast as NASCAR straight towards a cliff, towards total annihilation. It's being driven by Bush, Cheney, Gingrich, Trump; Arlene Hooker, Pat Robertson, Alex Jones – with people like my dad here cheering them on and throwing empty whiskey bottles out the window. But if you try to grab the wheel and save *everybody's* life, they beat the shit out of you. They call you Traitor and say God loves America so God's gonna save us. Bull shit. God may save our souls but he's not gonna save our asses. Not from the consequences of our own willful stupidity. *That's* the biggest danger to America. Not Muslims. Not immigrants; and sure as hell not transgender people in the wrong bathroom. Ha! – you think HB2 was bad…Not artificial intelligence, but natural stupidity. Criminally, treasonously, *Satanically* willful stupidity. 'We don't care what your so-called "facts" are! Unless they're from Breitbart they're not facts.' Well, I don't give a *shit* what Breitbart says: facts are *facts.* That cliff coming up is a *fact,* and it doesn't give a *fuck* whether or not you believe in it. If you drive off it, you, we, we're all going SPLAT!" He smacked his hands together with a loudness that made the interviewer jump. "When a *whole country* chooses massive suicidal willfully stupid *evil:* all you can do is get the hell out of harm's way and wait 'til they've destroyed

menace Va. Democratic campaign office...Washington man, citing Trump,

themselves. That's what we'll do, me and my friends out there. We know where to hide, and how to hide."

Rick was witness to another, unsanctioned, interview. He was back in Grantsville the last weekend in October, helping with more hurricane relief. Aidan, in the back yard, doing tai chi routines in just his gym shorts. Sunlight caught hints of stubble beneath his chin and a small swath of pale red hair between his pecs, the muscles beneath flexing and moving with fluid strength. Lin came loping round the side of the house. "Got some friends of yours here," he told Aidan, with a wolf's predatory grin. Behind him were Randy Hewitt, and Kayleigh Werthan with her father.

Aidan slowly turned, strong arm and leg extended. He acknowledged them with a silent nod, and continued his routine. A long pause. "Are you going to even talk to us?" Kayleigh demanded.

"What about?" Aidan replied, calm and open.

She goggled at him, opening and shutting her mouth several times before she could speak. "Well – like, maybe about how you *destroyed* my *life*."

"In what way?"

"What – like – do you know what's *happened* to me?"

Aidan continued his motions. "Your dad sent you to one of the best private schools in the country. They gave you regular trips to New York City. You saw *Hamilton*, and got a selfie with Lin-Manuel Miranda. Your roommate let you spend August with her family, in the Hamptons."

"How do you know?!"

"Your posts. And people told me. They thought I might be interested. I wasn't. But I saw you didn't seem to be suffering."

stabs kissing interracial couple...Alex Jones: Bernie Sanders like Hitler;

"I HAD to go away! Everybody was saying they were going to kill and rape me and burn down our house and, and – Everybody HATES me, all over the world, and YOU did it! You MADE them hate me! Are you happy now?" She paused for breath, and tears. If she was wearing makeup, Rick wondered, would it start to smear like Tammy Faye's? An unsympathetic thought; but after how she'd treated him...*Don't back down, Aidan.*

"You did and said things to me." Aidan remained calm and rational. "I showed them to other people. They didn't like them, and said so. Your actions have consequences."

Mr. Werthan put his daughter aside. (Square-faced and thick-bodied with thinning blond hair and disco-era sideburns. Lacrosse player in college. He'd lumber elephant-like across his dealership floor at new visitors, trumpeting welcome with a huge smile. He wasn't smiling today.) "You know what, buddy? So do yours. There's crimes you could be charged with. Invasion of privacy. Lawsuits. Anything happens to my daughter, you, and your daddy are gonna be looking at *the* biggest wrongful-death suit ever hit a courtroom." His finger jabbed towards Aidan's face. "And maybe more. There's things I know. About your daddy's finances. What your queer uncles get up to." Rick wondered if he was one of those "things." He kept out of Mr. Werthan's sightline.

"You know it's not polite to point at people," Aidan remarked. "And you also know Lin's recording all this." He nodded at his brother. "Recording a 48-year-old adult threatening a minor. Everybody watching this will see you pitching a fit," he told Kayleigh. "You'll attract a whole new crop of haters." A smile, of secret knowledge held in certainty. "You know, once you two calm down you should apply for jobs with Trump's campaign. You're just the kind of people he's looking for."

"I'm not recordin' nothin'!"

"I can see the outline under your shirt. That big black button, that doesn't match any of your other buttons, is the camera. And you keep fiddling with it. The picture'll be so jerky it might give people seizures. What brand? – DynaSpy, Super Circuits? Mine's a Brickhouse Security hidden-camera pen, since I always had pens in my shirt pocket anyway."

"Where the fuck'd you get that kinda money?"

"Only sixty bucks, with shipping. The bank accounts Dad set up for us when we turned ten, that Granddad put money in each Christmas. You spent all yours. I didn't."

"Everybody *hates* me!" Kayleigh wailed. "I can't go anywhere without people saying 'There she is, Suicide Girl, that everybody hates! Let's not talk to her!'…I didn't *mean* any of it," she pleaded. "I was just *teasing*! Don't you *know* that?"

"This how you hook up with girls?" Lin rasped. "Make 'em cry? That turn you on?"

"I'm not a mind reader," Aidan observed. "So I don't have any way of knowing what you meant. I go by what you said and did."

"I just wanted to make you *talk* to me! You never talk to anyone, you never even *look* at them –"

"Because when I did, they either laughed at me or bullied me." Aidan nodded briefly towards Randy, who'd been standing to one side, downcast, only occasionally glancing up. "If you'd tried talking to me, in a friendly, honest, polite way, like normal people do, things would have been different. Our typical 'talking' would be, I'm minding my own business, not bothering you or anyone. You corner me and attack me, for my weight or my hair or anything at all. I'm taken by surprise and can't think of a comeback. You and everybody watching laughs. I weep with frustration and humiliation. You point, laugh, and *gloat* because you made me cry, and run away giggling with your friends. Repeat on a daily basis. That's what my video shows. You saw them."

"I don't *care* about –"

"You saw them. You did and said those things." He was looking straight at her. His voice was cold.

"I –" She stopped. Her eyes were horror-wide, her mouth open.

"You did and said those things."

"I…did…and…said…those…things."

"You told lies about me."

"I…told…lies…about…you." She was trembling, more and more violently.

"You told me to kill myself."

"I…told…you…to –" (a desperate sob) – "kill…yourself."

"You *enjoyed* hurting me. You *gloated* at my pain."

She seemed to be trying, against a paralyzing grief, to shake her head. Her face twisted. Perspiration beaded her forehead, and tears flowed ceaselessly. Her father too seemed struck motionless, red with fury. "You *enjoyed* hurting me."

"I…enjoyed…hurting…you."

"You enjoyed hurting me."

"I…enjoyed…hurting…you," in a tiny voice.

"You will never deny it again."

rally violence: Far-left agitators not victims, "they were asking for it"...69-year

She pissed herself. "I…will…never…deny…it again."

Lin was bewildered and not a little scared. Randy looked outright terrified. *"What are you doing?"* Rick shouted. Kayleigh almost crumpled to the ground; then flung herself onto her father, sobbing hysterically and shrieking *"Make it stop, make it stop, make it stop!"*

Mr. Werthan dragged his daughter into his arms and fled. "You missed your chance, budro," Lin said with fake regret. "You coulda gotten you some serious great pussy. She wants it, I'm tellin' you. Now that you're all Mister MMA buffed up, she thinks you're hot."

"You really think I'm ever going to believe your bullshit again?" Another smile, of true regret, for Lin's pathetic hubris. "How do you know it's great? – have you already had it? If so, I wouldn't touch it with a ten-foot pole. I wouldn't touch it anyway."

Randy finally spoke. "Damn bitch's always tellin' me I'm trash and ain't shit 'cause my daddy's been in jail."

"People who call other people trash are trashy themselves," Aidan replied.

"I did a lotta fucked up shit…"

"You're not gonna pussy out, are you?" Lin urged. "He says he spent all his time gone learning how to beat the shit outa you. I think he's lying. Try him. All the shit he caused you?"

"Again with the pussy," Aidan remarked. "He's got it on the brain."

"Fuck you," Randy snarled at Lin. "Fuckin' goddamn pervert. *You're* the one started all this shit. Stole his stuff and tried to make him suck your dick. *Fuck* you." He spat on the ground and stormed off.

"What did you *do?*" Rick demanded again.

Aidan looked at him. "Tai chi."

Mr. Werthan gave Dad an earful about the incident. Dad was livid. He confiscated Lin's camera, sent him back to Greenville, and forbade him to be in Aidan's presence without adult refereeing. "But Aidan, I can't do a damn thing with him," Dad reported. "It's not like he backtalks me – I ask him to do chores and he says Okay and does them, doesn't make some big drama out of it. And he's polite, more so than ever. He's – Lord, I don't know…With Eunice it's even worse. She can't make him do what he won't do. No matter how much she begs and pleads and cries, he will not promise not to run away if Trump wins…Give me your honest opinion: you think Hillary'll beat him?"

"I hope so; but I don't know. All the polls say she will, but then I see stories that her lead's narrowing…I don't have an accurate reading. Everybody I know is Democratic, but driving out in the country, away from Chapel Hill, I see Trump signs everywhere. But remember how the polls had Werthan over you?" Kayleigh Werthan's father had carried out his threat to primary Dad; he'd lost, but not by much.

"Primaries are a different ball game. They're when all the fanatics come out. I'll admit I was worried. I'd go round town and folks I've known for years, now they wouldn't look me in the eye. It's feeling the same this time. Everybody in Grantsville's one hundred per cent Trump, even some yellow-dog Democrats. And they're wondering why I'm not speaking out for him. The man is – Somebody needs to do a serious sit-down intervention on him, and say 'Look, if you really want to move our agenda forward

state Senate candidate brutally beaten with brass knuckles at campaign event

you've got to do this and this and this. You've got to take this seriously.' Goddamn, that's what it is: Aidan doesn't take anything seriously. All the stuff that used to set him off; now he just smiles and says 'Ain't gonna be my problem.' Like he knows something we don't."

"Uh-oh. That worries me, Dad. That might mean suicidal."

"I thought the same thing. I asked him to his face, 'You're not gonna kill yourself, now, right?' He laughed! He said 'Hell no! I'm finally enjoying life!'…Eunice; she's been saying he was brainwashed; now she seems to think he's *possessed*. Talks about having Wolsley come up and *exorcise* him." (Reverend Wolsley was the senior pastor at First Methodist in Grantsville.)

"*Exorcise?* Crap! That's nuts. You're not going to let her…?"

"If she gets the bit between her teeth, I can't stop her."

"Look, like I've said, you can send him here for a while. If it'll help. Like a time-out for both of them."

Dad sighed. "I can't send him anywhere he doesn't want to go. He won't budge."

*

Post-election Wednesday was grey, wet, breezy, and unnaturally warm for November. Rick was at Mason and Danny's farm, helping with hurricane-relief care packages. (He'd voted early in Pittsboro; for Clinton, of course, and all the other Democrats.) Aidan was there, for the same purpose. Waking at seven from fretful sleep and figuring he might as well get it over with, Rick padded to the living room and turned on MSNBC. Things hadn't been looking good for Hillary when he'd gone to

...U.S. elections ranked worst among Western democracies...Breaking point

bed round eleven; but then again the Pacific Time states hadn't closed their polls yet; and he remembered how in '12 Romney had seemed to be leading throughout the evening until late returns put Obama on top. The first thing he saw, though, was Joe Scarborough mouthing over a red bar with the words DONALD TRUMP ELECTED PRESIDENT. Rick's jaw and the pit of his stomach both dropped. *"What?? –* No way!"

"Way," a voice said behind him.

He jumped. Aidan stood in the doorway, in sweatpants and a t-shirt from some Long Island bar called Callahan's. (Had he been sneaking into bars during his missing years?) Rick was again struck by how his plumpness had morphed into bouncer / bodyguard muscle. His face and his eyes were empty.

"We're all fucked," he remarked, and walked away. But had Rick heard him right? – had he said "We're all," or *"You're* all?"

The bad news just kept on scrolling. Governor McCrory, Buck Newton, Senator Burr; all the HB2 schemers and Amendment One touts, all were re-elected. Marijuana was legalized in several states; though getting legally stoned was not likely to be the main thing on anyone's mind for a long while. Dad won the Lieutenant Governorship, but by a slim margin; and when he and Eunice came out to the farm he didn't look victorious.

Cousin Mason and Danny were sullen. Some disagreement seemed to be simmering between them as they fixed lunch, neither of them looking at the other, and Danny banging the pots and pans on the stove louder than usual. "…not going," Rick heard Mason assert. "I'm not gonna cut and run."

"Then I'm not either."

After lunch, Rick and Aidan returned to package assembly from the piles of supplies (toothbrushes, soap, shampoo, tampons; breakfast cereal, baby formula, canned foods) stacked in the dining room. Aidan said little, and set his phone to stream the college radio station out of UNC Wilmington. Danny, and Mason with Dad helping, worked on separate repairs outside. Rick now and then heard Dad and Mason's indistinct voices, or the *plink, plink, plink!* of Danny hammering something. The greyness of the sky seemed to be growing darker. The wind had picked up, throwing rattling clusters of fallen leaves and an occasional twig against the house. The air felt weird and heavy.

An hour or so later, some cars drove up. Eunice hurried along the hall and opened the door. "He's in there," Rick heard her whisper. Cal's brother Luther Boulware, pastor of Sixth Street A.M.E. Church, came in; along with two of his largest deacons, and Eunice's friends Mrs. Haywood and Mrs. Pinyan. The women were wearing their Sunday best, and carried Bibles. Reverend Boulware was in his robes. The women looked apprehensive, while Boulware and the deacons had the expressions of guys bent on an unpleasant but important task. More whispering between them and Eunice: "...*pray* we don't have to bind him..."

They came to the dining room archway. Eunice stepped forward. "Aidan?"

Aidan turned. "Yes?" When he noticed Mrs. Pinyan and Mrs. Haywood he greeted them courteously.

"Aidan, could we talk to you a minute?"

"Go ahead."

"Privately?"

Aidan glanced at Rick. The psychic temperature of the

room seemed to drop a couple degrees.

"Please. It's important." Eunice's hands were trembling.

"I have no problem with Rick hearing it. He's family too. Is that all right?" he asked Rick.

Holy crap, was she actually going to try it? "If this is what I think it is: yes. I'm staying."

"Maybe it's some kind of intervention thing..." Aidan noticed Boulware's robes, the Sunday best and Bibles, the deacons poised as if ready to tackle him. He turned to Rick. "And you think it's...?"

"I think they want to 'exorcise' you."

Aidan didn't react in any of the ways Rick expected. He didn't react at all. His voice did not rise nor his expression change. His tone implied nothing more than polite detachment. "Oh?" he said.

She began sobbing. "You're...not...*you*...any more! You're *cruel,* and *heartless,* and *hateful!* That's not *you!* You were *never, ever, ever* like that! Something's taken you over and *made* you this way!" The women were patting her on the shoulder or arm. Aidan's face remained neutral. "Aidan, *please!* I know the real you is in there. We want to *help* you! Please, please, please; can't you do this one thing, this one little thing, to make me happy? Don't you remember how sweet you used to be when you were little? You'd say you'd do *anything* for me..."

"Your happiness is not my job. Not mine; or Dad's, or Mason's, or Rick's. It's your job. And my happiness isn't anybody's job but my own. The only way I could make you happy is by committing total psychological and emotional suicide. Lobotomize out everything that's my own soul. And that's not gonna happen. You're just wasting your time." He shook his head. "You still will not understand. You won't understand, you don't want to understand. I'm *growing up*."

"Eunice, if he's not going to do it, he's not going to do it," Rick said. "You're not going to make him." He was planning to intervene if they seemed about to harm Aidan in some way. But Aidan didn't act like he had any worries, even though both deacons were as large and threatening-looking as Lieutenant Worf from *Star Trek*.

Aidan stood. "I didn't say I won't do it. I just said they're wasting their time. But the only way they'll ever see that is by trying. So why isn't Wolsley doing this?"

Mrs. Haywood timidly took it on herself to answer. "Reverend Boulware's the only one willing. He has experience –"

"You've exorcised people before? Interesting. What kind of demons did you take out?"

"It's not wise to name them and attract their attention," Boulware warned.

"Have you got a herd of pigs somewhere, and a cliff for them to run off? Maybe with a hog waste lagoon at the bottom. And are you filming it? You should. It'd be a hit on YouTube."

Did Dad and the others know about this? Rick hurried out to the back porch. But Dad and Mason were way off by the well house, their backs to him, and Danny was invisible in the barn. Maybe they did know and were staying out of the way. Bastards. The wind nearly tore the kitchen door from his hands.

Aidan was reclining on the living room sofa, which the deacons had lifted away from the wall so everyone could surround it. His arms were comfortably crossed behind his head and his feet propped up on the other armrest. Boulware was reading from his own Bible, which had dozens of orange and yellow Post-Its sticking out everywhere. He had to grab a page of notes that slipped out towards the floor. He was stout like his brother, and looked like he'd have the same rich sonorous preacher voice, but his was more like a sheep's bleat; a male sheep perhaps, low in timbre, but still a sheep. "…This is the Word of God."

"Thanks be to God," the others murmured in an uncertain jumble. Mrs. Pinyan dug in her purse and pulled out several sheets of paper, which she handed the others.

"The Church," Boulware continued, "holds that the ritual of exorcism involves the casting out of an objective power of evil which has gained possession of a person. The authority to exorcise has been given to the Church as one of the ways in which Christ's Ministry is continued in the world. Is there any among you who does not believe that God is able and willing to deliver this soul?"

Me, Rick thought, *because of course he's not possessed. Not by anything more than teenage snark. And sure as shit, he doesn't believe.*

"We believe He both can and will deliver him this day," came the responses, still uncertain but a little less non-unison.

"Almighty Lord, God the Father, Lord of all creation; who was pleased to grant your holy apostles the power to work miracles and cast out devils; I humbly call on your holy name in fear and trembling, asking that you grant me, your unworthy servant, the power, supported by your mighty arm, to confront with confidence and resolution this cruel demon. I ask this through you, Jesus Christ, our Lord and God."

"Amen."

Aidan stretched to get more comfortable, making them all jump. His eyes were closed. Boulware upraised his hands. "In the name of our Lord Jesus Christ, I cast you out, unclean spirit, along with every Satanic power of the enemy. Begone from this creature of God. For it is He who commands you, He who flung you headlong from the heights of heaven into the depths of hell. It is He who commands you, He who once stilled the sea and the wind and the storm. It is God Himself who commands you." He took a breath and glanced at his notes. "Why, then, do you resist, knowing as you must that Christ the Lord brings your plans to nothing? Fear Him, who in Isaac was offered in sacrifice, in Joseph sold into bondage, slain as the paschal lamb, crucified as man, yet triumphed over the powers of hell. Begone, then, in the name of the Father, and of the Son, and of the Holy Spirit. Give place to the Holy Spirit by this sign of the holy cross of our Lord Jesus Christ, who lives and reigns with the Father and the Holy Spirit, God, forever and ever."

"Amen."

Nothing happened.

There was a long silence. No voices sounded outside, and Danny had stopped hammering whatever he'd been hammering. The air felt even weirder. Another scattering of leaves lashed against the windows and everybody jumped again, even Rick. Aidan remained comfortably spread across the sofa. Eunice tottered forward, trembling as though a breath would blow her over, and in a tiny voice asked "Aidan?"

"Yes?" He enunciated the word like a formal courtesy.

"Are you there?...Is it you?"

"Yes, it's me." In one easy motion he rolled off the

cushions and to his feet. He picked up the heavy sofa without any apparent effort and put it back. Then he turned to face her. "The same me as before," he smiled.

She burst into tears like a broken water main. "It's *not*, it's *not*, it's *not*! Try it again, try it again!" she begged Reverend Boulware, who'd looked out of his depth the whole way through, and now raised his hands as if to comfort or placate or just defend himself. The wind had risen, and Rick became aware of some kind of strange, subsonic sound or vibration. "It won't do any good, Mom," Aidan was saying in that same light conversational tone. "I could've told you if you'd *asked* first; but you never do."

"Aidan – Aidan – please *listen* to me! *I am your mother!* Your *mother*! I know – I *know* – with every bone in my body, that this is *not* you! The real you is *kind*, and *sweet*; and *loves* me" –

"That's too bad," he replied, as a swath of asphalt shingle slammed past the window. "I know with every bone in *my* body – and boner," he added, glancing at Rick. (*Did he say that, or was it in my mind? Did he just wink at me?*) – "that this is the real me. You'll just have to deal with it. You'll have to accept me as I am – or lose me permanently." He turned to the others. "I'm sorry you came all this way for nothing," he told them politely. "Would you like something to drink?"

Eunice fled, pushing past Rick without seeing him, and ran towards the back bedroom. Boulware and his party stood nonplussed. Outside, a jet stream of leaves was now racing across the yard; leaves, branches – wait a minute, a lawn chair? Somebody's mailbox? A sheet of *roofing tin*? The grey sky had turned greenish. The sound was no longer subsonic but a massive energy of rumbling, a jet about to take off or a heavy freight train.

the paranoid right-wing reality, where terrorists are literally everywhere...Ohio

Rick realized that for some seconds he'd been aware of the windows doing something odd. The glass itself was bowing in and out. Wavery figures of Dad, Mason and Danny were running for the house. Rick's ears popped.

Holy fuck.

"TORNADO!" he shouted. He dashed across the living room to the kitchen. "IT'S A TORNADO!" he yelled again at Boulware and company, standing even more nonplussed. He tried to grab Aidan but couldn't move that bouncer / bodyguard bulk off its feet. Open the cellar door, down the creaking stairs to Mason's wood shop, throwing himself under the huge heavy workbench. Covered his head. Barriered himself. Sounds, voices, outcries, as others followed.

Then reality exploded.

Eureka! I have found it!

Oh my good Lord have mercy.

Today we rode a trolley – a *trolley* – from Bynum down to Pittsboro, and a commuter train into Raleigh. I have the timetables in my hands. In my hands.

[*laughing or weeping*]

Hourly service from five A.M. to eleven at night, every twenty minutes during rush hours, and owl service out from Raleigh until one in the morning. And what did I see on my trip? For one thing, a Haw River you could swim in, that you could *drink* out of, by God. It's all true like he said; it's all true! Solar roads, hemp fields, backyard chickens, sky and air as clear as wine...I couldn't list it all. In the papers a sample ballot for a primary, *the* primary; held the same day, a holiday, all across the country, that everybody can vote in; *cumulative* voting where you get multiple choices. Oh, yes, Art Pope, bend over and spread for the fist of capital-"D" Democracy. Ha! – as if that rat bastard fatso could even set foot here. And what *didn't* I see? – besides Pope and his ilk? Freeways. Sprawl. Shopping malls. Wal-Marts. McMansions. Private racist charter schools battening on public taxes like leeches. Obama Derangement Syndrome. Shearon Harris. Anti-abortion and pro-gun bumper stickers. What I didn't see, won't see, will never see here, no matter how hard I look. No lampreys in the Great Lakes, no cane toads in Australia, no Tea Partiers anywhere – by God if *they're* not a hostile invasive species, tell me what is!

[*pause*]

I'm babbling. Giddy as a schoolboy. Scrooge after the three ghosts worked him over. After all the years, decades, of experiment after experiment, all the brainwave tapes and Rube Goldberg devices bought from New Age snake-oil salesmen, a waif and stray, *from my own home town*, no less, shows up at my door with the missing subroutine that makes it all fall into place.

From a mere word of comfort, posted to the comments on his amazing video. A word of comfort, and an offer of hospitality, while thinking "What am I thinking? What am I *doing*?!" even as I did so. He was from my home town, and what he did was so brilliant; and, he reminded me of *me*, fifty years ago.

[*pause*]

What else I saw?

No one was afraid. *No one was afraid.*

There were all the typical worries. Someone's grandfather was dying. Somebody had a big exam coming up. Someone was starting a new business, risking their savings. A girl was about to start her two years' national service, working in Glacier National Park. Everyone had different concerns about the different candidates, for or against, and was happy to explain them. But with no *anger*. Anger from fear. Fear that some huge power, in the hands of some faraway inaccessible people who didn't – who *wouldn't* care, was going to crush them in an Armageddon of stupidity. They knew their *own* power. Individual; and the power from, from joining together. Healing circles. They were going to have a healing circle for the man whose grandfather was dying, for him *and* the grandfather. Everyone was friendly – but not intrusive, which is a relief – when they heard it was my first time through. They didn't make a big deal about it. All in a day's work.

[*pause*]

They weren't afraid of *me* either.

Laura used to say I made people nervous. Then their nervousness would make *me* nervous; the sideways glances and whispering behind hands; and it would escalate, become an infinite loop. I stopped bothering after she died. Trying to socialize. Being social for the sake of being social. An infinite loop of failure. I'm not going to become Chatty Cathy all of a sudden; but...

This invisible *burden* seems to have lifted off me.

[*pause*]

When they argued about the candidates they weren't afraid. It was as if they knew that even if their guy didn't win it wasn't going to be a disaster. Because if things went wrong they could pull together and fix it. Before it got out of hand, before it was too late. Then they'd smile and say "That wasn't as good an idea as I thought, was it?"

Not like here. "How dare you say we're doing something wrong? Why, you – you traitor, you terrorist, you...you liberal! Try to challenge *our* power, *our* profits, will you? We'll destroy you! We'll destroy your academic career; we'll tell your university to revoke your tenure or they can kiss our donations goodbye. We'll make your job fire you. We'll buy your newspaper, magazine, website and shut it down...We'll hound you day and night with death threats. Rocks through the window, or worse. Slashed tires. We'll tar and feather you on the Internet. Burn you in effigy on the TV news. Convince the mob you're worse than Manson, Son of Sam and the Zodiac Killer put together. And Morton Downey will dance on your grave. How *dare* you point out our failures?"

You'll never eat lunch in this town again.

Vengefulness, on top of arrogance, on top of hate, on top of fear. And they'll never change, they'd rather murder the whole world instead of change, until all those walls can be blasted away and leave only the fear.

We sentence you to be exposed before your peers! Tear down the wall!

A therapist on the train was saying – They have therapists there too, because they have – people there have the same mental issues. Lots of them come with the damage that's been done to them here. "What are you most afraid of?" she asks. That's the core; that's where the cancer begins. The matter – antimatter chamber. The greater the fear, the greater the power. Laura said, "Your greatest fears are dragons guarding your greatest treasures." Hippy-dippy horse puckey, I thought. But my young friend explains that that's a powerful key, to what I've been seeking. Not the only one; there are many other combinations that –

[*break*]

A portal, right outside *my* old back door.

My Young Friend discovers it forty-two years later, and tells *me* about it. Ha!

Though maybe it wasn't there then.

One of the variables seems to be, how desperately the traverser needs a portal, or wants. Or needs *and* wants. But it isn't always necessary. He wasn't even thinking about portals that night. He thought he heard a train, even though the tracks are long gone, and went to look. He met a couple of travelers, traversers, getting wood for their bonfire, and they asked him over. He thought they were just some hitchhikers camping in the house. Then when he realized –

[*pause*]

I get choked up.

The way his face lights up with *pure joy*, even telling about it. When he realized what they were telling him, what they were *offering* him...

This enterprising kid, enterprising and determined like Edison – no, more than Edison, like Tesla! – he plays the latest tech of spy cameras and Internet like a symphony. God bless the Internet, and to hell with Steve Jobs. To hell with him anyway, for screwing Woz over. Yes, it's unleased the greatest pandemic of foot-in-mouth disease humanity has ever seen; but... My young friend uses it to blow up the whole, the whole *conspiracy* of willful stupidity against him, leaving them with egg all over their faces for all the world to see; and then escapes.

American enterprise is not dead. The kind that'll save true America from Ameri-capital-"K"-with swastikas-Ka.

[*pause*]

He says the house has been empty as long as anyone can remember.

I never went back. Never tried to contact them. Back then they could still have me thrown in Dix even as an adult. I found out eventually they had passed.

And nobody remembers us, he says. Even though Daddy had been station agent since before the war, even after the Coast Line merged with the Seaboard and they discontinued 49 and 42. They kept the agency open so he could reach retirement.

Companies cared about their employees back then.

I didn't want the house. I didn't want anything to do with the town or anyone in it. I had my new life. I wouldn't have this place if a client hadn't relocated to Argentina. He inherited it from an aunt and wanted to unload it. He thought it was useless land in the middle of nowhere. But I had a hunch how valuable it would become. After watching the Santa Clara Valley become Silicon Valley? Farm to sprawl almost overnight? Half an hour up to Chapel Hill, an hour to Durham or Raleigh...

[*break*]

Then of course: Laura. Laura at San Simeon. And me thinking "I have the power to make her fantasies come true." People don't realize how dangerous that is. Getting your heart's desire. She would have been miserable, which would have made me miserable.

I was never meant to marry.

[*pause*]

[*singing*] *Laura; a face in the misty light. A laugh on the summer night, that I can never quite recall...*

Not any more.

She'd rather have dreamed about it than lived it, I see that now.

[*pause*]

She never believed the world could be as evil as it was. Just wouldn't believe it. Convinced that good would always come out of bad. That would've killed the marriage. I'd be seething at her, "How can you *possibly* not *see*??! You –" She was so – She didn't, couldn't realize how *naïve* she was, about what – what evil lurks in the hearts of men. No kidding. The Shadow, she was not.

I'm no Lamont Cranston either; but…

Optimism's always naïve. At least in this reality. Something someday was going to crush hers. It was inevitable. It would have hurt too much to watch…I wanted to shield her from it, while at the same time I wanted to shake her until her teeth rattled, for *not* seeing that it could, *would* happen…

And now?

Oh boy.

Laura, thou shouldst be living at this hour. Maybe…The marriage still wouldn't have worked; but now she'd have good cause for optimism, instead of tra-la-la hippie fantasies. If we can pull this off; and everything I've seen tells me we can. If we can keep it on the right track; and everything I've seen tells me –

[*break*]

I wonder if the portal affects one's sight. Sometimes when I stand up suddenly, in the corner of my eye parts of the room seem to shimmer, like heat waves on pavement. Like my old acid-head friend used to describe his visions.

Never tried LSD. I held my brain too precious to risk on doubtful drugs. You couldn't even be sure what you were getting *was* LSD, unless you were lucky enough to be a friend of Owsley's.

Y.F. said some people find their way through with it, though more often with mushrooms or other natural – natural? psychoactives. Sometimes in conjunction with electronic or magnetic brain stimulation. Like those New Age devices I kept trying. I'll give them all to the UNC Psych Department. They did work for some people, sometimes, though it may have been the placebo effect. But I expect most of them will end up in medical museums, in the "How Stupid Can We Get?" display, next to the Civil War doctors' bloody saws. And bottles of Ritalin.

But every person's access code, as it were, is different, he says.

Not that I need it any more; but…what if one soaked the electrode sponges in water infused with psilocybin? I'll have to suggest –

[*End of tape*]

Aftermath

Rick dreamed of Ellis Island: a fantastically expanded Ellis Island of halls and corridors and gangways in impossible but functioning multi-dimensions, as if designed by M.C. Escher. It was full not of immigrants, but of people emigrating, sailing away to a better world. He could see out one window a train terminus, with a fleet of Ghost Trains that had brought the travelers. He was amused to note that they all looked like hippies. They could have come directly from the original Woodstock. They carried in their luggage things like bongs, carefully wrapped lava lamps, Grateful Dead bootlegs, and copies of the *Whole Earth Catalog*. They were boarding an ocean liner, whose name he could not make out but knew to be the same as the land they were bound for. There was a poignancy about their leaving, for it was a land like Avalon in the Arthurian legends; or Narnia; or the Valhalla-ish realm the elves and Hobbits sail off to at the end of *Lord of the Rings*. He also knew, for a certainty, that Aidan had passed this way.

The ship's whistle was about to blow. It was a cartoon whistle, anthropomorphized, whose valve became a mouth. It took a deep breath, and let loose. Its sound was not a whistle but a human shriek.

The shriek was real. It sank into a wail of horror and grief and unbearable despair. It was Arlene Hooker. It was TeShawn Williams. It was Leslie's doxxer. It was the terrorists, murderers, refugee traffickers, religious fascists the Wizard kept annihilating. It was Kayleigh Werthan. It was his and Claire's would-be mugger. It was Eunice.

Rick dreamed of Aidan. He saw a ring of giant, horrific

floods in West Virginia, Louisiana; thousands displaced...Call the Bundy monsters, a million times more terrifying than Godzilla. No one could pass them; anyone who tried would be annihilated with apocalyptic force. Within this ring, a little child: Aidan. He had been abandoned there, forever. He had been completely rejected, by everyone and everything, for eternity. He would be absolutely alone, for all the rest of his life, and for eternity afterwards. His heart had been broken, beyond repair, for all of eternity. He was innocent of any wrongdoing, of any desire to do wrong or even knowledge of it. He meant no harm to anyone; the very thought of hurting anyone was as far from his mind as the East is from the West. He had done nothing but *exist*: be himself, think his thoughts, wonder at his world. Yet that world, everyone and everything in it, even those who were the very source and reason of his existing, had betrayed him, rejected him, abandoned him; condemned him with fanatic, murderous fury, solely because he *did* exist. They had done everything in their vast power, greater than a million Hiroshimas, to annihilate his soul. So the monsters had come forth to protect him. He would live within their circle for the rest of eternity, never rescued, never reclaimed, never vindicated; with nothing to do but half-hearted attempts at play with a pathetic handful of broken and misfit toys, and to weep in heartrending despair. The monsters could only defend him; they could never comfort him. The vastness of that despair was so great, no words could ever encompass it. It was larger than all Existence itself.

Such despair, such suffering of overwhelming injustice, could not exist without equal rage. The rage was those monsters. The accumulated fury of that forced helplessness channeled itself into martial-arts training, with blazing-eyed teeth-gritted singleminded passion. Relentlessly they kicked and punched and chopped. Punching bags burst at the force of their blows. Tackling frames crumpled like tinfoil. Boards, bricks, cinderblocks, even steel bars, snapped like twigs. Bones broke too. Arms, legs, kneecaps, elbows; shoulders dislocated with a smash; jaws and pelvis and ribs shattered. Eyes were gouged out, ears bitten off, mocking tongues ripped from mouths. Testicles were crushed with a blacksmith blow from a sledgehammer. To everyone who'd ever dismissed him, patronized him, condescended to him, mocked his pain, refused to even acknowledge, let alone believe in, his truth, his monsters would show no mercy; no more than the man in Freeport who'd ripped the gun-lover's head off in defense of his babies. "I will FORCE you to *face the facts*, if I have to rip open your skull and burn them with red-hot irons into your very brain." He would be so mighty that no excuse, no attempt to shift blame, no counselor or minister-type negotiations, not even the most desperate pleas, could stand against him. Any *I didn't mean it, I was just teasing, I was just having a little fun*, would be blasted to ash by the monsters' atomic breath. *Can't you tell I didn't mean it?!* "No. Because I am not a mind-reader. It doesn't *matter* what you meant. The *only* thing that matters is what you said and did to me."

There was a shape, an outline, like a gingerbread-man cookie cutter. The shape was Aidan. All the forces of everything, vast and mighty, were pressing against it, trying to bend it into deformity; or worse, to rupture its barrier so it would collapse completely and be obliterated, like a cell crushed by too much weight and spilling out its life-plasm. But the Aidan-silhouette held its form, with the power of its heartbreak and its rage and its

man, arms raised, pleading with police moments before being shot...Native

absolute determination. The pressure grew and grew and grew, valves bulging, dials cracking, overloaded control panels bursting into flames. Layer after layer of concepts were melted away. Family – Dad's frustration, Eunice's tears, Lin's ass-covering prevarications: gone. The sympathy and willingness to help from Cousin Mason, Mom, Leslie, Rick himself: gone. The support of all the people who'd been moved by Aidan's video and taken his cause to heart – irrelevant. School policies and state laws were not enough. Platitudes like "it gets better" or "what goes around" or "you're better than this" were vaporized with a blast of bitter cynicism. Concepts like compassion and do-unto-others and there-but-for-grace couldn't help and were cast aside into nothingness. Civilization didn't matter. Human survival didn't matter. Nature didn't matter. The world, the entire physical universe, didn't matter. Time itself didn't matter. This was Aidan's *You shall not pass!*, his final showdown, between Absolute Life and Absolute Death. The Aidan-shape held its truth to be irreducible, in defiance of everything, even God God's-self, the very core and Source of all existence. (A tiny faraway voice Rick heard was Mr. Scott on the U.S.S. *Enterprise* telling Captain Kirk *"She canna take any more, Jim; she's gonna blow!"*)

Finally, like a sheet of plate glass compressed beyond its tolerance, the whole of Reality shattered through all dimensions against the invincibility of Aidan's truth, exploding into infinite razor-sharp shards that came avalanching down into a jumble of total chaos, from which they'd have to jigsaw-puzzle themselves back together, accommodating themselves as best they could to the permanent Fact of the Aidan-shape. The voice of Aidan's soul boomed out through all time and space and dimensions:

American student's grade docked for refusing to say Pledge of Allegiance...

YOU. WILL. STOP. HURTING. ME.

Rick was a tiny figure in the corner of a medieval manuscript, sitting on the Isle of Patmos and trying to comprehend this Revelation. He then saw a giant lever, controlling Forwards and Backwards. Trying to pull it Forwards were the progressives: meek, gentle, fair, honest, small in numbers and in strength. Dragging Backwards with all their might were the barbaric hordes of the reactionary "Right": the racists, xenophobes, LGBT-bashers; gun-worshipers, women-haters, antiabortionists; science-deniers, polluters, corporate plotters; religious fascists (Al-Qaeda and Fundamentalists side by side); all screaming in fanatical fury at the very thought of anything "fair" or "honest" or "compassionate." When Aidan's soul-shape spoke its ultimatum, there was a worlds-shattering crack; and then *two parallel realities*, one for each of the opposing forces, each with its own lever. In one, the progressives were finally able to pull it Forward and lock it into place. In the other it snapped brutally Backward, smashing and scattering the haters, their side ripping away and spinning down towards total destruction, all the consequences of their wrong and evil collapsing in upon them. They cried, in pain and terror and despair, so many tears that it formed a gigantic tsunami, crashing down with terminal force. But the good people were safely sheltered on their shore; and after the last of the wave had washed away, there was sunshine, and a lawn sparkling with dew. They emerged from their shelter, and walked into the beautiful morning of a clean bright new world.

*

Rick could hear lumber rattling. He realized he was still under the workbench, which was still against the cellar wall, but

War between police, NRA: Open-carry laws make cops' jobs virtually

blocked in on all sides by debris: joists, plywood, plastic, the lid of a washing machine. The rattling got closer. Some of the rubble tumbled away, and a strange face looked in on him. "Are you okay?"

"I think so."

The fireman turned and shouted something to colleagues. They dug Rick out. The house was gone, except for the corner of the guest bedroom where Eunice lay on the bed, face to the wall. She too was unhurt, at least physically. Danny was being loaded into an ambulance. Dad's face was bloody from cuts and his clothes ripped, but he was still standing. Reverend Boulware and his party, covered in dirt and shreds of pink insulation, were being helped from beneath the cellar stairs. The tornado's brutal gash in the landscape stretched away northeastwards as far as Rick could see. The clouds roiled overhead.

A few feet from Eunice, the trunk of a huge oak had been hurled to earth. An arm and leg were motionless beneath it. "You don't want to look," the fireman warned Rick. "It's Mr. Bates. I'm afraid he didn't survive." *Cousin Mason.* They were walking up to the ambulance, where one of the EMTs, not noticing them, made a crack about Mason and the tree being "too big even for his hole."

Rick punched him out.

Dad and the fireman were restraining him. *"You fucker! You fucker! He's my family, goddammit!"*

There was no sign of Aidan.

*

Grantsville had taken a bad beating too. The school where Aidan had suffered so much was a long ridgeline of rubble.

Buildings along Caswell Street had their insides torn out and were now only façades, like a studio set. The courthouse clock had been smashed. Nothing remained of First Methodist but the sanctuary's east wall, its Gothic windows all blown out, and the rose garden below. The site of the old Robbins place had been stripped bare. The very few people they saw walking about, Dad pulled over and called to, asking their situation and what they might need. Eunice, sitting in the back, seemed to see or hear nothing.

Their house still stood, missing shingles and with debris scattered across the yard. The power was out, of course. Dad and Rick spent half an hour trying to start an emergency generator, a machine that Mason (Rick thought with grief like a stabbing knife) that Mason could've got up and running in two minutes. Not long after it finally sputtered and chugged to life, Chief Laney pulled up. His cruiser had a cracked side window and its antenna was bent double. His face was grey. Rick knew there was more bad news.

A body had been found hurled against the brick wall of the old train station. The head was gone, smashed to nothing. But the clothes and ID were Aidan's.

*

Grantsville's wrecking paled in comparison, though, with what they saw online. Another tornado, equally strong, had plowed through North Myrtle Beach, simultaneous with a series of huge "rogue" waves crashing ashore. The surge had reached five stories high. Beachfront highrises slumped to their knees and pitched face-forward into the ocean. Tiny figures tumbled from a balcony, clutching in vain at a TRUMP / PENCE banner hung from the rail. Then an hour later, a funnel of gigantic power had

arrest for exposing use of attack dogs, pepper spray on Dakota Access

touched down near Bonsal, on the Chatham / Wake County border. On the "Fujita" scale of measurement, from F1 to F5, pale and shaken specialists believed it to have been an F8. At that level, its wind speeds could have exceeded 600 miles per hour; though every measuring device in the storm's path had been ripped from its moorings. Not even the thickest concrete, the strongest steel, could stand against it. At times it reached a width of two miles, with side funnels breaking from and rejoining the main vortex. It struck, and completely destroyed, the Shearon Harris nuclear plant. Then, with radioactive debris whirling within and raining behind, it smashed New Hill, Apex, Cary and Morrisville. It crossed I-40 west of Raleigh at the height of the evening rush hour, where traffic, already at a crawl due to heavy rains that preceded the storm and accidents those rains had caused, was helpless to escape. From there it turned north, to Raleigh-Durham Airport. Of the scores of travelers and employees busy behind the vast glass walls of the concourses, precious few had the presence of mind, and then the time, to shelter in interior spaces.

Then it crushed the shopping centers, hotels, office buildings and apartment complexes of Brier Creek, casting planes down upon the wreckage like childrens' toys. The car-crowded bridges of the I-540 / U.S. 70 interchange collapsed upon one another. Now eastward, through suburb after northern suburb, breaching Falls Lake Dam, letting flood waters down the Neuse River to damage Smithfield, Goldsboro, Kinston, all the way to New Bern near the coast. Finally, near Rolesville, it lifted itself back into the clouds. The next morning, almost sadistically, presented the shattered survivors with a sky of beautiful, innocent clear blue.

Pipeline protesters...U.S. using section of Patriot Act to justify detention,

Fifty-three people died in Grant County; including Danny, whose injuries took him down on the second night. Dad broke the news to Eunice as gently as he could about Aidan and Mason, with Rick standing by for support. At first they couldn't tell if she'd heard them; but then she looked up, and tears began to run down her cheeks. She stood, and clung to Dad for a few moments. Then she spoke. "Where's Lin?"

"Safe in Greenville. They weren't hit."

"I want to call him."

"The phones are all down. The Internet's working, though. He Facebooked us."

"Let me see."

She messaged him to come home. Dad had meanwhile offered shelter to some neighbor families whose own homes were unlivable, or gone; and the presence of "guests" brought her a little more back to herself. She changed clothes, and began piecing together a meal in the kitchen.

Rick stayed three days, helping wherever he could. He contacted Mom, Leslie and Claire. Leslie wrote back that she and Claire (and Baxter) were all safe; that Mom and Annie, also safe, were on their way to Philadelphia; and that the Court was unharmed. He asked her to contact all of their friends that she could reach and offer them the Court's shelter if needed. *Also staffs families. Ask Nate & Linda re supplies – how many can we feed & for how long? Also water, elec. Will try to get back ASAP.* He desperately wanted to return, but wasn't sure if he even could, let alone how long it might take. McCrory had declared a state of emergency, with the National Guard on patrol. Wake County was

incarceration, mass surveillance of minorities...Christian Fundamentalists'

under curfew; beyond, people were fleeing in all directions from feared radiation. RDU had only one useable runway, now closed to all but military flights. North-south rail lines and major highways were nearly impassable with debris and wrecked bridges. The death toll had already passed a thousand, with another thousand and more still missing. Instances of shock and madness were everywhere – like the viral video, whose source was never found, of a deranged man screaming at an Evangelical congregation as they try to hold prayers on the lawn of their shattered church, where campaign signs for Trump and other Republicans still stand. The man is in his mid-twenties. His well-tailored suit is filthy and ragged, as though he spent a very long time clawing his way out of rubble. *"How do you fucking explain it?"* he screams. *"You won everything! Every fucking election!"* He kicks down and stomps on the campaign signs. *"You own the whole fucking country now! You can persecute whoever you want! You can kill whoever you want! But God STILL fucking smote you! How do you explain THAT??!"* – until an equally wild-eyed youth, in a cammo shirt and "MAKE AMERICA GREAT AGAIN" cap, steps into the frame and blows the man's brains out with a semiautomatic.

Lin made it down from Greenville late on the third day, saying ECU was shut down indefinitely; the whole city was just an inch away from panic; and that there were rumors of self-appointed "militias" patrolling the highways out of Wake County and turning away anyone they thought "dangerous," the meaning of "dangerous" being whatever they wanted it to mean.

Rick left at dawn on day 4. They gave him food, bottled water, an extra can of gas, and a sleeping bag. Dad tried to give him a gun too, but he refused. "If they see me with it, they're *more* likely to shoot me," he insisted. They argued. "You think all that money and that big house is gonna save you?" Dad said. "You think me being your Daddy is gonna save you?"

"It might if they're some of your voters."

He had a detailed atlas, showing every back road in the state. He didn't know how reliable GPS would be, with cellphone towers blown down. He planned a long roundabout route south and west of Fayetteville to Pinehurst, up through Carthage to Siler City, then east-northeast towards the Court, staying well clear of Wake County. (Maybe down some detour he'd cross another "barrier" and meet another charming, helpful hippie pagan 57-gender-varieties family. He wished he'd been able to find that place again.)

He was exhausted, and not just physically. He'd spent much of the three days helping clear wreckage, uncovering injured – or dead – neighbors. He had to pull over often and take naps, from which he awoke disoriented, not knowing where he was, unable to fix the time or even the day. He'd drift awake out of confusing dreams, sometimes to discover that his waking was just a dream too; dreams that seemed to have him in multiple places at once, all with different pasts and presents. There had been a wave of devastating tornadoes; there had been only thunderstorms. Trump had won the election; or Clinton. The Wizard had performed his myriad wonders; the Wizard had never existed.

In a park by the Cape Fear River he met a worried-looking boy of fourteen, needing a ride to his Daddy's up by St. Pauls. As they drove he told Rick a bizarre tale: that as soon as the election had been declared for Trump, a mob had stormed the White House, dragged Obama out, and lynched him right there on the lawn. They gang-raped his wife and daughters, then surrounded them with all their guns and blasted away, until every ammunition clip was empty and the bodies blown to bits. "Weren't nothin' left bigger'n a McNugget."

"Are you *serious*?"

"Serious as a heart attack! Been nothin' else on the news ever since."

"How did they get past the guards?" And the Secret Service, and all the levels of post-9/11 security?

"They was in on it!" His Daddy had told him they'd been the first ones to turn their guns on the President. And now black people were rioting and burning shit all over the country, and shooting white people too. Right down in Wilmington they'd shot up a whole bus full of white tourists down on Water Street. He'd been staying with his Mama in Autryville. He'd had a bunch of black friends there; and even though they *were* his friends, and knew his Daddy had voted for Obama both times, they'd started looking at him funny. And when he told his Daddy this, Daddy'd told him how the Klan was running through the projects in east Fayetteville and shooting every black person they saw; along with Hispanics, and people they thought looked gay, and people they knew had voted for Clinton. And Daddy had said, "Son, you and me both need to get the hell outa Dodge." They were going to take the train from Laurinburg up to Cincinnati, where they'd crash with some friends of Daddy's while they decided where to go next, Canada or maybe Ireland.

They passed an old Volvo that had been wrecked against some trees and abandoned. A Bernie Sanders sticker was half-torn

professors warned after "campus carry" gun law passed: Don't teach

from the rear bumper. "Trains?" Rick said, concerned. "You better check on that. Amtrak's not running anywhere between Richmond and Savannah, because of the radiation."

"What radiation?"

"From Shearon Harris. That mega-tornado flattened it. *That's* been all over the news." The kid just stared. Was he getting his info from not just a different source, but a different planet? The road curved past a burnt-out ranch house with CLINTON / KAINE signs on the front lawn, now smeared with obscene graffiti. "Biggest one ever measured. It flattened everything from there all the way around North Raleigh. Cary, RDU Airport, Wake Forest – Three days ago. There've been tornadoes everywhere. We had one in Grantsville take out half the town and fifty-some people. Including some of my relatives."

The boy looked abashed. "Shit – that sucks. I'm sorry…There weren't nothin' in Autryville but some hail."

Rick set him down at a Huddle House, next to an I-95 interchange with all its ramps blocked by barricades and ominous, unsmiling state troopers. They blocked Rick's passage too, demanding every form of ID he could produce before letting him pass. A cruiser radio broadcast static-broken voices and strange snapping sounds that might have been gunshots.

Another nap east of Aberdeen; but here he floated out of a dream in which Sanders, with Hillary as his VP, had won in the biggest landslide ever measured, sweeping progressives to power all down the ballot; breaking the back of the Republican cabal forever and leaving it to die in a dark dead-end alley of history. Aberdeen, as he passed through, looked a peaceful tree-lined place. The air was autumn-crisp. At the trim railroad station, people with

"sensitive topics," anger students...California, EPA poised to expand pollution

luggage seemed to be expecting a train. His dream outside Goldston, though, was a nightmare of Midwestern fracking quakes compounding on one another until they triggered the New Madrid Fault, leveling Memphis, Jackson, Fulton and leaving them in flames; drowning Paducah and all who lived there beneath the Ohio River. Or, the flames were from fracking-gas explosions in Oklahoma chain-reactioning into a massive blaze, racing across the state so fast that its fire tornadoes outran fleeing refugees and roasted them alive in their cars. The dread that woke him was strong. He was parked across from a convenience store he didn't remember seeing before he'd dozed off. Hand-lettered signs at the pumps announced GAS $10 / GALLON NO EXEPTIONS and GIEGER COUNTER FOR RENT $300 / HR. The air was heavy and humid and smelled of burnt houses. The radio, which previously had picked up only distant strange music half-drowned by interference, between long spells of nothing at all, was now passing on updates from the Emergency Alert System. Radiation levels in Wake County were "stable" (whatever that meant – "stable" as in safely low or dangerously high?) but nonessential travel into the area was still not permitted...

As he got closer to the Court he wondered if everything there was running smoothly. Was it still there, even? A lot could have happened since he left Grantsville. His phone hadn't found any service throughout the trip. Would he be like Scarlett O'Hara coming over the hill to find Tara still intact; or Max de Winter in *Rebecca* saying "That's not the sunrise – it's Manderley!" as the house and Mrs. Danvers all burned down. Here was the turn to Lewis Ferry Road. He'd never come from this direction before and wasn't sure how far he had to go to reach the entrance. The sun was setting, light draining from the narrow strip of sky between the trees. It had to be right along here somewhere. But rounding the next curve he found himself in Lewis Ferry, with its crumbling bridge piers across the river and kudzu-haunted mill ruins. How had he missed the gate?

The store was closed and dark. No lights showed in any of the houses or trailers. He turned and drove back: a quarter mile...a half mile...three quarters. Fuck, where *was* it? He turned again and crept along slowly with his high-beams on, peering into the darkening woods. Three quarters, half-mile, one quarter. A few more curves and he'd be back in the village. WTF?? Then, glancing in the rear-view mirror, he saw the gatehouse reflected there.

It was all but invisible in darkness beneath the heavy overhanging trees. (Had they really gotten that bushy? He'd have to get the tree service out to trim them once things got back to normal – if they ever did.) He touched in the code from his phone. The gates swung open.

A lump lying on the drive sprang to its feet: Baxter! He scrambled in the opened car door and all over Rick, wriggling, whimpering, licking, then leaping back and forth to bark out every window. *Pack Leader is returned! Pack Leader is returned!* The gates closed behind them. Rick felt that same shiver, that thrill, he always got when he passed through the gateway. Relief; pride; that Danish word he couldn't remember which combined warmth, coziness, friendly intimacy, safely tucked in from a cold winter world.

Here near the hill's crest was that view out to the east, already black with night. No steam from Shearon Harris, of course; nor would there ever be now, unless they were idiotic enough to rebuild it. Here was the familiar vista down fields to the distant pasture where the "home farm" cows grazed, the gentle rolling hills beyond holding the day's last light. Familiar…and somehow not only from all the times he'd passed it. Another familiarity was pulling at his mind. A photo?...Yes, a photo; a recent one. (But Baum had never allowed photos, right?) Rick pulled over by the fence. And then the memory clicked. He went online (yes, thank god, the Court's WiFi was still up), did a search. Aidan's Polaroid, the very first one he'd sent. Aidan, insouciant and happy, leaning on that same fence, in front of that same vista.

Aidan had been at Haw Court.

He'd been here not long after leaving Grantsville. He'd been here when Baum was still alive. How had he gotten in? Had he met Baum? And had Baum taken him in; then somehow through his wealth and connections, enabled Aidan's travels? If so, he'd done it entirely in secret. Now Aidan as well as Baum were dead, any chance of explanations gone with them. The lawyers' files might mention people Baum had known, in places Aidan had sent his letters from. But if they were found – then what? Would Dad and / or Eunice still want to prosecute? Aidan had come back anyway…for all the good it had done any of them.

Rick drove on. Baxter had lain down in the passenger seat, head in Rick's lap. Round the crest of the hill, and another vista, an amazing sunset. And then, the distant outline of Haw Court: lights in various windows, trails of white smoke from various chimneys.

He took the service drive down to the garage. Closer to the house it was lined with parked cars, a U-Haul truck, even a scooter. (Did some poor fool have to ride a scooter all the way here? Damn.) When the garage door rose, though, he saw his space still open. Leslie's car was there too, but not Claire's or David's. Dinner smells drifted from the kitchen, along with Chris and Jésus's voices and the rattle of pans. He went up the stairs and down the corridor towards the entry hall. The tables in the big dining room were set, with warming pans ready on the buffet. Judging by the number of plates, he had a full house. Who would he find? "Hello? – hello?" he called as he went. Reaching the rotunda, he saw Leslie's silhouette at the far end of the center corridor. She shaded her eyes for a better look. Then she barreled down the hall to tackle him in a fierce relieved hug. "Oh my god, oh my god, you made it." Baxter leaped around them happily. She stepped back and held him at arm's length. "And it's really you, right? Not an avatar. (Please say yes.)"

Rick stared. "An *avatar*? Did radiation make me eight feet tall and blue?"

"Oh, thank god." She hugged him again.

"Guess what I found out!" He showed her Aidan's picture. "Recognize that? It's the view from the drive! Aidan was *here!*"

Her expression was strange. "You don't know the half of it."

She led him back to the Tudor room, where cozy lit lamps were reflected in the big Gothic window against the blue dusk. A fire glimmered in the fireplace. A figure rose from an armchair beside it and turned, calmly smiling.

Aidan.

Now Departing

Dogs can tell ghosts from people, was Rick's first thought. But Baxter trotted over, sniffed at Aidan's offered palm, wagged, and lay down by the fire. "*What. The. Fuck?*" Rick said. He didn't try to shake hands, fearing despite Baxter's approval that his own hand might find Aidan's death-cold, or pass right through it. Had he switched clothes with someone else, who was then killed by the tornado? Rick had a beyond-ludicrous image of two boys calmly changing in the wreckage of the school locker room as it whirled round inside the funnel. No, he couldn't have, there hadn't been time. "Do you know what happened in Grantsville? They found somebody in *your* clothes, with his head smashed like a watermelon!"

"That was my avatar."

"Your *avatar.*"

"It's a long and complex explanation, and I don't know all of the technical details. But to start with: alternate universes are real."

"You can explain later. Dad and Eunice need to know *now.*" Rick hit the Grantsville number in his contacts.

"You won't be able to get through," Aidan said. "Even if you did, they wouldn't believe you. They'd think you were playing a cruel trick."

"It's not a cruel trick to let them think you're lying in a morgue? With no head?" The number rang once. There was a long silence, with intermittent faint static – "Hello? *Hello?*" Rick called, to no avail – then the harsh *beep-beep-beep-beep-beep* of disconnection.

"When they test its DNA and fingerprints, they'll exactly match mine. Your avatar is like a clone, exactly the same on every level. Except it has no self-awareness. You can't clone peoples' *souls*."

"(Thank god for *that*, at least,)" Leslie muttered.

"Its brain has a neurochemical program that makes it do and say whatever you'd do in any situation, but there's no consciousness. So while it's out there getting destroyed by all the stupid evil shit Dad and his right-wing fascists will cause, it doesn't feel anything. And you're safe here."

"And where the hell is 'here'?" Rick demanded.

"An alternate reality, like I said," Aidan replied, in the half-condescending half-infuriated way of a teenager trying to deal with dense grownups. "One where we'll finally be safe from the consequences of their evil. Like global-warming tornadoes strong enough to wreck a nuclear plant. And killer hurricanes, and mega-droughts, and fracking earthquakes; and vote suppression and gerrymandering; and NRA gun-maniac bigots mass-murdering anybody who's not a white Christian Tea-Partier; and the Koch brothers letting us all die by the billions so they can keep gorging themselves on their wealth…Now that they've bought Trump the election, it's all going down. He and Dad and all the other Republicans'll finally get to do what they've always wanted and destroy every bit of progress we've made in the last hundred years. And that's going to destroy *them*. The whole environment, and civilization, and all of life. But now *we* won't have to suffer it."

"Are you ready for the Liberal Rapture?" Leslie asked sarcastically.

"*You're* not in this too, are you?" Rick demanded.

"Oh no. And I don't think I want to be."

"Are there avatars of us running around out there? Am I dead in Grantsville too?"

"No. You only get an av if you want one. If you want to stay here but not disappear from there, so you don't arouse suspicion, your av takes your place, until whatever disaster would've killed you kills it."

Confusion didn't even begin to describe Rick's attitude. His comprehension was banging around his mind like a tennis ball at Wimbledon. And he wanted to punch Aidan out, for fucking with everyone's horror and grief..."Are you the Wizard?...Was Baum the Wizard? You were here before. Look!" He showed the picture.

"Yes; and lots of other places. No, I'm not the Wizard, and neither was Baum. 'The Wizard' is, like, the psychic wavelength we use to communicate in dreams." He saw Rick's question coming and held up a hand. "'We' meaning all of us living here. Any time there's an important question, or a danger, we consensus our minds together, as many as we need, to answer it or repel the threat. The psychic part is so beyond known science that hardly anybody understands it. But we know it works." He smiled, as if he was actually proud of himself.

"This is – fuck it, this is a bunch of fucking science fiction bullshit, and I don't believe it. *You need to tell Dad and Eunice.*"

Aidan shook his head. "Not gonna happen. It can't. Even if I stood right in front of them they wouldn't believe it was me. They'd say I was an impostor. Mom'd be even more freaked...They spent my whole life not recognizing me. Now they never will."

"Then why the fuck come back at all? Or was that your damn 'av' the whole time?"

"I wanted to give them one more chance. I felt I owed them that much. They didn't take it. And I hoped, a little, that enough people wouldn't be totally pathologically Darwin-Awards retarded and vote for Trump. They did. As soon as he won, I switched out. I'm dead in Grantsville, and it's dead to me."

"Fuck this. And fuck you too, you selfish little shit. You know Cousin Mason and Danny are dead too. The tornado killed them too. Their house is *gone*. Did they have avatars too; or don't you care? Mason always stood up for you."

Aidan looked somber. "I don't know if they did. I hope so. They'd have been welcome here."

Rick stalked over to his den, opened the computer, pulled up Facebook. There, though, he found a message from Dad. The body's fingerprints had been confirmed as Aidan's.

Leslie came to see what had left him open-mouthed and staring. "Look at this," he said.

She leaned over, one hand resting on his shoulder. She nodded.

"I haven't gone nuts, have I?...I had bizarre dreams all the way here, every time I slept. I wonder if I'm still in one."

She looked back to the Tudor room, where Aidan had returned to his armchair and book. "He showed up yesterday," she half-whispered. "After I got your message he was dead. I had the same reaction. He told me the same story, about 'avs' and parallel universes. I didn't know what to believe. But I couldn't turn him away. I thought he might be in shock. I asked the others to keep an eye on him just in case."

"Who else is here?"

"I've made you a list." She indicated a paper on the desk. "We're about three-quarters full. Power and water are working fine. Chris, Nate and Linda say we have enough supplies for three weeks, more if we're willing to live on eggs, bread and canned vegetables. Nate says they could try to butcher a cow, but they don't really know how, so they'd rather not. We also have a couple of bowhunters who've offered to bring in deer. I don't know when hunting season is, but right now that's not likely to be a problem. The sheriff came to see if we were okay, and says to call if we need anything. They've got a shelter set up at the high school. I told him we could take people too if they run out of space. And Claire's gone."

"Where??"

"She's trying to get to her mother's." Mrs. Franchette lived east of Raleigh, towards Knightdale. "She's unharmed, but frantic. She's afraid to leave the house. She begged Claire to come."

"She'll never get there! Wake County's on lockdown. The only route she knows is 64 east, past Shearon Harris. Has she called?"

"No. I asked her to, but…I hope she's just forgotten."

"What about David? – where's he?"

"Wednesday – tornado day – he went to get his car tuned up. He was going to the Fiat dealership in Cary. Nobody's heard from him since, or been able to reach him."

"*Fuck*. Fuck, fuck, fuck." Rick slumped forward, shaking his head. He noticed a folder beside the guest list. "What's this?"

"The transcripts of Baum's tapes. They came Wednesday morning, but I haven't had a chance to look at them."

Rick glanced at the figure in the armchair two rooms away. He leaned in closer to Leslie and lowered his voice more. She did likewise. "Do you *believe* him?"

"As God is my witness, I don't know. Your parents have a body, with fingerprints and DNA. He says they'll match; but we could still test. We should! Get prints off a glass or plate he's used. DNA? Maybe from his underwear; if we can get past the '*Ewww!*' factor."

In spite of everything, Rick smiled a little. "Have we got anybody who can lift prints or test DNA?"

Leslie glanced at the guest list and shook her head. "I don't think so."

"There's no lab here, anyway. But when things calm down, I bet we can find labs in Greensboro or someplace."

"*If* things calm down."

*

Rick took a much-wanted shower and put on blissfully clean fresh clothes. He called Claire's mother, and David's parents, but got only answering machines. He worked on the operational stuff David usually saw to, signing necessary papers and writing necessary checks. (The banks were still functioning, Leslie said, but with armed guards and a limit on cash withdrawals.) He tracked down Sarah and Andy, in Durham. Sarah and her husband were staying close to home because of their children, but she regularly monitored the office's communications. Andy reported Aromamora was undamaged. Rick checked in with Chris, Jésus, Nate and Linda, and the rest of the staff. Of the maids, five were still working, either from loyalty or because they needed the money, while two had fled to other cities where relatives lived; the last, who'd been going to nursing school in the evenings, had volunteered at the refugee shelter. He got the landscaper's answering machine as well, but the owner soon called back, relieved to hear from Rick, and thankful that his crew would still have the Court job to go to. He tried to reply to Dad's message but it wouldn't go through; nor would phone calls to Grantsville.

Dinner was at six-thirty. They'd gotten into a routine, Leslie told him, of Chris serving simple buffet meals at regular times. Between meals and overnight, self-service snacks, drinks and dinner leftovers (if any) could be found in the Bavarian tavern, where there was a microwave. Everybody had been made aware that the Court's coffee stash could last two weeks as long as nobody drank more than a pot a day. Liquor and beer were running low, having been used as rough therapy by some of the more freaked-out arrivals, but Nate had two kegs each of Court ale and cider almost ready to tap.

That night there was lasagna, with or without meat; fresh-baked bread, a salad of autumn greens from the gardens. The guests were a mix of people Rick did and didn't know. Former co-workers from Duke Energy. Mom and Annie's next-door neighbor, five months pregnant, whose husband was an EMT working insane hours with search-and-rescue teams. Marcus and his wife Deborah; Scott with Rielle and daughter Meghan, now five. Friends of Leslie's, two families with children, whom she used to babysit. (Leslie was staying in the main house too, feeling safer among the Court's crowd of guests than by herself down at the gatehouse.) Acquaintances who'd lived in or near the tornado's path, who had been out on their daily routines when it struck, and now could not or dared not go back. They all expressed a vast amazed relief at finding such a refuge as Haw Court. Everybody wanted to thank Rick, tell the tales of how they'd managed to get there, praise the ways he'd set everything up. "Have you seen Aidan?" he asked, when he got a chance. Some people had, but they hadn't exchanged much talk. "Did he say anything about alternate universes?" No, they replied, giving Rick odd looks. Why; had he found one? If so, let us know; we're there in a heartbeat. They made jokes, the humor thinly stretched over worry and trauma, about wardrobes to Narnia or Doctor Who's TARDIS, or finding the nearest railroad in hopes a Ghost Train might appear. Had he heard the stories of Ghost Trains rescuing people at Burning Man and Rainbow Gathering? Now Haw Court, and Rick, were performing similar heroism. "Can we stay here until Trump goes away?" a little child asked.

Aidan came in late. He took his plate to a corner of the least crowded table. Rick joined him. "So what are your plans now? Since you're not going back to Grantsville. Are you just gonna hang around here?"

"You're starting to sound like Dad. No. You clearly wouldn't be comfortable with that. No, I've arranged to spend the winter at some friends' commune in the mountains. I'll leave Sunday night. I'll be helping them teach capoeira classes. Then…I thought I'd move to one of several places where other friends will put me up, and work while I decide where to go to college and what for. Unless something more interesting comes up."

"So you're sixteen, seventeen, and you're gonna find work that'll pay enough for college." Rick kept his voice low. He also kept an eye, as discreetly as possible, on Aidan's water glass.

"In our reality that's not a problem."

"Really. What'd you do, kidnap Bernie Sanders and have him give you free tuition? Was that his avatar running the campaign?"

The hint of a sardonic smile turned up one corner of Aidan's mouth. "Bernie Sanders. No, I don't think he knows about this, though he'd be welcome here. We'd probably make him President."

"Which reality are we in right now? Yours or mine?"

"Both. Your estate is a nexus. A 'wood between the worlds,' like in Narnia. The old Robbins place is another, hence the –"

"Was. It got smashed by the tornado too. Just like you."

"I was going to say, hence the ghost stories."

"How does it work?"

Aidan gave a shrug of innocence. "Again, I don't know. The naturally occurring ones seem to involve all kinds of factors: ley lines, magnetic fields, if there's certain crystals in the bedrock; solar flares, moon phases; even planetary alignments, according to some people; and the – the 'feng shui,' the shape of the landscape. That's why they're so rare, and why the few people who find them get treated like nutjobs when they come back with their stories. The balance of factors seems to be different for each person. And what's in your mind, too, the 'feng shui' of your thoughts. That's the most important part. It's learning how to do that along with combining all the other factors – and once you know how it's as easy as thinking the Wizard's barrier on – that lets us make our own gateways wherever we need to. And it's why anybody who wants to harm us won't ever be able to find them. When your social structures collapse under the weight of all the harm Dad and his kind are doing, you might find that useful. If some so-called 'patriot militia' decides they're going to strip Haw Court bare, and smash *your* head –" he pointed a fork at Rick – "like a melon if you try to stop them: they'll never, ever find their way in, no matter how desperately they try."

In spite of himself, in spite of thinking *They wouldn't let it collapse, the big corporations and the Pentagon, they've got too much to lose*, Rick felt a small but stubborn knot of worry at the back of his mind. Aidan sounded so completely assured, like it was all on the program. He wasn't ranting like some conspiracy nut. And how long might it take for 'social structures' to restart themselves in the swath of Wake County covered by radioactive wreckage? The fearfulness of those dreams he'd had during the trip flickered at the edge of memory. "Will Dad find it? Or Eunice or Lin? When they came to the housewarming they got here without any trouble." No, wait, they did; they couldn't find it and the security detail had had to flag them down, and then they'd made a wrong turn and ended up at the garage instead of the main entrance. But was that only because Lin had been driving?

Aidan ate a large chunk of lasagna, and thought. "Are you having to consult your 'consensus' on your psychic 'feng shui' wavelength?" Rick asked him.

"More like Dad every day. Half cross-examination and half campaign debate. That depends on them, not me. If Dad's caused too much harm to too many people; if they keep refusing to learn the truths they need to learn..."

"If everything does go to shit, you'd leave them out there in it, to die?"

"It's out of my hands," Aidan sighed, spreading them wide the way a magician (like the Wizard?) does to show his audience they're empty.

"Your own fucking family."

"My own fucking family. Who I'm dead to, and who're dead to me."

Rick stood. Tinged his fork against his glass for attention. "Announcement, everybody. Remember how I've been asking about parallel universes? Well, guess what: we're *in* one. Tell them, Aidan."

Some people looked surprised. Some looked puzzled. Some didn't react at all. Some didn't pay attention, too busy with their own conversations. Leslie was transfixed. Aidan calmly kept on eating. "Grantsville got hit by a tornado the same day you all did. Afterwards we found his body with its head smashed in, in his clothes, with his fingerprints. But now here he is, alive. How? He says this is an alternate universe, and that the body back in Grantsville was his 'avatar.' That right?" he asked Aidan.

Glances exchanged, hinting at unsaid knowledge. A woman – Frieda, Mom's neighbor – said "Have you had the dreams too?"

"What dreams?"

"About this being a 'safe world.' Or, kind of like a, a transfer point, to a safe world."

"Like Wizard dreams?"

"No, but – Everybody I talk to says the people who've had them but say they have – say they're all different. Some were like Wizard dreams and others just normal."

"Do they talk about you having avatars? And people who *don't* know about this quote-unquote 'safe world' and *won't* be let in?"

"You know what? Fuck 'em," Scott asserted. "They Brexited us, and Trumped us, so now we're gonna Brexit them. See how they like it."

"You can't fix stupid," several voices said. "And I'm convinced," Marcus added, "after all the eight years of vicious ugly shit they've thrown at Obama –"

"And us!" Deborah put in.

"Treasonous shit," a man growled. "Shutting down the government so –"

"*Treasonous* shit; that we can't ever fix racism. Specially when it don't want to be fixed."

"Shutting down the – they'd rather shut down, even *destroy*, the government rather than let people have health care?"

"They won't even *listen* to us!" Deborah insisted. "They hide inside their right-wing bubble and *refuse* to believe our pain's even *real!*"

Many voices, speaking at once. "And if you try to show them the truth they vandalize your house, key your car, threaten your kids –" "And call you 'cuck,' or worse –" "There's people out there I *work* with, who I thought were good people; but they actually *like* that Trump lies left and right and attacks the press! They actually *thanked God* that that vicious psychopath *rapist* won! I spent my whole lunch break crying in my car –" "But true facts are gonna hit them hard, and take them down harder –" "They say 'Burn it down!' What, they think they're fucking fireproof?"

Report students criticizing government policies, "Western corruption"...Right's

"Wait, wait;" Rick demanded. "How many of you know people who *won't* get through? Like, friends, or even family? What are you going to tell them?"

Another stew of voices. "Why should we?" "They need some hardcore tough love kickin' their ass." "Let them know? Are you nuts? They'd nuke us rather than let us escape." "Yeah, I'll tell people, 'Hey, I found me this portal to another universe,'" Scott mocked. "They'd have me in a straitjacket."

"Or Guantanamo," Rielle suggested.

Frieda tried to speak but got emotional. She'd been raped in college, she managed to explain, and now had had to tell her father and stepmother that if they voted for Trump – a monster who gloated in his power to sexually assault – she could never speak to them again. "I can't feel safe in my own *family*!" she sobbed. Rick thought he heard Aidan murmur "Been there, done that..." A therapist, one of Leslie's babysitting clients, made metaphors about toxic relationships, how at some point one had to cut one's losses, put up one's barriers and say 'No more." None of them knew for sure, he averred to Rick, if their friends, families, co-workers, etc. would be barred; they hoped not, hoped enlightenment would arrive in time. They'd even asked the Wizard in dreamtime to save this or that person, but received no answers...As for avatars? Reluctant admissions that some dreams had brought that offer too, an offer whose implications they were still trying to process. If it was true; IF it was true... activating one's avatar *might* reassure caregiver types, doctors, teachers, first responders and so forth, who wanted to take refuge in Safe World but not feel they'd deserted those they were supposed to care for. Maybe if things got really bad...which fractaled into diverse ideas of what "really bad" would look like. Trump's Muslim registry, concentration camps, eastern Carolina under water, a Constitutional Convention – "because you know they'd outlaw abortion, gay marriage, trans rights, gun control; everything!"

But how do you justify it to yourselves? Rick wanted to ask. *Abandoning them, like steerage passengers on the* Titanic. *Speaking of that; we're mostly all white and privileged here. What's happening to the homeless, the crackheads, the families in those Philly ghettos I was scared of? Are they being saved? What about red-state methheads and opiate addicts? Children too young to make their own decisions?* Before he could frame the question, though, Serena, one of the bowhunters, came charging in, thrilled to announce she'd bagged a nice big buck – plenty of venison and sausage! Nate followed, with the first keg of Court ale. By the time Rick settled these conversations, Aidan was carrying his tableware to the bins by the dumbwaiter. Rick watched; waited until Aidan left the room; then retrieved Aidan's glass. He wrapped it in a napkin and hid it in his bedroom.

He was exhausted. He flopped down on the bed and turned on TV. The Court had a deluxe satellite dish on the roof, which brought in several hundred channels, including some he'd never seen before. The news kept repeating the same clips: aerial shots of vast wreckage; traumatized survivors, exhausted rescue workers, McCrory haplessly trying to reassure everyone. FEMA still couldn't say when people would be able to return; but they had managed to set up a website with names of everyone located so far – alive, or dead. Rick found neither Claire nor David there. The Internet, of course, was even less help, with weird rumors and wild conspiracies arising from every quarter like zombies in *The*

inspired lunacy: Legislatures in Idaho, Pennsylvania, Utah moving to seize

Walking Dead. (Obama caused the disaster! With contrails! As part of a secret pact in the Paris climate-change treaty! For revenge against The American People for electing Trump! So he could impose Martial Law and hand the country over to UN World Domination!!) Rick growled. Baxter trotted over, looking worried. Rick scratched Baxter's head, and again noticed the transcripts. He picked one up, and began reading.

*

(*Transcripts – 6*)

I looked up the fellow's thesis. I was impressed. He doesn't merely make his points, he understands them. Instinctively, I think. The rituals he writes of, that codify the mutual respect each of the other, for their separate abilities and spheres. Respect, and even admiration. He understands "noblesse oblige." *And* that it needs to work both ways.

He's one of the few family member my young friend speaks well of. "He doesn't push himself into my shit all the time," Y.F. says. Sensible and detached.

Mutual respect.

He must have fallen far enough from the family tree to not become a poisoned apple.

Y.F. has left on his travels; first stop, he says, a dojo in Athens, Ohio. We took the trolley – I can't say it without smiling: the *trolley*! – up to Chapel Hill yesterday evening, where he met up with a lesbian couple also bound for Cincinnati, and saw them off on the *Carolina Special*. At Cincy someone from the dojo will meet him and bring him on to Athens. It's a roundabout trip because, he tells me, they're still rebuilding the rail network, and currently the only line into Athens comes down from Columbus.

But I'm forming an idea, that I want to run past him.

[*break*]

So: trolley to Pittsboro again, train to Raleigh. Train stations are engineered for portal ability, their materials and layout, their feng shui. And rituals, "blessing circles," they call them, when the stations are first opened. Everybody gathers and focuses, and mentally turns on the portal ability. Stations have natural potential already because they're places of transition, with the heightened emotions, the anticipation of travel. The trains themselves too. Y.F. says that when new routes are being beta-tested the trains sometimes slip through to the outside world.

Ah! – saying too much again. I'm as talkative as a Bond villain.

The ride is so fast and smooth. They've replaced all the road crossings with bridges. From Apex into Raleigh the tracks are below street level. There are stops at the state fairgrounds and the university, then the union depot. There trains on the Pittsboro and Sanford lines turn north to Wake Forest and Henderson, with a subway stop at Capitol Square. Then, look and sense for a place to traverse back. Carefully! – you don't want to find yourself buried beneath Fayetteville Street or trespassing in some bank vault. Not really, though. Y.F. assured me the portals never steer you wrong. And then walk a block or two to the lawyers. Noticing how different the air smells. Eau de "The World Is Our Ashtray."

[*break*]

It's done. The legacy is secured. The lawyers grilled me like Perry Mason, but Y.F. was all in favor. He says this place is at a convergence of all the right natural forces for a portal. Ley lines, whatever those are. It sounds like more hippy-dippy nonsense.

But it *works*. I *know*. When things start to collapse this will be a…a center of, for…decompression? Debriefing? Triage?...Safe harbor for the storm-wrecked, where they can pull themselves together and decide what to do next, where to go.

Ellis Island.

Where no one's sent back because of quotas. Nativist meanness. Because of "no Irish or Chinese need apply." Because they have tuberculosis, or a name the examiner can't pronounce. Because they look, merely *look*, retarded, mongoloid. Because like me they make others quote-unquote "nervous."

[*break*]

Young Mr. R. is in for quite a surprise…I don't know why that makes me giggle.

He little knows what I have done.

I hope his hands are steady. But Y.F. says they are, says the blood relation. Says with the same certainty with which he took me through the first time.

Was I looking for an heir? Not consciously. They'd been after me to make one, of course. A will. Naming an heir, or heirs. Create a foundation, they say, that will then disburse the money, to worthy causes. So upright, so noble! Pick a cause, any cause; and I could be listing them from now 'til doomsday. And which one would have any use for a place like this?

[*pause*]

No matter how worthy they were, what they're up against, it's like trying to put out a wildfire with an eyedropper.

Between the pathological greed of the ones on top and the pathological stupidity they've indoctrinated into the mobs…this world's screwed. Right off the cliff. It's patriotic to be stupid and slit your throat every time you go in the voting booth. At least you'll bleed to death red, white and blue.

But now...

[*pause*]

But now – you won't take us down with you.

Cry "Havoc!" and let slip the Darwin Awards, turbocharged by Murphy's Law. While we close the wardrobe door behind us.

[*break*]

And guess who came calling today? Young Mister R, Mister Thesis himself! With two lady friends. Just curious to see the place, they said. People do come by sometimes, wanting a look. More and more often I see them driving slowly up and down the road, peering out their windows as if they can't see anything. As if Marzipan Cottage didn't stick out like a sugar-frosted thumb. Does the portal also confer invisibility?

R and his companions found it with no trouble. The blonde seems to be his girlfriend. Reminded me of Laura, with half the intelligence. Now now, mustn't judge, I hear Laura's echo say. She might have been just as giddy if Hearst and Marion Davies had walked out the door of San Simeon to greet us. I let them go in and look around, swearing them to secrecy.

A healthy young man; looks like he takes good care of himself. Respectful but not intimidated. Would stand his ground if challenged. Well brought up. Ha! – though if Mama knew of his circumstances she'd have had conniptions and forbade me having anything to do with him.

He little knows what I have done.

[*break*]

My original name was Thomas Arnett Robbins. I was born August 22nd, 1949, in Grantsville, North Carolina.

I left home at sixteen because –

[*End of tape*]

*

He got up around seven. He washed and dressed quickly. He sent out an e-mail, announcing his plan; then started packing. Clothes; toothbrush and toothpaste, shaving kit; a handful of energy bars and bottled water from the cupboard in his den. Laptop and charger. Baxter's collar and leash. He'd grab a bag of dog food from the storerooms on the way.

In the middle, carefully wrapped and padded, Aidan's glass.

He pulled shut the doors to his suite. He crossed the Tudor room, went along the center hall to the entry. There he ran into Leslie. "Good news," she said, "Claire's safe. Her mom just called. She got there late last night –" Then she noticed his bag.

"I'm going back out there," he said.

There were footsteps above them. Aidan came walking casually down one of the curved stairways, wearing sweatpants, a hoodie, and running shoes.

"Where?" Leslie demanded. "What'll you do?"

Rick answered "First I'll make sure Mom's house is okay. Then I'll see if I can help with rescue efforts. I need you to handle things here unless David turns up. You along with Chris and Nate and Linda. I've let everyone know you're in charge."

Rick then turned to look Aidan in the eye. "And after that, I'm going back to Grantsville. And I'm telling Dad and Eunice that you're alive. And fuck whatever they – whatever *you* say they will or won't believe."

"It won't do any good," Aidan shrugged. "As soon as you cross the barrier all the evidence will disappear. For instance, the prints and DNA on my glass." He pointed at Rick's bag. "I saw you carry it out of the dining room. Even if you put your own barrier around it, the main barrier will override it. That shivery feeling you feel when you drive in or out? That's the main barrier. It's got millions of our minds maintaining it, all the time."

"Fuck it. What you're doing is *wrong*. This whole…parallel universe, apocalypse thing; if it's real, it's *wrong*. You're what – gonna let millions of people *die* because they voted for the – because *you* think they voted for the wrong guy??!"

"It's out of my hands," Aidan said in a long, patient sigh. "This train left the station long ago. All this has been building up for decades. Trump just tipped it over the edge. It would've happened even without the parallel universes, in which case *we'd* have been the first millions to die."

"If Rick leaves what'll happen to him?" Leslie asked accusingly.

Aidan had started strolling towards the front doors. "I don't know. But you'll always be able to get back in," he told Rick over his shoulder. "You're one of the Good Guys." As he went out he was murmuring to no one in particular, "Oh, Rhett, Rhett, Rhett, wher-*evah* will Ah go, what-*evah* will Ah do?"

Leslie turned to Rick. "I want to go with you."

Rick did a double take. "Why?"

"I worry about you. I care about you. This is freaking me out."

"We're all freaking out, and we need to *not* freak. If we do,

Americans would need 228 years to reach same wealth level as whites...

Now Departing / 385

he wins." He pointed after Aidan. "We need to keep it together and not let that happen. I care about you too. I trust you, most of everyone. That's why I need you to stay and run things. I *will* come back, and I'll call every day I'm gone."

She hugged him tightly for a long time. He hugged back. "Know what this reminds me of?" he said. "Disaster movies where the characters stop in the middle of everything for a romantic moment. I'm like, 'Are you fucking kidding me? Godzilla's two blocks away nuking everything, and you want to talk about our relationship??'" She shook, with amusement or worry or tears, or all three.

They separated, but his hands remained on her shoulders. "I want you to tell everybody here what he – and Baum – have been up to. Read the transcripts, you'll find out. Tell the sheriff too. See if he can arrest Aidan for faking his own death."

He kissed her. "I *will* come back."

"Don't you dare not."

*

At the crest of the hill, he guessed why he'd never seen Shearon Harris's steam plume: in this "reality," the plant had never existed. What else didn't exist here; and who else?

He thought his barrier on as he approached the gates, and asked for an extra layer of shielding round Aidan's glass. No response. Where was the Court's barrier exactly? He presumed it would follow the property line or the boundary wall, unless it flexed in reaction to outside forces. Recalling the previous times he'd passed through, it had always been at a slightly different point. Here were the gates; where would – It caught him by surprise, and he shivered...

...in the chill air beneath grey windy skies. Hadn't he turned on the heater? He checked for traffic. No pleaders, protesters, Aidan groupies, general crazies: now they had far more crucial things to worry about. Did a quick inventory. Laptop and charger, hidden beneath the back seat on which Baxter lay. Dog food in the back, snacks and bottled water on the passenger seat. His bag on the front floorboard, within quick reach. Inside it, carefully wrapped and padded, the gun Dad had forced him to take when he left Grantsville. (He hadn't wanted to, until they learned of the horrific events at the White House, and what those events had incited all over the country...) Would Leslie and the household be all right? He could only hope so. They had the security systems, the sheriff on call; as a last resort, the two bowhunters with their deadly arrows....

They'd no doubt buried Aidan by now, along Cousin Mason and Danny and all the other victims. They might do a memorial service later, though. He'd go, if he could. All that time Aidan had spent away, learning self-defense against bullies; only to be taken out by a force against which there was no defense. Death was the ultimate bully.

(Some tiny loose thread wavered amidst his thoughts of Aidan, some half-memory just out of reach. Something to do with a wizard. A wizard? Dumbledore, Gandalf? Oz? A wizard, and "ghost trains.")

As the gatehouse receded in his rear-view mirror, it became all but invisible beneath the vast shadow of the trees.

teach Pope of our "Biblical duty" to destroy the planet..."We are starting to